Praise for
A Truth to Lie For

"[Elena Standish is] a mature character who lives by her wits and builds on her previous experiences. . . . Attention to character development and plot, a fine-tuned sense of place and time, and well-crafted secondary characters [is] classic Perry."

—*Historical Novels Review*

"This is the fourth novel in the series and they keep getting better. [*A Truth to Lie For*] is another thrilling story with all the characters we've come to love. . . . Fans of the series will be happy with this one."

—Red Carpet Crash

"Unbearably suspenseful . . . Kudos to Anne Perry, who never disappoints and continues to surprise readers with a number of tricks up her sleeve in a story that pushes the envelope and succeeds on nearly every level."

—*Bookreporter*

A Truth to Lie For

ANNE PERRY

A Truth to Lie For

An Elena Standish Novel

BALLANTINE BOOKS

NEW YORK

2023 Ballantine Books Trade Paperback Edition

Published in the United States by Ballantine Books, an imprint of Random House, a division of Penguin Random House LLC, New York.

BALLANTINE is a registered trademark and the colophon is a trademark of Penguin Random House LLC.

Originally published in hardcover in the United States by Ballantine Books, an imprint of Random House, a division of Penguin Random House LLC, in 2022.

Originally published in the United Kingdom by Headline Publishing Group, London, in 2022.

This book contains an excerpt from the forthcoming book *The Traitor Among Us* by Anne Perry. This excerpt has been set for this edition only and may not reflect the final content of the forthcoming edition.

ISBN 978-0-593-35909-9
Ebook ISBN 978-0-593-35908-2

Printed in the United States of America on acid-free paper

randomhousebooks.com

2 4 6 8 9 7 5 3 1

To Scott Jeffers

A Truth to Lie For

CHAPTER

1

"I believe you have been complaining recently that your work is not challenging enough." Peter Howard raised his eyebrows very slightly. In the sunlight through the office window, he looked amused rather than surprised.

Elena drew in a breath, then slowly let it out again. "Yes," she said. She had been recruited to MI6 by Peter just over a year ago, in May 1933. Now, in June 1934, he was her mentor, and her commanding officer. "I'm doing what any halfway competent clerk would do just as well," she added.

A flash of amusement lit his face. "Then you will be pleased that I have a job for you that will require all your talents and abilities. Well, except photography."

Photography was Elena's profession, her art, and her passport to all kinds of places and situations. It was her expertise as a photographer that had resulted in her invitation to a conference in Trieste, where she had also succeeded in her first official MI6 assignment. And more recently, her photographic skills had added so much to

her family's celebration in Washington, DC—and ultimately led her
to solve two murders.

But she did not want to think about that now. It had been less than
two months since the incidents in Washington, which had involved
her grandfather, and which had ended so terribly. The pain was still
raw for both of her parents, but especially her mother. Elena had
hardly known her American grandfather, whereas she had a close and
loving relationship with Grandfather Lucas, the former head of MI6.

Peter was talking, and she had not been listening.

". . . Berlin again," he was saying. "You must not be recognized,
Elena. This is not an order—the mission is too dangerous for that—
but it is a request that you cannot refuse."

The irony of the distinction was not lost on her.

"We're sending another person as well, but you will not meet.
Nor will you contact each other unless it is absolutely necessary."

What had she missed? The humor of a few moments ago had
vanished. Peter was no longer smiling but squinting as he looked
past her, as if he saw something threatening approaching from far
off, something that was crowding out everything else.

He must have observed her confusion, because a gentleness appeared in his face. Not just in his eyes, but in his mouth as well.
"What is it?" she asked as politely as she could. Now fear brushed by
her. She waited, as if for the blow.

"I want you to get someone out of Germany who is currently in
Berlin."

She knew he would read the fear in her face, and yet she could
not hide it. That first assignment in Berlin had marked the moment
she had changed from a naïve—and frankly fairly boring—girl into
a young woman of courage and imagination. A woman who expressed a passionate anger against the indifference of those who saw
only what they chose to, which was primarily what fitted in their
comfortable lives.

Her throat was dry. "Berlin?" She only just managed to get the
word out.

"Yes," he said, watching her reactions. "There are two scientists we need to get out of the country."

"Physicists?" she asked, remembering her last mission, also one she had not chosen, but which had been thrust upon her.

"No, this time they are biochemists," he replied. "Two brilliant men. They form a research team, and the work of one depends on the other."

She remained silent, knowing that Peter would tell her only what she needed to know.

"One of them is creating new germs to be used in warfare, while we believe the other is on the brink of finding an antidote to those same germs, which is vital, of course, before using them against anyone."

He was still watching her intently.

"You were a child during the last war," he continued, "but you have learned enough about the use of gas in the trenches to imagine what germ warfare can be. What it can do, not only to armies, but to entire civilian populations, is—"

"Yes," she said sharply, cutting him off. The thought was obscene. "What do I have to do?"

"We're going to get these two men out of Germany. The extraction of one of them is your task. We'll send another agent, Alex Cooper, for the other."

"Why?" The word was out before she thought that perhaps she was asking for more information than she needed.

Peter's smile was bleak and there was a flicker of pain in it. "Because it's vital that we get both of them out. And if they leave separately, there's a better chance that they will survive. It causes less suspicion."

Elena was paying close attention. The last thing they wanted was to allow Germany and Adolf Hitler to have the upper hand in germ warfare!

"The Germans know that we're aware of this research," Peter continued. "And if they discover that we are planning to extract their scientists, they will make every attempt to keep these two men in a secure location, hiding them until their work is done." After a pause, he added, "And then they will kill them so they don't take their knowledge elsewhere. We need to get them out before this happens." He stopped. There was a rigidity in his body, even his face.

Elena knew that he hated having to say this, but he also knew that she needed the truth.

"It will be your job to get Professor Heinrich Hartwig out of Berlin. Cooper will go after the other scientist, Fassler, who, at this time, is not your concern. You need only focus on Hartwig."

She was certain there was more, and she waited. It was not long in coming.

"Elena, you need to understand. Fassler is vital to their germ warfare plans, but he's a Jew. The minute he delivers, he's dead. He knows this." Peter paused. "Both men are prepared to leave Germany immediately. Hartwig and Fassler are research associates, the Germans' top team in their field. They don't work together, or even in the same lab, but their work is complementary. One man's work is incomplete without the other's. Hartwig is developing an antidote to the germ. You can't use this stuff at all until you have a sure protection against it for your own population. If we only get Hartwig out and not Fassler, we will at least have the antidote ourselves. But Germany will still develop the germ. And then they will find someone else who will ultimately develop a vaccine against it."

"And Hartwig is willing to sacrifice his entire life in order to work in tandem with Fassler?" she asked. "Has Fassler no loyalty to humanity, if nothing else? What on earth does he believe in? Hitler?"

"I don't believe either of them cares about politics one way or the other. They care about knowledge, science, and medicine. But it's more than that," Peter explained. "Hartwig is a widower, no children, his life is his work. And he sees where Germany is heading. This is not a sacrifice for him; it's a necessity. Fassler? I know less about him."

"Peter—" she began, but was cut off.

"They both need to get out quickly, while they can," Peter insisted. "The Germans undoubtedly know that any of their enemies will try to lure these men out." His voice was firm, leaving no room for discussion.

"But you said that others would just take their places?" Elena asked.

"For some of the work, of course. Not for the creative genius. That's all you need to know."

Elena saw this as a polite way of reminding her how dangerous this mission would be. If she was caught, as long as she did not have certain knowledge, no threat, no torture in the world, could make her tell.

Peter moved a little toward the window and, in a trick of the light, the shadows vanished from his face. When he spoke, his voice was lower, harsher. "The Nazis are persecuting the Jews even more appallingly than when you were there a year ago."

"Worse than last year?" she asked incredulously, memory scorching her. "I saw a young man on the kitchen table of the people who took me in. The Brownshirts had flayed the skin from half his body. I don't even know if they managed to save him. I can't imagine the persecution being worse than that."

He looked at her steadily. Seconds ticked by. "Do you want me to send someone else?" His voice was not critical, just disappointed.

"No, of course not." She forced herself to say it, before she had time to consider whether it was really what she meant. But what a heavy burden! She was sure there was much he wasn't telling her, but she knew he was protecting her. Her grandfather Lucas would not have told her everything either. He had been protecting her from all sorts of pain for as long as she could remember, far back into childhood. Her memories of him had been of safety, discovery, of long conversations about all kinds of things: the ultimate friendship. She could remember weeding the garden with him, the immeasurable happiness of thinking she was helping. The memory was still so clear, and yet she had been only about three years old.

"Remember, Elena, Fassler is not your responsibility," Peter went on. "Your only goal is to get Hartwig out."

"And if I can't?" It was an unnecessary question, but she asked it anyway.

"Then think of the worst disaster you can imagine. Hemorrhagic fever, or something as dreadful as that. Uncontrolled bleeding, and then death. Entire populations disappearing. Corpses all over the place because there is no time to bury them, and maybe even no one left to do it."

"You don't need to paint that for me!"

"Or bubonic plague," he added. "The Black Death of 1348. It took a quarter of the population of Europe."

"I get the point, Peter. We must get them out."

"Yes, we must," he said sharply. Almost as an afterthought, he added, "You do know that we have our own germ warfare experiments?"

She froze.

"How the hell can we defend ourselves otherwise?" he said quickly, as if he might have said too much. "We don't know what the enemy has, but the more we know about where they are in the development of it, the better chance we have of stopping them." He shook his head fractionally, barely a movement at all. "Elena, if you can bring Hartwig here, he can help us with the antidote. But if you cannot get him out, you must see that the Germans don't arrest him. They must not take him alive. Can you do that?"

She looked at him with intensity. "Kill him? Yes," she said hoarsely. "I suppose there really is no choice."

She looked away. It bothered her that he would assume she would blame . . . and freely. "Is there more?" she asked.

"A lot. You need to know all you can about Hartwig. His life will depend upon you. That means you must learn about his history, his strengths and weaknesses. I will give it to you on paper, which you will memorize, then burn. You will have to contact him first, of course. Introduce yourself, and then say that you can and will help him."

"And who am I?"

"Ellen Stewart. Enough like your own name to recognize or remember it. Ordinary enough. I looked in the telephone book." He gave a very slight, bleak smile. "There are ten in the London telephone directory. I'll give you an address, too. You moved there recently. You will have a British passport, and a driving license. A checkbook as well. I don't expect you'll need it, but it will be attached to a real account. Your father is a schoolteacher of mathematics, and your mother had three children. They lost their son in the war. Their other daughter is a widow, also from the war. We'll stick to the truth as much as possible." Peter looked around the room, his face devoid of expression. "You'll need an explanation for your familiarity with Germany, both its culture and language. I suggest regular holidays, perhaps a childhood friend who came from Germany and wanted you to learn her language. And you studied German in school, and at university. Have it ready in your mind. Never volunteer information, but have it prepared. I think your major problems will be your appearance, your clothes."

She was a little stung by that remark, and then she realized it was not personal, it was strictly professional, and she thought she understood. When she had last gone to Germany, just over a year ago—although it seemed like another lifetime—she had learned that trying to hide was not the best way to disappear. Before Berlin, she had been unintentionally dowdy. She wore inconspicuous colors, soft blues and browns mostly, and dresses that were presentable, but ordinary. Boring, in fact. And no makeup, except a little lipstick to make her fair skin less colorless. When she needed to disappear into the background, her friends persuaded her to dye her hair from what she called "English mouse" to a sort of Nordic blond, which suited her wonderfully. She remembered that well-fitting scarlet dress. It was spectacular! And yet, when she changed into the dress, she disappeared. That was when she learned that people remember the clothing, and not the face of the woman wearing it. If anyone was asked to describe her, it was the dress they would remember.

She had liked the overall effects of these changes so much that she had kept them. Not the dress, which had been destroyed—and in a way she would rather not recall—but she had loved the style. That included the fairer hair, which was much the same as it had been when she was three or four years old.

So, was Peter asking her to become invisibly ordinary again, just like the image of her on the wanted poster that had been all over the streets in Berlin only a year ago? Not the striking blonde she had become, who walked with grace and assurance, as if she were beautiful and knew it?

She waited for Peter to speak. He was still hesitating, and she wondered what he was thinking.

"Leave your hair as it is," he said finally. "It attracts attention here, but blondes are less unusual in Germany. If the subject arises, your mother was Swedish. And stay with cool, sophisticated colors, possibly even black."

"In June?" she questioned.

"Why not? Or navy. And not a dress. Trousers are very fashionable now, if you can get away with them."

He looked at her carefully and she felt distinctly self-conscious. "Yes, sir," she said obediently.

He did not respond.

Elena guessed that he had known she would say exactly that, and that he had probably known the tone of voice she would use as well. It was the only answer she could give. They both knew the weight of what she was about to do, and the risks as well.

Peter relaxed a little. It was barely perceptible, just an easing of the shoulders. "You will spend the afternoon with Mrs. Smithers," he explained. "She'll see that you have everything you need. That includes money, a map of the Berlin railway system, bus timetables . . . I don't expect you'll need that but it's the sort of thing Ellen Stewart would carry. You can spend the afternoon however you think most useful, but you will sleep in a hotel tonight. And you will not contact your family. Any member of it! That includes Lucas. I'll tell him later."

She wanted to protest, but remained silent. It would be pointless anyway, and a trifle childish.

"That is an order, Elena," he said. "Disobedience will mean dismissal. And then we'll have to start again to find someone else to rescue Hartwig, before it is too late, which it might already be. Every day counts." He handed her a sealed envelope. "Your information on Hartwig. Memorize it, then destroy it."

There was not even the ghost of a smile on his face. She was quite certain he had not forgotten the scandal when she had worked in the Foreign Office. She had studied for years in Cambridge for her degree. She was good at her work, excellent. Even so, it was her father's post as British ambassador in Berlin, Madrid, and Paris that had resulted in that position for her. And then she had lost it because of her own stupidity. The disgrace had been deep and awful, especially to her family. For herself, she had deserved it. She was the one who had fallen in love with a traitor, but her family suffered for her, and with her. Peter knew how deeply it had cut, and he worded the warning specifically that way to impress it upon her.

"I trust you to tell them something so that they don't wonder why I don't answer the telephone," she said a little stiffly. "Or why I can't contact them at all."

That he agreed was evident in the softening of the lines on his face. "I might even tell Lucas the truth. Or perhaps not. I might wait until I know you are out again, and safe." His look was almost tender. "Be careful, Elena."

Lucas Standish stood in Peter Howard's office the following afternoon, in almost the exact place Elena had stood the day before. The June sunlight fell in the same area on the floor.

Lucas was well into his seventies, a tall, lean man with a slight stoop to his shoulders. His gray hair was thinning at the crown, but his eyes were the same steady, cloudless blue they had always been.

"So, Fassler has made a breakthrough," Lucas said. It was a conclusion, not a question. They had been discussing the subject of poison gas as a weapon of war and how, from there, germ warfare was the obvious next step.

Peter was half sitting on the edge of his desk. The two men had known each other since Lucas had recruited Peter into MI6, during the war of 1914–1918, which had spread until it was literally worldwide. The death toll had run into many millions. There was hardly a family in Britain who had not lost somebody. Peter had lost his brother, and Lucas his only grandson.

"Yes," Peter agreed. "Very recently."

"How far has he got?" Lucas asked. "Do you know?"

"That's one of the reasons we've got to get these two men out," Peter replied. "We don't know how quickly they could take that final step forward. Fassler for the germ itself, and Hartwig for the antidote."

"They could pass what they know over to others," Lucas added grimly. "What do we want with this Hartwig?" Lucas watched Peter, tension building in his chest.

"Both men have to be our focus. They are connected, though they don't work together. If they are both gone, the Germans' chances of succeeding in germ warfare decrease drastically. But . . . there's more urgency with Fassler. Not only is he a leader in this germ warfare research, but he's also a Jew. And we'll get them out separately. It gives us a better chance of success." His expression changed from appearing to care into something harder, a profound distress.

Lucas felt a chill run through him. "What is it, Peter?"

"So many German Jews think of themselves as being completely assimilated in the German culture: German first and Jewish second. This is a mistake, Lucas, and one that could be fatal."

"I know," Lucas said quietly. "I've heard the horror stories. You could persuade me to get Fassler out on humanitarian grounds alone. But if he's making major steps forward in germ warfare—or even if he hasn't, but is on the brink of such progress—we must get him out. It could be the most important thing we ever do."

"Alex Cooper will orchestrate Fassler's escape," said Peter. "He's already on it."

"Fine choice." Lucas knew Cooper. He was a good man, brave, imaginative, reliable. "What about Hartwig?" he asked.

"We sent someone late this afternoon. Should be in Berlin by tomorrow morning."

"Who?"

Peter looked away for just a moment. "Elena," he answered.

Lucas drew in his breath to speak, but no words came to mind, at least not any that he wanted Peter to hear. He already knew all the reasons why it was extraordinarily dangerous for her, and also why she was likely to succeed. The very fact that she was new at the job, that she was familiar with Berlin, growing up there as a girl, and that she looked like an overeager amateur, these were all in her favor. Above all, perhaps it was that she let her emotions show. A more professional MI6 agent would not do that. They would melt into the background, look casual. Elena did not act like any of their seasoned agents, and that was her best defense.

He saw how Peter waited, saying nothing. Did he still care what Lucas thought? Now that Peter was so close to the very top in command, he did not need to. Care, that is. He was head of his section of MI6, and he had earned it. In fact, it was the same section that Lucas had led during the war, and for some time after it.

Lucas thought about how they were alike in some ways. Peter had learned much of what he knew from Lucas. And yet, in other ways, personal ways, they were completely different. Unlike Lucas, Peter had no family other than a beautiful and distant wife, who had no idea what he did professionally, and his parents, who mourned their elder son, a hero lost leading his men on the battlefield, rather than a civil servant like Peter, who was, as far as their knowledge went, still pushing papers around in an office in Whitehall.

Peter could tell no one what he actually did. That was how it had to be, but it was not easy.

Lucas's family had gone for many years believing Lucas held mundane jobs in the government. When Lucas finally revealed he had been head of MI6, his son, Charles, and granddaughters, Margot and Elena, were astonished. He had kept his real profession from Josephine, his wife, for more than fifty years, and had learned only recently that she'd known all the time.

For his part, however, he had always been aware of what she had done during the war. Josephine had been a decoder of many of the most important secrets passed from government to government. It was while doing her own work that she had learned about Lucas's position, and had said nothing. Now in her mid-seventies, Josephine could still surprise him, and please him with her wit and courage.

Lucas felt Peter waiting for him to respond. He saw a shadow of anxiety in Peter's face. "Who does Elena have for backup?" He knew that Peter would never dare send her in completely alone.

"She can't go to Cordell," Lucas added, referring to their chief MI6 man in Berlin, working under the guise of cultural attaché in their embassy. To Cordell's displeasure, his daughter had married a young German, a Gestapo officer and Nazi. Initially, the Gestapo had been an honorable part of the specialist police, many of them university educated, particularly in law. But now they were changing, becoming increasingly violent, as was everything in Hitler's Germany.

"Of course not," Peter replied. "Going to Cordell would risk not only her life, but his as well. Much of our best information comes from Cordell. And I have to admit, Lucas, that he has recently surpassed our highest expectations. He's cautious, but he has courage when he needs it. Elena's backup is a fellow whose name you don't need to know. He's the hotel porter at the place where she's staying, almost invisible he's so ordinary. British-born, but knows Berlin like his own back garden. And he knows the necessary people to give her the help she might need."

As Peter spoke, his eyes were steady, his expression challenging. His relationship with Elena had developed over the past year. The first time they had met had been a disaster, and she'd left him semi-conscious and lying on a footpath! For her second mission, in Trieste, he had chosen her reluctantly, because of both her inexperience and her personal involvement with the principal player, which had already cost her a promising career in the Foreign Office. She had carried off the mission successfully, and with very little help from anyone else.

When Lucas had learned about his granddaughter's involvement, he was worried and unhappy about the extreme risks she was taking, but he respected her need to redeem herself. And in her place, he would have resented special treatment. It would appear like a lack of belief in her skill or her courage.

"I'm grateful for our man in Berlin," said Lucas. "That is, the hotel porter. Another invisible person doing a vital job. What would we get accomplished without them?"

"Very little," Peter said. "Most of them do it for the love of the cause, or revenge for friends or family lost already. Heaven knows, we pay them little enough. Sometimes we don't even thank them afterward."

"And sometimes they play both sides of the street," Lucas added. "Why do we do this job at all?" he said with a slight smile, but there was sadness in it, and also heartfelt emotions.

There was not a shred of humor in Peter's face.

"What other choice is there?" he answered. "We're talking about germ warfare. It only takes one infected person, or one exploded canister, to release the toxin and carry it over half the world! We can't let either of those men remain in Germany." His voice was intense, yet quiet. "It's not like the poison gas in the trenches, Lucas. This is so much more."

"You . . . said so." Now it was Lucas who was nearly at a loss for words.

"Think about the influenza that followed the war. I'm sure you remember that. It killed even more than the war itself. And it took the best and the strongest, much of the time. Against germ warfare, we have no defense. We're trying! But we can never underestimate the Germans. The cost of slipping up on this could be the creation of a germ that could wipe out a quarter of mankind."

Lucas thought this was probably an exaggeration, but that was immaterial. He could remember; everyone could. "Is it really in that order of horror?" he asked.

"I don't know," said Peter. "Is it worth taking that risk?"

"Of course not. But . . . are you saying that Hartwig might already know how to defend against it?"

"He's working on that, from what we can interpret," Peter answered. "But there's more to it than that."

He paused for a moment, and Lucas felt his sense of alarm grow.

"Some of our leaders in Whitehall are convinced the Germans are getting settled in, that there's a return of order and hope. There's food on most tables, trains are running on time. But we can't go to sleep in the sun and suppose that they will go on like this, meaning us no harm. Hitler means harm to anyone who gets in his way. Some of our leaders may not think so. There'll be battles in Parliament over it, until history proves who's right. By which time it will be too late to begin dealing with it. We have to prepare for the fallout, whoever is right, or whoever wins. Please God, let's hope that the people who are right are also the ones who win!"

"That's unusually optimistic of you, Peter."

"It would be optimistic if I said that the winners *will* be the ones on the side of what's good and right," Peter replied bitterly. He raised his eyes a little and met Lucas's with a hard, level stare, full of apprehension.

"What?"

Peter inhaled deeply before speaking. "Paulus has risen to power again. He's in charge of the department that oversees germ warfare. Just got word from Cordell in Berlin."

Lucas felt as if he had taken a step and the ground had given way under his feet. "Johann Paulus?"

"Indeed," Peter said.

Lucas struggled to disbelieve him. He found himself shaking his head. "He was finished! Disgraced," he protested.

"Yes, he was," Peter agreed. "In 1917. You made a laughingstock of him, and he disappeared without a trace. Except perhaps an echo of the laughter, which still scalds him like acid. But a lot can happen in seventeen years. He was only in his late forties then, a lot younger than you. You didn't bury a corpse, Lucas, you planted a seed. And men like him don't ever forgive. He's back again. In charge of quite a large section of the Intelligence Service, including germ warfare."

Lucas began to feel cold, as if an icy draft were coming from somewhere. "Why are you telling me this?"

"A warning. I had to tell you. From what little I know of your history with him, he won't have forgiven you." There was a trace of a smile on Peter's face. "What the hell did you actually do?"

Lucas shook his head slowly, as if he needed time to think all this through. "His hatred for me is based on more than professional victories and losses during the war," he said. "It became very personal. Paulus, in all his arrogance, bought into a series of 'top secret' messages that my people made sure he would uncover. Based on these, he led his crack team directly into an ambush, and most of his men were killed. The few survivors were taken prisoner."

Peter nodded. "So, Paulus was not only stripped of his rank, but his reputation was shattered as well."

"But not irrevocably if he's been reinstated." Lucas inhaled deeply and released a loud sigh. "Undoubtedly, he's never forgiven me," he said.

"He's from Prussia, right?" asked Peter.

"Yes, and brilliantly trained, of iron self-discipline. Not known for forgiving or forgetting."

Lucas forced himself to push aside thoughts of Paulus and return to his granddaughter's safety. "You haven't sent Elena using her own name, have you?"

"Don't be so bloody stupid!" Peter snapped. "Of course I haven't!" He took a deep breath, as if suddenly hearing the harshness of his reply, and to a man he deeply respected. "She's Ellen Stewart. She'll go in there quietly, and, please God, will bring Heinrich Hartwig out with her. We need someone German Intelligence doesn't know as one of our own, but also someone who is imaginative enough to improvise, to think of something new, if she has to. And who has the nerve to save Hartwig, if she can—but also kill him, if she must."

Lucas was startled. He remembered the little girl, the granddaughter he had known since the day of her birth. "And you think she can do that?" He tried to keep the disbelief out of his voice and knew at once that he had failed.

Peter rubbed his head ruefully. "Yes, I do. I still remember how she knocked me out in Berlin."

"She thought you were the enemy!" Lucas protested.

"She understands that Hartwig will be better off dead than in the hands of the Gestapo. That is, if he's caught escaping."

Lucas had no answer.

When Peter spoke next, his voice was a little above a whisper. "Germ warfare will be far worse, and—"

"I know," Lucas said, cutting him off. And then he drew a deep breath. Only minutes earlier, that very same thought had crossed his mind. "I know."

Lucas went home in the late afternoon. The sun was still high and bright, the color not yet deepening in the west. The days were long at this time of the year, and the heat soaked into the pavement, radiating it back. Lucas could feel it when he parked the car outside the garage and walked round to the front door. The climbing roses were in full bloom, yellow and pink, some even dropping petals already.

He opened the front door and stepped in. He was about to call out to Josephine when Toby came skating around the corner, slipping on the polished wood of the hall floor, and then throwing himself at Lucas. He was a golden retriever, still young, but Lucas was certain that his enthusiasm would always delude him into believing he was a puppy.

"Toby!" Josephine's voice came from the kitchen. "Don't jump all over him."

Lucas bent down and hugged the dog. "Do as you're told," he said gently, rubbing Toby's ears. He did not expect for a moment to be obeyed.

Josephine came to the kitchen door, smiling. Her face was unusual, strong boned, generous, and full of humor. It was the fashion now for women to have their hair short, but Josephine still wore her thick, silver-gray hair coiled up on her head.

She smiled at Lucas. "What if I tell Toby it's suppertime?" she asked. "That should get his attention!"

Toby took no notice of her. The magic word was "dinner."

Lucas stood up, smiling. "Come on, Toby, dinnertime."

Toby beat him to the kitchen door, tail wagging as he careened around the doorway and across to where his bowl stood. He picked it up and held it between his jaws.

"I don't know how he can do that without dropping it," Josephine said.

"I suppose it's practice," Lucas answered, putting one arm around his wife and kissing her cheek.

"Good day?" Josephine asked dubiously as she met his eyes.

He started to explain, then changed his mind. "I'll tell you, but let's eat first. I think I missed lunch." He vaguely recalled a sandwich with nothing specific in it.

"Cold bacon-and-egg pie and a little apple pie after?"

"Hot?" he asked.

She gave him a sideways glance. "Of course hot. And with very cold clotted cream."

He smiled with intense satisfaction.

After the meal, Lucas went into his favorite room and settled into his armchair. He stared out of the windows. This room opened onto the back, revealing the small lawn and the trees beyond. They were mostly poplars, towering above the rooftops, their leaves shimmering and turning in the sunset wind. He had lived here nearly all his adult life, and he loved it deeply. It was home. Memories were woven into the pictures on the walls. The way the light fell at the different seasons, the patches on the carpet worn thin with footsteps over the years. Except the rug by the fire. That was new. But it carried a different story, one to do with a traitor, a shooting, and death.

Josephine came into the room and sat on the sofa. She picked up her knitting bag and removed her latest project.

It was time he told her about Elena. During the war, they had each kept secrets, and it was one of the great comforts that they no longer had to. Of course, they probably should have, but they understood the need for total discretion.

"I saw Peter today," Lucas remarked quite casually.

"How is he?" she asked.

Lucas was sure she knew this was not about Peter; she was merely signaling that she was listening.

"Concerned about two German scientists," he replied. Was he going to share this with her to avoid carrying it alone? It seemed to him that she always knew if he was shouldering an extra emotional burden. He normally told her after the events occurred, but tiny things would give him away: something forgotten, reassuring habits repeated without realizing, the details a good agent would notice.

"German scientists," she repeated. "And concerned about what? Is this something more about the possibility of an atomic bomb?"

"In a way, it's far worse."

Josephine's hands were busy knitting. He liked the regular click the needles made, a very gentle, domestic sound. Now it stopped. She did not say anything, merely looked up at him.

"Germ warfare," he told her. "Not fully developed yet, not complete, but we need to get the men involved in the development out of Berlin as soon as possible. Peter has sent two agents, one for each of the scientists." He saw apprehension in her face. "One of them is Elena," he finished.

She did not change her expression, or even stiffen her body. The only difference he noticed were the two stitches that had slipped off the needle, and she did not bother to pick them up.

She breathed out slowly. "I see. But ... Berlin ... again?" She bent down to focus on picking up those stitches. "Mightn't they recognize her? It was only a year ago."

She was referring to Elena's last trip there, which had very nearly ended in tragedy. "It's a big city," he answered. "And we have to send our best."

"Is she one of our best?" Josephine asked, her eyes wide. "If she is, then she's not expendable."

"No one is expendable," he pointed out. "If the Germans expect anyone, it will be a man, and one they know. We can't afford to lose even one, Jo. We never can, but now more than ever. Elena has the best chance. She looks so harmless."

"Is it bad, this germ warfare situation?" she asked, her voice almost level. "I know it's been around for as long as we have fought each other, and perhaps since the dawn of civilization. A thousand years ago, two thousand, they used to throw the corpses of diseased cattle in the enemy's water supply. But I assume this is rather more sophisticated."

"Worse than gas in the trenches," said Lucas. "It can be used against civilian populations, entire regions wiped out with one round."

"What would be the point in poisoning a civilian population? You can't conquer anything then—no land, no peoples, no looting, nothing. Isn't it self-defeating?" she asked.

"For the first city you use it against, yes, it might be self-defeating, but after that, the threat would—"

"I see," she interrupted. "A bit like the threat of atomic bombs: half the world obliterated, so the other half will surrender. I don't think the Germans would do that."

Her voice sounded strong, but Lucas heard the doubt. Jo was an optimist, but also a realist.

"Jo, please! If we really thought about the end of things, we wouldn't do half what we do."

She bent down and focused again on her project, threading through the stitches carefully with a knitting needle, and then rolling the garment and putting the whole thing in the bag. "We do a lot of senseless things, Lucas. Like arguing against a decision that's already been made."

"Yes, I agree." He wanted to add more. He wanted to reach out and take her hands in his, but only for his own sake.

She looked at him steadily. "Is there going to be another war? And please don't insult me by lying. It isn't any comfort."

"Possibly," he said at last. "But that's better than blind submission. It depends on who's in charge. I understand those who say 'never again.' And I agree that we must never again send an entire generation to slaughter. But look at what's already happening in Germany. There's violence in the streets, the persecution of minorities, and imprisonment of political opponents in camps like Dachau and Nohra."

She said nothing.

Lucas sighed. "I know," he said quietly. "You and I are old. We're not of the generation that's going to be sent into the trenches. We'll probably be bombed in our own homes. And if we lose, we'll end up seeing the country taken over, enemy soldiers marching in our streets. Coming into our houses."

"We all know what happened to France last time," Josephine said grimly. "And before you say it, I'll say it for you. If we don't fight it abroad, we'll end up fighting it at home. And worst of all, losing to an alien ideology the very people we think we're protecting."

Lucas was very quiet for a moment. He had expressed his thoughts on this matter to Josephine on so many occasions. And yet they niggled away at him. "My fear is that nothing has changed in Parliament. Perhaps not in the entire country. So many of our leaders are blindly seeing what they want to. I have to remind myself to look very closely before blaming some of those who are saying we must never have another war, whatever the cost. These wounds don't heal, not completely. We lost our grandson, and that will always hurt, but it's important that I feel everyone's pain."

There was no need for Josephine to respond. She knew too well that Lucas still had nightmares over the terrible decisions he had been forced to make as head of MI6, and the men and women who set out on dangerous missions—missions that he controlled—and did not come back.

Now it was peacetime, albeit an uneasy peace, and Elena had been sent to Berlin . . . again.

Lucas closed his fingers over Josephine's and held them gently, but not so gently that, had she wanted, she could have withdrawn them. His mind teemed with things he wanted to say, but her knowing would change nothing, only make her fear more deeply for Elena. He kept his silence.

CHAPTER

3

Hans Beckendorff stood at attention in front of the polished desk with its scattered papers, blotter, built-in inkwell, and assorted pens and pencils. He was avoiding looking at the picture of the Führer in its silver frame, turned sideways so that both the man behind the desk and anyone standing where Hans was could see the face.

Hans had only had the privilege of working for General Johann Paulus for three or four months, but he knew better than to relax until he was given specific permission.

Paulus was a man in his mid-sixties, although it was difficult to tell his age from his appearance. He was solid, muscular, and in spite of his thick body, he moved with ease. But there was nothing of ease in his manner today. He was stiff, formal, very correct. It was almost as though he was on his guard about something.

Paulus held the high rank of general, yet there were whispers that he had been demoted in the past, and had only recently been restored to this position. The demotion had happened toward the end of the Great War, as it was called. Something had occurred that was never referred to, and Hans had no desire to know more of it.

Whatever his transgression had been, Johann Paulus was back in charge and leading a very important part of Military Intelligence.

Hans was ambitious. He was an only child, and his parents had great hopes for him. They had sacrificed much to give him the very best education, and he had justified their trust by getting top marks. He had graduated in law but chose the army, and then joined the Gestapo as an officer, which required a higher ambition than the law, especially in the present climate. The Gestapo was an elite police force, highly disciplined, many of them university graduates, not a group of rabble-rousers like the Brownshirts.

Hans knew that Paulus had gained the Führer's respect and, what was even more important, his trust. With this trust, there was no end to the heights one might reach, the opportunities available. Skill, patience, and above all loyalty were required by the Führer, and Paulus fulfilled them all. And one by one, Paulus was choosing the men who would form the Führer's inner circle, the men he could trust.

Hans waited for Paulus to address him.

The sunlight was bright through the window. It would have shown even a speck of dust, but there was none for it to find.

"I have been speaking with the Führer," Paulus began. His voice was very soft, as if he were imparting a confidence. It was a habit with him. It obliged listeners to watch him, partially read his lips, to be certain they did not miss anything.

Hans remained silent. It would be extremely foolish for him to do anything else, and Hans was not a fool. The expression on Paulus's face made it clear that the man understood his own power. There was a confidence, an assurance about him, as if he knew his strengths and his weaknesses and had tight control of both.

"He is concerned about some of the violence in the streets," Paulus stated, watching Hans closely. "It is not the Gestapo, of course," he added.

Did he want an answer? Hans judged that he did. He took a chance. "No, sir. The incidents that I have seen, or heard about, were caused by Röhm's Brownshirts." He did not try to keep the contempt out of his voice.

There was a flicker of satisfaction in Paulus's eyes. "You've seen that, eh? Good."

"Yes, sir."

"Do you happen to know how many there are of them?"

It was not that Paulus did not know, but rather a test to see if Hans did. "Yes, sir," he said. "Approximately three million. Thirty times the size of the regular army, at least." He allowed his disapproval of the number, even the danger of it, to show in his face.

"Exactly," Paulus agreed, his eyes narrowing a little. "It worries you?"

Hans knew that Paulus was asking for a commitment, and that was dangerous, but Hans had no choice. Paulus hated evasion. He considered it cowardice. After betrayal, that was the ultimate sign of weakness, and the worst of sins.

Hans stood a little straighter. "I believe there is a danger that their chief allegiance is to Röhm, not to the Führer. That means not to Germany."

The satisfaction in Paulus's face was clearly visible.

The general hesitated for several seconds before continuing. "And Himmler? What do you think of him?" he asked.

Now Hans was really caught. Paulus had given no indication of what he felt about the one-time chicken farmer suddenly risen to power. Himmler was a cold, neat little man, with a mustache that was a pale imitation of Hitler's. Hans felt a certain revulsion toward him, without knowing why. He decided to answer Paulus honestly. The man had a sixth sense for a lie, even a lie that was born of confusion, rather than an intent to deceive. Hans felt he must not appear to be evasive. "I do not trust him, sir. Perhaps I am being unfair to him, but I find myself cautious."

"Of what?" There was not even a shadow of a smile on Paulus's face. But then, Johann Paulus had never shown a sense of humor. If anything amused him, he hid it well. It was one of the things that set him apart, that and his present hard-won invulnerability.

"Of his loyalties," Hans replied. Had he taken a risk saying that?

"To what?" Paulus said immediately.

"Not to Germany, sir. But I wonder sometimes if he thinks his plans for the country might be slightly different from the Führer's. If we don't travel together, sir, we won't get anywhere we want." Even as he said it, he wondered if he really meant it, at least in the way it sounded. He had believed so a few months ago. But as he had given certain events more consideration recently, disturbing thoughts had arisen.

"And Dr. Goebbels?" Paulus asked.

"That's different, sir. I think he is single-minded, sir."

Paulus nodded slowly. "Yes, you would be wise to keep your opinions to yourself, Beckendorff. Tread softly, watch carefully." He blinked, but his focus did not alter. "Action may become necessary. I rely on you." He stared at Hans without wavering.

"Yes, sir."

For an instant, all Hans could see were Paulus's small, unblinking eyes. Hans drew a deep breath. He was about to speak when Paulus prevented him.

"Have you met the Führer, Beckendorff?"

"I've seen him, sir, but I've not met him."

"Then it's time you did. You must move forward, if you are to be of use to me. I have plans for you, Beckendorff." Paulus gave one of his rare smiles. He had remarkably good, straight teeth. Then the moment vanished. He rose to his feet. "Come," he ordered. He walked straight past Hans and left him to follow on his heels as he went out of the door, down the stairs, and into the street.

Hans caught up with him but did not say anything. He had no reasonable choice but to follow Paulus, having been ordered to do so. They walked in silence for the next ten minutes. Even when they went inside the building and were acknowledged by the guard, he still said nothing. Was he really going to meet the Führer? He felt tense, even nervous.

They went up a flight of stairs to an office on the first floor. The man guarding the area clearly knew Paulus, and nodded him past, with another soldier now walking beside them. Since Hans was with Paulus, he too was permitted to go in without question.

It was an extraordinary experience, to pass by all the formalities as if they were merely for other people. It was a mark of the general's rank, and far more important than all the gold braid on his shoulders, or even the ribbons from battles still remembered. It gave Hans a new regard for Paulus.

They stopped at another door. The soldier accompanying them knocked. At a word from inside, he opened it and nodded Paulus through, and Hans followed on his heels.

The room inside was large and sunlit, very tidy. Hans could even smell furniture polish. But it was the man standing in the center of the rug in front of the desk, as if he had been expecting someone to come, that took his attention. He was of average height, a trifle thick around the middle, which was the effect of a wide uniform belt around the outside of his jacket. His highly familiar face held Hans's attention. He had seen him before, always from several yards' distance. But now he was within six feet of Adolf Hitler, the Führer.

Hans noted the pallor of his skin, the dense thickness of his hair, and the startling crystal-clear blue of his eyes. He froze for an instant, then shot his right arm in the air. *"Heil Hitler,"* he and Paulus said in tandem. His mouth went dry. He felt his stomach churning.

"General Paulus," Hitler said quietly. "And who is this young man? Another of those for whom you have plans?" He turned toward Hans, then back again to Paulus, his eyebrows slightly raised.

"Hans Beckendorff, *mein Führer*. A young officer who supports the legal police, and the army. He is anxious about the rise of the SA," Paulus replied. Then he added, "The Brownshirts." His voice was suddenly heavy with contempt.

Hans listened and wondered if Hitler was offended by Paulus's explanation. Who didn't know that the army formally known as the *Sturmabteilung,* the SA, was commonly referred to as the Brownshirts?

Hitler turned to Hans again, staring at him with interest.

Hans looked back. He did not lower his eyes, as if he were afraid or trying to hide his thoughts.

"You don't trust Röhm?" Hitler asked him.

Hans felt his stomach turn over. "I am worried about the ever-increasing size of his force, *mein Führer.* It is thirty times the size of the regular army."

Hitler's face tightened, as if the answer displeased him. Hans felt the chill run right through his body. Why had Paulus brought him here? He must not speak. No one spoke without the Führer's permission.

Paulus cleared his throat.

"What?" Hitler said sharply, swinging around to face Paulus instead of Hans.

"Our young officer here does not entirely trust Himmler either," Paulus said quietly. "He is Gestapo, of course," he added, tipping his head toward Hans. "Good degree in law, and his loyalty is entirely to you, *mein Führer.* He may become useful to us, in time to come. I wished him to meet you. It is a privilege he will not forget."

There was a silence. Seconds ticked by.

"Good," Hitler said at last. "Loyalty. I like that. We need more of it." He looked from Paulus to Hans, and back again.

"We do," Paulus agreed. "And even more than that, we need to be sure who is loyal . . . and who is not. Particularly now."

Hitler's eyes narrowed. "Have you got something to say, Paulus?" he asked.

"We need men like Beckendorff, sir. Good family. Long history of service. And, as I said, a graduate of university. Law degree." Paulus took a deep breath and looked straight at Hitler. "Married last year. New baby." He glanced briefly at Hans, then back at Hitler. "Everything to live for. Live decently. Build a good society. The sort of young man never corruptible by the likes of Röhm."

Something in Hitler relaxed. He nodded slowly, as if he understood not only what Paulus was saying, but the meaning behind it.

A thought flicked across Hans's mind. There were ugly stories about Ernst Röhm, head of the Brownshirts. These stories included wild parties where young boys were assaulted. It was said of others in Röhm's circle as well. Hints about greed and indulgences. Drunken debacles.

Hitler was a vegetarian and abstainer from all alcohol. He abhorred vulgarity. Hermann Goering's gorging on food and the various other reported physical indulgences repelled him.

Or was Hans imagining some subtext? Glancing momentarily at Paulus's face, he thought it was real.

"I'm watching, sir. Every day," Paulus continued. "But we have enemies. Every great man does. Even more so when he is on the verge of making history that the world will not forget."

Hans did not know whether to be frightened or excited. He felt both.

"Gestapo, you said?" Hitler continued, looking at Hans. "Good. Regular police, regular army." He turned to Paulus before Hans was forced to think of a reply. "Thank you, Paulus, you're a loyal man."

Paulus snapped to attention and raised his right arm in the Hitler salute.

Hans instantly followed him, quietly breathing a sigh of relief. And then he held his breath until they were outside the door and it was safely closed.

He looked at Paulus.

Paulus smiled only slightly, but his eyes were bright. "You are fortunate, Beckendorff. You have earned your opportunities. But I have given you the openings to make the most of them. Remember that. Treasure it. Now go home."

"Yes, sir," Hans said. "Thank you, sir."

*   *   *

Before he went home, Hans stopped to see his parents. Gratitude welled up inside him and he wanted to tell them what rich fruit their sacrifices had borne. They deserved that, and part of his pleasure was the fact that he could thank them for all they had given him. It was not only the education, the time and place to study, but the encouragement, the belief in him. Maybe that was the greatest gift.

As he had expected, his parents were delighted to see him.

"I have news," he said, cutting across his mother's greeting. She was usually a very self-controlled woman, her emotions revealed only in words, not in the pitch of her voice, gestures, nor any changes to the color of her alabaster skin. But she responded to Hans; she always had. Now she looked at his face and her eyes were bright.

"I met the Führer," Hans told her immediately. "I mean, really met him, in his office, alone except for General Paulus."

"How did that happen?" she asked. "What did he say to you? Tell me!" Her eyes never left Hans's face. "He did speak to you, didn't he?"

"General Paulus told him I was a good man, and loyal, of good family."

"He said that about you, to the Führer?" she asked, her voice quivering with emotion.

"Yes. And the Führer said that we need more like me." He smiled, in spite of his resolution not to brag. He had to tell her. "Paulus said that I was reliable, and could be trusted." He could not help smiling again when he saw the gleam in his mother's eyes. "Thank you," he said more gently. He leaned forward and kissed her cheek. It was pale, smooth, and cool. "Thank you, Mother."

His father stayed back. He was not an emotional man, but his face shone with pride. Hans met his eyes for a moment. His father smiled and nodded almost imperceptibly.

CHAPTER

4

Hans continued on his way home. He was later than he would have been, had he not stopped off to see his parents. But it was worth it. Now that he had thanked them for all they had given him, he could devote what was left of the evening to Cecily and their baby, Madeleine.

He eased up his speed a little. Without meaning to, he had been driving much too quickly. The last thing he needed was to be stopped for speeding.

He slowed down and drove more sedately, as befitted a man so trusted by the Führer himself.

He had Paulus to thank for that, and he must not forget it. Paulus was not an easy man to like. Respect for him was another thing. One knew, even at a glance, that he was precise, meticulous. His work ethics were flawless: he always arrived early and left late. His concentration was phenomenal. Was that what made him different? Was it his dedication? His understanding of men, and what they could do?

Did he also recognize all their weaknesses? That was a thought

Hans did not want to pursue. One day he might have to, but not today.

He pulled up to the curb and parked outside his own house. It was small, and not special to anyone else—looking exactly like its neighbors on either side—but he loved it. It gave him that sense of belonging. There was now order in his life, where only a few short years ago there had been chaos.

Hans knew that his law degree was important, as was being chosen for the Gestapo. They were the new police of order, bringing safety again to the German people. So different from the hooligans of the Brownshirts, who did not seem to be aware of any law.

He switched off the engine, ensured that the brake was engaged, then stepped out and locked the door. He walked up the path, and lengthened his stride. He put his key in the door, pushing it open.

The air inside was sweet and cool, not heavy like the breathless, dusty heat of the street, with its smell of car engines and petrol.

"Hello!" he called.

"Hans? Hello! Upstairs!"

He took the stairs two at a time, then stopped on the landing. The light was on in the baby's room. He went to the door and pushed it wider. Cecily was standing beside the crib, their sleeping baby in her arms.

She was not a big woman. In fact, she still looked like a girl who had not yet reached her full height. The weight she had put on during pregnancy had almost disappeared. Was that normal to lose it so fast? Was she getting enough to eat? Was he looking after her properly? And little Madeleine had come early—by more than a month. She had been so small.

Cecily was smiling at him. Her dark hair was short, not really a fashionable bob. It was too curly for that: thick, soft, and dark. It was now pinned back, out of her way. It did not matter what she did with it, it always looked soft and clean. He loved the touch of it, like silk.

She spoke very softly. "She's just gone to sleep."

He could not speak. There seemed nothing to say, and he was

choked with emotion. He walked over and looked down at the tiny baby in her arms. His baby. He was mesmerized by her. She was so small, so perfect. She had such fair skin, absolutely blemishless, and so soft that his fingers barely felt it. Her wispy hair was dark, as dark as her mother's.

Madeleine was asleep, and he would not waken her, but he wished her eyes were open. They were sky blue. Darker than his, deeper, not brown like her mother's.

He looked at the tiny hands, only just big enough to grasp one of his fingers, and yet perfect. The smallest hands imaginable, with minute pink fingernails, and so strong. Whenever she clasped his finger, the warmth of it ran through his whole body.

Did she cling to anything she could hold . . . or did she know he was her father?

He touched her very gently. She was sound asleep. Completely unaware of him. He glanced up at Cecily. "Do you think she knows me?" he asked. Then he felt stupid.

Cecily smiled. "She knows she's safe." It was a perfect reply. It comforted him, without telling him a lie.

He wanted to tell Cecily about Paulus, and how he had taken him to meet the Führer. It was important, because it spoke to the future—their future—and to their safety and financial security. But he was not sure how to begin.

She broke into his thoughts. "Are you hungry? Supper's ready. We could eat while she's asleep."

Practical. Cecily had to be practical, always. One could not look after a tiny creature like Madeleine without being practical. Eat. Sleep. Be clean, dry, and safe. He had noticed already that from the day she was born, Madeleine had taken her mood from Cecily. If Cecily was afraid, anxious, or worried, if she was at ease—whatever she felt, then so did Madeleine. What a towering responsibility.

Cecily was looking at him, waiting for his answer.

"Yes, yes, please."

"Don't they even give you time to eat?" she asked with a frown, very carefully laying Madeleine down in her bed, on her back. There was a pillow nearby, stuffed with some kind of loose grain. It was not soft, as he had expected. When he questioned it, Cecily had explained to him how something soft could suffocate her. If she turned onto her side or, worse still, onto her stomach, the air could not come through. Cecily used this firm pillow to support the baby's back, if she was on her side.

The thought had troubled him. He sometimes got up in the night to check that Madeleine was asleep and breathing. It was absurd, but he could not help it. He knew exactly why Cecily got up so many times in the night, even though he was barely aware of the movement, the chill for a moment or two, then the warmth again when she returned.

They ate quietly in the dining room, off the kitchen. Hans had not realized how hungry he was. All day, he had not even thought of eating.

When he finished, including a second helping of strawberry flan, he sat back.

Cecily was staring at him. "What?" she asked. "You've been dying to say something ever since you came in. What happened?"

"I met the Führer, and it was face-to-face." He watched as her eyes widened with something close to disbelief. "General Paulus took me to his office. There were just the three of us in the room." He looked at her expression, the expectation, and a shadow of fear. Sometimes he forgot she was English, and that she had spent much of her childhood here in Berlin. Her father, Roger Cordell, was the cultural attaché at the British Embassy, and had held that position for a long time. Cecily spoke German fluently, probably because she used it more often than English. She was at home here. She understood the customs, the food, all the things that are familiar in a city: the best parks and places to eat, where to buy quality goods cheaply. She even knew the "in" jokes. She would not know as much about London, or any other city in England. And yet, with all of this adapting, she was still not used to the idea of the Führer.

"Paulus took me to the Führer to tell him that I was trustworthy," Hans began to explain. "That my family was good, my parents. And that I had a wife and a daughter now."

"What did the Führer say, and why would he want to know that?" She was plainly confused.

He put his hand out, across the table, and touched hers gently. "Because there's a lot of anxiety about Röhm, and some of the people who support him."

She colored faintly and looked down at the table. "So, it's true. Röhm really is as perverted as people say? I thought it might be just gossip." He did not reply. "Hans, don't be such a gentleman. I know what they say about Röhm. Everyone goes around in circles, just as you're doing, but I know what they mean."

He found himself suddenly self-conscious. He would rather she didn't know about such things, but perhaps that was unrealistic.

"Yes, I'm afraid it is true. But it's hard to know how to address it. Where even to begin. There are three million men in the Brownshirts now, which far outnumbers the regular army."

"Oh, please! Don't even think of such a thing!" she protested. "Is the Führer going to do something about it? How can he stop it?"

"I don't know. It's hard to know where to start. I think he has many enemies, people who are greedy for power and have no love for our country. I'm grateful to General Paulus for telling him that I am to be trusted. In all manner of ways."

She frowned and took a deep breath. "Hans?"

"What?"

"Do you think there's any danger?"

He felt suddenly cold. He knew she was afraid—not for herself. No, it would be for Madeleine.

"No," he said firmly. "No, we will take care to prevent any violence, threats to civilians, long before it comes close to us. But when you build a country, build it from ashes, there are bound to be bad people, greedy people who want more. The Führer knows of them. And it'll take time to get rid of them, get them out of power. He's a decent man, Cecily. He wants safety for the people, and prosperity again. He knows who the enemies are." Please heaven that was true!

"We are very lucky," she said softly.

"We are."

"I mean all three of us." She seemed to know what he was thinking. "You and me. And Madeleine. Thank you, Hans."

The wave of emotion almost drowned him. He tried to think of something to say that was strong enough, but no words came.

He was saved by the front doorbell sounding. "I'll go," he said.

On the step, in the sunlight blazing low on the horizon, was Cecily's father, Roger Cordell. She looked like him, the same dark hair, the balance of her features a smaller, more delicate version of his.

Hans searched Cordell's face. "Everything all right, sir?" he asked.

"Yes. I . . ." Roger smiled, slightly self-conscious, an extraordinary thing for him. He was a professional diplomat; nothing seemed to disconcert him, except a breach of courtesy, or an ill-tailored jacket. Real disasters were treated with quiet voices, outwardly at least, and always with complete control.

"Are you sure?" Hans asked, stepping back so the man could enter. "Please, come in."

Cordell did so and closed the door behind him.

"Did you come to see the baby?" Hans asked, then wished he had not. It was far more likely it was something diplomatic. Or else to reassure Winifred, Cecily's mother, that her daughter was recovering from what had been a difficult early birth.

Cordell smiled. "Actually, yes. I remember holding Cecily when she was just a few weeks old. Winifred wanted me to share her feelings, to love her as she did, and she could hardly let her go."

With these familial memories, suddenly, all of Paulus's good words and promotions, even Hitler, seemed irrelevant. Hans led the way inside, and into the small dining area, with all the familiar treasures collected over the last years: the blue and white Dresden dish, the ebony clock on the mantelpiece. Cecily had already taken the dishes away and had put them in the kitchen.

"Hello, Father," she said. "Like some tea? We've just finished dinner, so your timing is perfect."

Cordell relaxed. He was a handsome man, slender. His mustache was always trimmed, and his clothes, whether casual or formal, were always immaculate, even at the end of a long day. One had to know him well to read his deeper emotions. He normally displayed grace, consideration, only very occasionally anger.

Cecily shot a soft smile at Hans, and put the kettle back on the stove. "This will take a few minutes. Would you like to come up and visit Madeleine?" she asked her father.

Cordell smiled, and Hans could see that he relished this family time.

They all went upstairs. Cecily opened the bedroom door softly and went in first. She looked into the crib, then bent and picked up the baby very gently, handing her to Cordell.

Hans felt himself tense. He had to force himself not to step forward and intervene. He was impossibly taut, muscles aching, in case . . . what? He should drop her? He was being stupid.

Cordell moved very gently, rocking Madeleine in his arms, and smiled again. He looked across at Cecily. "You looked just like this when I first held you. Just as small, just as beautiful, and just as precious. And absolutely perfect."

Cordell lifted a finger and very gently stroked Madeleine's brow, and then up into the shadow of the silky, dark hair. She opened her eyes, gave a little hiccup, and then settled back, eyes studying her grandfather's face.

"You're right," Cordell said in whispered amazement, looking at Cecily, then Hans. "They really are blue! As blue as the sky!"

Hans felt a ridiculous surge of pride. Madeleine had dark hair like Cecily, but the blue eyes were his.

Cordell spoke to the baby, softly, for a few minutes, something about growing up and learning to read and write. It didn't really matter what it was, only that she listened, her eyes fixed on his face. She knew he was talking to her.

In that moment, Hans felt a wave of emotion so profound it took his breath away. It was something deeper than any act or belief, and it was unbreakable, in the blood. Cordell had held Cecily like this when she was a newborn, and he felt he would live or die to protect her. Hans felt that now for Madeleine. She was his own child. She was worth fighting for, and with anything that it cost, because he must make the future safe for her.

And for Cecily. Always.

CHAPTER

5

Elena flew from London to Paris the day after her briefing with Peter Howard, and then traveled by train into the city. She had been here dozens of times, having even lived here for a few years when her father was the ambassador. The outskirts of the city were always changing, and yet the heart was the same: the light on the river, the exquisite façades built after the Revolution, and in the quiet backstreets and the parks, trees in full leaf.

It was midsummer now. The sun set late and it was twilight far into the evening. Central Paris still filled her with the old magic. The City of Lights. Those soft lights were everywhere, warming buildings whose illuminated façades gleamed in the air, reflected in the river, moving in the headlamps of cars.

Elena wanted to stay, because it was familiar, beautiful, and because she did not want to take the next step: the long night train from the Gare du Nord into Germany . . . again. The last time she had taken that train she had been a fugitive, the German police close on her heels.

Being here brought back difficult memories, but it was not as if she could refuse the job. If she did that, she could jeopardize the whole operation. By the time they got someone else, it could be too late. And if she accepted a job, made the commitment, and then backed away, MI6 would have to throw her out. It would be, in effect, as if she were a soldier who ran away in the face of the enemy. Her family would be so ashamed.

She walked into the huge, high-ceilinged train station. It was quiet at this time of the evening.

She thought of her brother, as she often did when she was afraid. She was the youngest of the Standish children; Margot was older than her, and Mike had been the eldest. He had died on the battle-front in the last few weeks of the war. No matter how many years passed, she could still remember him vividly, his voice always in her head. *Hang in there, kiddo! See you soon!* That had been sixteen years ago now.

She straightened up, gave the guard at the barrier her ticket. With a warm smile, she said, "Good evening."

"Good evening, miss. Have a good journey. Your seat is in the front carriage."

"Thank you." She smiled again, then took back the punched ticket and walked forward, carrying her single case.

She found her seat. Fortunately, when the train began to move, the carriage was still half empty. She had room to stretch out across three seats, allowing her to rest.

A few of her fellow passengers were able to sleep almost immediately, propped upright, a thing Elena had never been able to do.

She dozed on and off, and after they had crossed the border into Germany and she'd shown her papers and passed inspection, she was able to sleep for nearly two hours. She woke up shortly before the train drew into the station in Berlin. It was already broad daylight. There were no more formalities now, just the need to blend into the crowd of early morning arrivals and to look indistinguishable from the droves of people arriving for their day's work.

As Elena got off the train, her suitcase felt weightier. She was carrying only an additional two changes of clothes for the week, underwear, a second pair of shoes, and of course the usual collection of toiletries, all packed by Mrs. Smithers at MI6. After too little sleep, the case dragged on her arm and shoulder. She had not brought any notes on Heinrich Hartwig, of course: they had been studied, memorized, and then destroyed.

He sounded like a nice man. Always studious, dedicated to his work, which was merely outlined so she knew the general area of science and medicine in which he specialized and excelled. But he was by no means boring. He liked architecture, and he could tell who had lived in a city by the buildings they had left behind, the stone monuments to their beliefs, each beautiful in its own way.

He spoke German and English, but he read in other languages also, particularly Italian, and he liked Russian poetry.

He had no children, although he had been married, but his wife had died several years ago. The very impressive record of his education was there, but no account of his friendships, simply that they existed. Perhaps that was wise.

Elena queued outside the station entrance for a taxi. Most other people did not have suitcases, but otherwise, she was exactly like anyone else in the crowd. People looked at her without seeing anything but another person not to be bumped into. Her appearance made her fit in quite well. She was a little above average in height. In a light coat, suitable for the midsummer weather, she looked of average build. Her thick blond hair was worn in a long bob with a heavy natural wave. With her clear, fair skin and blue eyes, she looked much like millions of other young German women. Pleasant, but not memorable.

Her turn came and she gave the taxi driver the address of the middle-sized and very ordinary hotel in which she had a week's booking, with the option of extending her stay, if she wished. She would like to have checked in with the British Embassy. She knew that Roger Cordell was head of MI6 in Germany. Perhaps he would be told of this operation, perhaps not. The embassy would be the place where she could get in touch with Peter, even possibly her grandfather Lucas. But to go there was impossibly risky and she had been warned off doing so: it would draw immediate attention to her. The slightest slip could be fatal. She must be ordinary, instantly forgotten. Completely average.

The taxi drew up outside the door of the hotel. It looked inconspicuous, but dulled by time, traffic fumes, possibly too little money spent on its upkeep.

She paid the fare and added the usual tip, took her case, and walked up to the large front door. It opened easily on a single push, and she was inside the lobby. The space was shabby, well worn, but extremely clean. Behind the reception desk, a young man greeted her with a slight smile.

"Good morning, madam," he said in German.

"Good morning," she replied in her own perfect German. She gave the name Peter Howard had assigned her, which was on her new passport.

"Yes, ma'am. We have your reservation. The room is ready for you. We were told you might manage to get here early in the day. Would you care for breakfast? Or at least a cup of coffee? Or a pot of tea perhaps?"

"I would love a pot of tea, thank you." Was that a mistake? Would it draw attention to her? So English! The English were laughed at, sometimes quite gently, over their endless cups of tea. She smiled at the man. "I had enough coffee on the train to last me quite a while."

He smiled back at her. "Ours would be better, I promise you. But, yes, tea. Would you like some toast as well? We have excellent pumpernickel, if you like?"

She remembered the dark-grained bread with pleasure. "Oh, yes, I would, thank you. Then I'll really feel as if I'm home."

He produced a key and handed it to her. "Your room is on the second floor, ma'am, right opposite the lift. I'll have the porter bring your case up."

"Thank you." She turned and went to the lift, then up to the second floor. The room was as she had been told: simple and clean.

The door opened easily, but it was heavy, and swung on silent hinges. Its weight surprised her. The lock would have been very hard to pick, and certainly it would take a battering ram to break the door down. She looked around. It was exactly like thousands of other anonymous hotel rooms. Generic pictures on the neutral-colored walls, instantly forgettable; one small cupboard for hanging clothes; a chest with three drawers. A small wall mirror reflected the light from the window. A single door led to a washbasin and toilet.

It was little more than five minutes before there was a knock on the door, and when she opened it, her suitcase was outside and a young bellboy was walking away. A second man, whom she presumed was the porter, stood there with a tray set with tea, a hot-water jug, a milk jug, sugar, and several slices of dark, toasted bread. Also butter and jam—black cherry jam, by the look of it. It was definitely one of her favorites. The sight of it lifted her spirits.

"Come in." She opened the door wide, and he passed her to put the tray on the small table, then went back for the case and placed it on the bed.

"Thank you," she said. She already had a suitable tip ready.

"No," he said, "thank you, miss." He closed the door, but was still inside.

"My name is Dietrich," he said, his voice low. "Mr. Howard asked me to be of such assistance as I can."

She felt the knot inside her becoming undone, and took a deep breath. "Oh, yes, thank you." She was so tired, it was a relief that someone from MI6 had made contact already. This was good, all going according to plan.

"Call me Dieter," he said.

"Thank you, Dieter."

"May I pour your tea, ma'am? And the toast is fresh. It's still warm."

"Oh, yes," she repeated. As he poured the tea, she spread the butter and jam on a slice of toast, all the time watching him. He seemed the most ordinary man, average in every way, except perhaps for the clarity of his light blue eyes, and the wry hint of humor in them.

"Drink your tea." He made it more of a request than an order, his voice low. "Little has changed since you left London. Just a few things you need to know, regarding Professor Hartwig and his work. He is very much a man of habit. It is both good and bad. He eats the same food every day without being bored. He will sit in the same seat, in the same café. It makes him easy to follow. If you lose him, you can easily pick him up again." He smiled a little bleakly. "He works at the same laboratory every day, with the same assistant. And he's doing something that matters more than anything the rest of us are doing, or possibly all of us together. Have you seen a photograph of him?"

"No. They didn't have a recent one. At least, I don't think so."

"Neither have I. Better that you don't carry one in case you are searched, for any reason." He gave a slight shrug. "Or your luggage is."

"I have to meet him."

"You will. But first I will update you on the latest bylaws and customs, so that you will not draw attention to yourself by being different. I will leave you with the layout of the campus at the university where Professor Hartwig works. All the walkways, rooms, entrances, and exits. But as well as that, of course, you must see it yourself, discreetly, and then look at and decide all your possible alternatives. Plan in advance so we can change anything if we have to. Tell me everything you need, anything you want, and I will get it for you if I can. I know the shops, who sells what, who can be trusted . . . and who cannot. And I have the money."

"I . . . I don't know what I need," Elena said. "Not yet." She was tired. The sharp, summer sunshine was streaming through the window. Her eyes ached, but there was no time to waste. She had a lot to learn. She could not afford even one mistake.

"I must go," he said quietly. "The management treats me well, but I can't afford to raise questions." He moved to the door. "If you need anything, just call the desk. If it falls within my knowledge, I will attend to it. Be . . . careful."

"Thank you." She meant it profoundly.

As Elena shut the door behind him, Dieter said, "I will come back when I am off duty tonight and take you to Hartwig."

When he was gone, she opened her case and hung the one jacket, blouses, and summer trousers she had brought. She knew the trousers fit, but she still felt a little strange about wearing them; they were so different from a skirt. She looked at the blouses that had been chosen for her, and thought that perhaps *shirts* would be a more accurate description, even though they were silk. They felt almost liquid running through her fingers. Hanging these, she looked at the tiny white birds on a navy background on one. The other was plain white. There was also a sweater, and a cardigan in pink, of all colors. She was certain that Peter Howard had not selected these.

She put the suitcase under the bed, then took a hot bath, washed her undergarments, and hung them to dry. She dressed in trousers, the dark navy ones, and put on the navy silk blouse. All she wanted to do was sleep, but she could not afford to waste time. It was still only a little after ten in the morning, and she had a full day's work ahead.

Elena went downstairs and outside onto the pavement. She had memorized the way to the university. It was not far. A quarter of an hour should be long enough to walk there briskly. The air was warm already. Berlin had a river, but it was very small compared to the Thames, and it had not chilled the air as a bigger water surface might have done.

She passed other women. Most of them were plainly dressed, as if they were walking to work of some sort. Very few wore trousers, as she did, and she earned a few stares, but those who stared seemed interested rather than disapproving. The trousers were flattering, and actually they were also extremely comfortable. And worn with flat shoes, as she was doing now, rubber-soled, they would be easy to run in, if she had to.

She moved gradually closer to the university. This is where Heinrich Hartwig worked, lectured occasionally, and had his laboratory. She found herself smiling in the sun and thought that she must look a great deal more confident than she felt. Quite a few cafés she passed had chairs and tables out on the wider pavements. If she stopped at one and ordered a pot of coffee, it might wake her up a bit.

She walked into a café area and sat down at one of the small tables, on a chair facing outward. A waiter came and she requested coffee. It was served steaming, even in the warm air. She thanked him, and waited a moment or two, allowing it to cool, before enjoying it.

A young man came in, glanced around, then sat a few tables away from her. Within minutes, he too was served coffee, and what looked like small biscuits. The movement of his being served attracted her attention and, for an instant, their eyes met. He smiled briefly, and then looked away.

Had she seen him before? Not in the hotel. She had seen no one except the staff: the man behind the desk, the bellboy, and Dieter, acting as a porter. Had he been at the railway station? On the train? Possibly. But she must look different now from the way she had looked then.

This was stupid! He was just being polite. And she did look good in the silk shirt with the white flying birds on it. It felt sleek and soft on her skin.

She drank the second cup of coffee, stood up, left a small tip on the table for the waiter, and walked away. She headed toward the university, so she could get a sense of familiarity with it.

Fifteen minutes later she was walking across the grass toward the school's formal entrance. There were groups of students standing and talking, others hurrying from one building to another with books in their arms.

One young man was passing her, coming from behind and moving quickly, then continuing beyond her. It was the young man from the coffee shop. Wasn't it? Then, he had seemed very casual. Was it a coincidence? How many women were dressed as she was, in navy trousers with graceful legs, and a silk shirt covered with birds? It wasn't so surprising if he remembered her, for at least half an hour.

Pull yourself together, she told herself sharply. That was the point of wearing attractive clothes, so that people did not notice the person inside!

She did not need to disappear, not yet.

She had studied the map of the campus. She needed to get a three-dimensional sense of the place, the ways leading in and out, the public places she could not pass through but had to go around; places where the crowds gathered and could block her way. Or, on the other hand, hide her. Who knew what getting Hartwig out of here might entail.

Elena mingled with students who were using the summer holidays to catch up on courses they had failed, or in subjects that were not part of their curriculum, but of interest to them. She also saw older people, possibly there to learn something new, or take a course in later life to improve their position, their skills.

She walked around for another hour, had a light lunch in one of the cafés, and then decided she had better go back to the hotel, in case Dieter had anything further to say.

She had gone at least three hundred yards along the road when she glanced behind her and saw the same young man. This time, she was almost sure it was he. Was he British Intelligence, keeping a discreet eye on her? To offer help if she needed it? Dieter could not do that. He must keep up his cover. And she knew him by sight anyway.

Far more serious, was he German Intelligence? Or worse, the Gestapo? Had they already recognized her? Did they still believe she had assassinated Scharnhorst a year ago? If they had any sense at all—and no one thought the Gestapo incompetent—they must have realized the truth. Or something close to it. Britain was not at war with Germany. Not yet. Maybe not ever in the future.

So, was this man's presence a coincidence? Was she being absurd, letting her imagination control her sense? Get a grip!

She continued on her way and went in through the front door of the hotel without once looking behind her. She entered her room, took off her outer clothes, and set her alarm clock for two hours.

The next thing to think of was finding a car to drive herself and Hartwig to the French border. Or if she judged it better, to catch the train back to Paris. The decision was up to her. However, on the train, they could not escape, except by getting off and then looking for another train, perhaps traveling in a different direction. She had fled Berlin on a train before, and that journey still came back to her in nightmares. No, she would be better to rent a car, then change it as soon as possible.

Elena woke up with a start, wondering where she was. Then it came back in a flood of memory. Dieter was going to come and tell her the next step. She had looked at the area around the university, memorized as much of it as she could, and now recognized the streets, the buildings, the one-way roads, the various routes in and out. She may never need to know this, but if she did, it must be instinctive.

She washed her face with cold water and dressed in the same clothes.

It was an hour before Dieter came back, now off duty, and momentarily unrecognizable out of hotel uniform and wearing casual clothes. "Are you ready to meet Professor Hartwig?" he asked.

She kept her voice level. "Yes." She did not mention the fact that she might have been followed. The more she thought about it, the less likely it seemed. So many students looked roughly the same.

"Good. I will take you. He speaks excellent English, and you speak very good German. I suggest you keep to German whenever possible." He gave a slight smile, gentle but completely honest. He was not telling her that this would be difficult, but he was not going to make any promises he could not keep.

She understood.

She reached for the navy jacket, casual and well cut, obviously intended to be worn over the shirt with the birds. It was an odd feeling, having someone you did not know choosing your clothes for you. But Mrs. Smithers at MI6 had excellent taste. Even Elena's fashionable and elegant sister, Margot, would have approved.

The air was still warm. There was no breeze at all. That might come after sunset, which at six o'clock was nearly two hours away.

Dieter left her room, and several minutes later she joined him at a prearranged spot not far from the hotel. They walked together in an easy manner, as if they were old friends who did not need to talk to be comfortable with each other.

Dieter finally said, and quite casually, "I will leave shortly after I introduce you. It will only add to the possibility of accidental recognition if I stay."

"We are being watched?" This was half a question. She was thinking of the young man she had seen three times this afternoon. Did he mean to be seen? If so, was it a reassurance from MI6 or, on the other hand, a threat from German Intelligence? If the latter, that would mean she had already failed. How could that be? She had not even contacted Hartwig. Had she been recognized as she entered Germany? She wondered if she should tell Dieter about the man who seemed to be following her.

She did not hear his answer to her question. "Are we?" she pressed. "Being watched?"

"Probably," he replied, smiling as if she had said something pleasant. "And there's no doubt that Hartwig is. They are not fools. As soon as you make contact, he will draw attention. Be prepared for that. I assume you are?"

"Yes." She knew that this was a half-truth. She was intellectually prepared, but not emotionally. Her name was Ellen Stewart, aged twenty-nine, a secretary in a large business.

During the war that had shaken the world, England and Germany had been enemies. That was no longer true. Even the new leadership of Adolf Hitler had plenty of connections in England. After all, he had brought order and dignity to Germany, and prosperity was in the near future. Who could be anything but comforted by that? Even hopeful?

"I am prepared," she said, with more assurance.

He did not look at her, but he smiled. "Of course."

They walked over the short distance still remaining, then stopped at a small, very casual restaurant that had tables outside on the street, as well as inside. She felt a moment's disappointment, as the tables she could see were already occupied. "Through to the back," Dieter said quietly. "Older man, sitting alone with a newspaper."

She looked, not staring, letting her eyes wander and then come back to him. He must have been roughly her father's age, mid-to-late fifties, but his hair was much grayer, white at the temples. His was a lean, intelligent face, almost ascetic. He reminded her quite a lot of her grandfather Lucas. In fact, it gave her a moment of mixed emotions, as if she had recognized him, until she saw the differences, and of course the fact that he was a generation younger.

"Is that him?" She said this so quietly, she was surprised that Dieter heard her.

"Yes," he replied. "Come. And then I will leave. I will always help you if I can, but you must take it from here. I'm working on another assignment now and must give my full attention to it."

"A car," she said quickly. "I need a car. How might I obtain one?"

Dieter's face was very solemn. "I would offer to rent one for you, but I think that would compromise my position, and yours . . . they could find me too easily. I—I'm sorry, but I think you would be better not to rent one. It could be traceable to you. And the connection between us would be fatal . . . for both of us."

"Steal one?" she said, with only a slight waver in her voice, and then conceded, "Yes, it's the only choice."

"Be careful," he warned. "There's something brewing, but I don't wish it to involve you."

"Does it have to do with Professor Hartwig?"

"No, it has to do with Röhm. I'm sorry, but I can't share more."

"Thank you," she said quietly, but was not sure what she meant. Did this somehow change all their plans? She started moving forward between the tables. When she reached the one where Professor Hartwig sat, she knew from the very slight stiffening of his body, nearly imperceptible, that he was aware of her, and possibly of why she had come.

"Do you mind if we sit here?" Dieter asked politely, pulling one of the chairs out for Elena as if he had already received permission.

Hartwig lowered his newspaper and stared at them with clear blue eyes. He looked briefly at Elena, then at Dieter.

"How do you do, Professor Hartwig?" Elena said with a slight smile, but she met his eyes unhesitatingly. "My name is Ellen Stewart."

He looked at her with curiosity. "How do you do, Miss Stewart?" He started to rise to his feet.

Hartwig looked momentarily awkward. Clearly, he was not used to either being told what to do or not exercising what he considered good manners.

When they were all seated, Dieter began speaking quietly, entirely to Hartwig. "Ellen will make arrangements with you, as you both think fit, but speed is advised. Tomorrow, if possible; at latest, the day after. Something is in the wind. I don't know what, nor do I intend to tell you the signs that suggest it, but the word is reliable. You know how to reach me, if it is vital. Better that you don't. Ellen has everything you need." He turned to Elena. "I will be back on duty until midnight. If you need anything, request assistance with your luggage, getting theater tickets, calling taxis, and so on."

Elena nodded. "Thank you. If I need a taxi, I will ask you." She smiled at the lie. "If you hear nothing, either I am in trouble, or I have already left."

He gave her a quick, flashing smile, which made him look completely different. Then it was gone again, and he was just a hotel porter. He stood up, nodded to Professor Hartwig, and walked away.

It was uncomfortable. The only other time she had had to get someone out of the country, it was a man only a little older than herself, whom she had known at one time intimately, but later realized she had known not at all. That situation was different in every possible way. He had been handsome, and he knew it, a man you could not ignore physically. He was also duplicitous, well trained by MI6, and physically violent, if necessary.

The only thing the two men had in common was that Hartwig was also tall, an inch or two above six feet. His glance seemed very direct, almost innocent. His humor at this highly artificial situation was gentle in his face. A quick glance would tell anyone he was not interested in appearance. He had things in his pockets, so his jacket hung a little crookedly. It would be the last thing he would care about. He reminded her again of Lucas.

"Professor Hartwig, we don't know each other, but we need to trust the people who know us both. You need to get out of Germany, and I believe you want to. We have to be very careful, and that means we also have to trust each other."

"I suppose that is necessary," he said. "I admit, I was expecting someone a lot older, and definitely a man." He smiled apologetically, aware that his remark was unfortunately candid.

"Good," she said with a wry smile. "Let's hope those who are watching you . . . us . . . are expecting the same thing."

After a moment, he asked, "Is someone watching you?" He seemed at once bleakly amused, and then profoundly aware of the seriousness of it. "Isn't that unnerving?" His voice was light, but it shook only just perceptibly, as if he knew what they were facing.

"I'm not sure," she said. "It could be German police, or MI6. British Military Intelligence. Or it could just be a young man who likes the way I look."

"I can believe that." He gave a shrug so slight it was barely visible.

She smiled. "Close your eyes."

He obeyed.

"Now, what color is my hair, Professor Hartwig?"

"Er, fair . . . more or less."

"How long is it? Wavy or straight?"

He said nothing.

"Can you describe my face?"

He opened his eyes. "I take your point. I took so much notice of your clothes that I did not notice your face. But you are tall and you walk with grace. And your eyes are blue."

She smiled. "So are the eyes of at least half the people in Germany. Or, for that matter, Denmark, Sweden, and Norway."

"Your German is colloquial. I can't place it exactly, but close to here."

"Yes," she answered. "I spent a long time here in Berlin when I was younger." She gave a slight shrug. "Both of us look quite ordinary from the outside. You could be my father. Sorry for the impertinence, but you actually look more like my grandfather. Not his age, of course, but I've known him all my life. He used to tell me stories, what we call 'shaggy dog stories.' They go on and on and on, wandering all over the place, and they make you laugh. Even when he had told them to me before, and I knew the end, I still enjoyed it . . . and laughed."

He smiled. "Even when we know the ending, that's part of the delight. The best comedians understand that, like hearing a familiar piece of music."

She knew he was speaking of something he understood, that they both understood.

She let a few seconds tick by, then she returned to the present. "Are you ready?"

"Tonight?" His face reflected grief, but very little surprise.

"No, but maybe tomorrow night. I only got here this morning. I need to know a little more before I make any decisions. That is, unless something happens to make it necessary to get out quickly. If you were going out quickly, which way would you go?"

"Why? Those who know me could work it out."

"To avoid that happening, of course," she replied, smiling back. "And be careful what you say from now on. If you leave any kind of message, make it casual. Not only your life may depend on it, but mine too." She lowered her voice a little more. "No goodbye letters. I'm sorry."

"I had planned to say nothing much, except that I was seeing the dentist, so people would not worry."

"Good. When you do not return, they will realize you've fled. The Nazis will search your home and your office. Please destroy your vital work papers—any that record the progress of your germ warfare studies. And do so discreetly, of course."

Hartwig nodded in agreement.

"Now," Elena added, "shall we eat?"

He raised his hand and beckoned the waiter over, then asked for some menus. He handed one to Elena. "I'll have the Belgian pâté, please. Plenty of toast, and unsalted butter. Add a slice of Brie. Small. And a glass of red wine."

"That'll be nice," said Elena, then looked at the waiter. "Yes, the same for me, please. Except I'd like sparkling water instead of wine." She smiled. "Thank you."

"A good choice," he said.

The meal came and it was as good as Professor Hartwig had indicated. They talked of everything that came to mind. Everything, that is, except politics, mass contagions, or getting out of Germany unnoticed . . . and quickly.

They talked about music. She loved Italian opera. He liked it, particularly *Rigoletto*, but he also liked Wagner, *Die Meistersinger* especially. He told her what he enjoyed in it and why. For nearly an hour, Elena forgot where she was, and even why she had come.

When they were ready to leave, she insisted on paying her part of the bill. "Are we going to quarrel so soon?" she asked him with a smile. "Once we are going, you give the advice, and I give the orders. Do you understand?" She said it gently, but she meant it.

Outside, she hesitated on the pavement and looked at Hartwig steadily, to make sure he knew she wasn't joking. "Let's go as far as the main street," she suggested. "Then I'll go to my hotel. In the morning, I'll start looking up a route or two. I will contact you again. Please be ready to leave very quickly."

"Yes. I think time is . . . short."

She gave a tight little nod and turned to walk away, nearly bumping into a Gestapo officer. There was another one standing a yard away from Hartwig. He could not have passed unless the man had stepped aside.

"Is this man bothering you, miss?" the first officer asked Elena.

She felt cold. She swallowed hard. "No, not at all, he's a relative. I've not met him before, but it's so nice to be in touch with the other side of the family again." She forced herself to smile.

The officer turned to Hartwig. "That right?"

"Yes," Hartwig said smoothly. "I'd like to show her some of the beautiful parts of Berlin. Most people don't know what a great city it is."

"Right, sir." He turned to Elena. "Welcome to Berlin. Good night."

She smiled again. "Good night, Officer."

She turned to Hartwig and repeated, "Good night," and then began walking along the pavement, her heart thumping in her chest.

Elena was disturbed by the Gestapo stopping them. She thought it extremely unlikely that it was she who had attracted their attention. It was far more probable that, if it was not by chance, then it was because they were watching Hartwig. This was something she had half expected, yet it was chilling to think that it was undeniably real, and to find that out so soon. This mission was not going to be easy. There was no room for even the slightest mistake.

She went to bed expecting to lie awake and turn the problem over and over in her mind, but exhaustion took hold and she fell asleep within minutes.

She had uneasy dreams, including one nightmare she had had every so often for as long as she could remember. She was in a city that, at first, she knew, but then she realized that all the streets were unfamiliar, she was lost, and it was getting dark. She was looking for someone, but she could not remember who.

Her traveling alarm clock woke her at 7:30 A.M., and she washed and dressed straightaway. She went downstairs and had a quick breakfast of boiled eggs, then dark toast with black cherry jam. It was excellent, the way it used to be when she lived here and her father was British ambassador. That was childhood, a time of relative innocence. Only the jam was still the same.

She drank a second cup of coffee slowly. She would need help getting Hartwig out of Berlin, beyond anything Dieter could do: someone who could help her steal a car, drive out of the city, and get them heading probably to the south. She knew that Alex Cooper, the other MI6 agent, would be here, but she had no way of contacting him, and anyway, to do so could endanger them both, never mind the two scientists they were here to help.

There were only a few people in Berlin she could trust, and Jacob Ritter was at the top of her list. He had saved her life when she was here a year ago. He had introduced her to his friends, and they had taken her in, hidden her from the Gestapo, and eventually arranged her escape, all at risk to themselves. She had not been in touch with them since May of last year, thirteen months ago. Her entire world had changed in that time; perhaps his had, too. She had not kept in touch with Jacob but she had thought of him often, worried for his safety, even his survival.

When she and Jacob had finally parted, it had been wrenching, almost a tearing away. She was never able to tell him that she had escaped, all the way to her grandparents' home in England. Or what had happened to her after that. And she did not know if Jacob had survived the increasingly nightmarish situation in Berlin. He was an American journalist, but he was also a Jew. He took risks saving others, and more risks reporting the truth as he saw it, events enacted in the street, the prisons, and these new internment camps, like Dachau, which were growing larger week by week. Places into which an increasing number of people entered but none came out.

She had read Jacob's articles and they had vibrated with rage and pity. Not numbers and statistics, not types, but individual stories. Without fail, Jacob had written well, and was published by American newspapers with worldwide recognition. How he had continued to write, she did not know. It had been some time since his last article appeared, which led her back to the most pressing question: Was he still alive?

So much had happened to Elena since their last meeting, things that might well surprise Jacob, but he would understand. Perhaps he would even approve, if she were able to share with him all she knew.

Elena knew that she would jeopardize Jacob by even trying to contact him, but he was the only person she could think of who could help her, apart from Roger Cordell, whom Peter had insisted she not contact.

If Jacob was still living, would she be able to find him? She felt sure he would fully approve of what she was going to do, getting Hartwig out of Germany. If she succeeded, it could very well change the balance of power. If she failed, the thought of a devastating germ-fueled disease raging across the world would have to be faced. And what sane person wanted that?

But in finding Jacob she might be drawing attention to him. Was he still reporting the truth and seeing that Americans knew it, whether they wanted to or not? Perhaps they were just like the British: they would believe what they wanted to believe. America had not suffered anything close to the degree that Europe had during the Great War, but they certainly had suffered in the Depression that followed. How naïve Elena had been before her recent trip to Washington, DC. Much of her ignorance had been swept away then . . . and in the short space of time since.

How could she find Jacob? She knew the places he used to frequent. But, surely, no one whom Jacob could or would trust would tell her anything. And if she asked the wrong people, even one of them, she would draw attention to him, which she knew he could not afford. And . . . it could be viewed as the ultimate betrayal.

Jacob would not live just anywhere. He kept a deliberately low profile on purpose. Not only for his own sake, but for the sake of his friends and allies. She thought of the Hubermann family, Jacob's friends who had taken her in, at high risk to themselves. It seemed to her that they had never thought twice about their own danger. They were Jewish, like Jacob. The difference was that he had seen the dark shadow of Hitler long before they had. And like so many German Jews, they too thought it would pass. They saw themselves as Germans first, and then, incidentally, as Jews. Did they still?

For that matter, were they even still alive? To ask, if she *was* being followed by the German police, might prove fatal for them.

Elena thought hard. She was not sure that Jacob was even in Berlin.

She could wander around the city looking for him, but that wasn't an option. No, there was no alternative but to go back to the Hubermanns' house and ask. She hated to put them at risk but they knew she could be trusted. And if Jacob was still here, maybe they could at least tell him that she was here, in the city again, and needed to contact him. Then he could make up his own mind whether to get in touch with her.

Elena left the rest of the now-cold coffee, thanked the waiter, and went up to her room to get her jacket in case the weather turned. Then she left the hotel and caught a bus, changed to another line and then another, like a tourist, and alighted finally at the familiar shopping center that was walking distance from the Hubermanns' house. Despite her precautions, she knew not to let down her guard.

She sat on the wooden bench, situated at the edge of the green by the bus stop. She could see no one walking aimlessly, or hanging around as if waiting for someone. Finally, she stood up and went along the road.

She stopped outside the house. Standing there, she was carried back in a tide of memory. For an instant, she was with Jacob as he took her inside and she met the Hubermanns for the first time. Then other memories flooded back. The night she had gone down the stairs to find the young man lying on the kitchen table, his raw flesh bloodied where his skin had been flayed from his body. Even then, only a year ago, that he was Jewish was enough for such a hideous crime to be considered acceptable. He had lived through that night, but she did not know what had happened to him since. What she did know was that the atrocities had increased, especially those perpetrated against the Jews.

Did the Hubermanns still live here?

She reached the back door. It was exactly as she remembered, only a little more faded. What would she do if a stranger answered?

She knocked.

Nothing.

She raised her hand to knock again, but the door opened and she saw the cheerful, familiar face of Marta, the Hubermanns' housekeeper. She looked blankly polite.

"Marta," Elena began. "How nice to see you."

"Who are you?" Marta was careful, but politely so.

"I understand," Elena said quietly. "You were very good to me when I was in trouble, just over a year ago. Last May, to be exact. Does Frau Hubermann still live here?"

Marta still looked confused.

"Jacob brought me. Do you remember now?"

Suddenly Marta smiled. "Oh, yes, I remember. You were here when that young man was injured."

"May I come in? Just so the neighbors don't wonder who I am. By the way, my name is Ellen Stewart."

"Ellen Stewart," Marta repeated, slightly confused.

"For the sake of prudence . . ."

"I see." Marta opened the door wider and let Elena in, then closed it again. "You want to speak with Frau Hubermann?"

"If I may?"

Marta smiled, not uncertainly this time but with real warmth. "I'm glad you got away. Just surprised to see you back again."

"Oh, yes, and quite safely." That was something of a lie, but it was all Marta needed to know. "Please tell Frau Hubermann I'm here to see if she can give me a piece of information."

"Yes, miss. If you'll excuse me." She pointed to the chairs around the table.

Elena sat down. It felt, for an instant, as if she had never been away. Even the warm cooking smells were exactly the same. A memory of fear touched her like a fever chill.

Seconds ticked by.

Then the door opened and Zillah Hubermann came into the room. Elena automatically rose to her feet. At first glance she looked exactly as Elena remembered her from a year ago, but then Zillah came in further and Elena could see her more closely. It was not the same black dress Zillah had worn before, but it was similar. She wore her dark hair the same way, which would have been severe, were it not naturally wavy and soft, always escaping its pins. It was her face that was different, still gentle, but lined far more deeply around the mouth and eyes, and a little thinner. The real change was in her eyes.

The women shared a quick embrace, and Elena felt for an instant ashamed to ask this woman for anything at all. If she succeeded in her assignment regarding Hartwig, she would be alive and well, soon at home in England, and back to the safe jobs that allowed her to go to her own flat every evening. Lonely sometimes, doing repetitive work most of the time, but safe. Always. Unlike Zillah, who was dedicated to saving Jews, risking her life. Day after day.

"I'm glad you got home safely," Zillah said. "You look different."

"I did," Elena replied. "After one or two adventures. Somebody I was foolish enough to trust very nearly succeeded in killing me." She gave a tiny smile. "I've learned a lot since then. But now I need to ask for Jacob's advice." She drew in her breath, holding the moment. There was the question she was afraid of asking. Maybe the answer would be tragic. And final.

"I'll ask him to come," Zillah said quietly. "But I won't urge him to do it. Things have become much worse since you were here."

Elena felt a rush of relief, knowing that Jacob was still alive. "I know," she said quietly. "And I believe it will only get worse still."

Zillah's face tightened almost imperceptibly. "Yes, of course, and it's only a matter of time before Hitler takes over Austria. Maybe . . . not very long."

Zillah smiled with sudden warmth. "Wait here. I'll contact Jacob, then we'll have a cup of coffee. I've still got some of the best in the tin."

"Thank you," Elena accepted.

Zillah went out of the room and was gone for a little while, perhaps fifteen minutes, before she returned, smiling. They sat and made friendly conversation, until there was a knock on the back door, and before Zillah could rise and open it, Jacob came in, closing it behind him.

He could not know why Elena was here, but she was quite sure Zillah had told him it was important.

"I'll leave you two," said Zillah, standing up, giving Jacob a quick hug, then slipping quietly out of the room to leave them alone.

Jacob turned to Elena. His face was thinner than before, the lines deeper than she remembered. And he looked tired. She felt a twinge of guilt.

She stood up, not sure why. It was not a requirement of good manners, more perhaps of respect. She wanted to hug him, but he was a stranger now. Both the frightened young woman she had been, and the man only a few years older who had saved her, the man who had kissed her goodbye at the railway station—they had both vanished into the past.

Should she ask how he was? They knew so much of each other . . . and so little. She had intruded, as before, without asking him first.

"I'm sorry," she began uncertainly. "Last year I was here because I was thrown into it. Now I do similar work, but I do it all the time." She sounded ridiculous, even to herself.

He was listening, but she could not read his face.

"Please, Jacob, sit down, and let me tell you, briefly. Would you like tea or coffee? Zillah has coffee ready."

He smiled. It altered his face, like sunlight on a landscape, except it was still clear that he had seen the nightmare coming, and now it was here.

"Are you all right?" she asked. There was a gentleness in that question, concern rather than criticism. It was foolish to waste time going around in circles. Either she trusted him, or she did not. "I have to get someone out of Berlin, someone very important who is being watched."

"Why? Why is he being watched? What has he done?"

He needed to know why it mattered so much. She could do this alone, but if she tried, it would be slower, and far more dangerous. "He has a scientific expertise that's important to Hitler's future plans, Jacob." She saw the understanding in his face. "We have to get him out," she went on.

"Or what?" he asked.

Elena swallowed. She found it difficult even to say it. "We have to get him out . . . or kill him." She saw the color drain out of his face and felt the need to rush ahead and explain. "His research is very important and, if it's successful, it could add immeasurably to Hitler's weapons of war. No one would be safe."

"All right!" he said hoarsely. "I see."

"Do you?" The words were out of her mouth before she had weighed them. Had she done so, she would not have spoken them. "Jacob," she said, her voice softening, "the research will go ahead with him or without him. If we get him out, he can work to develop a defense against it, whatever it is, for the rest of the world. If he stays, the Nazis will use him." She searched his face. "You know what Hitler can do to him, and will. To him . . . and to the people he's working with and his friends. If he refuses."

Jacob took a breath. "And what are you going to do if you get him out?"

"I don't know," she admitted. "But he has no immediate family. What do you suggest? What would be better?" She knew there was no answer to that. Other, worse thoughts crowded at the back of her mind. There was too much she did not know, too much she could not guard against.

Jacob said it. "What if he's a plant? A double agent?"

"He's a pawn in the game," she replied. "Whatever the case, I need what you can give me to get him out."

"Is he willing to leave? Do you know?"

Elena nodded. "I've already made contact with him. Aside from a car, it's just practical information I need from you, the things that you already know. Roads out of Berlin, which trains, buses, and routes are watched, or blocked. I can't afford a mistake. Just one could be . . . dangerous." She had been going to say "fatal," but changed her mind.

"A car," Jacob repeated.

"Yes," said Elena. "And here is some cash you can use to purchase one." Jacob accepted the stack of currency that Elena handed over.

"I'll see to it," he replied, folding the money into his pocket. "As for the roads, the information changes day to day," he answered. "Do you trust this man, the scientist?"

"Yes, I do trust him."

He smiled. "One of these days, if we have time, you must tell me what happened to you since we last met. It must have been . . . spectacular."

She remembered it so vividly, perfectly. It was an escape, or she thought it was, from the threat of death. How desperately she had wanted Jacob to come with her. At the same time, she would have admired him so much less had he left what mattered to him. At another time, in another place, would it have been different? Might they have been different, too? But if he had joined her, she knew that it would have lessened them both.

"Which direction do you want to go?" he asked.

"Preferably to France, but I need a choice. Maybe Belgium. Or even north, if we have to."

"Is he fit? How old is he? Will he do as you tell him? Is there a danger he could change his mind, want to say goodbye a last time?"

Her mind went back over what she knew of Hartwig. Did he really know what he was about to attempt? Or what extremes his enemies—and rescuers—would go to in order to stop him? Had he trusted friends he should not have? If he shared his plight, would bad things happen to them? Would they be tortured because of him?

Jacob's voice interrupted her thoughts. His face was very earnest. "Elena?"

She looked directly at him.

"Do you have any proper support at all?" he asked. "What the hell were the people who sent you back into Berlin alone thinking?"

"Ellen," she corrected him. She drew in a deep breath and let it out slowly. How could she be loyal to Jacob and the desperate past they had shared, and also to MI6, which represented more than Peter, more even than Lucas? She must not lie. The refusal to respond would be better.

"Ellen? It doesn't suit you," he replied with a wry smile.

"Good," she said, while still trying to decide. And then the decision was made. "I'm only part of it. There are others involved."

Jacob did not answer for what seemed like minutes. "What happened to you on the way home?" he asked finally. "After you left on the train?"

"I discovered who was behind it all, and why. He tried again to kill me. And, obviously, he failed." She would not tell him about Lucas. He did not need to know. "He's dead."

"Did you kill him?" There was incredulity in his voice.

"No." She would not tell him what she had done since then, how much she had changed.

He smiled slowly. It was in the curve of his mouth, but also in his eyes. "We can't meet here again. But we must plan carefully."

He did not bother to explain, but she could imagine the danger to Zillah and her family. She felt an immense relief that he was going to help her. "Then where?" she asked.

"Where are you staying?"

She named the hotel.

"Go out the hotel's front door, turn left, and walk a quarter of a mile. You'll come to a small Italian café called Tonio's. I'll be there tonight at eight, maybe a bit later. Can you drive?"

"If I have a car back in London, yes. Actually, I'm quite good," she added, with a winning smile.

"How un-English of you!"

"That's rubbish! Plenty of Englishwomen drive! We had women ambulance drivers on the Western Front, near the trenches, and they were damn good!"

Jacob laughed. "What's un-English is for you to say you are good! Some of you are brilliant, but it's not customary to say so."

"Are you making fun of me?"

"Only a little."

She put out a hand and touched him gently, just momentarily. By the time his fingers closed, her hand was no longer there. "I need help in knowing the backstreets that are open to traffic on any given day. Roadworks, detours, things like that. Guesses are not good enough. Just get us out of the city. Please?"

It was a bridge crossed.

Lucas glanced at the tall clock in the corner of the room, then rose to his feet. "Come on, Toby," he said. It was quite unnecessary. Toby had stood up the moment Lucas moved. Wherever Lucas was going, he intended to go, too. Lucas smiled. "Yes, I'm taking you," he told the dog. "What would a walk be without you?"

Toby trotted beside him out into the hall, wagging the plume of his tail. In fact, wagging his whole body.

"Just going for a walk," Lucas called out to Josephine, assuming she was in the kitchen, or perhaps the scullery, where she kept the vegetables, such as freshly dug potatoes or newly picked French beans. It was also the room where she arranged flowers every few days. She left most of them in the garden on their stems, but she liked at least one vase in the sitting room and, in the summer, another in the hall. It was part of the pleasure in having a garden. At the moment, he was drawn to the huge old English roses, each bloom having dozens of petals in various tints of the same basic color. Lucas liked them all, but the pale gold-to-peach-to-apricot were his favorite. At least, they were today. Tomorrow, it might be a crimson rose with a blood-red heart.

He picked up Toby's lead from the hall table. He always took it, but it was symbolic rather than useful.

Toby began going round in tight little circles of excitement.

"We're not going to the woods, we're going to the fields," Lucas told him. "And we're definitely not going to the river. Do you hear me?"

Toby had no idea what he meant. He knew lots of words, but not those. He just liked to be talked to.

They got in the car, Toby in the back, and drove further out of the built-up area and into the open countryside. Lucas had been called to this meeting by Peter Howard. He wasn't sure why, but it couldn't be good, not with Elena on a dangerous assignment in Germany.

The fields spread out in a patchwork of meadow and crops watered by the spring rains and growing strongly. The hedges were abundant, and there were all kinds of trees, bushes, and flowering weeds, even the sporadic tall purple foxglove seeds, wind-carried from the shadowed woodlands and copses of trees. The occasional chestnut held its flambeaux high and white, like real candles.

Lucas parked the car and climbed out, Toby leaping into the front seat and then out the door. Lucas reached down to clip on his lead, but Toby was refusing to be caught.

Lucas gave up easily. "Come on, then." He set out toward the gate. It led onto the path around the edge of the field, and then up the slight rise where he could see at least a mile in every direction. "But stay close! That's an order, Toby!"

Toby understood "stay" and "down." He subdued his enthusiasm a very little bit.

They walked up the slope in companionable silence. There was no sound but the slight wind in the grass, and far away the occasional bleating of sheep. This year's lambs were getting quite big. Toby knew better than to go anywhere near them. "Bad dog!" were the most miserable words he ever heard. He was a golden retriever, bred to fetch things, not to chase sheep, although it could be fun!

They reached the rise and saw a figure standing a couple of hundred yards away, on the next long slope upward. Toby stiffened.

"All right. Off you go!" Lucas told him. "Go on!"

Toby leaped forward, charged up the gentle incline, and hurled himself at the figure.

Lucas's face was wreathed with a smile as he watched the man bend down and hug the happy, wriggling dog. As far as Lucas knew, Toby was the only living thing that Peter Howard completely allowed to take over his emotions.

Toby wound himself round and round, then just as suddenly turned and came galloping back to Lucas, as if telling him Peter was here. As though he did not know.

Lucas looked at Peter and saw his face, and suddenly the summer field, the grass whispering in the wind, even the sweet song of the skylarks somewhere so far above them seemed to recede, as if all were suddenly on the other side of thick glass.

"Getting worse?" he asked quietly, when Peter was only a few feet away. Lucas wanted to ask specifically about Elena and her safety, but he held back.

Peter's face said it all. He gave a small, tight nod. "All the news I have tells me that Hitler is losing his grip. He sees enemies everywhere. And as far as we can tell, he's right. He's not imagining them. And they are his most dangerous enemies. Ernst Röhm heads the list. But God only knows where Röhm is going; I'm not sure that even Röhm himself knows. He has three million men, Brownshirts, in his force. That's thirty times as many as the regular army, and Röhm's men are out of control."

"Peter, I need to know about Elena."

"No word," he said, "which I consider good news."

Lucas frowned, and then nodded. "As for Röhm: Are his men more unrestrained than, say, six months ago?"

Peter turned sideways toward the sun. "Yes. But what disturbs me most is that the SA is out of control at the top. Röhm himself is hated. He knows it."

"He's likely to move first?" Lucas asked. "Before Hitler?"

"That's the issue, my man tells me. And if Hitler falls, what then? Bloody chaos."

Lucas thought for several minutes. They were close to a bush with purple flowers. A cloud of butterflies flew up, swirled around, and then settled again. "Hindenburg would take charge, at least for the first few days," he said thoughtfully. "But he's old, and he has no chance of being effective. And I think he doesn't want to fight for leadership."

"I'm sure he doesn't," Peter agreed. "Hitler may not have been his pick, in the beginning, but he is now."

"Will he stick with Hitler?"

"That's the question, and I don't think anyone knows the answer. There are people in the wings waiting, watching. Like Reinhard Heydrich, Himmler, Hermann Goering, Goebbels. We don't know enough!"

"You've got people there . . ." Lucas began.

Peter's body stiffened, as if awaiting a physical blow. "Plenty, but not inside, not deep enough. There are too many people to watch. And something else." He stopped.

The wind was warm; it smelled of earth and grass. It wasn't enough to stir the wild roses in the hedge, those small pink flowers with a single layer of petals, the ancestors of the lush garden rose.

"Something else?" Lucas prompted.

"There's this situation with Paulus," Peter said simply.

The words hung in the air. Lucas wanted to deny them, but he knew immediately that Peter would not have brought this up again were he not concerned. Concerned about the future, concerned about Elena. "What precisely is he doing?" Lucas asked.

"Not certain," Peter replied, frowning slightly. "Still involved in Intelligence work, of course. It's being said that he's very close to Hitler. In his personal cabinet, so to speak. Hitler seems to trust him, because he's not after the leadership, just the first position of whispering in his ear." He glanced momentarily at Lucas, then away again. "What's important is that Hitler's going to pieces. He trusts hardly anyone, which is a sure sign of paranoia, but that's also probably founded in quite a lot of truth." He shivered. "Goebbels is a dreadful creature, but he seems to be loyal to Hitler. Goering, I'm less sure of, but there's no doubt that he has plans of his own. Himmler definitely has ambitions. And worst of all, Ernst Röhm, who not only has ambitions, but that vast force at his command. And then there's Heydrich, who's a loose cannon, a compulsive sadist. Actually, if Hitler wants to trust anyone, Paulus is not a bad choice."

"He's ambitious, too, and cleverer than the others going about it," Lucas said.

"Of course he is," Peter agreed. "And he'll get rid of anyone in his way, sooner or later. But he'll use them first. As you know, Paulus is patient. For the time being, he'll be content with second place. He'll manipulate Hitler, when he's safely in his trust. He knows that the people all but worship the Führer, and there are many who actually do worship him. Paulus has enough sense to build Hitler up, while securing his position. Above all, he's a realist. That's his greatest strength. He knows the difference between difficult and impossible. He's cruel, but only when he considers it necessary. And as far as I know, and was ever able to discover, he has no weaknesses of appetite. He isn't addicted to alcohol or sexual encounters. He likes power, but he doesn't need to display it, to parade around in uniform and be admired. And he's in Intelligence work because he's brilliant at it, not because he's a coward or an incompetent soldier, like some."

Peter continued, "In Cordell's opinion, if Hitler loses, Paulus is finished. And I think he knows what he's talking about. His son-in-law, Hans Beckendorff, is working for Paulus now, and is just the sort of young man Hitler favors. Not that Cordell gets much information from him, except indirectly."

"Are you working up to telling me that Paulus is more involved in these germ warfare experiments than we first thought?"

"Yes," Peter replied. "Not the scientific side, of course, but the military. He would be the tactician of its use, whispering in Hitler's ear, telling him where it will be the most effective."

"So, Paulus is definitely involved," Lucas stated, his flesh suddenly cold.

"Yes," Peter replied. "I wouldn't have sent Elena into Berlin to get Hartwig out if I didn't think there was a real and very urgent danger. I worry for her as your kin, but I can't bring her back from this mission. Too much is at stake. I know how much you love her, and you made me promise that your feelings would make no difference to the jobs I gave her. Incidentally, I made the same promise to her."

Lucas thought for a moment or two. He did not want to go back over that particular piece of the past. In fact, he did not really want to relive any of it. It was a bitter victory. All losses hurt. Too often, they cost lives. It was war. There was fellowship, sublime courage, and sacrifice that could still make him weep, and there was loss that would never be recovered. There were wounds of mind and body that would ache for the rest of men's lives. And, of course, there were those who were robbed of the future, the promise of all that they might have been. Lucas knew that sanity could be lost if time was spent going over and over the decisions he had made. Or had not made. The alternatives meant little when it was too late to change.

"Then you must keep that promise," he said quietly. "Your promise, that is." He turned his eyes toward the nearby field. "Where's Toby?"

Peter looked around. There was a disturbance in the longest grasses, where something was thrashing around. "There," he answered. "I think he's chasing butterflies."

"Don't worry," Lucas assured him. "They are in no danger. He's like a man chasing dreams. He doesn't really want to catch one, he just enjoys trying."

Lucas looked away and raised his voice. "Toby!"

There was no response.

"That dog is selectively deaf," he said. "If I'd have called 'dinner,' he'd have come running."

"But you wouldn't have done that," Peter pointed out. "No decent man ever lies to his dog. He knows the dog trusts him absolutely."

Lucas smiled. It was true. "Toby!" he called again.

This time, Toby jumped, again missed the butterfly he was chasing, then came bounding back, flattening the grasses as he ran over them, unaware as they closed behind him, as if he had never passed that way. He arrived panting and wagging his tail.

Lucas patted him several times. He didn't say anything. It was unnecessary.

They began to walk down the slight incline, then back to the brow of the hill and toward where Lucas's car was parked.

"Was that all you had to tell me?" Lucas asked, breaking the silence. "About Paulus?"

"Isn't that enough?" Peter looked at him steadily.

"I know," Lucas said quietly. It weighed heavily on him, knowing that Elena might come face-to-face with the man who hated him. And, for that matter, might hate anyone with the Standish name. "Please God, she'll be in and out without Paulus ever hearing of it."

Toby settled beside him, blissfully happy.

"You told her not to contact Cordell, didn't you?" Lucas asked.

"Of course I did. She has no other MI6 contacts, except for the hotel porter. Trust her, Lucas. She's bright enough not to be unnecessarily brave. The only difficulty she'll have is if she has to kill Hartwig. As a last resort, of course."

Lucas felt his throat tighten.

Peter glanced sideways. "She will have known him just a few days," he said.

"I fell in love with Josephine the moment I saw her," Lucas replied. It was irrelevant, except to convey that caring had little to do with time. Had Peter ever felt intensely, passionately about anyone? That was the only thing about Peter that Lucas did not know.

CHAPTER

8

Hans had been working hard over the last couple days, getting together his report on the possible internal threats to Hitler, which Paulus had requested shortly after their visit. The list included private armies, groups both small and large, and individuals, all of whom might attempt a takeover. He needed to pare them down to the main facts. The list had to be precise, meticulous. Paulus would expect this of him.

Now that he had them all in order and ready to present to Paulus, he could go to bed at last.

Cecily had gone upstairs over two hours ago. He had heard her with Madeleine, comforting her, and singing softly. He had meant to tell her how lovely it sounded, but the long silence told him she had already fallen asleep.

Hans climbed the stairs and entered their bedroom. Cecily was indeed sleeping, her dark tangle of hair on the pillow. He set both alarm clocks; one was never enough for him to relax and sleep. He put them on the ledge beside the bed, undressed, and slipped under the covers.

He was almost asleep when he thought he would check on Madeleine. He wasn't checking really, he just wanted to look at her again, perhaps touch her, not enough to waken her. It reminded him of another world, safe, where when you cried, someone always came to you, held you, would give their life to keep you safe.

The door to the nursery was open. Cecily always left it ajar, so that if Madeleine made a sound, she would hear it.

He walked the few steps along the hallway and looked into the room. The night-light was on. It was always on after dark, so Madeleine would not waken and be unable to see. She was sound asleep. He could not even hear her breathing. He had to do that, hear her, just to make sure.

He tiptoed over to the bed and put his hand out, touching her cheek. It was warm. She gave a little sigh but did not waken. In the dim light, he could still see the shadow of her eyelashes on her cheek. Was she going to be as beautiful as her mother?

He must not wake her. He turned and walked to the door, leaving it exactly as he had found it, and went back to his own bed.

It seemed only minutes before Cecily was shaking him by the shoulder. "What is it?" he mumbled. "What's wrong?" There was light in the room. Why had he not woken with the alarm? He had checked both clocks, twice.

"Nothing is wrong," Cecily replied softly. "I just turned the alarms off because it makes such a noise. It wakens Madeleine, and she's just gone back to sleep. Get shaved and dressed and I'll make you some breakfast. Would you like eggs?"

He sat up slowly and rubbed his eyes. It seemed as if he had only just gone to sleep. But it was full daylight. Of course it was! It was only days past the summer solstice, when there were only a few hours of darkness.

"Thank you. Yes, please. I could cook it myself. How long?"

"Half an hour. And I'd like to cook it for you. Perhaps you want me to leave you alone to work?" There was sadness in her face, and he knew she needed to feel she could help.

"No. I mean, I'd like to have breakfast with you." He stared at her and saw the shadow leave her eyes. She smiled back at him.

He very gently pushed the hair off her forehead. He wanted to say something gentle and meaningful, but his emotions were too deep to find words that were big enough, carefully thought out, not flowery things that could not hold what he meant.

Hans was in the office by eight o'clock, feeling as if he had been there all night. He had reread his report and could think of nothing to add. Knowing this, and that Paulus was awaiting it, he entered his superior's office and left the document on his desk.

It was nine thirty when Paulus came into Hans's office—without knocking, of course. For practical purposes, every office in this part of the building was his. He looked tough this morning, solid, and as always seemingly unaffected by any afflictions of the imagination.

Hans swallowed hard, and stood up, raising his arm in the automatic salute and saying *"Heil Hitler,"* as he had been taught. Everyone did it. "Good morning, sir," he added.

"Good morning, Beckendorff," Paulus replied, making a gesture toward a salute. He was holding Hans's report. Clearly, it was to be the subject of their conversation. He met Hans's eyes steadily. "Sit down," he ordered. "I want to talk to you about this." He took the other chair and pulled it closer to Hans, who remained standing. "Sit!" he snapped. "I don't intend to crane my neck to look at you!"

Silently, Hans obeyed.

Paulus studied him for several seconds, but it felt to Hans as if he were dragging the silence into a full minute. "Did you show this to anybody else?" he asked.

"No, sir. I assume everything is for your eyes only, unless you tell me otherwise."

"Good," Paulus said, barely moving his head. "Where did you get this information?"

"Several different sources, sir. I never trust just one opinion. Even the most honest man in the world can be mistaken, see things as they wish them to be or . . ." He hesitated, not sure how candid he could be with Paulus.

"Yes, go on, man!" Paulus snapped again.

"Or as they fear them to be," Hans finished.

"What do you believe?" Paulus examined Hans's face, his eyes cold and penetrating.

"I see this as a place to start," Hans replied.

"Ask many people, did you?"

"No, sir. That's inviting . . ." He stopped again, uncertain how frank he should be.

Paulus was staring at him. "Inviting what?"

"Embroidery, sir."

"What?" Paulus's eyebrows rose.

"It's inviting people to add details that aren't accurate," Hans replied, carefully keeping his voice level. "I want the truth, nothing more. Of course, opinions are important, but only after the facts are collected."

"Good. Very good." Paulus held up the report again. "And you have not shared this with anyone?"

Hans was aware that Paulus had asked that same question only moments earlier. Was he testing Hans's loyalty? "No, sir. Only for you, and whoever you wish to share it with."

"And?" Paulus leaned forward a little, staring at Hans.

Hans was not sure what Paulus meant. And . . . what? Finally, he answered. "I think the Führer would want to see it, sir, and perhaps it would be up to him to decide who to tell. Some of these people—" He looked at the pages in Paulus's hand. "Some of them are men we would have thought we could trust."

"Have you checked those figures?" Paulus asked. He did not specify which ones. They both knew he was talking about Röhm's army, the Brownshirts.

"I have, sir, and I consider those numbers conservative. They might underrepresent a little. It's somewhere more than three million and less than four million. Over thirty times bigger than our regular army, which is what we should worry about. What would it take to—" He stopped. He had been about to say more than he intended. He knew he needed to be very careful.

It seemed that Paulus was also about to say something, and then changed his mind. "Reinhard Heydrich?" He made it a question. "Opinion, Beckendorff?"

Hans could not afford to hesitate. Months ago, he had decided that Paulus was unconditionally loyal to the Führer. Whatever position the man wanted to achieve, it was as a subject to Hitler, not a replacement. He had been a senior Intelligence officer during the war, and he knew the reality of it. "Heydrich's reputation is that he is a loose cannon, sir. Too much uncontrolled emotion, temper, political hatreds. As far as I can see, that's a fair comment. No one I respect trusts him. I . . . I don't think he has any beliefs, sir."

Paulus's eyebrows rose. "Really. You think a soldier should have beliefs, do you?"

Was that intended as a trap?

"Yes, sir," Hans said decisively. "You don't give your life, or take an instruction, if you don't believe in what you're doing. And in whom you're doing it for."

Paulus nodded very slowly. "Who taught you that?" he asked, but his voice was softer, curious.

Hans met Paulus's unblinking eyes. "It's self-evident, sir. You look at all the great leaders. They have a star that all courses are set by. And if they are temporarily beaten, even to their knees, they get up again and keep on going." He was thinking of Hitler's time in the army, toward the end of the war. And then the struggle afterward, and the despair, the hunger, the confusion and misery. And, of course, the man's belief that they had not really lost. The army had been deceived, robbed of victory when the civilian government had caved in. They had felt utterly betrayed, but there was nothing they could do about it. Some of them sulked or were lost in anger and self-pity.

Hans moved a bit closer. "But the Führer began to rebuild, and nothing could stop him. No setbacks, no failures, or even betrayals by the self-pitying could stop him. And we have a long way to go, sir. But we are moving. Every day we become a little stronger. It takes one man with a vision, and then all of us, or nearly all of us, can start to hope again. And to give the best we have. I know there are a few who love their own glory more than the good of the Fatherland, but they will fall by the wayside, sooner or later. Or better still, they will realize their folly and start doing something useful." He stared at Paulus's expression and felt a sudden wave of self-consciousness overtake him. He had spoken far too much, but it was what he meant. He could not now deny it.

Paulus nodded slowly. "Yes. You are a trifle more perceptive than I thought." There was surprise in his tone. "But remember, Beckendorff, you're in the Intelligence Service and you must keep your own counsel. Unfortunately, you cannot always be sure whom you should trust. Even I can't."

"Yes, sir."

"And it is our duty to warn the Führer of what we know."

"Of course, sir."

"Then come!" Paulus ordered. "You prepared the report. It's fitting that you should present it to the Führer. He needs to know that there are men he can trust."

Hans was startled, but he tried to hide it. He felt suddenly very young and very inexperienced.

Paulus smiled, as if he had read all that in Hans's face. "It is an honor you are more than ready for," he said, handing the list back to Hans.

"Thank you, sir." He swallowed.

"Then pull yourself together, man, and follow me!"

Hans stood to attention, clutching the papers, careful not to fold them. He needed to have them in hand so he would be certain of his facts, and in case Hitler wanted to keep them.

Hans followed Paulus out of the office and along many corridors, and then across a courtyard until they came to the Führer's office. It was the same destination, but Paulus had taken a different route from usual. Hans wondered if this easier access was only for those people close to Hitler.

Paulus announced his mission to the guards.

They snapped to attention. One of the guards led the two men down the hall and then knocked on the door. After a moment, he went into the room. A moment later, he returned.

"The Führer will see you now, sir."

Paulus gave him a nod, then led Hans into the room, closing the door behind him.

Hitler was standing in the center of the room, as he had the first time Hans had met him. He was staring at the two men.

Hans was struck by the tension in him, the rigidity of his body. He stood very straight, emanating energy and commanding attention. Although Hans had been face-to-face with Hitler before, this felt like the first time. They both saluted him.

"General Paulus," Hitler said sharply. "What have you to report?"

Paulus saluted stiffly. Hans followed half a second later.

Hitler nodded. "So, what do you have to tell me?"

"I am afraid you are right, *mein Führer.* Lieutenant Beckendorff here has prepared a thorough report, and of course has brought a copy for you to read. And with respect, I would suggest that you consider carefully to whom you show it."

Hitler breathed in and out very slowly. His face looked a little stiff. "What does this report say? I presume you've read it, Paulus?"

"Yes, sir. I made my own check of it, of course. I would not show you anything I had not checked myself. All the details are listed, for your reference, but Lieutenant Beckendorff is here if you wish to ask him anything, or question anything in his reports. Rumors and so on."

Hitler turned his attention to Hans, and his look was intense, almost mesmeric. "What did you find? Beckendorff, is it? Yes. Tell me."

Hans thought of several ways of answering, but now that he was standing in the same room as one of the most powerful men in the world, all prepared answers seemed pompous and rather absurd. This was real, and very serious indeed. "I'm sorry, sir, but there are many who put their own ambitions before the welfare of Germany, and of the German people in general."

"The people in general? What do you mean?" Hitler demanded. "What are you saying?"

Hans hesitated. Should he be direct and forget about diplomacy, respect for others, senior officers far ahead of him? Was he speaking about men Hitler thought his allies?

Hitler was glaring at him. He must answer truthfully, not evasively. That might give the impression that his own loyalty was wavering.

"Röhm has a great deal of power, sir," he began. "And he is looking to see how he may use it. Our sources say he has more than three million men, and he is increasingly demanding their personal loyalty ahead of their loyalty to the Third Reich." His voice was dry in his throat. "I fear he cannot control so vast an army, which does not have a regular army's rules or structure. And I have come across many instances of loyalty being displayed to gain money or power, rather than for the good of Germany. I have given examples in the report, sir." He swallowed hard.

Hitler continued to glare, as if he had found a caterpillar crawling in his salad.

Hans had left himself no room to retreat. All his life, he had wanted to serve his country, help rebuild after the ruinous war, which had reduced Germany to a heap of rubble. And now that he had the chance to serve the Führer himself, he was feeling tongue-tied.

Hitler remained there, standing stiffly, his hands clenched.

Hans took the plunge. "Sir, the Brownshirts are out of control. They have little respect for their officers, and they are frequently too drunk to behave like guardians and protectors of the people. They are more like an occupying army of enemy troops." He saw the flicker of disgust on Hitler's face. He knew that Hitler did not drink alcohol at all. Never mind getting falling-down drunk. Hans admired that. A man who could not control his own appetites was not fit to command others, either in a literal war of blood and iron, or in the war of ideas and will. He wished he were in a situation where he could say that aloud.

Hitler was staring at him. He must have seen that Hans had something more on his mind. "What?" Hitler said sharply.

"Sir, they dishonor the real army. Men who cannot control themselves, or will not, do not serve Germany."

Hitler looked at Paulus, then back at Hans.

Hans felt himself go cold.

"What does Röhm plan?" Hitler asked. "Tell me!"

Hans swallowed again. "All the evidence we can be certain of, sir, tells us that he is feeling his strength, the loyalty of his men. Reinhard Heydrich is not loyal to Röhm, and he is far too clever to back a losing player. But there are those whose ambitions are less under control."

"Such as?" Hitler's voice was scratchy, altered in pitch.

Hans had no choice but to answer. Everything was in his report, so there was no purpose in trying to hide this information now. And he had checked and then double-checked all of it.

Hans's mouth was so dry, he was not sure he could speak. But what choice did he have? "The power hungry, the disloyal, sir, greedy for their own profit. The ordinary people know not only that you were elected by the majority of the people, but that you are building a strong nation. We are restoring the railways, roads, factories. People have food on the table. Come the winter, we will have warmth and light. But more than that, we are regaining our self-respect that

is the . . . food of the soul." Did he sound pompous, as if he were trying to ape the Führer in his speeches to the people?

Hitler smiled. His whole body eased. He turned to Paulus. "What
is the matter with you? You said it was bad! What are you talking
about?"

Paulus looked at Hans. "Tell the Führer why you are worried,
Beckendorff! Stop dithering."

"Well?" Hitler was again staring at Hans.

As calmly as he could, Hans listed the men who had quietly, step
by step, changed their allegiances to someone who would promote
them, pay them more. But, above all, who would turn a blind eye to
their indulgences in alcohol, sexual appetites of every sort, often
with violence and extortion.

Hitler's face twisted into a mask of disgust.

"Go on!" Hitler snapped. "What else?"

Hans continued, "It seems they're building a big enough, violent
enough force to take control." He said the words and it chilled his
flesh that they were true. "Many of these men will go in the direction of least resistance. I have looked over the men who have made
their loyalties to you plain, and who keep order and decency." This
time, when he swallowed, he all but choked. "And also, those who
look to undo all that you have done . . . sir."

Hitler's face was white. "You see, Paulus?" His voice shook. "I was
right! They are betraying me. Our most dangerous enemy is within!
What have you done about it?"

"Nothing yet, without your permission, sir," Paulus began.

Hitler swung around to Hans. "How long have you known this?
When did you tell Paulus? Tell me the truth!"

"Yes, sir. First, I had to verify the information. I must not guess,
or give you a report that is flawed."

"When?" Hitler shouted. "How long did you keep it without telling me? I am your Führer!" His fists were clenching and unclenching and his whole body trembled.

Paulus started to speak, but Hitler swung his arm round as if he would hit him. Paulus froze.

"Well?" Hitler shouted at Hans.

"Late yesterday evening, sir. We put it together only this morning, to make sure there was no further news to incorporate. And then we brought it straight to you." That was not exactly the truth, but it would be fatal to allow any blame to fall on Paulus.

Hitler remained silent for a few seconds, then turned to Paulus. "Is that true? All this . . . this treason has just come to light?" He turned back to Hans again, without waiting for Paulus to answer. His body was shaking as if he were standing in an icy wind, and yet his face was flushed. "You see treason. Betrayal. And yet you do nothing? Why not? Are you one of them? Are you?" He was shouting now. If the guards were outside in the passage, they certainly were able to hear him, hear the wild pitch of his voice. He sounded like a man struggling to waken from a nightmare, and failing, or perhaps who suddenly realized that he was not dreaming, and this was real.

Hans's mind raced. He glanced at Paulus, who was no help at all. Had he expected this? No. That was impossible. He appeared to be as appalled as Hans.

"Don't stand there like an idiot, man!" Hitler shouted, his voice shrill, his face scarlet.

Hans had to answer. "At first I could not believe it, sir. It was so disloyal. So stupid! How can any man with eyes and ears not see what you have done for Germany? To turn against you is to turn against your own country, your people, your future. It is to put your insane appetite before everything. I could not believe what the evidence seemed to be telling me."

"Seemed to be?" Hitler shouted. "Seemed to be? Do you doubt it? What else could it mean?"

"My own misunderstanding of the situation, sir. I could not bring you news like this without checking again and again that it was true." Actually, he had reported it to Paulus, who clearly knew that it was true. He was now realizing that Paulus had brought him along to this meeting not as an honor, but as a buffer to take the brunt of Hitler's rage. If the information turned out to be a mistake in any way at all, Paulus wanted to be sure it was Hans who took the blame. Hans knew how skaters must feel on a frozen lake when the ice melts and they are pitched into water that is heart-stoppingly cold.

Hitler turned to Paulus. "You let this . . . boy do your work for you?"

Paulus looked flushed. "I needed him to confirm what I suspected, *mein Führer*. I had to be sure my suspicions were correct, and it was not just my loyalty to you, to Germany, that made me suspect these men. It was hard to believe they could betray you, betray Germany. It was almost impossible to grasp their treason."

Was that the truth, Hans wondered, or a quick scramble to save himself? No, he had not known Paulus more than a few months, but he had never seen him act without thought.

Hitler was still speaking, fists opening and closing.

Should Hans speak? If he did, he would be preempting Paulus, who must surely have some defense for himself. If they made an error now, would Hitler lose control of himself even more? Hans was certain the man would not forgive anyone who witnessed that!

Then another thought struck him, a far colder thought. Paulus needed him here not just to bear the brunt of Hitler's anger, but also to take the blame if their intel leaked. If the word got out that Hitler had been terrified? Had lost control of himself? Paulus would never shoulder the blame for having spread such information. It would be Hans Beckendorff who would be in the perfect position to shoulder that. And Paulus would see to it that he did.

What could Hans do to save himself? It must be now. It would be too late once it happened. He could feel the sweat break out on his skin and turn cold. Anything he said would be remembered and quoted back at him. No wonder Paulus had survived so long! Like any first-class Intelligence officer, he played six moves ahead of the game.

Hans cleared his throat. "*Mein Führer*, I felt it prudent to be certain of every fact. As I've said, after I had verified them, I could scarcely believe it. Everyone else I know, the men I see every day, have nothing but praise for you, and believe that you are guiding us back to the path we ought to be on." He hated saying this. It sounded so pompous. He sounded like his own father. "There are many men who see that, sir. This is our destiny. They share my belief that no greedy, misguided view will be allowed to stand in your way." That sounded ridiculous, but he saw Hitler's face lighten, his shoulders relax. "It is a small faction that does not share this faith," he finished.

"Yes, you are right," said Hitler. "We will deal with them. That is clearly our duty." He looked at Paulus. "Thank you for bringing it to my attention. It is as I feared, but they will not win. I shall deal with it! Bring everything you learn to me, do you understand? Straight to me! Not to Goering, or Himmler, or anyone else. Is that clear?" He glared at Paulus, as if the man had been arguing with him.

Paulus stood to attention. "Yes, *mein Führer*."

"Good." Hitler turned Hans. "And you . . ."

Hans also stood to attention, but did not speak.

"You," Hitler continued, his eyes riveted to Hans. "You report to Paulus, and Paulus only, unless I summon you myself. Do you hear me?"

"Yes, sir!"

"You will speak of this to no one. Do you understand? You will report everything to General Paulus immediately. A day lost might be crucial. We cannot afford to fail." His voice dropped to a whisper on that last word. He still looked very badly shaken. "If one word of this reaches anyone, and I hear of it, it will be the end of your career. Traitors deserve to die!" He glared at Hans, his blue eyes blazing, a little bloodshot, as if tiny vessels could have broken under the pressure of his rage. Or could it be his fear? Whichever it was, it resembled Hans's idea of madness, insanity.

Hans's throat was now so dry that his tongue felt stiff. "Yes, *mein Führer*. You are Germany's only hope for the future, and that is clear to anyone who puts country before appetite or personal gain. Those who think otherwise are not fit to hold office."

He saw Paulus shift his weight and draw breath as if to speak. Then he looked at Hitler and changed his mind.

"You will go far, Beckendorff."

"Yes, sir."

"Good. Is that all, Paulus?"

Paulus was still standing rigidly. "Yes, *mein Führer*."

Hans and Paulus saluted, then turned and went out of the door and into the passage.

Hans looked at Paulus, but the man was deep in thought, and seemed entirely unaware of him.

Hans felt sweat trickling down his sides, and yet he was cold.

The day dragged on. Hans was more shaken than he would have believed by Hitler's complete loss of self-control. And that was certainly what it had been. For those long, dangerous minutes, the Führer had looked terrified, panicky, and desperate for reassurance. Why had Hans assumed Hitler was above that kind of emotional crash?

And what about Paulus? He had made certain that Hitler knew that some of this discovery of treason had been made by Hans. Was that to protect himself? To date, Hans had uncovered no tangible betrayal, just the usual bad behavior of an army with no real battles to fight, no fear of its mortality or even serious injury. In the case of the Brownshirts, led by Röhm, no one had the weapons to oppose them. In truth, Röhm's men, all three-plus million of them, thought themselves immune. What was their purpose? Was it to find something to do for myriad young men with no discipline and no manufacturing skills? German youth who might otherwise have found it hard to get employment, whose idleness and poverty might make them vulnerable to any ideology, even Bolshevism? They needed someone to blame for their having lives without purpose or hope. Hitler had intended giving them purpose, unity, even power. And yes, hope. But Röhm seemed to have different ideas.

Hans tried to go over in his mind just how that massive force had been recruited, and for what purpose beyond keeping all these men occupied. Or maybe, to some extent, to keep control of them. He had not considered this before.

But now, at this moment, he was tired and longing to escape the whole situation. And yet he could not let it go until he understood it better.

Paulus had made no reference to Hitler's crazed behavior. The man merely had continued, at least outwardly, as if nothing had happened.

Despite Paulus having said nothing about Hitler's raging, Hans knew better than to refer to it at all to anyone. He had a strange feeling that it must never be mentioned again, because there was no acceptable explanation. Was it a privilege that he was being trusted with such knowledge? Or was it an unexploded bomb that he was obliged to carry into the future? He had seen something he should not have. Was this hysteria a sign of Hitler's mental state? Hans wondered if the memory of it would slip silently into oblivion, or be something he would regret having seen. Not because it destroyed his belief in a superhuman leader. No, it was more as if he had interrupted someone in the bathroom, someone who was momentarily vulnerable, an ordinary human being.

Hans realized that he had previously thought Hitler impervious to the consuming fears that haunted most people. But perhaps the Führer was as vulnerable to fears as anyone else. And because his aspirations were higher, so was his chance of failure.

It was a little before six o'clock. Still deep in thought, Hans walked out of his office and along the street. He continued for a couple of blocks and then crossed the road to a flower shop. Even at this late hour in the day, there was an abundance of blooms of many different kinds.

He wanted to say something to his mother, who had shown such pride in the recent signs that her only child was destined for success, but he was not sure exactly what he would say now. "Thank you for all the time and care you have given me" was a possibility, but those words sounded formal and flat, however sincere they were.

Hans realized, with some surprise, that he did not even know what blooms she liked. She was his mother! In some ways, physical ways, the mother-child relationship was perhaps the closest that can exist. And yet, as a person, an adult son, he knew little about her that mattered. Perhaps this was because his parents always appeared to agree on matters of importance, so he never heard his mother's opinion except as supporting his father's. Was that because they did think or believe the same things? Did she really agree with every-thing his father said, or was she deferring to his opinion because it was easier and more comfortable than arguing?

There was also the possibility that she wasn't informed enough to think independently, or there existed a world of thoughts and beliefs she preferred not to share. He doubted that. But at the same time, if he was being honest with himself, he did not want to know.

As for his father, the temptation to argue with him was always in the background of their conversations, but it was never the right time, or the right issue. Besides, he knew the pointlessness of dis-agreeing even before he drew breath to begin.

Still, it bothered him that he did not really know his mother, or what thoughts, beliefs, and dreams hid behind her agreeable expres-sion.

He would take her flowers, a large bouquet bearing their beauty, and they would convey whatever message she wished to hear. Noth-ing so beautiful could be misinterpreted.

The woman behind the counter was looking at him impatiently.

"My mother," he said, trying to smile naturally, as if he were cer-tain of what he was doing. "I'd like something a little different, and at the higher end of cost."

"Her birthday?" the woman asked.

"No, just to thank her. It's difficult to find words, but flowers express it nicely."

"Would you like a card to go with them?" she suggested.

"Yes, please, that's a good idea."

She turned and looked at the array of blooms, considering the choices. She seemed to be indecisive. He was about to interrupt her when she turned back to him and spoke. "How about one of these orchids? They're all a little different, and very beautiful. And, above all, they last a long time, if you water them regularly, but not too much. I can add a little card telling you about it, in case you're not familiar with them." She smiled and pointed to the most unique-looking flower Hans had ever seen.

He knew straightaway his mother would love it. "That's perfect."

He could already imagine his mother's pleasure. She would read into it all the thank-you messages he could not find suitable words to express. And she would be free to show the plant to anyone she pleased, because it would be prominently displayed. "Oh, that lovely orchid!" her friends would declare, to which she would proudly respond, "Yes, my son gave it to me." And then she would add anything more she wished to say about him. And when the orchid ultimately faded, at the least, the pot would still be there, an elegant thing in itself.

He hailed a taxi, not wishing to risk getting the flowers crushed or even broken by people crowding onto a bus, tired at the end of the day.

His parents would be pleased to see him—they always were. All their future dreams rested on him, their only child. They had worked hard, extra hours, extra responsibilities, and given up their own pleasures to afford the best education for him, anything he needed.

His mother must have seen him out of the window, because she opened the front door before he reached for the bell. Her face was alight with welcome. "Hans! How good to see you. Come in! Come in! Are you staying for dinner? We can easily set you a place."

"No. But thank you. I just came to give you these." He took the protective cellophane off the orchid plant and held it out for her.

Her face filled with amazement, an illumination of pleasure. Her eyes were bright, her marvelous enamel-perfect face creased only by a luminous smile. "It's so beautiful, it hardly looks real." She looked from the flower to him, then back again, as if to be sure she had seen its substance and that it wasn't merely a dream.

"It's to say how much I appreciate all you have done for me over the years." He still felt the weight of it in his hands. "Let me carry it for you into the sitting room. The instructions on how to care for it are on the card. Apparently, it needs special handling, like not too much water."

"Oh, yes, please!" She turned and walked to the sitting-room door and opened it. "Karl!" she called out. "Hans has come to see us, and look what he has brought for me."

Karl Beckendorff rose to his feet with a smile. It was a reflection of genuine pleasure. He had been brought up with excellent manners, but little warmth. He expected people to know that he cared for them by his actions, without having to explain himself. "Beautiful," he said appreciatively, looking at the orchid, then at the delight in his wife's face. "Very good." He turned to Hans and regarded him more closely. "You look tired. Would you like a little wine before dinner?"

Hans knew that this was as far as his father would go in expressing any understanding of what he felt. "No thank you, Father," he replied. "I have not eaten for a long time, and I'm on my way—"

"No need to explain," his father interrupted. "Still working hard for General Paulus?"

"Yes. But today I again reported to the Führer myself."

His mother clasped her hands together, her face shining. She seemed to be too excited to speak.

Hans tried to smile, aware of how mixed his feelings were. What should he say to them? How much of the truth? If he led them to the wrong conclusion, he would not have a chance to correct it. They

were waiting. He understood their hopes for him. And now, as a father, he realized that he could never have imagined this before Madeleine was born, and he felt that surge himself. The love was fierce,
protective, higher and nobler than any sort of reason. It was heart
deep, gut deep, far more profound than could be explained by logic.

"He let me speak for myself," he went on. "Directly to him. Just
three of us in the room. Hitler, Paulus, and me."

"What about?" his father asked. "What are you doing that took
you there?" His face was keen with interest.

Hans had thought how to tell them enough to make them feel
included, and yet not reveal anything he ought not. He wanted to
avoid the word "secret."

"Confidential things, Father." He saw the shadow on his father's
face. "I'm sorry, but I have to be able to say I spoke to no one. They
trust me; it was the Führer's personal order to me, and I must keep
my word." He felt self-conscious, even absurd. But he meant it. "I
just had to come and thank you for all you taught me, all you made
possible for me." He gave a bleak smile. "I gave my word. What
would you think of me if I broke it?"

"Right," his father said. "You must be worthy of the trust we have
all placed in you." He nodded in agreement. "The Führer trusts you!
That is a high honor. I'm proud of you, son."

"Thank you," Hans said soberly.

"Never forget your privilege," his father went on. "You serve the
Fatherland, and the Führer as well. Live up to it. Honor, loyalty,
obedience above all. In doing so, you have lived up to every sacrifice
we have made."

Hans did not know how to answer. He drew in breath, but words
deserted him.

"How's Madeleine?" his mother asked.

Hans relaxed. He turned to her, smiling. "She's fine, Mother.
Growing all the time. She seems to learn something new every day.
She is . . . beautiful."

"Of course she is," she agreed.

"Maybe the next one will be a boy," his father said.

Hans froze. His father must have meant it kindly, or at least not as the bitter criticism it sounded. He wanted to lash out, but no answer came to his mind that was not angry and hurt.

"It's been a long day," he finally said. "I'm hungry and I'm looking forward to going home." He bit back the angry words on his tongue. He wanted to add ". . . to my family." Instead, he bid them a good night and went out the door without waiting for a reply.

By the time Hans arrived home, he had cooled off, but the hurt was still there, and so was the regret that he had not found something better to say in reply. More than anything, he wanted to be alone with Cecily and Madeleine. He wanted to hold his baby, feel the warmth of her little body, maybe even see her smile. People said her expressions at this age were only wind, but the look in her eyes said that she knew him, and that she knew she was safe in his arms.

He pulled the front door open and found Cecily with her father in the sitting room.

Roger Cordell was seated, holding Madeleine, and he was smiling. The emotion was naked in his face as he looked down at the baby. It was as if he were holding something magical, and so precious he could hardly believe it.

Cecily heard the door move a little on its hinges and she turned and saw Hans. Her face lit with pleasure. "Father just came to see us," she said. "He came to see Madeleine. I've been replaced in his affection." She said this lightly, but Hans heard the gentleness in her voice. They both knew this was not true. Cecily, with a child of her own, understood so well that, to her father, she would always be special as no one else ever could be. That was the magic between parent and child.

Hans found himself smiling back at Cordell. It was a sharp, clean feeling of happiness. It was a problem for Roger, he knew that. Such a correct Englishman could never genuinely approve of his only daughter marrying a German, and an officer in the Gestapo at that. Even if its members were more disciplined and better educated than the regular police. Indeed, many had law degrees, as did Hans, but they were still so essentially German that foreigners instinctively feared them.

Fear. That was the key word. It was felt by those who had been beaten, humiliated, who lived with the threat of hunger and cold and loss, people who too easily became the bullies.

Cecily had been talking to him and he had not heard her. She was smiling, looking at him, waiting for an answer.

Cordell understood, at least something. "Hard day?" he asked. It was a word of understanding, not a question.

"Yes," Hans replied.

Cordell smiled and then stood up. "Then come and see something totally beautiful, and what the world is really all about." He looked down at the baby in his arms, then gently passed her to Hans. He did not hesitate. It was as if he trusted Hans as he trusted himself. He had stood exactly the same way when it was Cecily in his arms. His emotion was only too easy to read, and to share.

Hans took the baby, surprised at how heavy she was. He had not remembered. It was a while, several days, since he had actually picked her up. She was wide awake, smiling and making little gurgling noises, as if she knew she was the center of attention.

Hans's eyes suddenly filled with tears. How could he protect her from a world other than this one, in the safety of his home, his daughter in his arms? Cordell would understand that, surely. He would know what was happening outside this protected world that Cecily knew. Or did she know more? He was not certain. But right now, all he could think of was Madeleine, who looked at him with such total trust. She gave a little hiccup, and smiled. He had been told that this was usual, just part of digestion satisfaction, but he did not see it as that. He thought again how that little hiccup was a sound of safety, complete and absolute trust, and happiness. Please God, he would never break that trust.

Reluctantly, he passed Madeleine back to her mother, and Cecily went upstairs to put her to bed.

"She only got her up for me to see her," Cordell explained, although no explanation was necessary. "It was the baby I came to see, really. I could ask you not to tell Cecily that, but she knows. She's beautiful, Hans, absolutely perfect. If she brings you as much joy as Cecily has brought me, you are a fortunate man." He smiled a little ruefully. "But be prepared to worry about her for the rest of your life. Now tell me, how are you?" He was not asking for information—he knew Hans could not give it to him—he was only being polite, and perhaps kind. Did he see how tired Hans was? Was his anxiety transparent in his face?

The fatigue was not due to being up at night because of the baby. Cecily did all that, and sometimes he was barely aware of the empty space beside him in the bed. It was the stress in the air, the quick tempers of his fellow officers, the demands of working for Paulus. But today it was more. It was the aching disillusion of seeing the Führer hysterical, out of control with fear that men with far too much power were turning against him.

It was an old pattern, this jockeying for position. General Paul von Hindenburg, the great hero of the World War, was president of Germany, but he was old, tired, and had little idea what was really happening. In theory, he still held the ultimate power, but it was slipping further and further out of his hands. People awaited and expected his death.

Today, Hitler was the one who mattered.

Did Hitler know his ancient Roman history? Did he remember what he had learned in school about the assassination of Julius Caesar by his own men? *"Et tu, Brute?"* "You, too, Brutus?" Caesar's closest friend had been one of the first to drive the knife into his heart.

"Hans."

Hans smiled at Cordell. "Sorry, sir, it was a difficult day. General Paulus seems to approve of me. Or else is setting out for me to take the blame for something." He stopped. Would he have said this before? Even yesterday? Above all, to an Englishman who was with the British Embassy?

Hans wondered what more he might learn that would not be obvious to anyone who did not have access to Hitler. Only yesterday, he had believed that the Führer was invincible, but today that dream was shattered, as was all the comfort that went with it. He could find no rational explanation for the tantrum. But that scene, that emotional outburst, had left him trusting Paulus even less.

Had Paulus known how Hitler would react to this information about threats to his power? Surely, he too had been taken by surprise. Or had he? And worse, was Paulus, or even Hitler, somehow going to blame Hans for the news itself? Hans would have to guard himself against attack from a direction he had never considered before.

He felt Cordell watching him, not critically, but certainly with a probing eye, and that was fair. He could see Hans's face, but not into his heart. Was he judging him as a father? What sort of man would be good enough to look after Madeleine?

Cordell was smiling, but he was a diplomat, and Hans was beginning to appreciate how well he did his job. His smile could hide anything. For heaven's sake, Hans had seen his father-in-law even be civil to Goebbels!

"Paulus is not easy to work for," Hans said. "It's a privilege. But like most, it comes at a cost."

"Of course," Cordell agreed. "I'll leave you to have a meal in peace. Thank you for making me welcome."

"Always." Hans was surprised. It was perhaps the polite answer, but he meant it.

That evening, as arranged, Elena and Jacob met at Tonio's café, where they sat at an outdoor table in the warm summer air. At any other time or circumstance the evening would have been a pleasure. Now, however, Elena sat on the edge of her seat and stirred her coffee unnecessarily. There was no sugar in it to dissolve, no cream to stir through; her movement was merely a reflection of nerves, uneasiness.

Jacob sat opposite her, the last of the sun in his face.

They were there to finalize their plans for getting Hartwig out of Berlin. They had spent most of the meal discussing routes, alternatives to make sure of, in case they met with a blockade caused by crowds gathered for any unforeseen reason. It was important to know about scheduled roadworks that could slow them. There was no way to predict a traffic accident, but secondary routes needed to be considered. Such simple things could run them into a blind alley from which there would be no escape.

It was all tedious and time-consuming, but necessary. Possibly the difference between success and failure, especially since Dieter had fulfilled his responsibilities and she was on her own. She wondered if he was now in touch with Alex Cooper and Fassler, but there was no way for her to know, and that troubled her.

"I'm ready," she said quietly to Jacob. "The nearest border is Poland, but we have no connections there. Denmark is best. France is too far, and we would have to drive through most of Germany to reach it."

Jacob looked amused. She knew that he was accustomed to danger and that he saw humor in the strangest things. She had heard people say that this was a gift of his culture, falling back on humor to soften the pain of reality. God knew, the Jews had been hunted, alienated, and persecuted for untold centuries. Perhaps that dry, self-deprecating humor was Jacob's tool of survival. And a sign of courage.

She did not know what had happened to him in the year since she had last seen him. What she did know was that she had escaped death only because of his help. If she knew about his experiences after that, she feared it might open a window onto suffering that would stay with her forever. There were already things she had trouble forgetting, and people who occasionally haunted her dreams.

Now here she was, sitting with Jacob, drinking coffee like any other couple, while at the same time deliberately courting new danger.

"Is he ready?" Jacob asked very quietly. There was no tension in his voice. He might have been asking her what she would like for dinner.

"Yes," she replied. She had managed to meet Hartwig briefly earlier to warn him to be prepared to go the following morning. "As ready as one can be when about to leave behind everything you own, all the people you know, without any explanations or goodbyes."

A sharp anxiety filled his face. "You directed him to destroy his research, yes? Are you sure he hasn't said his goodbyes to anyone he would rather not leave, or lose? It only takes one person to leak information about his plans to go. Even a change in mood can give him away. Has he put together any family photographs, for instance, or his favorite books?"

She was not certain. She had warned him, but surely family photographs were safe to carry, if not in a frame? And a book, if he took only one. What would a book lover take? Nothing was so special that it was worth risking his life. "I'll make sure," she answered, "when I go to tell him the meeting point."

Jacob's look softened, his eyes gentle. "It isn't only his life that will be at risk," he told her. "It will be yours as well. Ours. He should bring fresh underwear and a clean shirt, nothing more. Once we are clear of Berlin, it will be safer."

"What about me? Can I bring my case?"

He thought for a moment or two. "It's a toss-up. What's going to attract more attention? A girl carrying a case, or one who has obviously slept in her clothes?" He had a twisted smile as he said it. "They'll be watching him."

She smiled. "I know. We are as ready as we are going to be."

Jacob nodded slowly. "Tomorrow morning, when the traffic is heaviest, at eight thirty. Meet him for breakfast. Is your hotel room paid for?"

"Yes. I don't have to check out."

"Come to think of it, don't carry the case. Can you put your clothes in a shopping bag?"

"I don't have a shopping bag, but I could get one."

He bent down and came up with a cloth bag. Inside was a jacket, and he removed it. The bag was as wide as it was deep. He passed it to her. "You can carry a week's groceries in that."

She took it, folded it, and put it in her lap.

Her coffee was still hot, so she stirred it until it cooled. When it was the right temperature, she sipped it. She met Jacob's glance and saw the tension behind it. There was nothing to say. They had already decided everything they must do.

CHAPTER 10

Hans arrived at work early, but not because he was eager to be there. Like jumping into icy water, it was better done quickly. The more you thought about it, the worse it seemed.

Even so, Paulus was already there. He looked up from the paper on his desk, his eyes bright and hard, unreadable.

"Good morning, sir," Hans said, standing at attention.

"Morning, Beckendorff. Lot of work here for you." He waved his hand as if indicating a mountain. "As you are aware, there is a very real threat from certain quarters. We need to know precisely where." He suddenly tapped his forefinger on the desk. "I trust that you now appreciate how deeply this problem runs?" He was still staring at Hans. "Did you mention to your family that the Führer now trusts you?"

Hans was startled. He had not expected anything so candid, or something demanding an actual answer. "No, sir. I told my parents that I had met with the Führer, and that it was an honor. I told them I was grateful to them for their support and I wanted them to share that pride. Nothing more."

For several seconds, Paulus said nothing.

He knew everything there was to know about Hans's entire life, from his birth, his schooling, his university courses, the marks he earned, his law degree, and his career since then. And this included the family of his wife. Paulus would not utilize the skills of anyone about whom he did not know everything!

"We have a lot of enemies," Paulus said at last. "Ambitious men who need to be stopped." Again, he looked steadily at Hans, as if he could read the thoughts behind his eyes. "We need to find them, Beckendorff, and strike first!" He blinked several times. "Do you understand me?"

"Yes, sir." It was the only possible answer. "But I feel we need to know more specifically who poses the most immediate danger." He hesitated, not certain how far to go. What did Paulus really feel, that Hans did not? Was he even surprised by the violence of Hitler's hysteria, or had he expected it? How was Hans to learn who had sown the seeds that had caused it? He stared at the man's face, with its heavy flesh, the brilliant, pale eyes, and he began to realize the extent of what he did not know.

Paulus was waiting. Hans felt he would go on waiting until his silence forced an answer.

"There is a great deal I don't know, sir," Hans began. "I think I saw only the surface. I don't know the people behind the scenes, the ones with the real power."

Paulus was nodding his head slowly. "I wondered if you would say that. I think you are far more observant than you pretend to be. 'Yes, sir; no, sir,' but all the time you are thinking, always thinking."

Hans felt a chill, like a warning breath that landed cold on the back of his neck. Should he retreat? Or take a step forward? Retreating would be a lie. Paulus would smell a lie before the words were spoken. "Anyone can take orders, sir, when those orders are plain enough. The Führer needs men who can anticipate orders before they are given." What was he saying? That the Führer needed men who could think for him, when he lost his nerve?

He thought of flattering Paulus, but the man would see it for exactly that: meaningless praise. And yet if he did not, it could be worse. Had he just boxed himself into a corner? No, Paulus had boxed him in, and he had let him. But if he had stopped him, would that have been the end of Paulus's trust in him?

He told himself to face the truth: Paulus might respect him, but he would never trust him, or anyone else. Therefore, he must take the lead. He must not allow Paulus to realize that he was planning, that he would never be the disciple Paulus wanted him to be: loyal, obedient, eager, and if need be, self-sacrificing. Paulus knew of Hans's family. He wanted to remind Hans that he was vulnerable— desperately vulnerable.

Hans took a breath. Paulus was going to force him to break the silence, or by his own silence reveal his distrust, his willingness to plan, to deceive. It was imperative that he speak. "I think we have struck the decisive blow, sir, but we need to do more than that. It is unwise to assume victory, just because it appears as such. When you pull a weed, sir, you need to get out more than the leaves and the stalk. If you don't dig deeper, all the roots will grow back."

"Gardener, are you?" Paulus's eyebrows rose.

"No, sir. But there are a few good general principles to be learned from a garden."

"Like pruning the roses, to get the best blooms?" There was satisfaction behind the gleam in Paulus's eyes.

"Yes, sir. We need to make sure of the people who are loyal to the Führer. And that those who are not will soon learn their lesson. It needs to be done quickly. The loyal rewarded, the overly ambitious pruned away."

"You have more courage than I thought," said Paulus, looking at him with a slight smile. "We must get rid of the Führer's enemies. And our own." The smile widened on his mouth, while vanishing utterly from his eyes. Hans was reminded of water crystallizing into ice.

The silence hung heavily in the room. Somewhere, there was a fly buzzing. Hans tried to think of something to say. "I heard this morning from a source that Schleicher and von Papen have fled." He thought this was no rumor, but the truth.

Paulus stared at him. "Why do you think they have fled?"

"Because they are ambitious," Hans replied. It was the judgment he had heard expressed discreetly.

Paulus stared at him. Again, he would outwait him in silence.

Hans stared at Paulus's face, and he began to realize the extent of what he himself was only now beginning to understand. All sorts of little pieces of information started to form a picture, ugly and dangerous. Hans could now see that Hitler had been overcome by his own fear of the truth, the growing violence, like a storm on the horizon, or a large tidal wave seen far out to sea. The man considered by many to be the most powerful person on earth had stood for a few agonizing moments like someone overcome by terror, unable to hide it even from his subordinates, including a man who idolized him.

But . . . did Paulus idolize Hitler? Or was he using him? Perhaps he had seen this behavior before and concealed it for his own reasons. Hans would be a fool if he thought Paulus would not use him as well, however it suited him. And Hans was beginning to see that he, Hans, could be in danger. He had to remain safe. Who else would look after Cecily and Madeleine? They were so vulnerable. "Tell me where you would like me to start, sir," he said, his voice steady and sure.

Paulus thought for several moments before he spoke. "There are things you do not know about, but I think perhaps it is time." His eyes searched Hans's face slowly, not hiding the fact that he was looking for something.

Hans opened his mouth, then closed it without speaking.

"Your father-in-law is in British Intelligence, isn't that so?"

Hans froze. "Sir?"

Paulus smiled. "You didn't know?"

Hans shook his head. "I did not." Did Cecily know? He was sure she didn't either. If Cordell was part of MI6, this changed every-thing. Most importantly, the safety of his wife and child. What else did Paulus know? How much? And what should Hans say? He felt like a dark moth pinned to a white board, with the pin impaling his chest.

"You really didn't know?" Paulus said, but this time with a slow smile.

Hans swallowed. "I know he works at the embassy, sir." His tongue was thick, as if he could barely say the words. "Cultural attaché."

Paulus's smile widened. "He used to be a friend of Lucas Standish, who was once head of MI6. It surprises you that I know?" He sud-denly sat bolt upright, slamming the legs of his chair against the floor, making Hans snap to attention. "Of course, he isn't with them anymore. Retired, Standish is."

There was nothing for Hans to say. He tried frantically to think of something, but his mind was empty.

Paulus was looking at him, laughter behind his eyes. "Well, now you know it, Beckendorff, as you should if you are to rise to the heights that you only imagine now. There is a great path ahead of you, if you are man enough to take it. Are you?"

There was only one possible answer. Hans raised his chin and pulled his shoulders back. "Yes, sir!" There was no room for hesita-tion. The tide had not only turned, but the undertow was now strong enough to reach for a man and drown him.

And then a thought ran through him like a powerful volt of elec-tricity. If Roger Cordell was MI6, was this why Paulus had chosen Hans to be his right-hand man? Not because of his intelligence, his education, or his courage, but because of his family relationships? His mind was repelled by this thought, but he must never let Paulus know. He must change the subject. "You mention Mr. Standish, sir. Is he important any longer?"

Paulus's face froze.

For the first time in Hans's short career with Paulus, he saw pain in the man's expression, something he could not disguise. It was not grief, it was vulnerability, and humiliation. And it had something to do with an old man, Lucas Standish.

He averted his eyes. Paulus must never imagine that his young protégé had seen these powerful emotions. It would cost Hans more than any promotion; it could cost him his life. He looked at Paulus again and gave a slight shrug of his shoulders.

Paulus stared at him without blinking. "Leave me be."

"Sir?" Hans said quietly.

Paulus blinked. "Well, get on with it!"

"Yes, sir."

With no answer to his question, Hans turned on the spot and went out of the room, the sweat pouring down his body, his mouth so dry he could not swallow.

Elena had a restless night. She had to be up early, pack what she could fit into the shopping bag, and walk the short distance to where she and Professor Hartwig were scheduled to meet.

Jacob would bring the car. The previous day she had given him money to purchase a vehicle. He knew to choose something old, but well maintained, and able to travel at a high speed. They could not afford engine trouble. It also needed to be filled with fuel, regardless of the price.

It was as good a plan as they could make, and Elena was confident that this was what she would have decided had she been forced to do this alone. The only difference was that she would have secured the car last night, and left it somewhere near the hotel.

She turned over, realized she had a stiff neck, and punched the pillow into better shape. She was too hot and threw off the top blankets. Then it was too cold and she needed them back.

Everything had been carefully planned, and it should work. In any case, it was too late to change plans now. And this mission was far too important to leave anything to chance.

* * *

She awoke sometime later and saw that it was still early. She was drifting off to sleep, when the alarm went off. It was broad daylight now. Was she late? No, of course not. This was midsummer; it was light for half the night.

She rose, washed, and dressed in black trousers and the white shirt, with the jacket over it. It was striking, especially with her blond hair. Sometimes she missed her ordinary light brown color and thought about dyeing it back. But she did not want to re-create the same ordinary young woman she had been before, and possibly re-awaken someone's memories.

She packed everything into the shopping bag, surprised to find it all fitted in easily. Then she left a tip for the housemaid and went down to breakfast, which, for all it was good, tasted like sweet sawdust.

She went back upstairs to the bathroom for the last time, looked around quickly, checked all the drawers and the wardrobe, under the bed, even though she knew she had left nothing. She went downstairs and out the front door into the street, without speaking to the young woman at the desk. She had just under half an hour to walk to the meeting place. It would be a serious error to be late.

What would she do if Hartwig did not come? He said he would when they last met, but he could change his mind, because his nerves had failed him, or he could be arrested. She knew that he was being watched. If the Germans were clever, they would not arrest him, but follow him to see who he met, and then arrest them all. Alarm suddenly rang out in her head. *Stop it! Just stop it!*

Her instincts kicked in and warned her that she was walking too quickly, that she must slow down and not get to their meeting place too soon. She would only have to wait, and waiting would draw attention.

Elena ended up being nearly five minutes late and Hartwig was already there, sitting with a cup of coffee and reading a newspaper, or pretending to. The sunlight made a halo of his graying hair and reflected in his glasses when he looked up at her. He did not appear to have any baggage at all, not even an attaché case for papers. He rose to his feet.

"Good morning, Uncle," she said, with what she knew was a forced smile. "How are you?" She lowered her voice.

"Coffee?" he asked.

"Yes. Yes, please. I really don't need it, but it gives me something to do until the car comes."

He waited until she had taken the seat opposite him, then he sat down.

"Comes?" he questioned.

"Yes." She forced herself to smile very slightly. "When it does, we'll get straight into it and keep going."

"Do you drive?" he asked, his voice very nearly level, as if it were an ordinary conversation.

"Oh, yes. In fact, I enjoy it," she replied. "But I don't know Berlin so well, and my friend does. And we need to get this right."

"Indeed."

"And you have brought nothing with you?" Her imagination went vividly to all the precious things he must have left behind. He must hurt appallingly.

"One book, in the inside pocket of my jacket, and a few photographs. After all, I am only out for breakfast, and a late cup of coffee. I told the lab that I had a dentist's appointment so it will be at least lunchtime before anyone notices I am not there. Or that all my files are missing." If there was pain in his face, it was well hidden, no more than a shadow in his eyes.

"What book did you bring?" she asked. It was not merely a matter of thinking of something to say; she wondered what on earth anyone would bring, if they could only choose one. She had no idea what she would choose.

"Dante's *Inferno*," he replied. "An English translation I rather like. There are some memorable lines, but the meaning is the same whichever language you choose. I have read the English, the German, and with a little difficulty the medieval Italian. Or, perhaps I should say, the Tuscan. It was written around the year 1300, you know. Yet it still stands up."

"Does it? In what way? For meaning, or . . . ?"

"Yes, for meaning."

"A journey through hell?" She saw an extraordinarily sweet expression in his eyes and, just for a moment, it was as if they had known each other for years.

"No, my dear," he said. "A journey of understanding, telling us that we are not punished for our sins, but by them. If I do something wrong, I may hurt others, but they can recover, or be healed. But because of what I do to myself, I have changed who and what I am. And that cannot be undone by any miracle of healing. I can be forgiven, but that is a blessing mainly to the one who forgives. So yes, I alone can change what I have become."

She stared at him, seeing in what he said the beginning of reason and all logic. She wanted to tell him that she understood, but it was too comprehensive a word, and so big an idea. In the end, she said something quite different. "That changes . . . everything, doesn't it?"

"It certainly changes a lot," he agreed. "And even a scientist can agree with that."

In the street, a car slowed down as if to stop.

Both Elena and Hartwig stiffened, then let their breath out slowly. It was not Jacob. She looked at the professor and saw the moment's alarm, then self-control reassert itself, and how he smiled ruefully.

A moment later, another car slowed as it approached. This one stopped. It was a matter of seconds before Elena recognized Jacob.

"Come," she said to Hartwig, while trying to keep urgency out of her expression. She picked up her bag, startled by the weight of it. She had forgotten how much she'd filled it. She made sure she left money on the table to cover the cup of coffee, and then walked to the curb. She heard and felt Hartwig on her heels. Although she was certain that the driver was Jacob, she checked again before she opened the door.

Hartwig climbed into the backseat, and Elena took the passenger seat next to Jacob.

He began to pull away before she had the door firmly closed. He glanced at her, then put his foot on the accelerator and slipped the car into the stream of traffic.

For several minutes, Jacob concentrated on negotiating the hectic chaos of rush hour. Elena glanced back and saw that Hartwig was outwardly calm. In her short time with him, she had learned that he appeared like this habitually. But this was so different. Today, he was leaving the city he had lived in all his adult life, the friends and colleagues of years. In fact, he was leaving every certainty he knew. It was a leap into an unknown, perhaps a dangerous future, and it was too late to turn back.

Elena wanted to reach out and take his hand, to say that she felt deeply for him, admired his courage, but that might be an intrusion. She was a stranger to him. She had no idea what ties he was breaking, what friendships he was leaving behind. Or, for that matter, which of the people in his sphere the authorities might pressure to learn anything they could. Might they execute someone who refused to divulge information? Would they ever make it public that he had left Germany?

She dismissed these thoughts. They were paralyzing.

Elena was certain there was nothing she could say that would not be intrusive, perhaps absurd, as if she could read his emotions. She thought back to some of the worst times in her life, such as when she was dismissed from the Foreign Office. That was the most bitter shame she had ever felt. And it was deserved. She had behaved like an idiot, and for a man who had never loved her, or possibly anyone else. She had atoned for that.

Elena could only guess what Hartwig was feeling. But what must the alternative be? The growth of germ warfare, tens of thousands, if not millions, of people ill or dead? Terrified, sick, and in pain, the dying and the dead. Carts going to the streets to pick up the bodies. Mass graves.

She had been reading too much about the Black Death. For heaven's sake, that was in 1348! This was more than half a millennium later; another world.

The car was slowing and came to a stop. The traffic all round them was at a complete standstill. Horns were blaring. Was it an ordinary traffic jam, this time of the morning? Or had the Gestapo already discovered that Hartwig was gone? Could they know that so soon? She felt the sweat of tension prickle under her arms.

Moments ticked by. No one spoke. Elena glanced back at Hartwig, but he was looking forward, past her and through the front windscreen.

Then they began to move at last, creeping.

Jacob changed lanes, shifting more to the outside, as if he were going to peel off and take a side street, but then continued in the same direction.

"You're not turning?" Elena asked, swallowing hard.

"No," Jacob replied, not taking his eyes off the road.

Elena knew that even the slightest accident would mean everyone stopping, examining the damage, exchanging names and addresses. Perhaps even calling the traffic police. Or maybe they would come anyway, just to get everything moving again.

Elena realized her fingernails were digging into the palms of her hands.

Seconds went by, and still Jacob did not take his eyes off the road, nor did he speak.

Slowly, the traffic eased and they began to move a yard at a time, then five yards, and then in a slow and steady fashion.

Elena felt her muscles unlock.

They were now cruising steadily, slowly, and then picking up speed. Not fast, because it was just the normal traffic flow of early morning in a busy and highly populated city. At this rate, she calculated, they would be on one of the main roads heading west, and well out of the city, in half an hour.

And then, with no warning, they were forced again to come to a complete stop. There were police ahead of them. The uniforms identified them, even at this distance.

"They've set up a checkpoint, it seems," Jacob said quietly. "Get out and slip between the cars and along the next side street to the right. It's about a hundred yards to the railway station. Wait for me at the clock by the Reibekuchen stand. In fact, buy one for each of you and eat them, so you'll appear to be killing time before you catch a train. Don't look for me, I'll find you. Talk to each other, and don't look anxious. And if the train comes before I do, you should continue on."

There was no time to argue. Elena opened her door and slipped out and onto the road, looking both ways at the traffic and for any police on foot. Hartwig did the same, standing close, his door remaining open. There were cars, endless cars, but no one on the pavement.

"Be careful," she said quietly to Jacob.

He merely nodded.

As soon as Hartwig closed the door, the car moved back into the traffic and was gone again. Within seconds, it was invisible in the mass of vehicles.

Hartwig took Elena by the arm and started to walk forward, forcing her to go with him. "Do you do this often?" he asked, as if this were a perfectly ordinary situation for her, and they were a perfectly ordinary couple—perhaps a father and daughter—taking a leisurely walk.

She wanted to laugh, and cry. "Not very," she replied, as if it were the usual thing to say. "The last time it was . . . I suppose it was less than a year ago. I was in Trieste. It's a very beautiful city."

"I've only been there once," he replied. "It was for a conference. Just a few days. Not nearly long enough. And you're right, it is very beautiful."

"I wasn't there very long either."

"Holiday?"

"No, a bit like this. Only . . . worse." She preferred not to think of it, it was all so painful.

"Clearly, you got out," he said with a slight smile.

She needed to keep this conversation light, two people chatting. "I got some wonderful pictures. Some of my very best."

"More picturesque than Berlin. All that water. It changes the light, don't you think?"

She smiled, looking at him with interest. "Yes, I do. Do you take pictures?"

"Only for my own pleasure. But we Germans make very good cameras." He led her across the road, dodging traffic. If they waited until there was none, they would be here all morning.

"I know," she agreed when they reached the other side and turned toward the railway station. "I have two Leicas. Wouldn't use anything else."

"Excellent." He smiled, as if that were a moment of real pleasure, a slip into a different reality where beauty mattered. Without speaking again, they increased the pace a little until they came to the main crossroads, with the high roofs of the railway station ahead of them. There were crowds of people fanning out and hailing taxis, walking quickly along the main road and into the side streets, heads bent, all knowing where they were going.

Hartwig increased his hold on her arm. She was glad of it; they must not lose each other now. They would probably reconnect again, but it would be a few minutes of fear before they did . . . and time lost. There were too many possibilities for mistakes.

They made their way through the crowds, occasionally getting knocked, bumping into other people who were carrying cases, boxes, bags, muttering apologies. At last, they reached the Reibekuchen seller. The fragrant smell of hot potato fritters and applesauce would draw her wherever she had been going. Hartwig bought two, even if there was too little time to eat them. As Jacob had suggested, it would at least make them look less conspicuous, as if they were here, possibly grabbing a late breakfast.

She looked around. There was no sign of Jacob. She had little idea of where he was going, or how long he intended to be, or even if he had any concept of that. What would she do if he did not come at all? The answer was unavoidable: get Hartwig out on the first train west. She had enough money. She could not afford to wait for Jacob, still less to go and look for him. It felt pointless, a betrayal, and yet it was her duty, and what he would expect.

Hartwig was standing in front of her, holding out the first potato fritter. The aroma of it made her mouth water. He was smiling.

"Thank you." She accepted it. It was too hot to eat straightaway.

They moved to where they could stand, which was not exactly under the clock, but close to it. Who would people assume them to be? Friends? Not colleagues. She was too young to hold a position anywhere equal to his. He looked distinguished, even in the ordinary, casual clothes he was wearing. It was in his features, his stance.

"What will people take us to be?" he asked, almost as if reading her thoughts. "Anything but what we are, I hope. Not fugitives anyway. You are good at looking so totally matter-of-fact."

"I don't feel it! Perhaps they will think you are my grandfather?"

He looked startled. "Grandfather?"

She realized her mistake immediately and felt the heat rise up in her face. "I'm sorry. I think I mentioned before, you remind me of my grandfather quite a lot. And that is not an insult. When I first really knew him, when I was two or three, he was about your age. And he was my best friend from the time I could talk. He still is. Of course, he's older now, but not in my mind." She smiled. "I don't allow him to get older, because I want him always to be here. I know that isn't going to happen, but in my mind it will. And I will believe it as long as I can."

"What does he do, this grandfather of yours?" He took a bite of his fritter and chewed with clear pleasure.

She would like to have answered him, but one mistake could be one too many. "He's retired now, and his favorite thing to do is to go for long walks with his dog, Toby."

"Isn't that every sane man's favorite thing to do?" Hartwig said quietly. Then he glanced beyond her. "That looks like your friend."

She turned and saw Jacob walking toward them, his dark hair making him more visible above the blond heads of the jostling crowd. She felt a wave of relief, both to see him and to escape from a conversation that was becoming too emotional.

Jacob reached them, and immediately they set off through the crowd, until they stopped by a very ordinary black car, in much the same shape as the one they had been in twenty minutes ago.

"Come on!" he said sharply. "Somebody's going to miss this soon, and then the word will go out. We must be on the main road before that."

Elena drew in her breath to make some comment on stealing a car, and then let it out again. Thank heaven she had not had to do this herself. She was a pretty good driver, even in a chase, and she could steal a car if she had to, but that only added to the complications. She could even start a car without its key, but she didn't feel fully adept at that. When she returned home, if she made it, she would get Peter to help her sharpen those skills. It was an area she needed to strengthen.

She nearly asked Jacob why they had bothered to buy the first car when he could have found one to steal, but she said nothing. And then it struck her that, had he stolen a car yesterday, the police would have been searching for it all night. And if he had waited until this morning to steal one, he might not have found what they needed. It made perfect sense.

They drove in silence for quite a long stretch. This time, Elena sat in the back with Hartwig. At a glance, they might look like they were being driven by a chauffeur. Jacob was wearing a dark jacket and trousers, easily mistaken for a uniform.

The car twisted and turned through the backstreets, following anything but a straight line. For a long time, no one spoke. Elena knew what Jacob was doing. If they were being followed, that person would think they had missed their way and were trying to find it again, either along the same road or on a parallel one going the same direction. But they did not keep in any direction long enough for someone to guess where they were going. This route was longer, but less dangerous. Thank heaven Jacob knew Berlin so well.

They stopped to top up the petrol tank. If they had to keep going over the open highway for a long time, at least they would not be caught for want of fuel.

They were out of the city and on the main road north when they ran into a roadblock. With a wave of emotion almost suffocating, the fear returned. Elena met Jacob's eyes in the rearview mirror. There was nothing they could do but slide to a stop, four feet from the rear bumper of the car ahead of them.

"I can't see what it is," Jacob said, before anyone could ask him. "It's too far ahead."

"Can you see any police on foot?" Hartwig's voice rasped slightly in his throat.

Jacob peered through the windscreen. "No."

"Do you want me to look?" Elena asked, putting her hand on the door handle.

Jacob said "Yes" and Hartwig said "No" at the same time.

"Good," Elena answered with a smile. "It gives me a choice. I won't go far."

"Stay where you are!" Jacob said sharply, changing his mind.

"You start moving, if you can," she replied. "I'll be back before then."

"What are you going to do if it's the police?" he demanded. "We can't get off this road."

She ignored him and got out, turning for an instant to give him a sweet smile, then closing the door. He said something, but she didn't hear it.

Her legs were cramped, because they had been locked into one position. It felt good to stretch, but she did it in a way that would draw no attention to her. Everyone seated in these cars was a stranger, and everyone presented a possible threat. She thought about Dieter, her contact at the hotel, and how secretive he had been about his other assignment. Could Dieter have betrayed them? Was he a double agent? Or was he simply one man trying to deal with multiple crises at once? What was the other thing he sensed in the air, intimated in unfinished sentences? Was it something to do with Alex Cooper and Fassler, the other scientist? There was nothing she could do about this, not now. No matter where Dieter stood.

She shook her shoulders, extended her arms, and walked forward, passing several cars with their windows open to let a little fresh air into the hot interiors. It was only nine in the morning, but it had been light, with the sun bright, for many hours already.

Elena continued up a slight incline and felt the pull in her leg muscles. When she reached the crest of the rise, she stopped. She was now able to see the road for several miles ahead. Halfway along, the cars were beginning to move. One car was being pushed to the right lane, toward the shoulder, and slowly the other cars were moving. She could see a couple of police cars parked to the side.

She turned and hurried back.

A woman called out from one of the stationary cars. "What is it? Are we moving?"

"Yes," Elena replied cheerfully. "An accident. They're getting it cleared."

She suddenly could not remember how far she had gone, or what the car looked like! Where was it? She stopped. Had she passed it? Ahead of her, someone touched a horn.

It was not Jacob. Where was she?

Fear drenched her for a moment. This was absurd.

The cars beside her were beginning to move.

A car door opened twenty feet ahead and the man stepped out. It was Hartwig. The sun shone on his gray hair and accentuated the very slight stoop of his shoulders.

Hartwig went round to the other side and climbed in.

She reached them just as the cars were moving forward.

"It's an accident, not a blockade," she said, shutting the door as she settled in.

"Thank you," Jacob said quietly. "And if you do that again, I'll leave you to drive. I'll sit in the back and give you directions."

"I won't," she said. "That is, do it again."

The car inched forward, then picked up speed until they were moving at a slow, steady pace. Again, no one spoke. They passed the scene of the accident and traffic began to move.

But before they could relax, there was another jam.

"I can take the next exit," Jacob said quietly. "We can't go on trusting our luck. The authorities might not have missed you yet, Professor. But even if this is so, it can't be longer than a few hours. And then they'll expect us to go to the nearest border. I think our best plan is to do what they don't expect, and that is to stay in Germany." He glanced at the rearview mirror and met Elena's eyes.

She saw that he looked worried. The part of his face she could see was tense, the muscles tight. She understood his reasoning, but wanted to be out of Germany, somewhere the German police could not stop them.

"We could be stopped at the nearest border," Hartwig put in. "They could have telephoned all the border police." There was a thin edge of fear in his voice.

Elena felt it as one does a paper cut. Sharp through the flesh, slow to bleed, then the pain. "Yes," she agreed quietly, turning to Hartwig and seeing the bleak acceptance in his eyes. She tried to think of something to say, but there was nothing that had honesty or meaning.

Jacob glanced once more in the mirror and then moved to the right-hand lane and took the next turnoff to the south, and the road that would ultimately lead them to Munich.

It had been a long day and Hans was keen to get home. He yearned for a quiet evening of Cecily telling him how Madeleine was growing.

Each time he held his daughter, he felt she was heavier. Perhaps only an ounce or two, but still noticeable. And she knew him, he was sure of that. He talked to her quietly, telling her how his day had been. Of course, she did not understand a word he said, but she did know that he was talking to her, and her eyes never left his face. He found himself telling her all kinds of things that worried him, or pleased him, and occasionally he told her his problems.

But this evening his thoughts were bearing heavily on his mind, and it occurred to him that a visit with his father-in-law might help. Paulus might have been able to dismiss the incident when Hitler had lost his emotional balance and come to pieces in front of them, but Hans could not. Paulus could even deny it—they all could—but that did not remove from Hans's inner eye the indelible vision of the Führer shaking with rage, then white-faced with fear, his head swinging from side to side, as if looking for someone to help him.

Paulus had controlled the situation, but only after a moment or two. Later, he had not forbidden Hans to mention it, but Hans was no fool. If he had not the intelligence to keep quiet about it, Paulus would no longer trust him. Perhaps Paulus felt Hans was less dangerous if he remained close to him: if this young man made a slip, said anything at all, he could very quickly be silenced.

It was mainly for that reason that Hans had said nothing, as if the incident had not occurred. But he was aware of Paulus watching him, very aware. He was certain that Paulus intended to use him somehow. Was that an honor? Was it because he trusted Hans's ambition, and it was because of his ambition that he would keep himself in line and discreet?

Hans had no delusions that he was still by Paulus's side because of any kind of respect, or even affection. Paulus had nurtured protégés before, and Hans guessed they were chosen because they could do the tedious work of watching Paulus's back. Or were they there to be blamed, if something went wrong? Or connected to someone whose position could benefit Paulus, such as being the son-in-law of a British agent?

He told the taxi to stop a couple of streets short of where the Cordells lived. He thanked the man, paid him, and walked the rest of the way. It was a lovely evening to be out and about, but it was discretion that made him walk first away from the house, then take a roundabout route until he was sure that he was not being followed, until finally he arrived at their front door. It made sense if Paulus had Hans followed, just to see if he would visit Roger Cordell. To Paulus, that might constitute an act of betrayal . . . or worse.

The door was opened by the maid, who showed Hans into the sitting room, the one with French doors that opened onto the back space that Winifred had transformed into a typical English garden. She had lived in Germany nearly all Cecily's life, and she had wanted to create a little bit of England around her.

At first, Hans had not liked it, simply because it was alien. Now, as he got to know his mother-in-law better, and could see where

Cecily got so much of her gentleness and some of her mannerisms, not to mention her domestic skills, he enjoyed the garden and was learning to appreciate Winifred.

She was even-tempered. In fact, Hans had seen her offended, even angry, but she had never lost her temper. When she had a belief, she seldom changed it, but she was not aggressive. She did not follow fashion in clothes, or far more importantly, as Hans had begun to realize, neither did she follow other people's opinions, tastes, or ideas. He used to be impatient with her, without showing it. And then, without realizing it, he began to like her.

Quietly, in her own fashion, Cecily resembled her mother. And now he was beginning to hope that Madeleine would be like her, too.

He stepped into the garden as Roger walked toward him and looked steadily at his face.

"Nothing wrong," Hans answered the question that mattered. "I just felt like talking to you."

Most of the anxiety cleared from Cordell's brow. "You mean the family's all right, and it's something else?"

"Am I so readable?" Hans asked. It was disconcerting, and yet comfortable at the same time.

"Yes," Cordell answered with a smile. "And anything wrong with those we love matters profoundly. Political or professional difficulties we can deal with, or at least try. But family? It's not the same."

A year ago, Hans would have said that was self-indulgent nonsense. Shortsighted, even selfish. Now he understood completely.

He walked further into the garden. It was set out in a deeply satisfying way. There was always something in bloom. The colors varied with the season. He had noticed that spring was all blues and golds: primroses, daffodils, bluebells, and perhaps a little purple in Dutch irises. Summer, as it was now, was bright colors, reds and greens, blue lupins and delphiniums, white daisies, clean and vivid. And, again, there was purple, this time magnificent irises. Winifred had told him that in England they were sometimes called German irises, stately flowers standing tall with plumed petals and gold stamens. That pleased him. In autumn, he could remember from last year, there were red and tawny-gold asters and chrysanthemums, and a second blooming of the roses. And again, something purple, always something purple, as if it somehow made everything else blend together.

He thought of a time when he had dismissed Winifred as dull and predictable. But that was until he had grown to see how much Cecily was like her, in ways he loved: thoughtful little things that could be missed if one did not take notice.

He realized with a quick stab of something like shame how much more comfortable he was with Cecily's parents than with his own. Of course, there were still subjects they could not discuss, specifically politics. This would only result in tension. But when it came to family, they were now able to talk with pleasure: the family-shared moments, their mutual love for Cecily, and now a precious new baby. But the first, the political, was becoming a heavy weight Hans could hardly bear.

"I am honored to work with Paulus," he said suddenly. "But I don't like him."

"And I don't like the British ambassador an awful lot," Cordell said, with a slightly rueful smile.

"But you trust him?" Hans was being far more honest than he'd intended, now that the weight was pressing down on him.

"Yes," Cordell said without hesitation. "And I think he knows his job, which is actually the most important thing."

"I'm not quite sure what Paulus's job is," Hans admitted.

Cordell did not reply immediately. He was standing in front of one of the larger flower beds filled with color. A cascade of pink roses in full bloom covered a trellis at least six feet high. The flowers arched over the top, as if each blossom were trying to outstrip the others. There were purple vines in front of it.

"There's always something purple, isn't there?" Hans observed. "Is it Winifred's favorite color?"

"You noticed that," Cordell observed. "I asked that, too. It isn't.

It's apparently the one shade that ties all the others together. I didn't know that, but now I can see how it does. Everything is planted where it is for a reason. And Winifred puts different kinds of fertilizer around them, depending on what the soil around each plant needs."

"She loves it," Hans said, and then wondered if it was too personal a remark.

Cordell smiled. "I sometimes think everything does better if you love it."

"Like plants?" Hans tried to keep his tone of surprise, rather than incredulity.

"Or food," Cordell replied, keeping his tone light as well, as if he was not certain whether he believed what he said. "Food prepared with love tastes better." After a moment, he asked, "What's really worrying you, Hans?" He turned sideways to read the young man's face.

"There are a lot of plots against the Führer," he said. "But I expect you know that, or at least suspect it."

"Yes," Cordell agreed. "Is it Paulus's job to hunt them out?"

Hans hesitated only a few seconds. "It might be others' as well, but it's certainly one of his." He would not add that Paulus was also in charge of germ warfare. Roger Cordell would not learn that from him. Hans wanted to tell Cordell that Paulus had ordered him to help uncover the plots, but that would be a betrayal of his duty. Paulus would most certainly not want him to do that! Or . . . would he? Was Hans chosen for the job precisely to get this information out? And to whom? The British ambassador? Or British Intelligence? Cordell was meant to be a cultural attaché, and he certainly did the job well. Anyone with any sense of how Intelligence actually worked would know perfectly well that there was a senior, well-experienced Intelligence officer in any embassy. Hans was realizing all too clearly now the hideousness of his position working for a top German Intelligence officer while being the son-in-law of an equally senior British Intelligence officer.

Had Paulus asked for Hans to work for him to use him as an un-witting go-between linking the Germans and the British? Then a worse thought struck him. What if Cecily and Madeleine were the pawns in a game to make sure that he, Hans, and perhaps even Cordell, would do whatever Paulus wanted? That could be anything! If he thought about it, was there anything he would not do to save them? Or anything Cordell would not do?

"Hans?" Cordell's voice was sharp, making Hans realize his father-in-law had spoken before and had not been heard.

Hans stared at him.

Cordell did not pretend. "What is it? What have you just thought of?"

Hans started to shake his head. Then he felt Cordell's hand gripping his arm so hard it hurt. He pulled away. Not from Cordell's question, but from the sheer physical pain. "I'm just wondering why I've been given such an important job with Paulus." He almost wanted to laugh and cry at the same time. "I thought it was my skill and my loyalty. Or perhaps even that my father had put in a word for me or paid the right people." He gave a little shrug of disgust. "How naïve! I never even thought of it being my family. My wife's family. I'm sorry." He was sorry, profoundly. But he did not know any path that would have been better, not one that led to the same place in the end.

Cordell put his hand on Hans's arm, but this time it was gentle. "Don't apologize. We can only do what we think best. Just look after Cecily and Madeleine."

Hans's mind raced. He was horrified by the realization that had just come to him. Now he was in turmoil, and fear welled up inside him, threatening to paralyze his brain. Who could he turn to? The answer was another unavoidable truth: no one.

He wanted to persuade Cordell of the hope he had felt only a few days ago. But everything that came to his mind about hope was based on the invincibility of the Führer. And now he must face it: he had watched as Hitler lost his nerve and panicked. It was Paulus who had kept control.

Was Paulus really keeping his own nerve or had he created the situation in the first place? And how much did Hans actually know for himself? Not enough. He did not know for sure if Röhm was truly trying to take over power from the government, using his gigantic army of Brownshirts. And for what? Self-indulgence? Unchecked power? And then, ultimately, what? Chaos.

Suddenly, Hans was afraid of Paulus. And at the same moment, he knew that he was one of the very few who could do something about it. But what? And at what cost? Not at the risk of harm to his wife and child.

Cordell removed his hand from Hans's arm. Hans saw this not as a denial of anything, just a step forward on this very difficult road.

How honest could Hans be with his father-in-law? Admit that he knew the man worked for MI6? But what was the purpose of talking to him at all if he was going to lie? Cordell would not trust him and Hans would not blame him for that. He glanced sideways. Cordell was looking at the garden, at Winifred's work. A partial truth would have to do. "Hitler really is at risk from plotters," Hans finally said. "From among our own people."

"That's what I've heard," Cordell agreed. "He'll put a stop to it pretty soon." He smiled slightly. "I don't expect you to answer me on that!"

"I don't know the answer," Hans replied honestly. "I look at Paulus and I think he knows what's going to happen. In fact, I think he might have actually planned something . . . or at least guessed it."

"An attempted coup?" Cordell said with apparent surprise. "A change of direction?"

He sounded incredulous. Did he really find it so hard to believe?

Cordell was waiting for him to answer. Maybe he thought Hans might not have a balanced judgment. He might have had it a month ago, even a week ago, but perhaps not now. He remembered Paulus's face as he watched Hitler's panic. His expression conveyed exasperation, disgust, perhaps fear—but not surprise. Hans realized that now, in hindsight.

Perhaps the Führer's outburst was because of the pressure of having a whole nation—beaten, starved, and humiliated—depending on him, this one man, to re-create it, raise it from the dead, as it were. And this was not an exaggeration: everything centered on Hitler.

Hans thought of Röhm, a disgusting man. He had heard stories of Röhm's excesses, and knew several people who had seen them. Himmler had his ambitions, too, and Goering, even of becoming Führer. Hans knew that he needed to take them all more seriously.

How could he have been so . . . not innocent, but ignorant? And willfully blind, not looking honestly at what he did not wish to see. Was it all apparent to Cordell?

The silence grew heavy between them. Hans could hear the faint buzzing of an insect in the flowers, probably a bee. How far should he trust this man? Cordell was an Englishman, on the outside calm, reliable, and not terribly imaginative; loyal and predictable. Possibly, to anyone who did not know him, Hans seemed to be following in the same path. Maybe that was what appealed to Cecily—his comparison to her father. He hoped not. It was nothing like what he felt inside. His was a protective covering, far more effective than a suit of armor. Sometimes he thought Cecily saw through that.

Was Cordell very different underneath?

Everything he had relied on, those matters he no longer needed to think about, was falling apart. It was as if the Virgin Mary had come to life and had let out a flood of foul language. Hitler stood for courage in the face of adversity; faith even when victory seemed impossible; imagination, loyalty, and more than anything else, the unquestioning, unwavering conviction that Germany was on the way to greatness again.

Was Adolf Hitler a man wearing a crown that was too heavy for him? Did Cordell realize that?

Hans turned to look at him.

Cordell smiled. "Does Hitler know how flawed some of his lieutenants are?"

That was a simple question, and Hans could give an honest answer without betraying anyone. "Yes."

"Then be careful, Hans. If they attack, instead of retreating, there could be a nasty rats' nest beneath it. Choose your sides very carefully. And if I may offer a small comment of advice . . ."

Hans's mouth went dry. "Yes?"

"Don't turn on Johann Paulus. He is, above all, a survivor. I know one or two things about him that you might not. He's been through some hard times."

Hans had heard stories. Something about a fall from grace that Paulus had suffered. He had tried to look at Paulus's record one day and learned very quickly that this was a bad idea. There were secrets locked inside those documents. If Paulus wanted them kept secret, it would be dangerous to uncover what they were. "I know," he said. "But I don't know what they are." His mind was racing. "Do you?"

Cordell answered him bleakly. "I don't know the details myself. But Cecily had a friend at school, Margot Standish. Her grandfather is Lucas Standish, and the story somehow involves him. But, Hans," he added, his expression stern, "don't let that name slip into your conversation. Standish is not a common name, and it certainly is not one Paulus will ever forget." He studied Hans closely, anxiety in his face.

It occurred to Hans, with surprise, that Cordell not only cared for him but also trusted him. He was concerned about Hans surviving all of this. He was hoping that Hans would climb the ladder of ambition, professional success, financial stability, rank, but in different ways, for reasons other than his own father would have judged important. For an instant, emotion choked him. How often had he tried to explain to his father his ideas, his beliefs, and no matter how well it had started, it always ended in frustration, even pain? Hans wanted to agree. He wanted to please his father, but he couldn't. He felt boxed in, no longer in control of himself, his beliefs, and the ideas he needed to think about, argue about, explore. Ideas and ideals. He felt ungrateful, and he resented it.

"Be careful." Cordell's voice interrupted his thoughts. "Remember that Paulus is very clever indeed. For God's sake be careful. And . . ." He did not finish.

It was clear to Hans that he did not know how, or which words to use.

"I will," Hans replied. "It helps to come and see you. And talk about it, without watching what I say all the time. Something is changing, isn't it?"

"I think so," Cordell answered. "But I don't know which way. It's—" He stopped.

Hans wondered what he was about to say. That it was frightening? It would have been the truth, but he didn't want to admit that to Cordell. He cared what Cordell thought of him; he wanted to earn his respect.

Cordell spoke, his voice softer. "It's time you went home for supper. Give my love to Madeleine. And, of course, Cecily."

Hans swallowed hard and smiled. "I will."

It was a long, steady drive from Berlin to Munich, but once Elena, Jacob, and Professor Hartwig were on the highway and well clear of the traffic jams and blockades, they made good time. It appeared that if anyone was looking for Hartwig, they were concentrating on the roads that led to the Danish or Belgian borders, or possibly the closest border of all, which was eastward into Poland. With no roadblocks, Elena assumed that either the professor's absence had not yet been noticed, or no one was looking toward Munich, which was Hitler's stronghold. It was public knowledge that Hitler had a deep love for the nearby mountains of Bavaria. It was where he felt most at home. Elena had taken holidays there as a girl, and she could very easily understand the peace that wrapped around one with those immense mountain views, the clean air, the sun. Even the occasional storms were dramatic, both frightening and beautiful.

This time it was different. They were fugitives who, if they were caught, would almost certainly pay with their lives.

Elena watched out the window, staring at the passing scenery. "I can drive, if you like," she offered.

"Have you a driving license in the right name?" Jacob asked with raised eyebrows.

"Actually, I have," Elena responded with some glee. "The people I work for aren't stupid, and they don't miss much. The only thing they wouldn't be able to do would be to alter German registration records and get my name on them."

"Doesn't matter really," Jacob answered. "If they're looking for the professor, they'll have his name and they'll know what he looks like." He glanced in the rearview mirror and met Hartwig's eyes. "Sorry, Professor, but you have a distinguished look about you. Intelligence is stamped on your face, and you wouldn't convince me you were ordinary, even if you tried. But not being able to go north, as we wanted to," he went on, "could be a blessing in disguise. It will be the opposite of what they expect us to do."

An answering smile flashed for a moment on Hartwig's face, and then vanished. He did not say anything.

Elena, beside him on the backseat, felt a deep sorrow for him. She wondered who he was leaving behind. Peter had told her that Hartwig had no family, but there was always some relative, even distant. It was better she said nothing, in case it reminded him of something that might weaken his resolve. Getting him out of Germany and safely to England was her job, however much it cost him. Whatever they did, he could not be left in Germany.

"When will they miss you, Professor?" she asked. It was a loaded question. What she was really asking was who would know that he was gone.

"Probably not until late afternoon," he answered, not looking at her, but staring straight ahead. "My students will realize soon, perhaps today. But with me saying I had a dental appointment that would take some time, they may not feel the need to check in on me. I'm not ill, and I don't need the attention."

"Good idea," Jacob said. He glanced in the mirror quickly and met Elena's eyes.

"So . . . by this evening?" Elena asked. "That's when they'll suspect?"

"Possibly. If someone comes to ask how I am, or they need a question answered."

"And your closest friends?" Elena pressed. She wondered if he would be doing this, fleeing Germany, if he had a wife and children.

As if Hartwig were reading her thoughts, he said, "My wife died several years ago."

"I'm sorry," she said quietly.

Hartwig was looking at her. Had he any idea that she understood even a little of what he experienced? At least she knew it was real, not stories or things made up to frighten people, make them obey.

She looked at Jacob's face in the mirror. As if aware of her, he took his eyes off the road and met hers again, but only for an instant.

"I'm American," Jacob answered. "My family are safe in Chicago." They had been speaking only in German, and his American accent had nearly disappeared.

"Do you speak Yiddish at home?" Hartwig asked.

Elena wondered how he knew that Jacob was Jewish.

"In the family, yes. But at work: English, always," Jacob replied with a tight, amused smile.

"America . . ." Hartwig said slowly. "And yet you work with the British, helping to get certain people out of Germany. Or is it a co-operative operation? I want to go to England, to Cambridge." He stopped, took a breath. "Although I shall be grateful simply to be away and alive. I don't mean to sound so ungracious. It is only that—"

Jacob interrupted him. "No, I don't do this regularly. I'm a journalist. I write for American newspapers. I just happened to meet Ellen when she was in Berlin. She's a photographer, by the way. We collaborated on a piece."

To Elena, that seemed like a different lifetime, yet it was just a year ago. When she had arrived in Berlin, she had been naïve and stunned by grief. Now she felt ten years older, and far more aware of the horrors no longer on the horizon, but very close. Too close.

No matter what was said, the point of all these words was that Jacob was American, and Jewish, and he lived in Berlin. Not only was he the only person she could turn to, but he had barely quibbled when she had asked for his help. And now here he was again, this time driving Elena and a fugitive scientist across Germany, hoping to heaven they were not caught.

Elena was gripped by guilt. She should not have asked him. She had given him no room to refuse, no opportunity to choose helping her or not. If something went wrong, she would not know how to live with it.

But . . . this was germ warfare. There was no choice.

Elena sat silently while the countryside sped past. They stopped at a café by the roadside, and Jacob went inside for all of them. Elena reached to open the car door so she could go with him and help him carry the food.

"No!" he said abruptly. "You draw attention."

"I won't!" she protested.

He gave a twisted smile, and she was sure he was on the edge of laughter. "Yes, you will. You're different from the way you were the first time, when you were plain, a little shy, and had no belief in yourself. I think the change came when you lightened your hair, and got that red dress. You saw yourself in a mirror and realized who you really are. With your striking blond hair and stylish clothing, you look wonderful and graceful. And memorable."

Elena smiled. "Not too memorable, I hope."

She leaned back in the seat. After Jacob closed the door and walked away, she laughed quietly and turned to Hartwig. He was laughing, too, kindly, but with genuine humor. For a moment, they forgot they were escaping.

* * *

It was late in the evening, about dusk, when they reached the outskirts of Munich. Most of the traffic was coming out of the city, into the suburbs and beyond.

"The traffic is rather heavy," Jacob observed. He was looking at Elena. "Do you think we're safer in a crowd, or out of it?"

Elena had been thinking about it. "You've been driving all day; you must be tired."

"If we keep going," Jacob said, "we'll turn toward Austria, but that will be further east from where we ought to be." He frowned and his voice dropped. "German power in Austria is growing, and it's getting more all the time. They're on the edge of taking over altogether."

She remembered vividly her time in Trieste, less than a year ago. It was one of the most beautiful cities she had ever seen. She would never get tired of the way the light lit the stones, the ripples in the canals, the shadows under the arches of ancient bridges. And it had been part of the Austrian Empire for years. It was not long reunited with Italy. The Austrians were still there, German-speaking, and the city was of their culture more than it was Italian. The Germans she had faced there were Hitler's supporters, keen on Austria's alliance with the Führer. But Chancellor Dollfuss, who wanted his country's independence, had prevailed so far. For how much longer, no one could be certain.

"We can't go into Austria," she argued, without explaining herself.

Jacob glanced at her, questions in his face, but he did not ask any of them. "We can start early in the morning, before rush-hour traffic, and go straight for the border, and then into France. We'll make it before nightfall," he said.

At nine in the evening, they drew up to a middle-sized Munich hotel. The car park adjacent to the building was packed. They had again bought food at a café and were carrying it in the car. By this time, they were so tired and hungry that any place giving them lodging was welcome.

Jacob pulled into one of the few parking spaces. "We'd better settle for this place, no matter what it's like," he advised. "Everything else looks busy. We'll be lucky if they have room for us here either." He bit his lip, as if stifling what he was about to say.

He led them into the building and to the reception desk, where a middle-aged man stood waiting, his face filled with anxiety.

Elena had a miserable feeling that there were no rooms available. She would have been willing to sleep on the floor, as long as the door locked!

Jacob took the lead. The receptionist would find it more natural to deal with him than with Elena, and Hartwig did not wish to draw any attention at all.

"Have you any rooms for tonight?" Jacob asked. Elena knew him well enough to be aware of the slight tremor in his voice. They were facing the possibility of having to spend the night in the car, all three of them, with no chance to lie down, no bathroom, no privacy at all.

The receptionist pursed his lips unhappily and shook his head. "Sorry. I have only one room left. Just can't do it. Don't know where else to recommend. The whole city is jammed with people. You might have to drive further on, another forty miles."

"We'll take the room." Jacob put his hand in his inside pocket.

"But the lady . . ." The receptionist's eyebrows shot up.

"For heaven's sake, man!" Jacob exclaimed. "She's my wife! You want us to sleep in separate rooms?" His voice was high-pitched with disbelief.

"And the other gentleman?" the receptionist asked uncertainly.

"It would be nice if you had a separate room for him, but we'll be glad of anything, if you don't. He's her uncle. You don't mind, do you?" He looked at Elena, not at Hartwig.

"No, of course not," Elena replied. This was survival. They were exhausted, and at least they would be comfortable, and safe, until tomorrow morning. They were far too tired to continue tonight, which might draw attention anyway.

"I have to warn you, sir, there are a lot of Brownshirts staying here. They are celebrating . . . something." The receptionist looked a trifle embarrassed about his unwillingness to say precisely what.

Elena guessed such gatherings were pretty frequent events, along with the Brownshirts' growing power. "We don't mind," she began, then stopped. The receptionist's face was filled with embarrassment. "We'll be happy to have a room."

"They are pretty noisy," the man went on.

She smiled at him. "Thank you for the warning."

The receptionist nodded, then asked for the money in advance. He handed the key to Jacob. "Breakfast is at seven thirty, and served until ten, sir."

Elena could see Jacob force a smile.

"Thank you," said Jacob. "You are very kind." He took the key and looked at the number on it.

"Top of the stairs, to the left," the receptionist said. "No more luggage than this?"

"In the car," Jacob answered. "We don't need it tonight."

"I hope you locked the car, sir. There are lots of people roaming around the streets."

"I have," Jacob assured him. "And the luggage is not where anyone can see it. Thank you. Good night."

"Good night, sirs . . . madam."

They climbed the stairs, which were long and steep. At the top, Jacob turned to Elena.

"This is fine," she said in a whisper, before he could ask.

Jacob nodded, then lifted the key and went to the door. The lock turned easily, probably from frequent use. He pushed the door open. The room was not very large, and the one double bed took up most of the floorspace. There was a large eiderdown rolled up at the foot of the bed, probably used only during the colder months, and there were two pillows on either side, pushed up against the headboard.

Without waiting, Hartwig took one of the pillows and the eider-down and found the one space on the floor where he could lie down full length. "This will be fine," he announced.

"I apologize in advance if I snore," Hartwig said with a rueful smile. "It was a very good piece of quick thinking. You're risking your lives to get me out of the country. I should be honored to be your family, until further notice."

Jacob and Elena faced each other across the bed.

"Do you have a preference?" he asked with a slight smile.

"I don't care," she answered. "I just need to wash, take off my outer clothes, and lie down."

He nodded. "Good. I have a small alarm clock. We should not be here too long. We want to get out of Munich by nine at the latest. But we need breakfast, in case we don't get lunch."

Elena saw the concern in Jacob's eyes. "For tonight," she said, "we should be safe."

CHAPTER

13

Elena was dreaming of darkness, chaos, loud shouts. Someone screamed. Only it was not a dream. She found herself sitting bolt upright in bed. Beside her, Jacob was awake and he, too, sat up.

They had been warned of noise, but not like this. It was not celebration, even a drunken one. It was more like rage, or fright.

There was more shouting, voices, high and harsh-sounding, like terror. No, more than terror, hysteria.

On the floor near the bed, Hartwig sat up slowly, looking at the door, and then at Jacob and Elena. He was blinking, newly awake, but Elena also detected fear in the stiffness of his body.

Outside, there were heavy footsteps, as of men in army boots. It was daylight, but the light was sharp, blue-edged, not long after dawn.

Jacob threw the bedclothes off and stood up. "Get dressed," he ordered in a low voice, struggling to remain steady. "We need to get out of here. I don't know what the hell is going on, but it isn't good. And it's not a celebration of anything!"

Hartwig obeyed, moving swiftly, picking up the eiderdown and pillows and throwing them onto the bed. "I don't think they're looking for me. They would want to do it more discreetly than this. But if they are, and they find me, don't make a fuss. It will make no difference, and they'll shoot you. Don't die without a purpose, please."

Elena drew in her breath to argue, but she met the professor's gaze, and in the broadening daylight of the room, she could see his features clearly.

There was no time to fumble with her clothing, but she must be careful not to put the garments on inside out. "I don't intend to die at all, on purpose or not!" she said sharply. "And certainly not with no clothes on. They'll take me for a tart. Two men at a time!" She did not care if either of them was embarrassed. Anything was better than the kind of fear that paralyzed.

"How very English of you," Hartwig said with a bleak smile.

Jacob froze, staring at him.

"I spent some time in Cambridge, years ago," Hartwig explained. "I like the English sense of humor. Dry, abrasive, and really very funny."

Jacob's expression eased for a moment, as if he was being reminded of another time, an older time more civilized than this. No one had known then that they were heading into the most lethal and violent war in a thousand years of history.

"We laugh." Again, Jacob said it tersely. "But now—" He stopped and reached for his shirt.

There was another scream, this time a man's voice high-pitched with terror, somewhere near the hotel, then a volley of shots.

Elena froze, her throat so tight she could barely breathe. It sounded so close! And within the hotel. She swung round to look at Jacob.

He was looking at Hartwig.

"You'd better leave," Hartwig said, peering out of the window. "Quietly." He looked at Elena. "Are you up to going out through the window? It's a drop, but it's in the shadow, and there's a vine of some sort that should hold your weight. Jacob can go first."

"And leave you behind?" she said with open disbelief. "Getting you out is what we—what I came for. Jacob is helping because he knows how important it is."

There was another volley of shots, and more shouting, this time outside, in the car park.

"We'll stay here," Elena stated, not because she was afraid of heights, although she was, but because they would not be better off in the courtyard. And while climbing down, they would be easy targets. Even a bruised bone or a twisted ankle would slow them, perhaps fatally.

There was no time to argue.

Someone crashed against the door and it burst open. A Gestapo officer stood in the doorway gripping a submachine gun in both hands.

"Do you want something, Officer?" Elena asked before anyone else could speak. The man stared at her. Clearly, she was not what he was expecting. He looked from one to the other of them, then at Hartwig.

"My husband and my uncle," Elena told him. "There was only one room left."

The man stared at Jacob. "Put your clothes on," he ordered. And then he swung around to look at Hartwig but kept the gun pointed at Elena. "And you! Put your clothes on, too."

In long, breathless seconds both men obeyed, stiff fingers awkward, fumbling with buttons and bootlaces. Finally, they were finished and stood upright.

"May my wife dress as well?" Jacob asked.

"All right! You better get out of here. It isn't safe."

Jacob drew in breath to answer.

"We will!" Elena cut off whatever he had been going to say. "Thank you, Officer."

The moment the soldier left them alone, they went into action.

"We have to leave now," said Jacob. "This seems like some sort of raid."

"The Gestapo against the Brownshirts?" Elena could not grasp it. "A mutiny?"

"Perhaps," Jacob replied. "There are Brownshirts all over the place, and there's damn little discipline. They are drunk out of their minds, from the sound of it." His voice was more level now, but quiet, with a sort of anger that carries the grief of defeat.

"Any mutiny won't necessarily succeed," Hartwig responded, but his voice was also low, almost flat. "Hitler will suppress it."

The door opened again and the officer was standing there. "Move on," he ordered. "Now! And go out the back, not the front." He gestured with the muzzle of his gun.

Elena finished dressing as rapidly as she could, including a jacket on top of the very nice blouse she was wearing. She did not want her face remembered, or any other part of her, for that matter. She went to the sink and collected her few toiletries.

Both men also collected their things, and within a few minutes they were ready to go. They left the key on the bedside table.

There were lights on at the far end of the corridor and the noise of shouting below, in the entrance from the street. Someone screamed again, and the sound was cut off abruptly by two more gunshots.

Elena felt Jacob yanking her arm, half pulling her off her feet. "Come on!" he hissed. "We don't want to get caught in this."

They were outside now. It was broad daylight, the sky sharp-edged, and there were people all over the place, mostly half-awake guests of the hotel, but many of them Brownshirts. Also, there were several Gestapo in uniform.

More shots rang out and a woman screamed. Men were shouting. And then more shots again. A man came running out of the hotel, blood streaming from his arm, his face twisted in pain and horror.

Jacob pulled Elena even more sharply. "We need to find the car and get out of here."

Hartwig took her other arm and the three of them moved past the front of the hotel as the shooting continued. There was yelling, but no words were distinguishable.

Elena struggled with Hartwig and Jacob gripping her arms. She all but fell, scrambling to keep her balance.

The three of them pushed their way past half-awake Brownshirts, some of them still not properly dressed, having been awakened from sleep. Many of them staggered, as if they were drunk.

The Gestapo officers, on the other hand, were wide awake and carrying their guns ready for use. They seemed to be trying to herd the Brownshirts into one place.

"Come on," Jacob urged again. "We need to find the car. It doesn't matter where we go, we've got to leave Munich."

Elena stumbled again to keep up with him; Hartwig kept her from falling.

"What do you think is going on?" she asked, gasping for breath. The whole area was in chaos. There were dozens of men, even hundreds. No one seemed to be in charge. "Is it a revolution?"

"I think it's trying to be," Jacob answered, angry with himself. "I should have seen it coming. And I should have known that Röhm would start it. There were enough signs. I thought it might blow over because Hitler was in full control."

A drunken, terrified Brownshirt, with half his uniform torn off one shoulder, staggered across their path. Jacob pulled Elena sharply out of the way. She lost her grip on Hartwig's arm, then tripped and fell as another man lurched into them.

Before Jacob or Hartwig could help, a Gestapo officer pulled her to her feet. "You all right, ma'am?" he asked. "You should get out of here! It's not safe for a woman!"

She looked to her side. Hartwig was gone, and Jacob was being questioned a couple of yards away. And then more Gestapo passed between them and she lost sight of Jacob as well.

"You here on your own?" the Gestapo officer asked with concern.

"No," she answered, trying to keep her voice steady. "They ... my husband and my uncle ..." She looked around, not even sure which way the hotel was, because the crowd had carried them so far. "We were in the hotel. There were shots, so we—" She snatched her arm from him and turned round to try to see Jacob, or even more important, Hartwig.

"You don't live here in Munich? You're traveling?" he asked her.

"Yes, but it got late and we were tired. Too tired to go on safely." Always stick to the truth if you can, she reminded herself. It is the fool who gets caught out in the unnecessary lie.

Somebody banged into the officer, and he turned around and grasped the man, letting go of Elena. For a moment she thought of running, and then good sense prevailed. If she was innocent, why would she run?

The officer steadied the man, looked hard at his bleary face and shaking body. He shouted for another Gestapo officer, a few yards away, to come and take the man. "Lock him up to cool off," he ordered. Then he turned back to Elena. "It's been a bad night, ma'am."

"What happened?" she asked.

"The Führer landed a couple of hours ago."

"Landed?" She was confused.

"From Berlin. We had to put down this attempted coup. Don't worry, I think Röhm may be dead already. Many of his chief men have been arrested, or shot. And we'll get the rest. Communists, Bolsheviks, and heaven knows what else. You should get out of here. Find your husband and your uncle and leave the area. This could take a day or two to clean up. Don't be afraid for the future. We'll be all right."

"I thought the Brownshirts had millions of men." She should not betray too much knowledge. "At least that's what I heard. Haven't they?"

"Yes," he agreed. "But they aren't trained like we are. The Brownshirts are pansies dressed in uniform. Cowards, and drunk half the time. We'll get control of this, and in a few days' time we will return our country to order. Don't worry," he said again. "They won't try again. Just find your uncle and your husband and leave. Half the Brownshirts are drunk out of their minds and in bed with each other, but you could be in danger."

"Thank you," she said a little hoarsely. "I— Thank you." She didn't know what else to say.

Where were Jacob and Hartwig? The area outside the hotel was chaos. She finally saw the back of Jacob's head. Then he turned round and it was a stranger, nothing like Jacob at all.

Hartwig was tall. In this early midsummer morning, the light was so bright, so hard, that it reflected off many heads that were light, fair, or gray. She couldn't see him. Panic welled up inside her again. She could not recognize anyone. Jacob was gone. Hartwig, too. They could have been captured, for all she knew. Her heart pounded so violently it seemed to rob her of breath.

Calm down, she said to herself. *Calm down, kiddo!* She heard her brother's voice in her head. He was always alive in her thoughts, especially at those times when she was frightened, on the edge of panic.

She knew that Jacob would make for the car park, if and when he could. The car was their only way out. Hartwig would know that, too. As far as she could see, no one suspected them of being anything other than three travelers caught in the Gestapo attack on the Brownshirts.

The car park was beside the hotel. She could see no clear way ahead, but if she swung too far away, she might find she could not get back. She must find Jacob and Hartwig, but especially Hartwig. She must force herself not to look for Jacob until she had found the professor. That was what she was here for. Hartwig was an important scientist... and he was defenseless. What irony! He had the scientific knowledge to kill half the nations on earth, but not the anger or the skill to kill one man. And, quite honestly, she did not think he would kill, unless he had no other choice. Or perhaps he would, if it was to save her or Jacob.

A man bumped into her, knocking her off balance. She could not tell whether he was Gestapo or Brownshirt. His tunic was smeared with blood and torn down the front. He staggered and fell. She over-balanced when she was shoved from behind and landed hard. She scrambled to her feet, nearly lashing out at the man who had trod-den on her, who was now trying to master his own balance.

She must get out of this melee before she, too, was badly injured and unable to reach the car or help Hartwig. She hoped he was mak-ing his way to the car, but he could also be looking for her, to help her. That would be the noble thing to do, or even the instinctive thing, but it was his survival and his escape that mattered. Would he remember that? Elena wondered if he would know to make his way to the French border, if she was no longer able to help him.

He wouldn't, she told herself. Not escape to save his skin, leaving behind the two people who were risking their lives to get him to safety.

She doubled her efforts to reach the car park. Jacob had the keys. If only she had more experience in starting a car without the keys. She could do it, but her skills were limited. It might ruin the ignition system, but if it became a choice between survival or capture, what did a damaged car matter?

She stepped over the body of a Brownshirt, his pistol still hol-stered, submachine gun beside him. She pushed him onto his side and took his pistol. When she straightened up, there was a Gestapo officer perhaps four feet away from her.

"Be careful with that, miss," he said.

She forced herself to smile at him and wished she had not. The situation was utterly without humor. She wondered if she looked insane! "Only to save my life," she answered, and then wondered if he knew what she meant.

"You should get out of here," he told her grimly, gesturing away from where they stood. "Go on!"

"I'm . . . I'm trying to reach the car park," she said, managing to get the words out intelligibly. "But I need to find my uncle and my husband."

"Saw an older man just now," he answered her. "Gray hair, tall, and a bit thin. Looked dazed. Maybe—"

"Where?" She cut across him. "Where were you when you saw him?"

He swiveled round and pointed toward the hotel. "Other side of that door, but don't go in there—"

His words were cut off by a scream, and then a prolonged volley of shots.

"Thank you," she said, but her words were lost in the noise.

She raced toward the door as rapidly as she could, rounding the side of the building and then changing direction, away from where the Gestapo officer had indicated. Now she was heading for the car park.

When she got there the area was a disaster. Some of the cars had shattered windows. From the star-shaped cracks in the roofs, the splintered glass of the windscreens, plus the holes visible on doors and side panels, it was evident that much of the damage was from stray bullets.

Elena stopped abruptly. There were two Gestapo officers near what seemed to be a kitchen door, with something held between them. Half a dozen yards closer, an older man was standing in the shadows, looking out toward the rows of parked cars. Elena moved toward the man. He looked stiff, frightened. It was not in his face, which she could not see clearly, but in the rigid lines of his body.

She walked closer.

It was Hartwig.

She quickened her step. A gut-deep wave of relief ran through her. She was about to call his name, then remembered with a jolt that she had told everyone he was her uncle!

"Uncle!" she said urgently.

For an instant, he did not realize what was happening, and then his face changed, as if he suddenly recognized her voice. His body eased and he came forward in long, quick strides.

She threw her arms around him, as if he had been her father. "I haven't seen Jacob yet," she said into his ear.

Without letting go of her, he replied, "I've lost him, too. I thought the car was the best place to make for."

"It is best." It hurt to say that, but she knew there was no choice: they had to get going. Jacob could make his way back to Berlin. It would be acutely painful if they had to go without him, but it must be done if there was no alternative.

"We had better go and find a car," she said. "If ours has been damaged or taken, we'll have to find another."

"If we steal one, won't that get us into even more trouble?"

"Possibly. Can you think of a better idea?"

He waited only a few seconds before replying. "No, not yet."

There was another series of gunshots. Another terrible scream, and then an explosion, followed by a flash of light.

"If Jacob isn't at the car, then he might be hurt," Hartwig said urgently. He pulled Elena away from the noise, but not in the direction where they had left the car. And then he stopped. "You wait here while I go to look for him."

"No!" She hung on to his arm and pulled him closer. "If you insist on going to find him, we're staying together."

"Perhaps he's wounded," said Hartwig. "Possibly badly."

He had no need to emphasize those words. Elena had only to look into his face. The gravity of his words was impossible to misunderstand. "I'm coming with you," she insisted. "Don't argue."

He was not arguing. Instead, he was already leading the way back toward the courtyard.

Gestapo were rounding up Brownshirts; a few hotel guests were looking dazed and angry, but even more seemed frightened. Several people lay on the ground, some struggling to get up, others strangely motionless. It was impossible to tell if they were dead.

Elena and Hartwig skirted round the corner of the building.

Hartwig grasped her by the arm and pulled her sharply to a stop. Ahead of them were three Gestapo using their guns to forcefully direct six or seven Brownshirts against a wall. The men were protesting desperately, but they were ignored.

One of the Gestapo soldiers gave the order and shots rang out. One by one, the men crumpled and fell. None of the assailants spoke; there was not even a change in their expressions. They were completely impassive, nothing like the frenzy she had seen, and certainly not like the madness in the faces of the book burners only a year ago. This was different and, in a way, worse. This wasn't insanity; this was beyond that, as if they were now on the other side of some irreversible divide.

Elena and Hartwig moved on past bodies spread out on the ground. They slipped in pools of blood, frantically searching for Jacob. *Please God, let him be alive! And not arrested!* The place was milling with people, dazed, a few shouting angrily, voices shrill with fear. Elena nearly tripped over the corpse of a Brownshirt lying spread-eagled on the ground. "We must move!" she urged, and then realized she had twisted her ankle. It hurt, but she could not allow it to slow her down. She wobbled on it for a moment, and tried to ignore the pain.

"If you need to rest, then do." Hartwig looked at her anxiously. "Can you make your way back to the car? I can find you there. Could you get into it, and take the weight off your foot?"

"It's fine," she insisted. "If necessary, can you drive?" It was a stupid time to think of it, but the words were out before she weighed them. That was not the thought that was filling her mind.

"Yes, I can. Don't worry if you can't. Just make your way slowly back to the car."

"My ankle is perfectly all right!"

That was not what mattered. What mattered was that she came to Germany to get the professor out, the scientist who was working on breakthroughs in germ warfare. Even more important, Hartwig was the expert in antidotes. That was the whole purpose of her being here, and risking her own life was part of it. It was not such a long drive to the French border, no matter who was driving.

But Hartwig again insisted on finding Jacob, even at the risk of his own life. Why? The whole purpose of her being in Germany was to rescue him! He was a good man, but that did not matter. His work was the only thing that mattered, perhaps more than any scientist in Germany. Or in all of Europe.

14

Hans woke with a start. It was before dawn. He had come home late and gone to bed after eating a light meal, but not before holding Madeleine for a few minutes and speaking to her, touching her face until she opened her eyes and gave him a sleepy smile. And then he was satisfied.

He fell asleep before Cecily came to bed.

What was that noise? The telephone! He scrambled out of bed and lifted the receiver before it could waken her. "Beckendorff," he said.

"Paulus," the voice answered. "It's going forward. Tonight."

Hans was confused. He had no idea what Paulus was talking about. He glanced at the bedside clock. It was 2:35 A.M. "Do you mean later this morning? Or tonight?" he asked.

There was a brief bark of laughter, a sound seldom heard from Paulus. "I mean now, Beckendorff. Get dressed, have some breakfast. God knows when we'll get to eat again."

Hans blinked and shook his head. "Why? What's happened?" He felt a chill run through his body long before he heard the answer.

"That list of the Führer's enemies that you provided."

He could imagine Paulus's face, and see the smile on it. "Sir?"

"The Führer is acting on your list. This is going to be a night to go down in history." There was exultancy in his voice.

"Where are we—" Hans began.

"Your list of enemies!" Paulus snapped. "Get your clothes on, take your gun, and report to the airstrip. I'll send a car, so be ready in twenty minutes. And Beckendorff..."

"Yes, sir?"

"Nothing to your wife. Don't worry her for no reason. Now get on with it!" The telephone clicked and went silent.

Cecily turned over and opened her eyes. "What is it? Is Madeleine—"

"No," Hans said instantly. "She's fine."

"Then ... what?" There was fear in her voice. She sat up on one elbow. "Hans?"

"I don't know. That was Paulus, and he wants me to—no, that's ridiculous." After a moment sorting his thoughts, he said, "He has ordered me to report to the airfield. He told me to have something to eat and be ready for a car to pick me up in twenty minutes."

"I'll get you—" she started, pushing the bedclothes off.

He put a hand on her arm. "Stay in bed. I'll go quietly, not to waken Madeleine." He wanted to say something about not saying goodbye, then knew it would only make it harder for both of them. He leaned over and kissed her. She was warm and soft, smelling of sleep. More than anything else, he wanted to stay with her. But that was impossible, and even to entertain this thought caused unnecessary pain. He kissed her again, then stood up and carried his clothes into the bathroom to shave and wash. He collected his gun and ammunition from their safe storage.

Hans hesitated for a moment at the top of the stairs, then went down them rapidly. What was there to say to his wife before he left? That he loved her? He knew this would not comfort her. In truth, it would frighten her. He should tell her nothing, even if he wanted to.

There was a crisis, of that he was certain. Paulus would not send for him in the middle of the night, and tell him to be armed, and to rush to the airfield, if it were not an emergency.

He made a quick breakfast, put his dishes in the sink, and had not yet turned on the tap when the doorbell rang. He went to answer it before it could ring again and disturb Cecily. There was no one there, but a car idled at the curb. Hans closed the door behind him and went straight to the car. The driver seemed to recognize him.

"Sir!" said the man, saluting as well as he could inside the confines of the car. He did not attempt to get out, even as a mark of respect, nor did he stop the engine. He pulled away from the curb immediately and picked up speed before they reached the end of the street. All of these things confirmed to Hans that an emergency was afoot.

They drove through the dark streets. Very soon, Hans saw the dawn coming in, with a high wing of soft light broadening the white chill of early sunlight. No matter how many seasons he had lived through, the summer's long days of light and short hours of darkness fascinated him. He could fall asleep at near midnight, when the sky was still light, and awaken at five in the morning, with the sun having risen.

They passed very few people on the road: the odd deliveryman, a few workmen preparing for a dawn start, and the occasional cyclist. The driver kept up a speed that at any other time would have been illegal.

They were quickly out of the city and again increasing speed. It seemed too little time had passed before he saw the open space of the airstrip. One light, four-winged plane was clearly visible.

The gates were open and the car swept in and pulled to a halt.

"Sir," the driver said quietly.

Hans opened the door and climbed out. He gave a sharp salute. "Thank you."

"Sir!"

Hans closed the door and rushed across the open, windswept

grass to where Paulus was moving from foot to foot impatiently in the pale light, wind whispering through the uncut grasses bordering the runway. The plane beside him was small and fast. Where were they going? And above all, why?

"Come on!" Paulus snapped. "The others are already on board." He turned and led the way up the short flight of steps and into the cabin, where there were half a dozen uniformed Gestapo officers already seated. Paulus shut the heavy door and closed the handle. He pointed to two empty seats at the very back, for himself and Hans.

"The Führer is behind us," he said quietly. "He's due to take off at four thirty, but his plane is faster, so we'll get there only a little before him."

"Get where?" Hans had to raise his voice to be heard above the engines.

"Around Munich, of course," Paulus snapped, fastening himself into his seat.

Hans looked sideways at Paulus. The man was staring straight ahead, a slight smile on his heavy face, the curl of the lips, nothing more. In the gray dawn's light, it was impossible to read. But to Hans, it told him that Hitler knew what to expect, while Hans did not.

The plane raced down the runway. Hans felt the moment when the wheels left the earth and the craft climbed into the white, shining daylight.

The steady thrum of the engines was soporific. One of the other men, seated further forward, slipped sideways, starting to fall asleep, then jerked himself up. Hans wondered if he was afraid to be seen sleeping. He had probably put in long hours the day before, and had had little rest.

"You did a good job, Beckendorff, finding the ringleaders." This time it was not really a smile, just a tightening of the lips over his teeth. Still, there was satisfaction in his eyes. "There's nothing for you to do, until we get there," he added. "You might as well go to sleep, if you can. It will be a long day." He turned to look directly at Hans. "There will be a lot more to do after we land." This time, he really did smile.

It was not comforting.

When they landed at the airfield in Oberwiesenfeld, the dawn was mist-wreathed in silver, and there was more than enough light for Paulus and his men to see all around them. Hitler's three-engine Junkers Ju 52 arrived soon after. From the way they were bunched, it was easy enough to pick out Hitler. He was apart from the group and walking toward a waiting car, several men clustered after him.

Paulus opened the rear exit of the plane and gestured for Hans to follow. He moved gingerly down the steps the moment they were in place. This was not the time for an overwrought, elderly man to sprain an ankle, and still less to make a fool of himself by taking an unnecessary jump.

The rest of the men watched Paulus as he descended, the rickety structure of stairs shaking, but holding.

Hans went straight after him. Perhaps now he would find out what was going on. If some of the results were going to be attributed to information he had provided, he most certainly needed to know more.

Paulus marched quickly behind Hitler, across the open tarmac. It was not to catch up with him, Hans was sure, but to be part of the group. He jerked one arm abruptly to signal Hans to follow, and he did so reluctantly.

It was early dawn, but they were at a higher altitude than Berlin, and considerably further south. The midsummer nights were not quite as short, and it was cooler, and the air cleaner here than outside a huge, smoking city.

The mountains of Bavaria. This was the home of the Eagle's Nest, Hitler's luxurious estate. Hans could easily understand why the Führer was partial to this region. There was barely a breeze. The light had a clarity he had seen nowhere else. He would come here, if he could, and bring Cecily and Madeleine with him to hear the silence, feel the rising sun and the dawn wind on their skin.

He caught up with Paulus.

"Get that car," Paulus snapped, pointing to a nearby vehicle. His frayed nerves were betrayed in his voice. "We must follow the Führer. I think he's going to the Bavarian Interior Ministry." His face was tense, gray stubble just beginning to show on his jaw in the unforgiving light. "This is it! This is the showdown, Beckendorff. Be ready for anything. Röhm must be got rid of."

Hitler got into a car that pulled away toward the gate to the airfield.

Hans drew breath to ask what he meant, then closed his mouth again. Were they about to kill Röhm? He found that his voice was too choked to ask. Hitler would not do the killing himself, of course. But he had too many enemies ready to betray him, and Hans had helped Paulus compose the list of them. A few weeks ago, he would have said that they deserved it. Now the whole idea filled him with a different kind of fear. He had seen Hitler's panic, his ranting hysteria, and a loss of informed reason, as if this specific threat had dissolved the ground underneath his feet.

Hans strode forward, and through the car's open window seized the driver by the shoulder. "This car is for General Paulus!" He let the man loose and yanked the back door open. Paulus slid into the seat, with Hans half a step behind him. He pulled the door shut with a slam as the car lurched forward, following Hitler by only a few yards. What happened to the others? Hans could not see.

"Good. Well done," said Paulus. "Now keep your gun loaded and ready, and your mouth shut."

"Yes, sir."

The next hour was a nightmare. The car carrying Hans and Paulus followed Hitler, with Paulus ordering the driver to stay close behind. As they drove through deserted streets to the Interior Ministry, they did not speak. Paulus was so tense his uniform was stretched over his chest and belly. Half a dozen times he drew breath to speak, then changed his mind. He stared at the back of the driver's head; his eyes were unfocused.

The silence prickled. Hans swallowed hard. His body ached with tension.

As soon as they reached the building housing the ministry, they saw Hitler's car parking, along with several others. "Wait," Paulus ordered the driver. Then he waved his arm at Hans. It was a clear command. Hans followed him into the almost-deserted ministry, and stayed on his heels as the man barked questions and strode after Hitler.

They heard Hitler shout at two of the Brownshirt leaders ahead of them, and saw him reach out and tear the epaulettes off their uniforms.

"You will be shot!" His voice was high-pitched with fury. "Now! Traitors! Traitors to the Third Reich." He turned to see the men next to him. "Get them out of here . . . now! And get three cars! Where is Röhm? Where is he?"

"At Bad Wiessee, *mein Führer*," replied one of the men standing nearby.

"Where in Bad Wiessee? Where?"

"Pension Kurt-Hanselbauer, sir." The man stood rigid with fear, knuckles white.

Hitler swung round and marched out into the corridor. He stopped for a moment, noticing Paulus. "Come!"

Paulus snapped to attention, heels together. He did not turn to Hans, but followed Hitler at a respectful distance, not too close. Was it out of respect, or fear?

Hans went immediately behind him and said nothing. He wondered if Paulus had engineered this or whether he had merely lit the fuse.

Back in the car, they drove at a dangerous speed through silent streets, passing the occasional tradesman or delivery service as the town began to stir.

Paulus was silent. He ignored Hans as he would a servant.

Forty-five minutes later, they arrived at the pension. The driver drew up and stopped without saying anything. It was half past six in the morning.

Hans and Paulus got out of the car and Paulus went in the front door without turning to see if Hans was following.

Even from outside, Hans could hear the shouting within. A woman screamed somewhere close to them. A man swore loudly and rapidly, his voice shrill with terror.

Then shots rang out, and for several seconds there was silence.

Paulus turned to Hans. "Come!" he ordered, strain in his voice. "We must stay in control of this. If we lose control now . . ." He left the rest unsaid, but Hans felt its urgency.

Paulus strode forward, leaving Hans to keep up with him.

"Yes, sir," Hans replied. There was no other possible answer. He followed Paulus through the building, finding the bodies of more of Röhm's men along the way.

A man staggered out of one of the rooms, half-naked, and fell sideways onto the floor. He was bleeding heavily.

Hans went forward to help him and felt a blow on his back. Another man seized hold of him, yanking him back onto his feet. The man stared at Hans's uniform, then turned and shot the man huddled against the wall. He slumped forward and lay still.

"What the hell—" Hans began. Then he saw the man raise his gun again and froze. He was wearing an army uniform; it was not a Brownshirt.

There was a moment's total silence.

The man kept his gun raised, and he grimaced. "It's time we cleared out this garbage. That way!" he ordered, jerking his gun to the side to indicate the direction he expected Hans to go. And then, just as suddenly, he turned and strode away.

More men came down the passageway.

This time, it was Paulus who raised his gun. "Where is the Führer?" he demanded.

The men, five or six of them, came to an abrupt halt. One of them pointed upward and to the left. Then they must have seen Paulus's uniform and silence fell. No one moved even the muzzle of a gun.

Paulus flung up his right arm in a Hitler salute. Then he grasped Hans's arm and gripped him so hard the young man gasped in pain.

Hans almost tripped as he turned his back on the men and followed Paulus along the passageway.

Above them was more noise: shouts of fear and outrage.

"That way!" Paulus said sharply, pointing at the hallway. "Go down that wing. We must back up the Führer. Make sure he's safe. Got to get rid of these traitors. Now!" He pointed again, jabbing the air with his pistol, then went to the right, leaving Hans to go to the left.

Hans had no choice. He was driven to take Paulus's side, Hitler's side, or deliberately go against them. And then do what, side with Röhm? That was impossible. Röhm stood for everything vile, everything descending into chaos. Hans knew that. He had seen the evidence of it himself.

He banged on the first door, using his fist.

It flew open and a large, very dark man stood there, his trousers half on. Beyond him a youth with peach-fuzz cheeks struggled to gather a blanket around himself.

Hans drew in his breath.

The man swung his arm backward and struck out, violently.

Hans ducked and raised his gun.

The young man on the bed reached for his own gun to defend his . . . what? Hans wasn't sure. The boy's superior officer?

Hans shot the man, who swayed and then collapsed.

Hans had to move sharply to avoid being knocked over as he fell. Suddenly, shots struck the framework of the door, only inches from his head. He took one step into the room, aimed his gun, and pulled the trigger. It was a perfect shot. A red hole appeared in the youth's forehead, just above his eye.

Hans had no time to feel sick, or shocked, or to think at all.

There were heavy footsteps in the passage. In the next moment, he was surrounded by men. A door slammed somewhere further along the passage. In near silence, someone heaved the body of the big man out of the way and slammed the door.

Hans turned, the gun still in his hand.

When *"Heil Hitler"* rang out, everyone except Hans echoed it. He did not want to join them, but that was irrelevant: his throat was too tight to say anything.

The men pushed on, carrying Hans with them by the sheer weight of their bodies.

Paulus must be somewhere ahead of him.

More doors smashed open and sleepy, half-drunken men were caught too off guard to resist.

Somewhere nearby, there was more gunfire.

Hans watched men being captured, manacled, and taken away. Those who put up resistance were shot.

He stepped in a pool of blood, slipped, and landed on his hands and knees. He tried to get up. There was no use speaking: the noise would blur out his words.

It was a nightmare. There was blood everywhere: on the walls, all over his uniform, on his hands. The floor was running with it, like a slow-moving river, going on and on.

"It's all over!" a man shouted.

Did he mean it was finished? Or that this havoc was everywhere? And was he one of Hitler's men, or one of Röhm's?

Hans overheard a soldier saying that more than a hundred people were dead. But there were three million Brownshirts! A hundred lost was a pinprick.

Where was Hitler?

The clamor of boots pounding along hallways rang through Hans's head. There were shouts, screams, gunshots, more screams. He had never experienced such chaos. And so much blood.

He needed to find Paulus. It was broad daylight now. It seemed like hours since this had begun, but it had been far less. He stopped a Gestapo major and asked him where Paulus was.

"No idea," the man said.

"The Führer?" Hans pressed.

The man pointed. "I think he's found Röhm, the bastard!"

Hans thanked him and took his directions, pushing on, asking people. Everywhere he turned, he saw fear. Men were confessing, on their knees, terrified. What should they believe, or who?

There were more shots. And then a scorching scream. Hans could not tell if it was a man or a woman, or even an animal! He froze where he stood. Someone slammed into him and he almost fell again. It took a moment for him to recover his balance. He reminded himself that he was an officer. The Brownshirts might be hysterical with fear, many drunk, but he was Gestapo, an educated and disciplined man. He must take control of the few men he might reach.

It took another hour of fear and chaos and murder before he found Paulus. Like Hans, he was bloodstained, but he seemed unhurt. He was standing in a long hallway, his back to Hans. He was facing the Führer.

"Paulus!" Hitler said sharply. His face was flushed and his body so tense he moved jerkily. "We must do it all today! You were right, there are traitors all over the place. I should have put an end to this sooner, got rid of this filth. And half of them are drunk!" His lip curled as if he were smelling something sour, something foul.

Hans stared at Hitler. He knew that the man respected the real army, because he had been a soldier in the trenches throughout the war, from the first day to the last. He had even earned the Iron Cross for bravery, twice.

Hans suddenly realized that Hitler was staring at him. He straightened up and looked him in the eyes. How could he speak the truth to this man? What was the truth anyway? By sheer force of will, Hitler had rebuilt Germany, and had made the Germans believe in themselves again. He got the factories rebuilt, the roads fit to drive on, the trains running, and the army restructured and believing in itself.

But he was also the man who allowed, even ordered, the burning of books, the persecution and murder of Jews, the shadow of fear to hang over the streets. Why was he orchestrating such terror? Hans believed it was because there was fear in his own soul. He had seen it that day, in Hitler's office, when he had been feverish with fear, suspicious of everyone and everything. Hans expected that he would never be forgiven for having seen that. One does not witness the crumbling of a world leader's courage without terrible repercussions.

He knew that, and had thought seriously about it, but he was trapped by the fact that there had been only three of them in that room and that, during this emotional collapse, Hitler had looked straight at Hans.

Had anyone on that list surprised Hitler? He expected that most, if not all of them, had not. Still, no matter how little Hans had to do with names on that list, his presence, his witnessing, made him, in Hitler's eyes, a man who could be a threat. One of *them*. The fact that there had been no alternative—Paulus had demanded that list— would excuse nothing.

And possibly more important than Hitler's wrath was that Johann Paulus would not forget. He may have wished this tantrum, perhaps even engineered it, but only to bind Hans to the drama now unfolding. If a scapegoat was needed, Paulus had created the perfect one.

A cold jolt ran through Hans. It was no coincidence that he was here, observing, even killing.

Hitler was staring at him.

"Heil Hitler," Hans said, although the words choked him. He met Hitler's eyes and saw no emotion.

"What have you to report?" Paulus demanded, glaring at Hans.

Hans knew instantly that this was a mistake. He did not answer Paulus, but directed his attention to Hitler. "It is under control, sir. I know of at least fifty men under arrest, and"—he swallowed hard— "and I'm told another forty-five are dead. But that is only in this immediate area. I've learned that the resistance is contained, sir, and that most of the leaders of the ... most of Röhm's men ... have been either arrested or shot."

"Good!" Hitler said tartly. "Good." He was still staring at Hans, those eyes penetrating, mesmerizing. "Röhm is dead."

Hans could not think of anything to say.

"I killed him, shot him myself," Hitler added. He continued to stare hard and levelly at Hans.

Hans was sure Hitler would not look away until he answered. He felt as if he were in a dream, a fever dream, a nightmare. He breathed in the taste of sweat and blood. When he heard his own voice, it was as if it were coming from someone else, far away. "You led the way, sir. It is what I expected."

Seconds ticked by. Hitler drew in a long breath and let it out slowly. "What you expected?" He was still looking at Hans, ignoring Paulus.

It was time Hans brought Paulus in. Any longer, and it would be too late. "Yes, sir. You are the leader. We all know that. And General Paulus assured me you would not allow Röhm to continue."

Hitler was satisfied. He was not listening anymore.

Hans felt rather than saw Paulus relax. Despite the success, Hitler seemed somehow stunned, as if he himself could barely grasp what had just happened.

It was Paulus who spoke. "You have won, *mein Führer*. By my reckoning, and taking into account the many places we struck tonight, there are at least a thousand men either dead or captured. With Röhm dead, they will not rise again. No one would ever dare such a"—he looked for the right word—"a treasonous thing. The nation will be grateful to you." He stopped, as if for once uncertain how to go on.

Hitler seemed frozen. His face was ashen but for two spots of color in his cheeks. It made him look unnatural, like a man in clown's makeup. Finally, he spoke. "Clean up, Paulus. Clean up this charnel house!" Then he turned on his heel and went out, stumbling against the doorpost.

* * *

That afternoon, Hans managed to find time to wash, and then have a cup of coffee and a slice of bread. But he was still tired physically as well as emotionally when he reported to Paulus again. He had needed that quiet time, alone and without the man's expectations.

When he traveled to their preassigned destination, he did so again with a car and a driver, as he had been ordered. When they pulled up in front of the building where they were to meet, Paulus got into the car.

"Good. Good," Paulus said.

It was late in the afternoon; the sun was beginning to sink.

The driver asked for instructions. Paulus offered them, nodded when they were repeated correctly, then the man pulled away for their relatively short drive back to the airfield.

Paulus did not look at Hans.

Hans saw that he was smiling quietly.

"Do you understand what is happening?" Paulus asked. "Do you realize we have turned a page of history? A thousand men are dead. No one will ever rise against Hitler again."

Hans hesitated only a beat. "Yes, sir." He swallowed hard. "The Führer is taking control of the army. All of it. He's getting rid of all those who are against him . . . against Germany." He was not sure if that was true. His emotions were exhausted. But he was quite sure about what he was supposed to say. All he wanted at this moment was to drink clean, cold water, to wash the smell of death off his body. But would anything on earth take it from his mind?

Paulus stared at him, as if weighing his response. Then he gave a bark of laughter. "Beckendorff, you are a damn sight cleverer than you look. I think I can use you. Yes, you are right. It is a little house-keeping. Get rid of the vermin and clean up after them. Someone shot Röhm. The Führer said he did it himself. And it was a damn good job, too. Röhm was a filthy creature. I suppose he must have had his uses, although I can't see them. When they pulled him out of bed, there was a seventeen-year-old boy with him. We still have got some cleaning up left to do! If it were a house, we'd fumigate it. Get rid of all the vermin." He turned sideways in his seat and looked Hans up and down, carefully. "You can help, Beckendorff. There are other people who are dangerous, if not as obviously so. They would even be good people, if they were on the right side. But they are not. You did well today, Beckendorff."

Hans wanted to be sick.

"Thank you, sir," he said carefully. He thought of adding something, perhaps to show his understanding, but nothing came to mind. And he was far from understanding anything anymore. Did he look as exhausted as Paulus did? The man's face was bleached of all natural color. He looked as if he had not slept for several nights, and the stubble on his chin glistened white. Perhaps he had known this was coming? He must have been aware of the danger, been balancing the possible causes and losses in his mind.

Hans understood that Röhm had had to be got rid of. He had not been only a present and physical danger, with his massive force of armed men, but a political danger, too. A rebellion from him would have undone all of Hitler's work to rebuild Germany, to give order and prosperity back to the people. Hans would learn bits and pieces of reports about who was arrested, who was disgraced, and who was dead, but all he could comprehend was the smell of blood, the sight of it, and the shrill sound of terror.

He sat silently, watching Paulus, and he realized that the casualties included many of the men on that list he had produced and given to Paulus. After all, most of those men had been loyal to Röhm.

In return, Paulus was watching him. He must have seen the instant that thought entered his mind. It was the making of that list that Paulus was thanking him for.

Hans let out his breath slowly, not taking his eyes off Paulus's face. And then he inhaled fully, as if he were filling his lungs after a long day doubled up inside a car.

Paulus's eyes were bright. "Yes," he said slowly, stringing the word out as if it had more than one syllable. "You did well. Proud of yourself..." He left the sentence unfinished, leaving Hans wondering what he had not said. "Not that I doubted you, mind," he went on. "You have a new child?" That was not a question, it was an observation. "Your wife is English, right?"

Hans hesitated. Why did Paulus mention that? He already knew the answers. Hans was too tired to think, his mind drenched in unforgettable horror. It was a trap, however he answered. Be careful! Be very, very careful. "Her parents are English, sir." He said this as if Paulus didn't know, had never asked. "She has grown up in Germany. You would not know she is English, except for how well she speaks that language." That was true, but as an answer, it was an equivocation.

"Your child is German."

"Yes, sir." Don't add anything! Why was he asking? There would be a reason. There was always a reason for everything with Paulus.

The sense of dread was so powerful, Hans feared he might vomit.

"What does your father-in-law, Roger Cordell, claim to do at the British Embassy?" Paulus was staring hard at Hans, as if his answer mattered.

The plane would be waiting for them. If this conversation were to continue to seem casual, it would have to reach its conclusion soon. If Paulus picked it up again, Hans was certain it would not be casual any longer.

Did Hans want to know why Paulus was probing? Or did he want to avoid the subject going any further? His mind was exhausted. He knew he was vulnerable because he could not think clearly. And he knew very well that Paulus already had an idea of what Cordell did, but still, he could not afford to wait. "Lots of cultural exchanges, programs of music and literature. Exhibitions, and looking after student exchanges. We and the English have a lot in common. A German student goes to England, and an English one comes here. The English are good at science, but we're better." He gave a bleak half smile. "And we are the best in the world in music."

"I suppose it's interesting... to some," Paulus said, as if to dismiss it. Then he smiled, and this time it was even bleaker than before. "Our cultural attaché in London is head of our Intelligence over there. Gets to meet all sorts of people, including those who have great respect for the Führer. People high in government and, of course, many of them fought in the last war. Don't want another, at any price. Is Cordell one of them?"

Hans waited, all but holding his breath. Paulus had already told him that Cecily's father was with British Intelligence, which meant MI6. Did he just want Hans to repeat this, or did he assume Hans had since confronted his father-in-law to learn more of his true responsibilities? An implication was building up. It hung in the air, and heavy, like a thunderstorm about to break. He felt as if he were waiting in the heat for the first heavy drops. He wanted to say it himself, push Paulus to some conclusion about the British loyalties, but that was what Paulus was waiting for: to see if Hans would commit himself. Once he did, there would be no going back. He considered what he knew about Cordell. His ease of manner, his sophistication beneath the casual air that Hans had thought was part of his being English. But both he and Paulus knew it was far more than that.

"I've heard opinions about the British," he said. "They don't want another war, at any price." He knew instantly that that was the wrong tack to pursue. "Neither do we, of course," he added.

Paulus hesitated, as if on the edge of a decision. "What do you suppose your father-in-law reports to British Intelligence, Beckendorff?"

There it was! Spoken, but in equivocal words. What should he answer? Paulus had said this so directly, it was an obvious thought. He was reminding Hans that Roger Cordell was a far more powerful man than Hans had previously supposed.

Paulus was waiting for an answer, and Hans knew he must come up with one soon. But an ugly thought was filling his mind, growing bigger, heavier, crowding out all other thoughts. He thought again that this must be why Paulus was giving him preferential treatment.

Not for his skills, his ability, or his intelligence, but because he was the son-in-law of the man who was head of British Intelligence in Germany. The pieces were falling into place perfectly. What should he do? In any direction he moved, he betrayed someone. And Paulus had the perfect potential bait in his wife and child.

His mind was burning, and his body seemed paralyzed with cold. They were nearly at the airfield.

"He used to be friends with Standish, you know," Paulus said casually, as if somehow that followed logically from what they had been saying.

Hans's mouth was dry. "Standish." The name was familiar, but he could not place it immediately. And then he remembered Cecily's father mentioning it, and Paulus before that.

"Lucas Standish," Paulus said. "High in MI6 during the war. He became the head of it."

Hans was about to ask if this mattered, but the look in Paulus's face told him that it did. It was naked emotion, a hatred burned into the bone. "I will remember that," he said very softly. "Sir."

Paulus nodded slowly, as if satisfied, but he did not speak again.

CHAPTER 15

Hans returned to Berlin so exhausted he felt as if he were walking in his sleep. Every part of his body ached. He felt bruised all over, but mostly his mind was bruised with horror and grief that such brutality could happen.

Even Paulus seemed a little dazed, and unusually silent. He made no comment on the sudden, abominable violence.

"Go home. Eat and sleep," he ordered Hans. "There will be plenty to do. The Führer—" He stopped, as if he had forgotten what he intended to say.

Hans stared at him, waiting for orders. Paulus's face was unreadable, as if he also was too exhausted to command his thoughts. The man seemed to need to hide his own reactions from anyone. Perhaps it was self-protection. He never acknowledged fear, surprise, revulsion, or doubt. Did he not feel these things, after the overwhelming, almost insane slaughter in Munich? And, they had just learned, there had been a bloodbath nearly as bad in Berlin as well. Perhaps it helped, in all the chaos, that so many people were stunned, dazed, and uncertain how to react—or who to trust.

Hans also observed that the entire army of Brownshirts was in chaos, with Röhm, and God knew how many others, dead. Summarily executed. Or murdered?

Hans thanked Paulus and went straight home. When he was barely through the door and into the familiar light and shadows of his own home, with smells that wrapped around him with memories, Cecily appeared and ran straight into his arms, hugging him fiercely. He had not realized she was so strong. She drew breath to speak, and then wept with relief instead, drawing great sobbing gulps of air. He held her tightly, glad to feel the strength of life in her, to hear her voice, even if the words were choked and incoherent.

Then she pulled away and stared at him, moving her hands up and down his arms, as if to assure herself he was not hurt.

He drew a deep breath to steady himself. "I'm fine," he said with a crooked smile. "It was pretty awful, but it's under control."

"No, it isn't," she said quietly, looking into his eyes. "It's only going to get worse. Was it a revolution against the Führer? Do you know that?"

She was terrified, barely holding on to her self-control. His mind whirled with possibilities, fears crowding his thoughts. He loosened himself from her grip and met her gaze. "Madeleine?" he asked, although he knew she must be all right. He would have seen it in Cecily's face, felt it in her body, even through her clothes, if anything was wrong. It was, in a way, as if they were still one body. He had no idea yet how he would keep them safe, and it was the only thing that mattered to him.

She pulled away. "You must be exhausted. Are you hungry? Or would you like a hot bath? There's plenty of water." She looked away. "I'm sorry," she gulped, "I'm talking too much. What would you like?"

He buried his face in her soft hair, and the smell of shampoo. "Bath. I was able to get a clean uniform, but I still feel dirty. Then a hot drink. Do we have cocoa?"

"Yes. I'll run you a bath. Go and check on Madeleine. She's missed you."

He smiled. "Oh? She told you?"

She looked him straight in the eyes. "Yes, in her own way."

He went upstairs slowly, tired, but also relishing the moment. He was safe in his own home, with the people who mattered to him above all else.

The night-light was on in Madeleine's room, as usual. He pushed the door open sufficiently to go inside.

She was lying on her back, sound asleep. She was so quiet he wanted to go over and touch her, just feel the warmth of her body, feel her breath.

He resisted the temptation. It would not be fair. Cecily had probably spent a long time feeding her, changing her, and getting her to sleep. He stood still, just looking at her. He had been trying not to think of her all day. She was too precious, the thought of losing her unbearable. He had to be alive, to be here to protect them both.

Then without thinking, he bent down and touched her. She gave a little sigh but did not waken. His eyes filled with tears. It was ridiculous. Cecily would think he was so weak! He must get control of himself before he went down again. He wiped his hand across his cheeks and took a deep breath.

Then he felt Cecily's hand on his arm, gently. He was grateful for that. He put his other hand over hers. There was no need to say anything. There were no words that would not be clumsy.

Elena stood in the hotel courtyard with Professor Hartwig and tried to quell the panic inside her. She was exhausted, frightened, and again coming to terms with the dramatic necessity of getting Hartwig out of Germany alive. She wondered how Alex Cooper was doing with Fassler; whether they were already out of Germany.

Whatever the case, she must not stop trying. By now the authorities would have realized that Hartwig was gone, which could also lead them to Fassler's absence. An alarm would have gone out and their chances of being captured were far greater . . . if not assured.

These thoughts spurred her forward. They must get to France, which was the nearest border, or anywhere else, other than Austria, which was too much under Hitler's influence. She and Jacob had discussed Poland, Holland, and Denmark as backup plans. She now realized that the final decision would be made at the last minute, based on whatever route offered the safest passage.

Elena was not going to share her concerns with Hartwig. He understood all too well that there was no turning back: he desperately needed to escape.

But none of this mattered, not at the moment. What mattered was finding Jacob.

Elena felt the urgency. It was emotion, yes, but also an obligation that must be kept. No, "obligation" was the wrong word, as was "honor" or "duty." What was urging her forward was friendship, a loyalty to Jacob, who had been so loyal to her. Peter would tell her otherwise. He would remind her that the first duty was to the job. The argument that came instantly to mind was that these decisions have a way of catching up with you! One bad decision and no one wants to work with you, no one dares trust you. She would not trust herself. Nightmares would stalk wakefulness as well as sleep.

Hartwig understood that Fassler was also part of the plan, but he asked no questions, as if acknowledging that the less he knew, the better.

"We should go," Elena said a little huskily. Her throat was dry. She could not bring herself to say anything more.

"Yes," Hartwig answered, his voice perfectly level. "I think we should go back to the car park and see if we can find some vehicle with a working engine, and perhaps a full tank of petrol."

"Right." She had difficulty forcing the word out.

He smiled; it was gentle, and with only amusement, not anger. "And then what are you going to do to me? Shoot me?" The moment of levity come and gone, he stepped off the curb and followed the pathway to the car park, with Elena hurrying to keep up with him.

They moved between cars. "A black one might be safest," she said. "That yellow one is gorgeous." She pointed to a brightly colored car and gave a twisted smile. "I'd like to believe the sort of inside-out logic that says we'd never select a yellow car because it's obvious. But we can't take a chance."

He gave her a smile with laughter behind it, and a tinge of grief. They were keeping up with the humor, as if this were no more than a game, but they both knew it was anything but that. The price of losing was death.

They wove their way around bullet-scarred cars, many of them parked at odd angles, as if they had been through an earthquake, or had been abandoned quickly, while people had tried to back out, to escape anywhere onto the open road, but were stopped by the gunfire.

They walked close together, exchanging glances, as if to say, *This car? No. This one? Possibly!* They moved quickly. One car had its windscreen smashed, many had flattened tires. Elena felt increasingly desperate. What would they do if there wasn't a car that was drivable?

She looked at one car, a dark maroon saloon. She tried the door handle; it opened. The driver's seat was soaked with blood. She gulped, drew in a sharp breath, then slammed the door shut.

"Let's try the dark gray one, over there," said Hartwig, pointing.

"There's somebody in it!" she argued.

He was smiling.

She followed his line of sight. She could see the slight movement of someone in the driver's seat, leaning forward, perhaps looking for a lost object on the floor. Then he sat up. She turned to Hartwig. "Is it . . . ?"

"I think so," he replied.

"But how . . . ?"

The man in the car turned and looked toward them, as if aware of being watched. It was Jacob!

A wave of warmth enclosed Elena like a blanket. She was dizzy with relief. She grasped Hartwig's hand, and then felt him pull her from rushing ahead.

"No sudden moves," he said. "You taught me that!"

He was right. She was letting her emotions take over.

Jacob stepped out of the car and gestured toward it. "This one's pretty good," he said with a slight smile. "And it's got enough petrol for a hundred miles from here, at least. Let's get going." He looked at Elena more carefully, but said nothing further.

Five minutes later they were running smoothly on side roads, the car twisting and turning toward the outer suburbs and then, at last, into open country.

"So how did you escape the hotel unscathed?" she asked.

"I was looking for you both. When I couldn't find you I thought you might have sought refuge away from the fighting, further down the street. So that's where I went. When the gunshots stopped, I came back for you, knowing you'd try to make for the car lot if you could. And there you were. This one had keys in the ignition. It must have been abandoned when the shooting began."

"Thank God," said Elena.

"Breakfast?" Jacob asked. They were on a quiet country road with fields on either side, and the occasional copse of trees. The crops were deep and golden, ripening and ready for harvest. Jacob drove into the shade of a grove of perhaps half a dozen trees partially hidden from the road.

Elena opened the door and stepped out. The air was warm, and the silence like deep water. She stood still, breathing in the smell of the shadows and the still-damp earth.

Jacob stood beside her. "When the gunshots subsided, I stocked up. There's cheese, bread, and water in the trunk," he said quietly. "I'm afraid we can't afford more, and even less can we afford going on with empty stomachs. We might need all the quick thinking we have."

"It'll be fine," she said, meaning the bread and cheese, even the water. And yes, they might need all the money they had to purchase fuel.

Jacob kept his voice quiet, so Hartwig would not hear them. "It's fine at the moment, but it's still a long way to the border. We can't take anything for granted." He looked anxious.

She realized how exhausted he must be, and the fine lines on his face were clear in the sunlight. His part in this was all generosity, not duty. She had asked his advice, and he had given her his help, even to the point of risking his life. And he was still doing it.

"Jacob, I can drive from here on. I've had a lot of training since we last met."

She saw a curious expression in his eyes. Understanding, fear, and something that she was almost certain was pride.

"You came for Hartwig," Jacob said. As if she had asked for an explanation as to who he thought she worked for. "Someone sent you here. It could have been a request, but I thought it was far more than that: an order. Not that you would have refused, even if it had been possible." His face reflected a moment of pain. "May tenth was a turning point, wasn't it?"

He was referring to the night they had stood together in Berlin and watched in horror as students, capering around like mad creatures, gibbering and shouting, piled all the great works of literature and philosophy onto the huge fires and attempted to burn the ideas of the greatest minds in Europe. As if fire could destroy a belief!

But it was not the fire that had changed her, it was the hate-distorted faces of unreason. It was on that night that Elena had realized for the first time in her life that there were people beyond the reach of sanity.

Hartwig walked up to them, but he stood silently, as if realizing that he had interrupted a moment of profound emotion.

"Memories," Elena said, turning to the scientist. She did not want him to feel embarrassed, as if he were an intruder. She needed to explain that it was not a romantic moment, but a signal event for mankind. "May of last year," she explained. "When they burned the books." She stopped. It was painfully clear from Hartwig's expression that he, too, had seen that shattering display, if not firsthand, then in newsreels and in the papers.

"I remember," he said quietly. "That was the moment we realized that the wind had changed. The stench of ashes has been in the air ever since." His face reflected what he understood of it and, even more, what he felt. "Let's have breakfast, and forget for a few minutes that it ever happened. Don't let them steal our ability to taste the good things as well. We'll need those memories." He smiled with something like self-mockery. "Like the animals that eat in autumn to store up fat for their winter hibernation. There's going to be some part of us that will sleep through the coming years." He stopped, gave a slight shrug, and then held his hand out for Jacob to pass him a piece of bread roll, a slice of cheese, and a bottle of water.

They walked a little distance from where the car was parked in the shade and concealed from the road. When they were on the edge of the field, they each found a comfortable place to sit, close enough to speak to each other without raising their voices. There was silence, except for the wind rustling through the ripe heads of the wheat and the birds singing. In England, it would have been a skylark with that high, sweet song. Elena did not know what it was here, but it was a glorious sound.

At first, they ate in silence, hungrily. Without doing it consciously, they all lifted their faces to the sun, eyes closed, and drank in the peace of it, as if they were being consumed by their own dreams.

It was Hartwig who moved first. "We must leave. We need to think and plan. We might be able to slip into France tonight."

Jacob nodded. "Maybe, if there aren't any more roadblocks. I don't mean to belittle your importance, Professor, but I hope the authorities are too busy with the fiasco in Munich, and I imagine Berlin also, to bother about us."

"I hope so, too," Hartwig agreed. "But if anyone has missed me and thought to side with the army, they won't say, 'Professor of germ warfare wanted; apprehend at all costs.' They are far more likely to say that I'm a traitor to the Führer. Or if he is fallen ... please God ... then an ally of the Führer. I'll be described as some dangerous but interesting conspirator. Nothing has to be true, only believable."

Elena began to argue, then realized that he was right. She watched him gaze at the landscape. "Have you been here before? These hills, these roads?"

Hartwig smiled. "Yes, on my honeymoon, actually." There was exquisite memory in his face of something so sweet the ugliness of the present could not touch it. "But it wasn't this time of year," he said. "It was spring, everything just coming into leaf. The winter corn was pale green over the plowed earth. The grass was new, untrodden." He smiled again. "There were wildflowers in the hedges and under the trees. Everything was bursting with life, and trust. That was before the war, of course."

Elena nodded, but knew to say nothing. Hartwig's memories were bringing him such pleasure, a welcome break from the tension and fear.

"We had endless hope in the future," he said. "It seems now to have been so idyllic, such peace sunk deep into the earth, but it was real then." He was staring into the distance, as far as any of them could see: across the fields, a small river, and the sharp edge of a steep hill on the far side of the valley, and the higher rises beyond that. The sky was clear, just a few clouds shadowing across the hills far away, softening their outlines against the sky.

Elena had not imagined his wife and their life together. These things mattered. She wanted to ask, but it seemed clumsy.

"Such a beautiful place," she said softly. "Perhaps it's a good thing we had to come this way, instead of to the north."

He turned and smiled at her, but she knew his thoughts were far away, in another time. He was remembering, and she was glad he had precious moments to recall.

Hartwig stood up slowly, as if a little stiff. "We need to move. We must use all the daylight we have." He looked at Jacob. "Would you like me to take a turn at the wheel?"

"You think I'm likely to fall asleep?" Jacob asked with a twisted smile.

"Not while you're driving, or I would insist. But I think you would like a little rest."

Jacob hesitated only a moment. "Thank you," he accepted, standing. "I think you're quite right. I would be a better driver with rest." He stretched his neck, rotated his shoulders. "I learned to drive on the streets of Chicago. Good traffic practice. Have to look where you're going. In this"—he glanced around at the tree trunks, then up into the branches, now almost hidden with a full canopy of leaves— "I could get distracted by its beauty and forget . . ." He did not finish his thought. They were all too aware of how the sentence would end.

They removed any traces of having been there, except for a few crumbs, which birds or small animals would consume as soon as they were gone.

They walked back to the car and climbed in, this time Hartwig in the driver's seat and Elena beside him. Jacob stretched out on the backseat and fell asleep within minutes.

For a little while they drove in silence, watching the road for any signs of trouble. Elena wondered again about Hartwig's wife. She tried to imagine how hard all of this was for him. Leaving his home, his books, his favorite chair, perhaps art, paintings, all of which must be filled with memories. And, of course, he could not tell any friends, however close, what he planned to do, for their sakes as well as his.

There was another probable outcome to his sudden escape: he would be painted as a traitor to Germany. Friends and family could be deemed guilty by association, especially by those people who would see him as disloyal. Even the idea of escape, planning it, would be seen as treason. It would require sacrifice, and few people were willing to face that kind of loneliness, and the consuming loss.

She looked at his face. He was concentrating on the road, but there was a certain ease in his expression. It was as if, whatever the cost, he knew it was right. And perhaps this beautiful scenery with its intimacy and its sudden, vast views was full of memories of the best time in his life.

He smiled as he steered. "Ellen, you must come back one day, when you can do so safely."

"I will," she said. She had to say that, although she was not at all sure she wanted to. Other memories came back to her too sharply and she had a feeling he would understand. "I went for a holiday once, a driving holiday with my grandfather. I think I mentioned that he is my favorite person in the world. We drove through much of England, just the two of us. We ate bread and cheese and drank a little red wine, just sitting on the edge of a field. It was utterly silent, except for the wind in the grass. And the sound of bees in the heather." She let her mind drift back to that innocent time, before she had even heard of MI6, or all the battles that would never be over.

She was aware that he was glancing at her. She smiled. "He knew all the patter songs from Gilbert and Sullivan. He used to sing them. I can't sing, but I love to listen."

To her amazement, Hartwig began to sing very quietly one of the songs from *HMS Pinafore,* and in a very pleasant baritone. When he could not remember the words, she put them in, surprised that they returned to her. The whole world had changed since her trip with her grandfather Lucas. It was a testament to the happiness of their holiday that those memories returned now.

"*I never use a big, big D*—" he sang.

"*What, never?*" she responded, following the beat of the music.

"*No, never!*"

"*What, never?*"

"*Hardly ever!*"

They ended the song, laughing loudly enough to awaken Jacob. He sat up, puzzled.

"Gilbert and Sullivan," Elena explained. "But sorry, didn't mean to waken you!"

Jacob shook his head sharply, as if to clear his mind. "It's a good sound," he answered, leaning forward. "Where are we? Do you know?"

"On the right road," Hartwig answered. "We'll join the main road toward the south in a mile or two."

"'A big D'?" Jacob was smiling.

Elena could see his puzzled face in the rearview mirror. "Damn!" she said. "That was what 'a big D' stood for. The humor is that these are sailors, so a word like 'damn' was far from vulgar to them. But it's all very innocent. The music is marvelous, and the words sound like nonsense, which makes it even more wonderful. Because when you sing them, they make sense!"

"I understand," Jacob said quickly. "It's English. It means nothing, and everything."

"Yes," said Elena. "You've got it exactly."

Jacob tapped Hartwig on the shoulder. "Do you want me to take over now?"

"If you like."

"I'd better. If we hit a major roadblock, we want them looking at me, not at you," Jacob replied. "Pull over to the side."

Jacob and Hartwig switched places and they drove on.

Hartwig was right. In another couple of miles, they joined the main highway again. It was an excellent road, and they were able to maintain a good speed. That is, until they rounded a bend and saw a roadblock.

"We're nearly a hundred miles from Munich," Jacob said. "We'll need to fill the tank soon."

"They must still be looking for people who escaped, members of Röhm's forces," Elena suggested.

There were many cars already stopped ahead of them, and the ones directly in front of them were slowing down. The traffic was much heavier since they had rejoined the main road, but they had no choice.

Elena suddenly found herself tense again. Could these guards possibly be looking for Hartwig? This far south? But in all this turmoil, did they have time to care about one scientist? Yes, if it was the one who had made the breakthrough in germ warfare that could cause terrible, lethal diseases and the other who was working on the antidote. Unlike some tragic weekend of violence, this weapon could cause long-term chaos and destruction.

The traffic was slowing even more. Ahead of them, drivers were being questioned one by one. Elena felt all her muscles clench, as if suddenly it was difficult to breathe.

The car ahead of them was waved through.

Now there were men at their window. Jacob rolled his down. "Yes, Officer?" he asked.

"Papers!" the man said abruptly. "Who are you?" he demanded. "Where have you come from?"

Jacob gave his name and passed him the identity papers.

"What were you doing in Munich?" the man asked. He was young, fair-haired, a little overweight. In every way the opposite of Jacob.

Jacob told a version of the truth. "I'm a journalist. I write for an American newspaper, *The New York Times*. The whole world is interested in Germany."

Elena knew that, apart from any flattery, that much was true.

The officer looked at Elena. "Who are you?"

"Ellen Stewart, sir."

"What are you doing here?"

Jacob interrupted. He smiled at the officer. "She's with me." He gave the officer a knowing look, which seemed to satisfy the man.

The man peered into the backseat. Hartwig looked at him innocently.

"She is my niece. Her mother is my sister," Hartwig said. "Heinrich Hausmann. We were enjoying a day in the countryside."

"Papers!" the man demanded.

Hartwig took them from his inside pocket and handed them over.

Elena's sense that she could not breathe became even more severe.

The man read the documents slowly.

They waited in intense silence. The sound of other car engines seemed miles away, noises without meaning, from another world.

"Where are you going with these young people?" the officer asked.

"As I said, we had a lovely day planned together outside the city," Hartwig answered.

"Get out." The officer gestured, placing his other hand on his gun.

Hartwig obeyed. He was a little uncertain on one ankle, as if he had twisted it on the uneven roadside.

"Come here!" called the man to one of his fellow officers. "Do you think this is him?" he asked.

The other officer looked intently at Hartwig, who was pale, but quite steady. He peered even more closely. "Schneider? No, wrong height." He shook his head, then put his hand into his pocket and pulled out several photographs.

"Who do you say you are?" the first man asked Hartwig again.

"Heinrich Hausmann," he repeated.

The second officer shouted something back at one of the other men on the roadblock. A third man walked over, his gun raised. He looked at each of the photos, and then at Hartwig. "Not Schneider," he said firmly. "But he does remind me of someone."

Elena opened her mouth to speak, but realized she might make it worse. She looked at Jacob. He was very pale indeed.

Finally, the officer handed Hartwig back his papers and told him to get into the car. "Go on," he said. To his fellow soldiers, he added, "Let them go. No need to jam up the traffic any worse." He stepped back.

"Just a minute!" one of the other guards shouted. "Take another look at him! He could be that professor they're looking for!"

Hartwig got in the car, fumbling a little with the handle.

"Hey! You! Stop a moment!"

"Go!" Elena cried.

Jacob stepped hard on the accelerator and the car shot forward. There was a shout from behind them, unintelligible, followed by a volley of shots. They heard glass shatter.

The car slewed, then straightened and picked up greater speed. They were sending up billowing clouds of dust behind them.

Elena swiveled round to look. She could see other cars gaining speed, drawing closer.

Jacob put his foot to the floor and the car pitched forward and went flat out, careening around curves, missing the oncoming traffic by barely a foot, but gradually drawing ahead of the police cars.

Elena shouted to Jacob to take the first turn, but her voice was lost in the squeal of tires. They were slowly drawing out the distance between themselves and the police.

Jacob was intent on the road, his whole body tense. Then, suddenly, he swerved, skidded a few feet in the dust at the edge of the road, and veered around the corner of the next side road, where he drove into a clearing half-hidden by a clump of trees on higher ground.

Below them, several police cars raced along the main road.

Elena drew in a shaky breath, and said nothing.

"We could pull back onto the road," said Jacob, "but they might double back, then we'd be trapped. Better we stay here, well hidden, and wait." He turned around to face Hartwig. "Professor—" His eyes grew wide.

Elena turned also, then froze. Hartwig had slid down the seat, his face relaxed, totally at peace. There was blood streaming from the back of his head onto the car's seat.

Elena felt as if she were being choked. Tears welled up in her eyes and ran down her cheeks. Her emotions were overwhelming, as if an awful void had opened up to swallow her.

Jacob inhaled shakily. "There's nothing we can do. We'll have to leave him here."

"We can't!" Elena protested. She heard the passion in her voice and realized that calm was needed here. Calm, and a level head. "Anyway," she added, her voice reasonable, "we need the car."

"We'll leave him here, in the trees." Jacob's voice cracked. "I know it's bad, but we must go on."

"I vowed that I would get him out!" She tried to say more, but her voice choked. She let the tears flow.

"We have to move," said Jacob. "It's not easy, I know, but we have no choice. We can't take a chance that we're stopped, and he's in the car."

"But . . . the animals." She stopped. She knew what Hartwig would have said. They had done all they could. He was part of the trees and the earth now.

They got out of the car. Jacob put his arms around her, tightly, as if, for a few moments, they could be one and share their grief.

Elena could feel the beating of his blood in his bare arms. When he stepped back, she said, "I know," her voice hardly coming out. "I'm ready."

But that was a lie. She would never be ready.

CHAPTER

16

After the bloodbath, the German people were reeling from shock. Hans felt as if he had just witnessed perhaps the most appalling event in civilian history, already being referred to as the Night of the Long Knives. He had told no one of his feelings. Certainly, he had not even tried to explain any of it to Cecily. How could he? He had killed two men!

He wanted to weep, to release the pent-up horror inside him, the revulsion, and the pity. But men did not weep. At least those with any courage did not. He needed her to love him, he needed it desperately, because he did not love himself.

His mind saw his wife. She was so beautiful, but delicately so. At times, she seemed as fragile as a child, but there was strength in her. It amazed him. She did not ask him about that night, or about anything he was doing. Was that because she did not want to know? Hardly. It was on every tongue, one way or another. More probably it was because she did not want him to have to relive it, or admit it aloud. She let him believe whatever he needed to.

After the nightmare, he hardly dared to pick up Madeleine, won-

dering if she would smell blood on him. No, her total innocence was
a blessing so sweet it physically hurt him. When she lay in his arms,
smiling, her eyes full of trust, he wondered if he would ever again be
worthy of it.

He knew that he must stop this self-indulgence. It was not the
first time Paulus had implied that Hans's future lay in his hands, and
that it could be far greater than Hans realized.

At Paulus's orders, he was at the office by seven o'clock in the
morning.

Paulus arrived, freshly shaved and wearing a clean, pressed uniform, but he looked tense, muscles tight in his neck and jaw. He
stared at Hans as if he had to concentrate to recognize him. "All
right?" he said sharply.

"Yes, sir!" Hans replied, standing to attention.

"We have another meeting with the Führer," he said. "You are to
watch and listen, but do not speak unless ordered to do so. It is important for you," he added, meeting Hans's eyes gravely.

"Yes, sir," Hans said, but with a flutter of nerves in the pit of his
stomach. At the same time, he was relieved, since he had no wish to
speak.

"Come with me," Paulus commanded.

Hans nodded as he followed Paulus out of the office.

Paulus slowed his pace for just a moment. "Watch. Listen and
remember. I'm counting on your loyalty, Beckendorff. Everything
turns on this." He stared at Hans unblinkingly.

Hans felt a shiver run through him, although the passage was hot,
almost airless.

They arrived and Hans saw several men enter the room. Paulus
was the last of the group, and he left the door open for Hans, who
went straight in behind him.

Everyone in the room rose to their feet and saluted. Hans recognized Hermann Goering, the big bullet-headed Prussian who had
not only been president of his own province, but had founded the
national air force and was now second in command to Hitler him-

self. Goering looked satisfied, even smug. He loved the good life such power afforded him. He ate and drank enormously, collected fine art with some taste, and proved himself to be good company. Paulus always spoke well of him. But then he, too, was Prussian.

Joseph Goebbels took one of the seats near Goering. Goebbels was smaller, leaner, the pinch-faced Minister of Propaganda. He had hard, dark eyes and a mouth like a slash across his face, and he wore an orthopedic boot to compensate for a deformed foot, so his limp was barely noticeable. He was a womanizer and known behind his back as the Goat of Babelsberg. He was by far the cleverest man in the room. Almost certainly, he knew it.

After the first glimpse, Hans avoided looking at him. He always had the feeling that Goebbels could sense a person's thoughts, apparently their fears, at a glance. He did not see them so much as smell them, as a predatory animal does.

Hitler was talking. His voice was rasping. His hand on the table was tense, white-knuckled, strangely fine boned, as one might imagine the hand of an artist.

Glancing round the table, Hans saw a variety of expressions, from Goebbels's flat glare to Paulus's tense, careful watchfulness, evident by a tiny muscle jumping in his temple. His eyes never left Hitler. Anyone who did not know him would think it was respectful attention. Those who did know him, like Hans, would recognize it as judgment.

Despite what he might be feeling, Paulus's face was calm. There was no gray stubble today. Hans understood he was measuring everything Hitler said, only occasionally glancing at the others around the table, as if judging their reactions. Hans knew that he would make a point of remembering each of those reactions for later.

Goering was talking now, praising Hitler for taking control of the armed forces and getting rid of Röhm and his violent, undisciplined Brownshirts. Every word he said was infinitely predictable.

Hans tried to force himself to listen, and failed. He could have foretold it all. What was far more enlightening than listening was watching. Each man's face reflected something slightly different. Goebbels, in particular, appeared eager, sniffing the wind as if looking for opportunity. A change in direction? To be ahead of it? He had done that before.

Others were watching Goering, waiting for the Reich Commissioner of Aviation to move before they followed. What did they really believe? Was there anything at this table more than opportunism?

Goering had a few ideas. He had loathed Röhm and was full of praise for Hitler's decisions, including killing Röhm, now that the action was accomplished. Hans wondered what he had felt before.

Paulus was also watching each of them in turn. Hans knew he was reading all of them, these followers who had their ears close to the ground, while his fist was clenching and unclenching. Was he judging if perhaps someone in this room was planning treason against the Führer? It was more likely that he watched so he could use them to learn more. Always the opportunist.

There was more congratulating of Hitler's decisiveness. No one argued, but some were too eager, a few hollow-sounding as they repeated someone else's words.

As they sat there, more deaths were confirmed. Included in these reports were names like Kurt von Schleicher, who had been second in power to Hitler and his rival, murdered in the massacre. There was Franz von Papen, not executed but exiled for life. Of course, Röhm had been shot, as had the young man found in bed with him. Hans felt a flicker of pity for the boy. He probably had been given little choice. It was likely he would have been shot whatever he did. What alternatives did you have if you were young, a little soft, a little boyish in looks, and the commandant of three million Brownshirts told you to go with him to bed . . . or anywhere else?

Thank God Hans's father had got him into the Gestapo. He should be grateful for that for the rest of his life. He knew it had cost his parents some sacrifice to send him to a fine university, with expenses that included clothes, books, everything to keep up with the best boys there. He had worked even harder to reward them for it. It was a start in life beyond price.

He pulled his focus back to Hitler, who was alternating between intense attention, as if he was committing every word to memory, and a seemingly glassy-eyed stare into space, as if his mind was entirely elsewhere. Hans wondered if he was afraid of Hindenburg, who was still president of Germany. He was very old now and comprehension was slipping out of his grasp, but then it would occasionally return with full clarity. Only a fool would assume that the old man had not heard something, or that he had only partially grasped it.

It would be interesting to know what Hitler had told Hindenburg; how he had explained what seemed from the reports to be nothing more than mass murder. If he had included the death of Röhm, and the rest of the leadership of the Brownshirts, Hindenburg might be very pleased! He despised them as dangerous rabble. He himself was a brave, skilled, and occasionally rigid Prussian. Hans clearly recalled how Paulus, in an unguarded moment, had described him as having as much imagination as his riding saddle, and less than the horse who carried him.

Everyone was tense. The meeting dragged on.

In one silence, Hitler stared with intensity at Hans, and then he looked questioningly at Paulus. Paulus noticed, and stiffened.

"Sir," Paulus replied steadily. "Beckendorff's behavior in Munich was excellent—steady, level, and unhesitating. I am entrusting him with more responsibilities." He looked satisfied, almost smiling. "We need such men."

"Good," Hitler said, nodding. "Loyalty should be rewarded." He was not looking at Hans, but at Paulus. Then he turned to Goebbels and continued with his previous conversation.

Everyone was staring at Hans. He could feel the color flooding up his face. "Thank you, sir," Hans said quietly to Paulus, although he almost choked on the words. His mouth was dry.

Paulus nodded, and moved into the conversation.

* * *

The meeting ended late in the afternoon.

"Remember this," Paulus said quietly to Hans as they walked along the corridor and outside into the courtyard. "That meeting will be important. Tell me, what did you make of it?"

Hans had been waiting for this. It was the kind of question he would be asked—not about matters of fact, or who held what position, or what their duties were, but how he assessed it all.

Paulus was subtle in his questions. His message would not be in what was said, but what was not said, and who committed themselves, and who did not. It was the current of the ocean far beneath the temporary wind or the tide.

Hans knew he must answer honestly. Paulus was like Goebbels, although he would not welcome the comparison: he could smell fear, smell a lie. "I think it all depends on President Hindenburg, sir," he said. "If they can see the necessity of getting rid of people like Röhm and his influence over the Brownshirts, then they will understand that it will not take long for much of the uncertainty to clear up, and that it will be better. Much better." Had he gone too far?

Paulus's mouth turned down. "Didn't expect you to see that," he observed. "What's wrong with the Brownshirts?" He was not asking from lack of knowledge, but because, Hans suspected, he wanted to see what Hans would have the nerve to tell him. It was another test.

"No vision," Hans replied, as if certain of the answer, although it was coming to his mind as he spoke. "We have to go forward, and we can't do this if we have no idea where that should be. It is the test of a good mind that it envisions a future, and then works toward that future, and with belief." He stopped. Paulus was staring at him with a totally fixed expression, but one that Hans could not read.

"Did you hear the Führer say that?" Paulus asked at last.

"No, sir, I didn't think of putting it into words until you asked me." That was the truth. He had been too overwhelmed by the violence, the sheer chaos, to think more deeply about it. But above all else was the realization of how precarious the Brownshirt movement was, how it had seemed to come unraveled. And he was certain that it was not yet over.

Paulus was still staring at him. Hans was avoiding a discussion of the incident in case he sounded as if he considered himself equal to Paulus. He knew that it would be dangerous. Paulus had earned his seniority through long, difficult years in the wilderness.

"Good," Paulus said finally. "You've handled this very well, Beckendorff. I see a future ahead for you. And, in fact, I will be the one to determine it."

"Thank you, sir." There did not seem anything else to say. To praise Paulus would be impertinent. Or, worse, obsequious. And he knew it was all conditional. This was not a promise. He was on the verge of a giant step forward, if he remained cautious and vigilant.

On the way home, he called on his parents. He needed to assure himself that they were all right, although there was no need to fear for them. It was more a courtesy, as he knew his mother would worry.

He arrived and was greeted with too much relief, even for his normally controlled father. The man stood aside, not touching him as he entered. His father was not a tactile man, but he could not take the smile from his face. His mother hugged him fiercely, and it was seconds before she let him go.

"Do you know what happened in Munich?" she asked. "Did Röhm really turn against the Führer? What have you heard?"

Hans must explain it as simply as possible. Truthfully, but without the horror, the chaos. He stepped back from her hug. "I was in Munich. General Paulus took me on his flight."

His father was nodding slowly. "You've done well, son. I'm sure you conducted yourself with honor." He was not looking for an answer, more reassurance.

"I believe so, Father," Hans replied. "General Paulus expressed his approval."

"Good. Good. And you're safe?" That was a question. He needed to know.

"Oh, yes, back in Berlin, and safe, but . . ."

"What?" His father's voice was hard, sharp with fear. "What? Tell me!"

Hans had already let slip more than he meant to, not in words but by his expression. "I'm sorry," he said. "I have not slept much since it began, and it was very frightening. To realize that we have such betrayal, and on so many sides. At least, it seemed like that in Munich." He remembered the hysteria in Hitler's eyes, his voice, his clenched hands and wild gestures. "I was not afraid for myself, but I worried for the Führer." That was half true, but not in the sense he knew his father would understand it. "But he is safe now."

"Was he afraid?" his mother asked incredulously, arching her brows even higher than usual.

Hans knew the superhuman qualities she invested in Hitler in her mind.

"Not for himself," he lied. "He was a soldier, remember? All through the war, and on the front lines, not back where it was safe." Why did he say that? To deny the fear he had seen? He had faced death many times before. He was very afraid for the cause. "And I think the Brownshirts are . . . I prefer not to tell you, Mother. It could offend you, and you don't need to know."

She looked him up and down. "But you are not hurt?" That really was a question to which she needed an answer.

"A few bruises. And stiff, from sitting in a small plane. Nothing that won't be gone in a day or two. I wanted to show you that I am unhurt, and to thank you again for giving me such a good start in life." That sounded so pompous, and yet he felt the need to repeat this praise again and again. How should he finish, to sound honest? "I would have none of this without you."

His father nodded several times, and for an instant Hans thought he saw the sheen of tears in his eyes. He said nothing.

His mother smiled, and for a moment her face looked younger, a glimpse of what she must have looked like when she held him as a baby, the overwhelming gentleness. An image of Cecily flashed in his mind's eye, holding Madeleine. How had he and his mother traveled so far from that?

He must go home now, and spend time with his wife and daughter, let them know that he would always keep them safe, whatever the price. He would continue to work for Paulus, no matter what he felt about the man. He owed too many people the safety he could give them, and that above all he wanted to give them.

He looked at his parents, intimate strangers, people who had given him so much, invested, and not necessarily what he wanted, but what they wanted for him. He smiled and nodded, not meaning anything in particular, and then turned and went outside again. Hitler was back in control. Hans had done well, and Paulus was pleased with him . . . so far.

Maybe if he got up in the night to hold Madeleine, and if she woke and needed anything, he would tell her the truth. He was talking to her quite often in their quiet moments alone. She always stared at him with those huge blue eyes, so like his own. And while she did not understand a word he was saying, she knew he was talking to her, and that he loved her more than anything in the world.

CHAPTER 17

Lucas was standing in Peter Howard's office. Usually, their meetings were casual, a walk in the woods along the river path, or across the fields. The peace, the long view of the slopes in the land, the richness of seasons, were a balance to the things they had to speak of. For Peter, it was a freedom he seldom experienced otherwise.

This was, in large part, a unique friendship. Lucas Standish was the man he was closest to, and who understood the pressures and the loneliness in his life.

For Lucas, a walk with Toby was a regular practice, a reminder of the beauty of the earth, the healing of the seasons, unending ripening and renewal.

The two men often met for these walks, but today Peter could not spare the hours away from his desk, even for a momentary escape. There was news coming in, and it was vital that he share it with Lucas as quickly as possible.

"Hitler's been to see Hindenburg," he said, his voice grating with stress and exhaustion.

Lucas thought Peter had probably been up most of the night.

"From everything we can learn, so far," continued Peter, "the old man thoroughly approved the visit."

"He would," Lucas said wearily. "He's too tired and confused to fight, and possibly he knows it would be futile anyway. He hasn't much idea what's really going on. And the Brownshirts epitomize everything he despises . . . and fears. Rightly. God knows, they're an enormous force, with virtually no controls placed on them. But this was a bloodbath, Peter. They're calling it the Night of the Long Knives. There seems to have been no order or judgment in it, just mass killings . . . murder."

"It's a bit like cauterizing a wound," Peter observed. "You need a hot iron for it; a needle and thread are too slow. You would bleed to death before that worked."

"That's my point, Peter! Hitler left it too long to suppress this explosion of Brownshirt dominance. He dithered around, so that in the end he had to strike wildly. I hold no grief for any of the Brownshirts, least of all for Röhm himself, but this sounds like a massacre. They're estimating anything between five hundred and a thousand actually dead. I don't think anyone knows how many are wounded, or whether or not the action was effective."

"Effective?" Peter said dubiously, a raw edge to his voice. "Probably far more of a risk to go in carefully and try to root out the leaders. They'd have had warning time to take countermeasures. The vast majority of them are followers. But the leaders, Röhm and his like, are venal, self-indulgent, and often drunk." And then he added emphatically, "But they are not stupid."

"You think not?" Lucas asked with heavy suspicion. "Röhm got above himself. He endangered Hitler's hold on the army, not to mention offended his sensibilities. Hitler could have executed a few who were more or less innocent, stupid, young, who went along with the crowd. There are always those. But, by all accounts, this was butchery. And apparently Hindenburg, who is still president, at least in name, has approved. I'm not sure which is worse, Hitler or chaos.

Someone else would emerge, but if Hitler fell, who would rise to the top?"

"Goebbels?" Peter said. The expression on his face was unreadable. Was his opinion of the Goat of Babelsberg the same as Lucas's?

"Isn't he in charge anyway, prompting Hitler, pulling the strings?" Lucas said, only partly sarcastic. "Hitler will come up with powerful and terrible ideas, after Goebbels has sown them in his mind."

Peter hesitated only a few seconds. "I was hoping you wouldn't say that."

Lucas smiled wryly. "Why, so you could, and I might argue with you? You wouldn't believe me, and you wouldn't feel any better for having said it."

"I suppose not," Peter answered rather sheepishly.

"Anything else?" Lucas said. "Are you avoiding telling me about Elena because you have no news? Or because whatever you have is bad?"

"Because I have none," Peter answered, looking down at the carpeted floor. "But my people in Berlin tell me that Hartwig hasn't been seen for a couple of days." He looked up at Lucas. "She's left Berlin, but I don't know where she is. I presume she has Hartwig with her. I hope to God they weren't anywhere near Munich, which is where the worst of this bloodbath took place. I'm sorry." He paused for a moment. "I have heard from Alex Cooper, and he and Fassler are still in Berlin. He's going to wait until all this with the Brownshirts settles down a bit. At the moment, everyone is being watched."

"I expected this," Lucas replied.

There was silence in the room for a few moments. Thoughts, memories crowded Lucas's mind. So, Elena had been sent to Berlin to rescue this man who was working on the antidote to germ warfare. And, apparently, Fassler could not complete his project without him. Lucas was always interested in what was behind human connections. What drew people together?

"That's not all," Peter said, sounding as if he were apologizing for something.

Lucas felt the chill that he knew was only his imagination. "What else?" Peter had sent for him for a reason. Lucas already knew about the major parts of the massacre.

"You already know that Paulus is back," Peter said quietly. "But he's wielding far more power than we first thought. When I say 'back,' Peter, I mean back in control, and with far more influence over Hitler than we first believed. We're certain that he's Hitler's right-hand man in most decision making. I don't know how he did it, but he's often seen at Hitler's elbow." Peter hesitated, and then went on, "We had men in Röhm's secure levels to observe, and also to keep us aware of what was going on. Paulus discovered one of them, tortured and then killed him. We have to assume that he got a good deal of information out of him first."

Lucas said nothing. Nothing about Paulus surprised him. Memories returned in a flood, like a black tide rising to suck away all the light. He remembered operations during the war, on moonless nights, bitingly cold. Paulus had been clever, ruthless in the sense that he understood the price of lives, and ignored it. His judgment was acute, instinctive, and it had required all of Lucas's courage to beat him. Lucas brought Paulus to his knees and it had made Paulus a laughingstock.

Now Paulus had the whip hand again. It had taken him from 1917 until now, 1934, to regain his reputation. Half those men who had mocked him were probably dead by now, or retired from active duty. They had been the Kaiser's men. Now Paulus was at Hitler's right hand, Hitler had solidified his power, and Hindenburg was an old man who would probably die before the end of the year.

Hindenburg wanted assurances, and no more battles. He wanted to believe Hitler's vision, but did he understand what that vision was?

Lucas felt Peter watching him. "What do you want me to do?" Lucas said at last.

"Paulus oversees the germ warfare department, as far as security is concerned," Peter answered, except that it was not an answer. It was only a bridge between what had happened now and what he wanted. "Paulus knows that we have men planted within the German command. If he doesn't know their names, he'll find out. And he won't mind torturing them to get the rest."

"I know that!" Lucas said abruptly. "The only way to stop him is to kill him."

"Yes," Peter agreed. "You know Paulus better than any of us do. I want you to choose the man to do it, and I want you to prep him, and send him. I'm not ducking it, Lucas. I'm trying to get the right person to find Paulus, kill him, and then get out alive. I'm not vain enough, or stupid enough, to think I could do that as well as you could." His face was bleak, white. "It matters too much to—"

"I understand," Lucas cut him off. "Hitler is stronger than ever. Perhaps unassailable now. Hindenburg is old and tired. When he dies, probably before autumn, there will be no one to curb Hitler at all. And Paulus is his right-hand man in Intelligence. Paulus must be killed. It's either him or perhaps the entire network of our men in Germany."

"Yes," Peter agreed.

"Then I'll go myself."

"No, you won't! For God's sake, Lucas, you're an old man!"

"Exactly," Lucas said, and winced. "Nobody would expect me to be dangerous."

"You could be killed!" Peter choked on the words.

"So could anybody else who went," Lucas pointed out realistically. "I know him by sight. I can get through the barriers. I know him well enough that I can predict him, recognize him out of uniform. Think clearly for a moment, Peter—I'm the obvious choice. And I understand what's at stake. I'll kill him without hesitation."

"Just as he'll kill you. You know he will recognize you," Peter retorted.

"If he can. I taught you better than to be sentimental. Everyone's life matters. Mine no more than anyone else's. You've given me the job. Now let me do it." He took a deep breath. "We have to beat

Paulus," he went on. "Doubly so now, however it's done. Getting Fassler and Hartwig out of Germany is still as important as it always was." It was unjustified, he knew, but the pain and fear inside him needed some release.

Peter took a long breath. "You must kill Paulus. That's why, as much as I hate it, I will let you do this. You're our best chance."

Lucas tried to control his imagination. He must think. A mistake now could be fatal.

Peter waited. It cost an effort of will, and it showed in his face.

Lucas gave a bitter smile. "I understand. I'll go."

"How do you expect to find him, after all these years?" Peter asked.

"I won't have to: he'll find me."

"Lucas!"

"What? Too risky? Come on, Peter. If I show myself, Paulus won't be able to resist."

Peter snapped, "For God's sake, Lucas!" There was a thin, sharp note of desperation in his voice. "We won the war, at a terrible price. But we aren't winning the peace. This is no time for some quixotic gesture!"

"You know me better than that, Peter. I'm going to kill him. We can't afford to let him live. You agree, or you wouldn't have sent for me. This Night of the Long Knives is not over."

Peter stared at him.

"It's the reality, Peter," Lucas reminded him. "War is mostly about killing. Paulus can't be tricked, or used. He can only be destroyed."

"And what if he catches you?" Peter asked. His eyes were absolutely steady; only his voice shook a little. "If you imagine he would not torture you, then you have forgotten all you ever knew of him."

"I haven't," Lucas answered. "And he would also torture Elena or our man Cooper, or any of our other operatives, if he caught them. I know all the arguments, and I'm as afraid as you are. I don't know whether I could stand torture or not. They can dose you with all

---

sorts of things that make you do anything they want. You could wake up and not know what you have told them. And I know too much to let that happen. I'm an old man. And far more afraid of failing, of unintentionally betraying my own people, and all I believe in, than I am of dying."

"Meaning you'll, what, shoot yourself?"

"Not the most likely solution. I could miss, just be horribly wounded but still alive. I'll take a gun, of course." He made up his mind as he spoke. "And I'll take a few pills, the sort that act immediately. And I'll put them in different places, so that I can access them before they can remove them. Don't argue, Peter. I'm right, and you know it as well as I do. The only complete failure is not to try. I will tell Josephine before I go. And when I come back, I'll tell her whatever I think wisest. If I don't come back, you must tell her what she wants to know. Above all, tell her why I went."

"For—" Peter started, and then he met Lucas's gaze and knew that anything else said would only make it more difficult. "I'll get my aide to give you all the things you need."

"Thank you." Lucas gave a brief smile. Then he turned and went out before either of them could express all those thoughts and feelings for which there were no adequate words.

After Lucas received all the papers, gadgets, poisons, and two very small but deadly guns from Morrison, an MI6 quartermaster, he went home. It had been a long time since he had taken a flight across the Channel, and even longer since he had knowingly put his life at risk, understanding that he might not return.

He arrived home carrying a small case such as might be filled with business papers. He opened the front door. Toby heard his footsteps and came charging down the hall, throwing himself at Lucas. Josephine always told him not to behave like this, and so did Lucas, echoing Josephine's words, but their tone totally robbed them of meaning, and that is what Toby understood.

Lucas bent down and patted the dog, then held him tightly, until he struggled to pull away. The moment he succeeded he came straight back for more.

Lucas heard Josephine's footsteps. It was time to tell her. He looked up.

She was at the far end of the hall, walking toward him slowly. She stopped. Her face was very pale. "Elena?" Her voice cracked.

Lucas straightened up. "No. As far as I know, she's fine." He saw how her body relaxed, some of the fear slipping away, and guilt seized him.

He stood up straighter, one hand resting on Toby's head. "This isn't about the scientists, Jo. It's about Johann Paulus."

Her eyes widened. "Get to the purpose, please, Lucas."

"If they capture our agent taking out the first scientist, he'll be tortured, and he may reveal that a second scientist is also being brought out."

"Elena."

"She may already be well away; we don't know yet."

She was uncharacteristically quiet.

He, too, said nothing, trying to think of a decent way to reveal the next step. "Jo, I'm going to Germany . . . tonight. And no, Peter isn't sending me. I choose to go. I will not have to seek Paulus—he will find me."

"Don't play games with me, Lucas. You're going there to kill him!" There was neither praise nor blame in her voice, nor in her eyes.

He hesitated only an instant. This was not the time for lies, even by implication. "Yes. If he has the names of any of our agents—which we believe is the case—he'll torture them for information, and then kill them."

"Why do you think you can even get to Paulus?" she asked. She looked at him steadily. "Please, either tell me the entire truth, or say nothing. You are going to Germany to do a young man's job. And, my love, you are not young."

"I caused his downfall, and deliberately. I won't have to look for him. The moment he knows I'm there, and he *will* know, he'll come looking for me."

She drew in a deep breath and let it out again slowly. "Can we discuss this in the garden?"

There was nothing to discuss, but he agreed. "Come on, Toby." He led the way through the room and opened the French door. The perfume of roses and heat wafted in. He breathed deeply, then stepped outside. Toby came on his heels and turned to face him, looking up. "No, we're not going for a walk," he said. "Not now."

Should he take a long look at the roses growing round the door leading to the garden? Or walk on the lawn, and see the last sunlight on the tops of the elms? Take Toby for a walk? Should he even think of such things? They were vivid in his mind. Not only the look, but the sound of the wind in the leaves, the smell of the earth. This could be the last time he stood there, the last time he saw Josephine. He tried to shake off these thoughts, but it was impossible. He needed to focus on Paulus, and all he could remember of the man's nature, his intelligence, his tenacity.

And what about his weaknesses? The most important to remember was his pride! Paulus could take loss—every soldier had to, sometime or other—he could endure pain. He was master of his own fears. Unless he had changed a lot, however, there was nobody he cared for enough to make him vulnerable. Unlike Lucas.

He saw the pain in Josephine's face. If there was any way he could have taken this pain from her, protected her, this would be the moment to do it.

"I understand," she said quietly. She took a long breath. "What time is the car coming for you? Soon?"

"No point in putting it off. I'll sleep on the plane."

"Can I pack for you?"

His throat was tight. "I'll get my case from the study. Keep Toby from following me." He stopped.

It was quite late in the afternoon that a staff officer came to tell Hans that he was required to report to the Führer immediately. Hans obeyed, following the officer along the many passages and courtyards leading to Hitler's office. He knocked and was told to enter by a voice he recognized as Paulus's. He felt a wave of relief that he would not have to face Hitler alone. He gave the traditional salute. *"Heil Hitler!"*

As always, Hitler was standing in the middle of the room. His skin was pale, but his cheeks flushed. His eyes were feverishly bright.

"Well done," Hitler said to Hans. "Excellent. General Paulus has reminded me that you behaved with total loyalty in Munich."

"Yes, sir." Hans knew better than to say anything more.

"Good. Good. We need more men like you. I have just seen President Hindenburg."

Hans waited. Hitler's face was filled with life, with emotion, almost excitement, as if he had at last gained a hard-won victory. What had President Hindenburg said? Would they ever know? Did Hindenburg even understand what had happened?

Hitler was staring at Hans.

Hans looked back, focusing on Hitler's cheek; not looking away, but not meeting his eyes either. That might be taken for insolence.

"We have much to do," Hitler went on. "General Paulus recommends that I promote you. Lieutenant Beckendorff Weissman, you are now Captain Beckendorff." He glanced at Paulus. "You hear that, Beckendorff?"

Hans stood even straighter. "Yes, sir. Thank you, sir."

"Right. Good. We let the Brownshirts get far too out of control. This must never happen again. We must keep a much tighter hand on them. Divide them up. Discipline them, or they could bring down the whole government. You see that?"

"Yes, sir." Hans wondered why on earth Hitler was asking him this. Did he need assurance? Was he testing his loyalty again? Hans had the uncomfortable feeling that Paulus knew exactly what was happening, and that he had prompted it.

"We have much to do," Hitler repeated, now looking intently at Hans as if awaiting his response.

"Traitors who are enemies of the Third Reich," Hans replied. "Of the German people. They're a disease spreading among us." Had he gone too far? He was thinking of the Brownshirts in Munich, the way they treated ordinary people in the street, decent people just trying to survive. To call them enemies of the German people was not an exaggeration.

Hitler turned slowly to face Paulus. He looked him up and down.

Paulus did not move. Hans wondered what he was thinking. Paulus had seen the panic in Hitler before flying down to Munich in the middle of the night. It had been anything but a measured reaction to the discovery of political treason.

Was Hitler remembering that?

Again, Hans warned himself not to meet Hitler's eyes. He was always afraid of appearing challenging or arrogant, and he feared reading in the man's eyes something Hitler could not afford to have him know.

Hitler needed to believe in himself—nobody else could do that for him. The German people needed to hear that Hitler was in charge, that everything was under control. Some part of Hans understood that the Führer was an extraordinary mixture of utter blindness and brilliant perception.

Should he say what was on his mind? Was any praise too extravagant, perhaps suspect of sarcasm? Yet Hitler and Paulus were both waiting for him to say something.

"I am sure you are familiar with the labors of Hercules, sir," Hans began. "This was like the cleansing of the Augean stables. Mere buckets of water won't make any difference. We need to redirect a river through them. Violent, extreme perhaps, in some people's eyes, but necessary." Again, he asked himself if he was going too far. To his own ears, he sounded sycophantic. But when he remembered the disgusting things, the violence and the cruelty he had seen in Munich, the simile was not an exaggeration at all. "It won't need to be done again," he added. "History will remember this."

There was a prickling silence for seconds.

Hitler turned very slowly to Paulus. "You are right, Paulus, he's the promise for the future."

"Yes, sir." Paulus's face was hard, unreadable.

Hans glanced at Paulus's hands, held rigidly by his sides. He could see his left hand, a half-clenched fist, as if Paulus was aching to lash out, but there was no one to strike.

Paulus was speaking to Hans, staring at him.

"Yes, sir," Hans said swiftly, even though he had missed what had been said. He saluted Hitler, and followed Paulus out of the room and back to his own office.

It was early the following afternoon, and Hans was in Paulus's office when a messenger arrived. He was a thin, ordinary-looking man who might have been a clerk or a salesman in some shop. He was as inconspicuous as one could possibly be, and had no military manner at all, no command about him. He could have been any age between thirty-five and fifty.

Nevertheless, Paulus was willing to see him immediately. He even looked anxious to do so. "Yes?" he said, without dismissing Hans. The man glanced at Hans with eyebrows raised, as if in question, but he did not speak.

"What is it?" Paulus demanded.

The man took a deep breath before replying.

Hans felt a sudden chill, like a premonition. This man had come without warning or permission. And yet he knew Paulus would listen to him.

"Sir." The man did not stand to attention, or make any kind of a salute. "A plane landed from England yesterday evening, quietly. One of its passengers caught a local train to Berlin very early this morning."

"Spit it out, man! Who?" Paulus snapped.

The man stared at Paulus without blinking. "Lucas Standish, sir."

There was silence for a second, two, three.

"Are you sure?" Paulus said at last. "He must be in his seventies, at least."

"Yes, sir, I'm sure," the man answered. "I wouldn't have troubled you with a mere possibility. I have photographs, if you would like to see."

"Yes, yes, I would." Paulus put out his hand.

The man began to place several prints on the desk. Paulus snatched them up and stared at them. As he searched them one by one, a curious succession of emotions crossed his face. Disbelief, concentration, slow understanding, then a hard, bitter hatred overtaking everything else. He looked up at the man. "Thank you. You did the right thing. Who else have you told?"

"No one, sir." The man's voice was without expression, as was his face.

Paulus's jaw hardened till the muscle stood out on his neck. "No one at all?" he demanded. "Who took these photographs? Or developed them? Who might they have told?"

"I took them myself, and I developed them. I told no one. It is up to you, sir, if you wish to tell anyone. Or not."

Paulus took a deep breath and let it out slowly. "Good. Very good. Yes, I will choose who to tell. Or not. Well done, Brecht. I will not forget this service. You may go."

"Yes, sir. Thank you, sir."

Before the man could take his leave, Paulus said, "I shall mention your name to the Führer. He, too, will be very pleased."

"Thank you, sir." The man gave a rapid salute. *"Heil Hitler."* Then he turned and went out of the room, closing the door gently behind him.

Hans stood waiting. Paulus was looking at the photographs again and his face was filled with rage, and some other deep emotion that burned up not like fire, but like acid. Then, slowly, Hans watched as that expression seeped away and an ugly smile spread in its place.

Paulus turned to Hans and held out one of the pictures.

Hans took it and looked at it. It was an elderly man, gray-haired, with a slight stoop. He was lean, his face aquiline, with a strong nose and what looked to be a penetrating gaze from light eyes, blue or gray—in a black-and-white photograph it was impossible to tell. He was walking toward the camera, but not looking at it. In fact, he seemed unaware of it entirely. His expression was mild, even benign.

Paulus was watching Hans intently. He passed him a second photograph.

Hans took it and studied it carefully. It was the same man, but from a different angle. It was possible this time to see his profile. He looked up at Paulus. "Is this Standish, sir?"

"Don't you know?" Paulus look faintly surprised.

"No, sir. I've never seen him."

"Are you sure?" Paulus asked, searching Hans's face.

"I don't recognize him, sir." Should he apologize?

"So, you have not met him." Paulus was gazing at him intently, the lines of his face drawn tight.

"Not that I can remember, sir."

"Good. Good. Then perhaps he does not know you. Sometimes, I forget how young you are!" It was a throwaway remark, with an edge of condescension in it.

Hans did not answer. He held out the two photographs.

Paulus shook his head sharply. "Keep them. Study them. I want you to know that man when you meet him. There is no room whatsoever for mistakes. With him, one error could cost you your life. And more importantly, your mission."

"My mission, sir?"

"Yes. You are to meet him. I will tell you where and when."

"Yes, sir." A heaviness was settling over Hans, like a darkness shutting out the light.

Paulus stared at him, his eyes hard and cold, like river stones. "He is my enemy. And yours. Lucas Standish was head of British Military Intelligence during the war. But then, we've been through this, yes?"

Nausea was building in Hans's stomach. "And what do I say to him, sir?" He was on guard. What could Paulus want him to tell this man?

"Say anything you like," Paulus replied. "Anything—it doesn't matter."

Hans felt heat rise up in his face, and a viselike squeeze to his heart.

Paulus was smiling. "Oh, and one little thing," he said. "When you meet him, you are to bring him to me, and then you are to kill him."

Hans felt the vise tighten until he feared his heart would stop altogether.

"I've seen over the last few days what promise you have," Paulus went on. "But, of course, if you manage to kill an ex-head of MI6, that would be an achievement above all others. And since he is a personal enemy of mine, I should be grateful to you. But should you fail in this mission, I shall see that your family is taken care of. Your wife and a daughter." There was something gleeful, and terrible, in his voice.

Hans was in a nightmare. This could not be true. Paulus was asking him to murder, in cold blood, a man who used to be head of British Military Intelligence. "Would he not be more use to us alive?"

Paulus stared at him. "Don't be stupider than you have to be! Do you imagine he will tell us anything of use? If the British caught me, I would tie them in so many knots of truth and lies it would take them years to work them out."

"Is he as clever as you are?" Hans asked, and then knew instantly that it was a mistake. Somebody had beaten Paulus toward the end of the war. Beaten him badly. It was still spoken of in whispers, and even suppressed laughter. Hans knew better than to try to repair his mistake. And now he knew with a certainty that it had been Standish. "I'm sure you wouldn't tell them anything, except inaccurate information that would damage them, sir. And I'm sure that this Standish is not as subtle as you are." He despised himself for heaping praise on Paulus that he did not mean.

Paulus's lip curled a little. "No, he's not. He's grown soft. And he's old now. Much older than I am."

Hans dared not say anything more, in case he made another mistake. With Paulus, he had no chance of getting away with it twice. He felt the sweat run down his body, first hot and then cold.

"We need to do a lot of housecleaning, Beckendorff. We got rid of Röhm and quite a few of his closest lieutenants, and some political traitors as well. The others will see what happens to enemies of the Führer." He was staring at Hans now, as if he required an answer.

"Yes, sir," Hans said. He wasn't sure if he was agreeing, or merely acknowledging that he had heard.

"There are great things ahead of us, Beckendorff. At the top is the founding of a Third Reich, which will last more than a thousand years. Don't you think?"

This time, he was sure that Paulus required an answer. "Yes, sir!"

"Good, so you do see that!" There was a flicker of laughter behind the man's flat, clear eyes. "Then the next step is to get rid of Lucas Standish." He licked his lips, an extraordinarily obscene gesture.

Hans felt dizzy, as if he were losing his balance. He would not have been surprised to see the floor rise up and strike him.

"What are you waiting for?" Paulus demanded. He gestured toward the door.

"Sir?"

"Either you kill Standish, or we will kill your wife and daughter. Your baby is a girl, isn't she?"

Hans's mouth was dry. He struggled for words and could not speak. He tried to draw breath and failed. The room spun, as if he were falling.

It was a nightmare, worse than any dream of skin-crawling horror. He fought down hysteria. He thought of holding his baby in his arms. She trusted him with her life. This was more appalling than anything he had imagined. It was worse than his own death.

He stood straight up. "Yes, sir." He looked straight at Paulus. "I'll find Mr. Standish."

Paulus nodded slowly. "Good. Good. And, Hans, remember what it will cost you if you fail."

Hans left the office, closing the door behind him, and then followed the passage to the men's room. Please God, it was empty.

He walked inside. The mirrors all reflected him, bright lights hurting his eyes. For a moment he thought he was going to vomit. No, he must get control of himself and think! Plan!

He drew in a deep breath. Then he took a drink of cold water directly from the tap and swallowed it with an effort. Slowly, it became clear what he must do. He must save Madeleine, at any cost.

E lena was struggling to stay awake when she and Jacob finally drew into the car park of a small hotel just off the main road. To their intense relief, they found there were two small rooms available, even at this late hour. They both needed sleep, even more than food.

Jacob paid the bill in advance and was handed two keys. Wordlessly, he gave one of them to Elena.

She nodded and made an attempt to smile. As soon as they were sufficiently far from the desk, she stopped. "I wish we could call the police, or someone who will go and . . . ." She swallowed hard. Her throat was too tight to continue. Her eyes filled with tears. She had voiced this several times since they had left Hartwig's body near the highway, even though she understood how impractical—and potentially dangerous—it would be. "It's the night animals," she started, then her voice broke. She was embarrassed. "I'm sorry. That's so amateur, I know. Still . . ."

She drew a shuddering breath, almost obsessed with the ugly thought of Hartwig being unrecognizable, once those animals got to him. She knew how the scientist would respond to her fears, were he standing before her. He would tell her that millions had died on the battlefields of war, soldiers whose families would not have recognized what was left of them. Some were buried, some were not. He was no exception.

Elena turned away from Jacob, determined to get her emotions together and behave like an adult.

Jacob took her arm and held it for a moment, and she was glad of it.

"I've got an alarm clock," he said quietly. "I'll waken you in the morning." His face softened. "Sleep, Elena. I can't make that an order, but your bosses would, and you know that."

"Yes, I do know. And you, too." She drew a deep breath. "Jacob . . ."

"What?"

"Thank you. I know you are doing this not for me, but because it's right. But thank you all the same."

He smiled, and said nothing, leaving her to find his own room.

Her room was small, but clean. And the door locked from the inside, which made her feel safer. She thought of a hot bath, but while she was sitting on the bed considering it, she lay back and fell asleep.

She had mixed nightmares that slid one into another, each one packed with emotion. But she did not fully waken until sometime toward the early dawn. She got up and went into the bathroom. She washed thoroughly in water that was blissfully hot, then went back to bed and fell asleep again. It was about four in the morning. This time, as she slept, she was too deeply asleep even to dream.

She woke with the room bright with the fully risen sun, and Jacob sitting on the side of her bed, gently rubbing her shoulder. His touch was firm enough, however, that she was forced fully awake.

"Is it already time to leave?" she asked, with her eyes still closed. The sunlight coming in through the thinly curtained windows was too sharp, too bright. She was not yet ready for the danger of the new day, nor to remember that Hartwig was dead and there had been no choice but to leave his body in a copse of trees. They needed to return to Berlin, and not be caught. Jacob, at least, deserved that, whether she did or not.

And then a thought struck her. "Jacob, how did you get into my room?"

"It's not quite time yet," Jacob replied to her first question. "And you left your key in the door but didn't lock it." He held it up in one hand. "It was too easy for me to get in. Don't do that again."

"I'm sorry. I was too tired to think. They could probably pick the lock anyway, or break it." She opened her eyes, blinking against the light. She focused on his face. He looked so much older and drained of life than the young man who had rescued her in Berlin, just over a year ago. That was in another lifetime.

"Elena!" Jacob's voice cut across her thoughts.

"Yes, we must go," she agreed, sitting up slowly. "Let's have breakfast and then we'll drive back to Berlin. We need to tell Dieter that Hartwig is dead. He will see to it that the intel gets to the right place. From there, I suppose I should go home." She realized that his face held far more than just agreement. There was something he had not said. "What?" she demanded.

Jacob's expression barely changed. If anything, it was a little softer. "I don't agree, but I do understand."

She felt her body relax a bit. "I'll get dressed now." She pushed the bedclothes off and stepped onto the floor. She was wearing only her underclothes, but she had long ago ceased to indulge in unnecessary modesty, which actually only drew more attention to herself. In the face of such dangers, it would be absurd, self-centered, and irrelevant.

"I'll get some breakfast to take with us." Jacob stood up. "Fifteen minutes?"

"I'll come down soon, but let's eat here. It won't take long, and it's been quite some time since we sat at a proper table for a meal."

He touched her on the shoulder, gently. "See you at breakfast. It's going to be another long day."

He went out into the hallway, closing the door behind him.

Elena was dressed and downstairs in five minutes.

There were half a dozen other people in the dining room, all seated at one long table, with Jacob settled in among them.

He stood at once and pulled out a chair for her, and then turned to the others and smiled.

Elena forced herself to smile, too. "Good morning," she said, looking at the other guests, three men and three women, although they did not easily fall into pairs. The two elderly ones seemed to be a couple, while the two other women resembled each other in coloring and the bone structure of the faces. Perhaps sisters? The other two men sat apart and seemed to be alone.

Hard-boiled eggs, cheese, and sliced ham were offered around, and there was plenty of fresh dark bread and reasonable portions of butter, providing no one took too much. It was a good breakfast to begin the day, especially with fresh and surprisingly good coffee.

Jacob and Elena helped themselves to everything.

One of the sisters, if indeed they were so, peeled her egg carefully and, staring at the shells on her plate, remarked to no one in particular, "I say the sooner we get home, the better."

"Don't be stupid, Helga!" her sister said sharply. "It was just a few ill-behaved young men causing a fight. They won't be told, so they needed a bit of a sharp discipline. No one is going to bother a couple of women passing through."

"That's not what the papers say," her sister retorted. "They're calling it a massacre!"

"What newspapers?" one of the men asked. There was derision in his face, and he did not bother to hide it. "The Führer is in charge, that's all we need to know. As your friend says, those damn Brownshirts need a bit of discipline. The real thing, not pussyfooting around. Don't be a nuisance to people. Don't drink. Don't swear. Don't pick up street women. They're men, for God's sake!"

"Street women?" The other man looked at him with contempt. "You damn fool, half of them are picking up young men, not women!

Or each other! Hope you don't have a son in that lot! You don't want him assaulted by some drunken oaf, do you?"

"You're being hysterical," the first man accused. "Pull yourself together! If you think the Führer would allow that, you don't know what the hell you're talking about. And you better hold your tongue, before you get yourself in real trouble." He swung round and stared at Jacob. "Know anything about this?"

Jacob pursed his lips for a moment, as if deciding how to respond. "I was there," he said. "That is, my wife and I were. We barely got out of that hotel alive."

"You were there?" asked the man, his eyebrows raised. "My God, tell us!"

Elena froze.

Jacob hesitated only a moment longer, and then he spoke. "It was a whole lot more than a bit of a brawl," he answered, measuring his words, looking from face to face to see their reactions. "The Führer himself was there, too. I heard that he executed Röhm . . . and quite a few others. I think it will be the end of the Brownshirts running wild. Without Röhm in charge, there should be order again." He glanced along the faces, all turned toward him. "I hope so."

The two sisters looked at each other.

The elderly man took his wife's hand.

The man who had last spoken turned his mouth down at the corners. "If the Führer is overthrown, or if he can't keep order, we're finished," he said grimly.

Absurd as it was, Elena could see a certain logic in that. The disciplined behavior of Hitler's forces was better than the chaos of the Brownshirts. Wasn't it?

"They're calling it the Night of the Long Knives," one of the men told them. "Some people say hundreds of men were killed. And it looks as if the Führer is back in control, so we'll be safe now. Order. That's better for everybody."

"Yes, order," the man's wife agreed. "Don't you think so?" She looked at Elena.

"Yes." There was nothing else she could say. "Order. Nothing can be done without order. No one is safe." She felt sententious and idiotic as she said it. There was good order and bad. But perhaps there was only bad chaos. "We can all get back to work."

Jacob put his hand over hers. "It was an excellent breakfast. We must be going."

He did not look at Elena, but she could picture the expression in his eyes, the mixture of laughter and bitterness, perhaps even a grief that must be conquered. At least there was something they could do . . . or try to do.

"Yes, of course." She stood up and spoke to the others, half over her shoulder. "Travel safely." She took Jacob's arm, as any wife would. When they were safely in the car, she would tell him about passing on this vital information to Dieter. And then . . . home.

As they walked out of the hotel, Elena heard the man's voice in her head.

The Night of the Long Knives.

An appropriate name.

CHAPTER 20

The flight from London to Berlin was not a long one, but to Lucas it had seemed both interminable and far too short. Now he sat in his hotel room and reflected on what he had to do.

The idea of killing Paulus revolted him, but he had every intention of doing it. Their relationship could only end when one or the other of them was dead. If Lucas won, it would be a clean, swift death for Paulus. If Paulus won, it would not be a clean kill. He would torture Lucas to learn everything he could from him. The most valuable information with which he could supply Paulus was how much Britain knew about Germany's germ warfare program— not that Lucas would give the intel up, even if it meant losing his life. Paulus would torture Lucas not only to get this information, but for the pleasure of it. The man's need for revenge was insatiable.

Lucas could not afford to lose this battle and allow Paulus to win. If they both lost, that would be bad, but bearable. Lucas had enjoyed a long and honorable career. Not without mistakes, of course. But a career without mistakes was probably a career without risks, one in which he aimed far too low. Lucas had always aimed high. He was wise enough and seasoned enough to understand that his life in itself was not valuable. The value came in what he could accomplish with it.

No matter how he looked at his relationship with Paulus during the war, in the end it all came down to one truth: Lucas had won and Paulus had been disgraced.

But this time would be different.

What could Lucas possibly gain from Paulus? If Lucas lived, what would he take home at the end? The only thing Paulus knew of value concerned the progress being made in the development of germ warfare. If Elena and Alex Cooper got the scientists out of Germany alive, these men would provide far more accurate details than Paulus could ever know.

He was certain that Paulus not only needed to exact his revenge in person—it would be of no value to him if he didn't have the satisfaction of Lucas knowing he was behind it—but above all, Paulus would stop at nothing to learn the state of the British germ warfare program. That was why Lucas carried enough poison on his person for both of them . . . if need be.

When the plane had landed and Lucas had gone into the Customs area with nothing to declare, none of the Customs officers had seemed to take note of him. He did not know whether to be disappointed or to accept that the news of his arrival would reach Paulus discreetly.

From there he had caught a train from the nearby station into Berlin, then taken a taxi to this small hotel where he had booked a room.

His room was at the back of the building, neat and quiet. He had been here before, years ago. The window had its own fire escape down a rickety ladder leading to an alley that provided passage in either direction. Not that he had any expectation of escape. But knowing an escape route was habit and, as such, comforting. The idea of climbing out through the window and trusting his weight, not to mention his balance, to that old ladder would have been funny at any other time. At his age, however, it was worthy of a rueful smile.

It was a long night. He did not expect Paulus to strike immediately. Still, it was difficult to relax, never mind sleep. He must be rested, as wide awake as possible tomorrow. If Paulus did not come for him, he would have to attract his attention. Attack somehow. There was one thing of which he was certain: Paulus would come. Even after that shattering Night of the Long Knives, as the newspapers were calling it, Paulus would be back in Berlin, with Hitler, and he would not be able to resist seeing Lucas himself, probably even killing him himself.

Lucas had no idea how long any of this would last, but he was guessing months, at least, maybe years.

He told himself to stop thinking about it. It would keep him awake, and to no purpose. But he could not sleep.

He turned on the bedside lamp and took out the one book he had brought with him. It was G. K. Chesterton's *The Ballad of the White Horse,* an epic poem that was often by his side. He opened it to where Alfred defeats the invaders, the Danes, at the Battle of Ethandune. Lucas was soon caught up in the story, as well as the cadence. He was always lifted by this ballad, the words quickly morphing into vivid images racing through his mind.

He woke up when the book slipped out of his hands. The light was still on, quite unnecessarily, because it was full daylight. He sat up slowly, his head thumping, his neck stiff. He looked at his watch. It was after seven.

He threw off the covers and stood up. He was stiff. He was a fool to have gone to sleep reading, but at least he had slept.

He shaved, washed, and dressed quickly. Then he went downstairs, taking his packed case with him, and had a hearty breakfast in the dining room. Bacon and eggs, toasted black bread with butter and black cherry jam. At home he had marmalade, but when abroad he always chose the cherry jam. It was one of his favorites, and this one was particularly good. It was rich, full of fruit, and just a little tart.

He drank two cups of coffee. He had no idea when he would eat again.

He had almost finished when a young man came into the dining room. He was a little above average height, fair-haired, blue-eyed. He was not quite handsome. There was something bland about his face, making it difficult for Lucas to read.

The young man glanced around the room and his eyes settled on Lucas. Very slowly, as if he were uncertain of his balance, he walked over to Lucas and stopped. He was wearing the uniform of a Gestapo captain, a high rank for one so young.

"Mr. Standish?" he said very quietly.

Lucas looked up. "Yes?" For a moment he thought he recognized him, but the time or place he had met him escaped his recall. "Do I know you?"

The young man looked even more uncomfortable.

Lucas was certain that he reminded him of someone. Then the memory came back. He had not met him, but had seen him in a photograph from Cecily Cordell's wedding. "Hans . . . something?"

The young man looked even more uncomfortable. "Yes, sir. Will you please come with me, sir, so we do not disturb the other guests?"

Lucas stood up. "You work for General Paulus, I presume?"

"Yes, sir. Please don't make a fuss. It will alert the others."

"And no doubt endanger them," Lucas added. He bent down and picked up his case. He was certain that he would not be coming back to this hotel again.

"Sir, let it go," Hans said sharply, clearly trying to keep his voice low. Nevertheless, there was a distinct edge to it.

"Then will you bring it along for me, please?" Lucas asked. "There is no weapon in it, but you would no doubt be derelict in your duty if you believed me." He gave a brief, regretful smile.

"Yes, sir. Lift it and open it," Hans ordered.

Lucas opened the case and picked out the clean shirt and underwear, as well as the razor, toothbrush, and toothpaste, and the comb. The pen, with its hidden burden of poison, was tucked in his inside breast pocket.

"All right," said Hans. "Close it. You may bring it."

"Thank you. I assume we are going to see General Paulus?"

"Yes, sir. But as I said, please don't make this difficult; people could get hurt."

"I have no wish for anyone to get hurt," Lucas answered. He gave a slight shrug. "At least . . . not yet."

It might have been the shadow of a smile on Hans's face, or perhaps it was the slightest change of an angle in the light. Whichever it was, Lucas walked with him through the hotel dining room, across the lobby, and out of the door to the street easily, as if he had expected it, yet was surprised at the suggestion of sympathy in this young man's response.

This was part of his plan, to be escorted to Paulus. He wondered briefly what the people on the pavement thought of them. Did they see an elderly gentleman walking with a young officer in uniform, perhaps father and son? Or even grandfather? Or were they sufficiently used to it that they saw it for what it was: an elderly, unnamed gentleman probably under arrest?

Lucas and his escort did not speak. The young officer seemed to be troubled, even guilty. Was that because he was taking Lucas to Paulus, who would have him tortured until he had extracted all the information he sought? And was it this young man who would do the torturing? Paulus would prolong this torture in the hope of learning more, and then more, and then a bit longer for the pleasure of it.

Lucas had certainly tortured him in the past! Not physically: such a thing was contrary to international law, as well as his own principles. He strongly believed that there was no point in fighting against someone if the techniques we use make us become just like them. That was the ultimate defeat! And he also believed that torture was useless in obtaining information. More, it was an excuse for the sadistic pleasure of the person who administered it, and it was, in its own way, an admission of failure. Except, in this case, it would be reparation for the mental torture of disgrace that Lucas had meted out to Paulus so many years ago. Despite the passage of time, he was certain it still stung within Paulus. It always would.

Did this young officer realize that if he witnessed a failure on Paulus's part, his own future was jeopardized? He might see small failures, and get away with it. But Paulus was, above all things, proud. If Paulus tortured Lucas, and still learned nothing of use, and in the end killed him, would this young man be allowed to survive to re-peat it to anyone else? Only if Lucas had told some clever lies that Paulus believed. Then he would not lose face in front of his young officer.

What was his one hope of surviving? Feeding Paulus false infor-mation, with the tacit promise that there was more to come? And he passionately wanted to survive! More than he had expected, or had even taken into account. He wanted to walk the harvest fields that were scattered with blood-red poppies, reminders of the last war and all the young men who had paid the ultimate price. But could the inheritance of those same men now preserve the peace that they had paid for so dearly? And he wanted to live to be greeted by To-by's enthusiasm to see him. Above all, he wanted to see Josephine, spend hours talking, and still more hours in silent understanding, sharing without needing to speak. And Elena? Would she come home safely? To him, she would always be the child he had loved so dearly, who had trusted him without hesitation.

They rode in silence, Hans Beckendorff driving carefully through Berlin, and Lucas Standish breathing deeply, attempting to remain relaxed, despite what he suspected awaited him.

They arrived at a small office above what appeared to be a dis-used brickyard. The place was on a surprisingly busy street. Once through the main gate, however, it was a world apart.

The young officer pushed open the door after a brief knock, and then shoved Lucas in ahead of him.

The room was small, the windows filthy and cracked in several places. The floor was thick with dust and pieces of broken plaster and shards of glass. It smelled of heat and animal waste.

Johann Paulus was standing in the middle of the room, dressed in uniform, but without his jacket with its medals and insignia. Lucas saw it hanging over the back of a chair, the only piece of furniture in the room.

Paulus looked heavier than the last time he and Lucas had met. He had more bulging around the middle. His hair was thinner, and there was a lot of gray in it. He also looked far stronger, physically, than Lucas had ever been. At the same time, he had changed little. He was still heavily jowled, broad-nosed, his skin a little florid.

It was far too hot in this small, airless room, and he was sweating; it stood out on his forehead, and his shirt was stained with it.

It was clear to Lucas that his adversary oozed satisfaction. He could even smell it in the stale air.

"Well, well, Standish!" he said in English, looking Lucas up and down. "You look old! What have you come for? I have a list of all your men here in Berlin. I'll strike when I want. But you know who they are already, don't you? Isn't that why you've come? But what use is that to you? They are all in peril."

As Paulus had just done, Lucas looked him up and down slowly. "You've grown fat, Johann," he said. "Really fat."

"Life is good," Paulus said. If he was insulted, he refused to show it. "I'm in charge of a very interesting part of Intelligence. Germ warfare. But perhaps you knew that?"

"I had heard."

"Is that why you're here? To see what we are doing?" Paulus sounded interested.

"One of the reasons," Lucas conceded.

It was as if the years between them had been a long hiatus, and little more than a space filled with dreams. That was all they were: beautiful dreams. But now both men were fully awake, not even pretending that they were at peace, or had a common aim. No more dreams.

Lucas knew that he must keep Paulus talking. At the moment, they were standing seven or eight feet apart, and the young Gestapo captain with the gun on his hip was close enough to shoot Lucas before he could get the poison-filled fountain pen out of his pocket, let alone stab Paulus with it. Actually, one scratch would be fatal, but even that was impossible, positioned as they were. If he kept speaking, it might not only engage Paulus's attention, but also allow the young captain to relax. Whatever happened, it would be better, faster, if the captain shot him before he could be tortured. And there certainly was no point in regretting anything now. The die was cast.

"And the other reasons?" Paulus asked. He seemed to be in no hurry. No one would find them here; the place was obviously abandoned. Even the air was old. Nothing moved except the occasional fly; nothing disturbed the layers of dust.

"The reason?" Lucas asked. "To see for myself if you were lean and hungry, or if you were satisfied."

Paulus's features relaxed into a momentary smile. "I'm satisfied," he answered. "I'm surprised you came yourself. Did you think . . . ? No, I'm sure you knew that I'd be told the moment you landed. You know me so well. But did you think that I'd send somebody else, instead of coming myself?" He did not glance at Hans, but gestured very slightly in his direction. "You didn't know this young man here. He's a very promising officer. Could go far. Ironic, isn't it? His father-in-law is a longtime friend of yours. Did you know that? It makes you and me almost related."

His smile was wide now, showing his teeth, strong, like an animal's. "What shall I tell you about our germ warfare? What would you like to know?"

"Only what I don't know already," Lucas replied, keeping his voice level. "Dangerous stuff, germ warfare. No handle to hold it with. Before you spread it, you'd better be damn sure you can protect your own people!"

Paulus froze. It was only for a second, but it gave him away.

"I see," Lucas said quietly. "You haven't perfected that yet. Not even close to it, by the expression on your face."

"Neither have you," Paulus said. "You don't even know which direction to look!"

Lucas admitted it. "If we are looking at the same nature of illness, it's not who perfects it first, it's who perfects the antidote. I presume you can see that for yourself." From the look on Paulus's face, Lucas was not sure at all that Paulus had realized the necessity. But he did now! "And your scientists . . . how are they doing?"

Paulus waved away the question, making Lucas wonder if he even knew that Hartwig and Fassler were on the run.

"Two or three hundred deaths from our germ agents will be enough to terrify your people into submission," Paulus replied. "And they will know it came from us! Germs are brilliant warfare. But fear is even better." He smiled very slightly. "Fear paralyzes people, don't you agree? If they believe that this germ causes hemorrhagic fever, where they bleed and it can't be stopped, they'll pay attention! Imagine it, Lucas, blood from all over their bodies? And they won't know who will be next? And . . . no way to protect against it!"

Lucas struggled to remain silent. Was this the truth? If so, Paulus told him because he had no intention of allowing him ever to leave this building. The torture he intended was not only going to be physical, but it was in the imagination as well! Lucas could not suppress his thoughts. The warning of the terror and grief that would spread from one person to twenty thousand, and then to a million—and possibly even more—was enough to bring a country to its knees. And was this germ the kind to create disease for other species, crossing boundaries? Rats were infamous for carrying the fleas of bubonic plague, the Black Death. Lucas had read about how the night carts had carried bodies away, until more than a quarter of the entire population of the known world had perished.

"Fool!" Paulus said angrily. "We won't use it until we have an antidote!"

Lucas took a deep breath. "Perhaps the Americans will carpet-bomb you, to be sure to destroy the germ. Fire is probably the only thing that will kill it for certain."

Paulus was visibly shaken. "Don't be stupid! We'll contain it."

"Do you think you can?" Lucas answered. "While you're destroying most of the world? Or is that your intention? Nobody wins? Your victory is that you are the last to lose?"

"I wondered how you would react," Paulus said with a slow smile. "I have almost half a mind to let you go back home and spread this around. The fear," he quickly added. "Not the disease."

"You can't afford to have your men die of it either," Lucas countered. "Those who survive your purges, that is. Of course, you just killed a lot of them yourself, didn't you? Mutiny, was it?"

Paulus let out his breath. "Night of the Long Knives? Yes, we got rid of the rotten portion of Röhm's army. And of Röhm himself, of course. Think of it as ridding our country of garbage," he said bitterly. "You'll have to do that one day. Except you haven't the stomach for it."

"Fish rots from the head, Johann, maybe you don't know that." He was surprised to see the mixture of emotions in his adversary's face.

"The Führer will win," Paulus said softly, between his teeth. "He's the perfect leader for the time. I'm telling you any of this only because I won't allow you to return to England." He smiled again. "Did you think I would? Or did you mean to kill me? But I'm faster and stronger than you are. And I know you haven't a gun, or even a knife. Were you going to bore me to death?" He smiled more widely at his own joke. But the sweat was running down his face. This was not going to last much longer.

Lucas said nothing.

"Did you really think I would let you go?" Paulus repeated, but this time his voice was taunting, cruel.

Lucas saw standing before him a man filled with the hatred of the years, the short victories of the war, and the long losses between. "No," he said honestly. "Unless you told me something that would be a major harm to us, or misinformation so believable that I would carry it back to my government and create chaos, only then would you let me go. I believe you're telling me now because it pleases you. That is, to tell me of my death in advance, when I can't do anything about it. It's brief revenge for my victory the last time we crossed swords. You lost, and you let it eat at your soul. Revenge is only sweet if the victim knows that you are behind it."

A flash of rage lit Paulus's face. "You speak as if you know! Did you come over here hoping to beat me again? Stupid! Stupid! It isn't hemorrhagic fever we're working on at all. We only let your spies think that it is."

"Really?" Lucas said skeptically.

"We aren't stupid enough to start that!" The color became even higher in his face. "We know we'll never find a way of preventing it from spreading round the whole world. What we have is a variant of the Spanish flu, but even more deadly. However, you won't tell anyone that, because you are not going home." He looked around them. "This filthy hole is going to be your last resting place." He ran a finger across his upper lip to remove the sweat. "No one will find you, because no one will look. The feral cats will probably discover you, because they're always on the prowl for fresh meat. And the rats, of course. Vile little beasts, they'll even eat carrion. At first, your family will worry why you did not come home. But eventually they will realize that it's because you are dead. Or maybe I'll tell them. I would like that." He turned around to Hans. "Captain Beckendorff?"

Hans squared his shoulders. "Sir!"

"Shoot him," said Paulus. "Shoot him . . . dead."

Lucas wondered why he was asking this young man to do it, rather than doing it himself. To implicate him, of course. The protection of having him equally guilty.

Lucas turned to look at the young man. It would make no difference, of course, but he preferred to watch what this soldier was
about to do.

Hans removed the gun from its holster and gripped it firmly, his
hands not shaking at all. He raised it, took a few steps forward, and
pointed it directly at Lucas's forehead.

Lucas forced himself to keep his eyes open, as he silently said
goodbye to Josephine.

Hans stared at Lucas, his eyes narrowed. And then, in one swift
move, he swung round and fired.

Paulus had no time to register surprise. The bullet went straight
into his brain. He was dead before his body crumpled onto the
rubbish-littered floor.

Lucas gasped, and then let out his breath into a long silence.

"Sir," Hans said, his voice catching in his throat. "I think we had
better go out the back way. And rather quickly, if you don't mind."

"Yes, yes, I think so, too," Lucas agreed. He had no idea what this
young man intended to do. And what was more alarming, he did not
think the young man had any idea either. "Thank you," Lucas added.

CHAPTER 21

For the first few seconds after Paulus crumpled to the floor and lay motionless, Hans remained frozen. He stared at his gun for a long moment and then turned to Lucas. "We had better leave," he repeated, his voice astonishingly steady, even firm. It was far from what he felt. This was not the first time he had killed a man. The act was irrevocable. Not that he wanted to revoke it! But he must not get caught. What would Cecily and Madeleine do without him to protect them? And what would the Germans do to Cecily and their baby if they identified Hans as the killer? His little family were the most important people in his life.

He also needed to get Lucas Standish out of here. What the hell had the man really come for anyway? Was it worth his life? Paulus would have more than one copy of the list of British operatives. Surely Standish would know that? But perhaps killing Paulus would give the British time to warn them all, time to escape.

Maybe Lucas Standish had come to Germany not to learn what Paulus knew about MI6 agents, but with the sole intent of killing him. But he had no gun, Hans was certain of that. And he was an old

man. Even in his prime, he would have been no physical match for
Paulus. Had he learned anything from this visit to Berlin he did not
already know? Perhaps his purpose had been to give Paulus false
information? Did he not know that Paulus would kill him if given
the chance? And if not given it, then would he create it . . . seize it?

"We've got to get out of here. To an airport, I suppose. Out of
Germany. I don't know how long we have before someone discovers
the general's body." He swallowed hard. He was beginning to shake.

"Hold the gun steady," Lucas told him. "Or put it in its holster, if
you wish. If anyone stops us, you have to get your story straight."

Lucas looked as if he was about to continue, then changed his
mind.

Hans wondered if he had done this sort of thing before. This man
was the former head of MI6. The man who, during the war, had been
responsible for Paulus's final disgrace. Those who had known about
this, and who disliked Paulus, took less-than-secret pleasure in his
exposure to mockery. It was like pouring hot water on skin already
burned. Hans knew that Paulus never forgot. Even more chilling, he
was a man who could never forgive. Not . . . anything.

But that was no longer his concern: the bastard was dead.

"Yes," Hans said, reaffirming it to himself. "Can you drive? I
haven't got handcuffs to make you look to be under arrest. If I've got
my hands on the steering wheel and my eyes on the road, and we're
stopped, anyone will see that you're not my prisoner." He wanted to
laugh. It was all so absurd. Except that the air was stifling in this hot,
dirty room, and there was a body sprawled on the floor with a bullet
hole in his forehead that had hardly bled at all. Paulus looked short
and fat, with no spirit in him, no anger, no pride.

"Come on," Lucas said briskly. "We can't wait here any longer."

They walked out into the sun, a uniformed officer with an elderly
gentleman he had apparently arrested. People might assume it was
just another Jew.

Hans was surprised to find so many people on the street, and
relieved that no one seemed to take notice of them.

They climbed into the car, Lucas driving and following Hans's directions.

"We should be at the Berlin airport within the hour," said Hans, his voice tight with anxiety. "There are many flights to London. Or Paris, if necessary, then a connecting flight to London."

"It's been a long time since I've done this," said Lucas. "Been on the run, that is. I haven't been in the field for years. Since just after the war, actually. Time is a strange thing. Sometimes those years seem like a different century. At other times, it's only the day before yesterday."

Hans tried to keep his mind off the burning question regarding what he was going to do after he had seen this Englishman onto an airplane that would take him back to his own country and freedom.

It was an hour's drive and uninterrupted by any events. There was nothing remarkable about two men driving out of the city and into the hot, still countryside.

They were on the outskirts of the city when they were stopped at what seemed to be a security check. Hans could feel his heart lurch. When the traffic policeman stood at the driver's window and spoke, Hans was prepared to answer. He leaned closer to Lucas so the policeman would recognize his Gestapo uniform. He had to establish that Lucas was not in charge. He drew in breath to speak, but his whole mouth was dry, his voice stuck somewhere in his throat.

By a stroke of fortune, the policeman noticed Hans's insignia of rank before words were spoken. He looked startled. "Sir. Captain . . ." he began.

"It's all right, Officer," Hans said, forcing himself to speak. "You did the right thing. You have to stop everyone. I am escorting this gentleman, to be certain that he reaches his destination. I commend your thoroughness." He stopped. He saw the hesitation in the policeman's face, and then the relief.

"Thank you, sir." The policeman stepped back, signaling the car ahead to move to one side.

Lucas drove forward, accepting the efforts by this policeman to give him free passage, skirting ahead of the others who were in their cars watching. Only Hans, sitting beside him, could see his white knuckles on the steering wheel.

"Poor soul," Lucas said very softly. "I hope he never knows what he has done."

"So do I!" Hans said fervently. Sweat was running down his torso and leaving dark stains on his uniform. His mind raced with frantic thoughts of what his next move would be, after Standish was safely deposited at the airport.

"You will have to do a lot of things differently now," Lucas said.

Hans understood too well that his life, in the past minutes, had changed irrevocably. He closed his eyes and took a deep breath.

They reached the airport and Hans stood a few feet from Lucas, who was at the ticket desk and asking about flights leaving for the United Kingdom.

"The next flight out is to Edinburgh," said the agent.

Lucas thanked the clerk, said that would do excellently, and arranged for his seat.

"You need to go quickly to the gate," said the man, handing him a ticket. "Passengers are already boarding."

Lucas turned and gave Hans a smile, and also a gesture that some could have interpreted as a salute. When the young man nodded, Lucas turned and walked toward the boarding gate.

Hans drove onto the main highway but chose a circuitous route back to Berlin. It was less busy, so in the end perhaps just as quick. The thoughts that had been forming in his head began to take definite shape. Lucas Standish would be over the North Sea very soon, and safe. But Hans was anything but safe. Whatever he did personally was almost irrelevant. If he was identified as Paulus's killer, his wife and daughter would be in terrible danger. They could become hostages . . . or worse. Their lives were far more important to him than his own, and he would do anything to save them.

But he also must save himself. Without him, who would look after Cecily and Madeleine? Who would love them unconditionally, listen to them, teach them, hold them when they were frightened, when they wept, encourage them when they faltered, always believe in them, listen to all their dreams? That was his job, his purpose above all others. And he must survive in order to do it.

Was it possible that he was already being sought? Surely no one had found Paulus so soon. But it had been more than an hour! Even though that warehouse area was deserted, anyone off the streets could have sought refuge there.

With fear growing that the police might be looking for him, he gripped the steering wheel and drove as quickly as was legal and safe toward Berlin.

The minute he was near the city, he parked near a train station and found a public telephone. As he placed the call, his hands were shaking.

Winifred Cordell answered after the fourth ring, very politely, as an ambassador's wife should.

Hans had rehearsed what he was going to say. "Mother-in-law? This is Hans. I cannot tell you the reason, but please believe me, this is necessary." His voice was shaking. He must make her not only believe him, but understand, even feel frightened.

"There has been a very serious event," he countered. "I can't tell you about it now, but I must ask you . . . beg you . . . to go to Cecily at once and persuade her, however you do it, to put into a suitcase a few clothes for herself, and everything Madeleine needs for a few days. Also, clean underwear and clothes for me."

He was speaking too quickly, but he could not help himself.

"And my shaving kit and hairbrush," he went on. "And tell Cecily to get ready to leave. Our lives depend on it and . . . be quick! Don't tell anyone! Please, just do it!"

"Hans! Are you all right?" Her voice was almost steady.

He could imagine her standing with the phone in one hand, white-faced, frightened, making herself not show it. He used to wonder what Roger Cordell saw in her. She seemed so cool. No, cold! And so English. Only after quite a while was he able to see the stoicism, and the tenderness underneath. Perhaps, in a way, it was more interesting, and longer lasting, to discover a person slowly. Lately, he was seeing more and more qualities in Cecily that came from her mother: a grace, an unfading politeness, a quiet pleasure in certain things of beauty, a stillness of heart. Maybe Madeleine would be like that when she grew into a woman. That must happen, that she could grow into womanhood! He must not even allow his mind to imagine any other possibility.

"Mother-in-law . . . Winifred . . . I'm safe, but none of us will stay safe if we don't leave Germany as soon as possible. Promise me, please." How could he tell her this without frightening her? And betraying all of them. He held his breath, not knowing what else to add.

"Are you sure you're all right?" she asked again.

"I'm not hurt, but you must call Cecily at once; we have to leave. There's no other choice. And tell no one else, except Roger. Promise me! No one else at all! Not"—the words had to be forced out—"not anyone who might call from my office, inquiring about me. And not a word to my parents, under any circumstance."

"And if Cecily asks me why?"

"Tell her . . ." What should he say? He would have to tell her one day. It might as well be now. "General Paulus is dead. Once they start to investigate, I will be blamed. I should be home in an hour, maybe less. She must be ready. We haven't a minute to spare."

"I'll do this now. And . . . be careful, Hans." The weight of emotion in her voice reminded him that she had lived through war.

"I will look after them. I promise you," he added, his voice nearly a cry.

"I know you will."

He made an instant decision. "Is Roger at home?"

"No. He's at the embassy. Do you need him?"

"I need papers for Cecily and Madeleine. Does she need a passport? She's only two months old."

"I'll find out. Do you need one, too?"

"Yes. And . . . not in my name."

"I understand. I'll get Roger to see to it. At the embassy, they can do that quickly and—" She stopped abruptly.

He knew what she was about to say: that they had done this for Jews. To smuggle them out of the country. And why had she stopped and lapsed into silence before letting him know that? Did she really fear he would betray it? Yes, obviously she did. He could hardly blame her.

"If Roger can get the documents to Cecily before I arrive, it would increase our chance of safety. I'm coming home now." There was a pause, and then he quickly added, "I'm going to leave my car at the train station and take a train. I'll get a cab from the station to the house, so I'll need a car."

"Will you drive out of Germany? I'd think a train would be safer."

Hans thought about this for a moment. "Yes, a train."

"I'll arrange it all," said Winifred. "Everything will be ready very soon."

"Thank you. And Winifred—you should have Roger draw up papers for the two of you as well." He ended the call before she could reply.

He heard a train in the distance. It was time to go to the platform. He dared not miss the train. He bought a ticket, and then a newspaper at the kiosk. Not because he wanted to read it, but because he needed something to look down at, so he could hide his face.

The train was exactly on time. He felt stiff and clumsy as it pulled up, but there was no question about whether to board it or not. He had to, even if it was risky. Hopefully, no one would be looking for him here. Not yet.

The train arrived in central Berlin and Hans hailed a taxi. After a ride that felt interminable, he paid the driver and climbed out. He waited until the man drove away, drew a deep breath, let it out slowly, then walked the few yards to his own front door. He had the key in his hand, but before he could place it in the lock, the door swung open and he found Winifred standing in the hallway, white-faced but composed. She looked him up and down, as if to satisfy herself that he was not hurt. She smiled briefly, fear in her eyes. She stepped back and he followed her in, closing the door behind him.

"I'm sorry," he said, and he meant it profoundly. He was endangering her daughter and her granddaughter, because of his reckless action. He had had no time to think, consider. He had shot Paulus without regret. If he had shot Lucas Standish, he would not be able to live with himself. There would be no way of explaining it to Cecily, never mind her father, whom she loved deeply. One day, he hoped Madeleine would love him like that.

"Lucas Standish just came to Berlin," he said to Winifred. "To meet Paulus, who took me along. We met in a disused building. Filthy, but vacant. Safe."

"Hans—" she began.

He talked over her. "No time to discuss it," he said. "Just know that they talked, then Paulus turned to me and told me to shoot Standish."

"Oh God!" Winifred's hand flew to cover her mouth, her eyes wide with horror.

"I didn't!" Hans said, taking her by the wrist. "I didn't," he repeated, his voice suddenly lower, more self-assured. "But . . ." He paused for a moment to gather his thoughts. "Instead, I shot Paulus."

Winifred's eyes widened, as the gravity of the situation became clearer.

"They'll find Paulus, probably soon, in that desolate building. They'll look into who could have done this, and they will see that I was the last person with him. They will come for me. I have to get out of here. All of us. You have to come, too. They'll take you, and use you to bring me in, and I would come, before I let them hurt you. But if we're able to get out of Germany . . ." His voice trailed off. What more could he say?

Winifred nodded slowly. "And Lucas got away?"

"Yes. I saw the plane take off. It's a short flight to Edinburgh, then on to London. It was the best he could do."

"Thank you," she said slowly and with intense emotion. "I think you might always be glad of that. But you are right, you can't stay here."

"None of us can! Please. They'll come for you, too!"

"They may," she agreed. "But first we must get you and Cecily and Madeleine out of Germany."

"But you and Roger—"

"We are staying." There was no pleading in her face, no uncontrolled emotion. "You must look after Cecily and Madeleine. I'm sorry, but as you said, you won't be able to speak to or see your parents. They'll be waiting for you and will be devastated when they work out what you've done. It will be hard for them, and I'm so sorry."

"I know. But—"

"Cecily is nearly ready," she said calmly. "Don't waste time saying things we all know. We love you. We know you love Cecily. And I believe you love Madeleine in a way you have never loved anyone before."

"But you and Roger—" he began.

She shook her head. "We have given it a lot of thought, especially since a few days ago, after the Night of the Long Knives. Both of us believe it's only going to get worse. Our duty is here. Please, it changes nothing; it only makes it more difficult."

Hans kissed Winifred gently on her cheek. She smelled vaguely of lavender. And then he stood back. Cecily was coming down the stairs with a single case in one hand, and Madeleine held close to her hip with the other. She looked very slender, very young, and desperately vulnerable.

His heart ached so intolerably he could hardly bear it. He walked up the lower steps and took the case from her, met her eyes for a moment. He saw the fear in her, and the struggle to find courage.

"I'm sorry," he said quietly. "There wasn't anything else I could do."

"I heard what you said to Mother," she answered quietly. "I've been happy in this house, Madeleine was born here, but it's time to go. We're ready."

He saw such strength in his wife, so much of what he was seeing for the first time in her mother. At the same time, there was a shadow that filled the back of his mind. How would this affect his parents? They would be confused, their whole lives betrayed by the son to whom they had given all the emotion, the loyalty, and the means they possessed, sure that they had done what was best for him, for them, and for Germany. He could not help it, or change any of it, nor at heart did he want to. But he knew that his parents would be made to suffer for their son's betrayal. And there was no way to predict what their punishment would be. Shame, certainly. A deep, penetrating pain. But what else?

Hans had to push these thoughts away, in order to find the courage to leave. He would have liked to have explained so much to his parents, to tell them yet again that he was grateful for all they had given him. And explain to them that he could not betray himself, and what he felt without question was morally right. But would his parents understand? Would they forgive him?

Would he ever see them again?

He was sorry, deeply sorry, but there was no turning back. There was nothing he could change.

CHAPTER

22

Hans rapidly changed out of uniform and into casual clothes. He looked like any ordinary young man, but his heart was pounding and he could barely swallow. There was no time to linger; the risk was intense and there would be no escape once he was caught.

No one in the house said anything, but they all knew that their survival depended on not wasting a moment. One wrong decision, made from emotion rather than intelligence, and they could lose everything.

He was ready to lock up the house and hand Winifred the keys, but they couldn't leave until Cecily's father arrived with their travel documents. What was taking him so long?

They stood together—Hans and Cecily, and Winifred with little Madeleine in her arms—and there was nothing they could say. There was no choice but to leave behind all the material things that Hans and Cecily had accumulated, objects with far more than financial or practical value, things that symbolized their time together. Even those precious objects that had been given to them by their families, or that they had acquired over their short marriage, had to stay behind. They could carry only what Hans could manage. As for Cecily, she would carry Madeleine, and that was enough.

A car turned into the road and stopped immediately behind where Winifred's car was parked. Roger Cordell climbed out and slammed the door. His face was pale and he could not disguise the anxiety in it.

Hans understood the man's fear more deeply than he would have imagined even three months ago. Roger loved Cecily; it was in his blood and his bones to protect her, as it was in Hans's to protect Madeleine.

Hans went to him immediately, forcing him to stop. Winifred and Cecily appeared at the door, Madeleine being held by her mother.

"I'm sorry," Hans said desperately, his voice low so that only Cordell could hear. "I couldn't kill Standish. And it was him or Paulus. I . . . I wanted to kill Paulus. Standish is safely on his way to Scotland. First flight out."

Roger's grip was almost painful. "Yes, you must go," he said. He took his hand away and went into his inside pocket. He passed Hans two passports and sets of identity cards, and a wallet full of money. "Madeleine is on Cecily's passport. Now go." His voice broke. "Godspeed. Let us know when you are clear of Germany . . . and safe. No long conversation that can be traced. Just . . . safe. Use your initials: H, C, and M. Now go." He grasped Hans again, and his eyes filled with tears. Before he could let go, Hans leaned close to his ear.

"They know you're MI6," he whispered.

Roger said nothing, but Hans felt a change in the man's body.

Roger hugged Cecily one last time, quickly, desperately, and touched the few wisps of Madeleine's dark hair. He started to speak, but emotion caught in his throat. He walked to his car and climbed in. He never turned back.

Hans put the papers in his pocket. He removed the money from the wallet and placed it in his pocket as well. He did not want to take it, but he might need it very much before they were in England. In fact, he almost certainly would. He had not thought clearly about that yet.

He was angry with himself for the emotions that all but choked him. Perhaps this outcome could have been a lot worse. He picked up the case and put it in the back of the car, and then insisted that Cecily sit in the back, holding Madeleine in her arms, where she would be safer.

Winifred slipped into the driver's seat and Hans took the passenger seat beside her. Together, they watched Roger Cordell drive away.

Hans did not look back at the house. Everything about it was imprinted on his memory anyway. And everything that mattered, the present and the future, was with him in the car.

"The house . . ." he said.

"We'll worry about that later," said Winifred, pulling the car away from the curb. She handled the car with confidence, her attention now fully focused on the route.

"Are you quite certain that you wish to remain in Berlin?" Hans asked her, and then saw that she smiled. It was small, with only the corners of her mouth, but there was no bitterness in it.

"Roger must," she said. "Apart from the suspicion it would raise if he left, which could make a lot of difference to the authorities looking for you, he has worked here, he knows Berlin. Perhaps it is more important than ever that we stay, and my place is with him. It is not arguable, my dear."

She was watching the road, the traffic, and going as quickly as was safe, as if she understood that it would be foolish to draw the attention of the traffic police by making any error at all. "You have a baby to consider, more than yourselves. You must get safely out. Madeleine is very tiny; she cannot survive without you." Her voice choked for a moment, then she mastered it again. "As Roger said, we need to know only that you are safely out of Germany. Don't tell me anything other than that. I cannot give away information, however unintentionally, when I don't know. It is not far to the station."

Winifred silently navigated through the ever-thickening traffic, more and more congested as they drew closer to the platform entrance at the train station.

"There's so much to say," Cecily began, her voice low, strained.

"No, there isn't," her mother replied, her voice also thick with emotion. "There is nothing we haven't said, and more importantly, we know it anyway." She maneuvered through traffic and was nearly there. "When I stop at the curb, get out, and I will pull back into the traffic. There are no more goodbyes to be said. Telephone the house or the embassy when you are safe, or at least when you're outside Germany."

"Of course," Hans replied. "And . . . thank you." He was choked with fear, but also with relief, and the great effort of keeping his nerves and his imagination from crippling him.

A space near the pavement opened up and Winifred pulled into it.

Hans opened the car door and stepped out, then opened the back door, reaching in to help Cecily, who was carrying the baby close to her, tightly. She accepted his aid and straightened up, staring only once at her mother, and choking on tears.

Hans pulled the one case from the trunk; it was surprisingly heavy. He turned to Winifred, his tears almost blinding him. "Until we meet again," he said quietly. That was infinitely better than "goodbye." "I'll look after them, I swear. They are the most precious things in my life."

Winifred nodded, her hands clutching the steering wheel. "I know," she whispered. Then she put her foot on the accelerator and pulled away, finding her place in the stream of cars.

Hans led his wife and child inside, where they queued with other people to get their tickets. He looked at the board to see which train was next out, and moving in the general direction of northern France or Belgium. There was one leaving for Brussels in twenty minutes. They must be on that train! Without his Gestapo uniform, which would have granted him special consideration, he was simply another traveler.

The ticket line seemed interminable. Finally, he reached the head of it and presented to the man at the desk his false papers, his passport, and Cecily's, which also included Madeleine.

The clerk seemed to take forever examining them. When he looked up and asked, "And why do you want to visit Brussels, Herr Wilhelm?"

Hans felt his throat constrict with fear. He thought rapidly. "My grandmother lives there. She hasn't seen the baby yet."

The clerk looked beyond Hans at Cecily, and apparently noticed the baby for the first time. He glanced down at the papers again, and then smiled. "Very nice," he said gently. "You look after them! Next?" It was so normal, so pleasant, that it seemed like a breath of sweet air, compared to the filthy room in which he had left Paulus's body.

They went onto the platform and entered the train. It was a small train, and crowded, but it took only a few minutes to find a place where they could sit together in the second-class carriage. An old lady with bulging bags of shopping made room for them without being asked, and then changed seats to the opposite side so Hans and Cecily could sit together. Now she would be traveling backward, which was rarely a traveler's preference.

"Thank you, ma'am," Hans said a little awkwardly.

"Your first?" the woman asked, glancing at Madeleine.

Cecily looked at her baby, then at the woman. Suddenly, she seemed a little self-conscious. She nodded.

The woman smiled. "One day, she will discover the word 'no,' and the enormous power of it. There is a whole world around that word. It says, 'I am me! I'm not you! No! No.'"

Hans smiled at the woman. Her friendly conversation was helping ease the tension in his chest, and was helping Cecily relax, perhaps feel less frightened. The kindness of strangers.

The train pulled out of the station.

"Lovely," the old woman said approvingly. "My first was a girl, Ingrid."

"A beautiful name," Cecily replied. "If I have another girl, I think that is what I will call her. I hope you don't mind?"

The woman beamed. "I would be delighted."

They went on talking, mostly about children, their stages of growth, the great leaps forward, like first steps, first words, and second stages, such as seeing their own reflection in a mirror, knowing what food they liked, and did not like. The woman smiled warmly.

Hans was watching the exchange, and he thought about what that word "no" meant. It was the first realization of self, of the ability to decide, to choose. This stranger was right: the day would come when Madeleine would decide "I will!" or "I won't!"

In a way, that was what he had done today. Was it only hours ago that Paulus had ordered him to shoot Lucas Standish, and he had shot Paulus instead? It had shocked him when he had done this, and especially because it was done without any hesitation. It was as if the decision had been made ages ago, and this was simply a matter of acting on it. Clearly, Paulus had never even considered the possibility that his young prodigy would turn on him. Either Paulus had trusted him completely, or the man had been so arrogant that he had never deemed it possible that a junior officer would dare to disobey his orders.

Had Hans even contemplated what it might cost him? He would be a fugitive all his life.

It had been an insane thing to do! He had a wife and a child, and the responsibility to feed and clothe them, and give them safety, shelter. And even, one day, a knowledge of belonging. But at what cost? And if they escaped Germany safely, what country would they belong to? He must be the best father and husband he could be. Would he be able to teach them what he believed in? But what *did* he believe in? He was no longer certain, except that he felt the direction Hitler was taking Germany was wrong.

Did either of them want safety, at a price to be paid by others?

It was at that precise moment that he reminded himself that he had said goodbye to Winifred and Roger, but not to his own parents.

They would be mortified! Worse, they would consider him a traitor. And even more than that, their friends would judge them to be responsible. They took pride in his success. Would they be blamed for his treason? He doubted his parents would ever understand.

He sat silently thinking for a long while, the train rolling out of Berlin. Cecily was holding Madeleine gently, rocking her very slightly. She seemed to be asleep. The woman opposite them excused herself, explained that she would be back soon to tell them whether there was tea available. She closed the carriage door quietly behind herself, as if careful not to wake the baby.

Hans looked at Cecily.

"I'm sorry," he said, his voice low, yet filled with emotion.

She looked at him, then slowly smiled. It was gentle, radiant. "I know. But I'm proud of you. Really, very proud. You haven't explained anything to me, but I think I know, if only the barest facts." Her voice was soft, almost inaudible. "I knew Lucas Standish, did you know that? He's Margot's grandfather, and she talked about him often."

Without thinking, Hans said, "He was head of MI6 during the war." He told her quietly, although there was no one else in the carriage now. "It's hard to imagine. He seemed like a rather vague, polite professor. He defeated Paulus over something. I'm not sure what, but he did so very thoroughly, toward the end of the war. I don't know how this has anything to do with germ warfare."

"Germ warfare?" Her face darkened. "You mean that?"

It was too late to take it back. How could he have been so stupid! Now, with this knowledge, her life might be in even more danger!

"It wasn't about that," he said quickly. "It was an old score. I think Paulus wanted me to shoot Lucas Standish because I would take the blame, if it all came out."

"Hans, if anything had gone wrong . . . or goes wrong . . ." Her voice was low, angry. Then she looked up. "I'm proud of you." She reached out as far as she could and still hold Madeleine. He leaned toward her. She touched his cheek and smiled.

He lowered his head, to hide the tears in his eyes. This was what mattered. There was time to tell her all that he had done. But not now.

The woman returned, made a few polite remarks, and then leaned her head back and drifted into sleep.

The train slowed to a stop and border guards came into the carriages. They were in uniform, reminding Hans of himself, only hours ago! The whole world had changed since then, like a kaleidoscope where all the pieces were the same, but a violent shake had obliterated the picture out of the old elements, creating an utterly different one.

"Papers?" The guard was standing before him now, his hand out. He looked at the sleeping baby and lowered his voice. "I got one about that size. Bit bigger. Changes every day."

Heart pounding, Hans passed him the papers, and smiled. "Boy or girl?"

"Boy," the guard replied, his smile widening.

"Do you talk to him?" Hans asked. "He won't know what you're saying, but he'll know you are talking to him, confiding in him. That's all he needs."

The guard shook his head, but he was smiling. He looked carefully through the papers. "These look new," he observed.

"They are," Hans agreed. Suddenly his throat was tight. He could hardly breathe.

"We're taking her to see her other grandparents," Cecily put in. "Just for a day or two. Pictures aren't quite the same."

The guard handed back their papers and passports to Hans, who took them with an unsteady hand.

The guard then checked the woman's documents and left the carriage, moving on to the next car.

Hans felt the sweat trickle down his skin under his jacket. He did not dare look at Cecily, or at the old woman in the seat opposite.

The rest of the journey drifted by. Cecily dozed while Hans held Madeleine. The woman opposite woke up several times, saw him with the baby, and smiled. And then she drifted back into sleep.

* * *

At last, they pulled into the station at Brussels. The relief that Hans felt when they stepped off the train was immeasurable. A new country, a new life. There were quite a few people speaking German, although the majority were speaking French and Flemish, with English in the mix.

The next matter was to find a bed for the night, and then plan what to do in the morning. Hans had been so engaged in this current emergency of escape that he had given little thought as to what they would do when they reached relative safety. He would have to find some kind of work to support the three of them, before the money he carried ran out. He had not wanted to accept it from Roger and Winifred, but he realized how much it would be needed. Winifred's insistence that it was for Madeleine brought any argument to a stop.

First and foremost, he knew that they needed to be practical.

He asked the taxi driver about hotels. The man was used to such inquiries, and his German was quite respectable. He took them to a large hotel, the kind that guaranteed anonymity.

They checked in and went directly to their room. He watched Cecily feed the baby and then they sat quietly as Madeleine fell asleep.

Hans remembered his promise to Winifred. He went down to the lobby and found a telephone, where he could make an international call. Until she knew they were safe, she would be frantic.

It was Roger Cordell who answered.

"Yes? How are you?" Cordell said, his voice shaking with emotion when he realized it was Hans.

"We're fine. In a hotel in Brussels." He was so emotional, hearing this caring voice, that he forgot the warning to use codes and keep it short. "We'll go on, I suppose, in the morning. I'm not sure where, but we need to." After a moment, he added, "I'm sorry." It was all his fault for getting into the Gestapo in the first place, for his ambition to work for Paulus. And it was too late for any of it to be changed. "Is Winifred all right?"

There was a silence, then Roger's voice came back full of emotion, pride, and something like laughter. "We had a formal visit from the police this evening. Of course, they treated me like an official of the embassy. And Winifred was perfect. You would have been proud of her. I was." His voice wavered only a little. "She was marvelous. She welcomed them as if nothing on earth were wrong. She told them we were having a private celebration as new grandparents. She showed them photographs, told them Madeleine was our only grandchild, and with tears in her eyes. I was so proud of her! It was a performance worthy of an Academy Award."

After a lengthy pause, Cordell said, "H, you need to write this down."

"Give me a moment." He took a few steps to the front desk and grabbed a small pad of paper and a pen. "Ready," he said, the phone pressed to his ear.

"Make your way to London and the Foreign Office. Ask for Mr. Ogilvy. He'll be expecting you. He'll have documents, work papers."

"Work?" Hans asked. "How can I—"

"You're an attorney. The Foreign Office will make good use of your knowledge of German law. And I imagine that Lucas Standish might want to give you a hand, adjusting to English life."

Hans felt hope rise in his chest. "I'll tell C. And . . . thank you. She's just put M to bed for the night. It's impossible to believe that only hours ago—"

"I know," Roger cut across him. "But you did the right thing. Don't doubt that. Whatever the cost. Just look after your family . . . our family. And tell C and M that we love them, and that we'll see them soon."

"I will," said Hans. It was more than an answer; it was a solemn oath.

A s soon as Jacob agreed that returning to Berlin made sense they drove north, only stopping when they were exhausted. If Elena could pass on the information from Hartwig, she could ease some of the weight she was carrying.

It would take them at least eight hours, more if there were delays. "If we're too tired, we can find a hotel," he said.

Elena saw the road sign informing them of the distance to Berlin. "I want to make a wish ... and we'd be there," she told him.

As they traveled, Elena learned that, after they said goodbye a year earlier, Jacob had stayed on in Berlin writing articles of increasing perception and warning, and sending them back to New York, and occasionally Chicago, his home city. She also learned his view had grown darker since then, as had hers. Germany might be in a resurgence of economic growth and prosperity, but the price could prove greater than most Germans realized.

"With Hitler rising in power," she said, "I can't imagine there won't be a war."

There was a heaviness weighing over her, a darkness that was a combination of grief and fatigue. She felt as if she were on the run again, much as she had been not so long ago. And, again, a life had been lost.

By the time they reached the outskirts of Berlin, it was very late and they were both struggling to stay awake. Despite this, Elena knew what she had to do. She had been specifically ordered not to contact Roger Cordell, and she would obey. But there were other possibilities.

"You can drop me at the hotel," she said. "Then go home and get some sleep."

They rounded the corner and Jacob parked the car. "I'm going in with you," he said. "And that's not open for argument."

She wanted to disagree, but there was a voice in her head telling her that she could not do this alone.

She took her bag from the car and walked into the hotel. It was risky, she knew. They recognized her here. But she had no choice.

The clerk welcomed her, acknowledged that her same room was available, and handed her the key. He saw Jacob standing nearby, but said nothing. If a single woman wanted to take a gentleman to her room, it was none of his business.

When Dieter approached her and offered to take her bag, relief washed over her and she had to struggle to suppress her appreciation.

With Jacob following closely, they took the elevator to her floor and followed the carpeted hallway to her room. Once inside, with the door closed firmly, she quickly told Dieter about Hartwig's death. The man was clearly surprised, as well as concerned. Before he could speak, Elena gave him the location of the scientist's body.

"Off the highway?" repeated Dieter.

"In a copse," she added. "We had no choice. But please, please send someone there. It's so . . . he deserves much more."

"I'll report back. You can wait here until I've confirmed that they have all the information they need from you."

Elena moved toward the door and opened it for Dieter. He stepped out and she locked it behind him.

Just minutes later, three knocks on the door interrupted Elena and Jacob's conversation. Jacob crossed the room and turned the knob, finding Dieter on the other side.

He stepped into the room and carefully shut the door behind him. Dieter cleared his throat, then ran his fingers through his hair. "We have a problem," he said. "It's Fassler."

It was Jacob who spoke. "Is he injured?"

Dieter looked at him for a moment, as if unsure that he could have confidence in this stranger.

"He's trustworthy," said Elena. "More than that, he has saved my life. And not once, but twice."

Dieter nodded. "Someone betrayed us. We don't know who, but there's no question that we have a mole somewhere. Yesterday, late, the safe house was breached and Alex Cooper was injured. Not life-threatening—if he's looked after well, he'll recover. And he drove away the attacker."

"But, if that's the case," said Elena, "that leaves Fassler unable to escape."

Dieter's eyes were steady, his smile almost rueful. "They want you to take Cooper's place now that you're back in Berlin."

She said nothing. It had always been a possibility. She should have expected it, but it was still a shock. It felt to her that she was substituting Fassler for Hartwig, as if they were interchangeable. Perhaps in some ways they were, since both men would draw the attention of the Intelligence force protecting them. And now she was alone and responsible for the safe passage of this second scientist.

She knew nothing about Fassler—that is, Fassler the man—but it was too late to worry about such details. It was her job, and she had no choice but to do it. In effect, Hartwig and the whole experience with him, knowing him, liking him, caring, had taught her that, as professional as she was, she still had feelings, heart. But Hartwig was dead. Now it was Fassler who mattered.

What did she need to do next?

"Where are they, Cooper and Fassler?" she asked.

"In another safe house," Dieter said. "You need to get to them, make sure Cooper is getting the care he needs, and then get Fassler out of Germany."

She nearly asked if MI6 trusted her to perform this task, considering her failure with Hartwig, but she said nothing. It would sound like self-pity, a very unpleasant characteristic in which she refused to indulge. At least, not until this was over. Still, she could not shake the belief that she had failed with Hartwig. That thought still hurt. Not so much her failure—that she could accept—but his death. The pain of it was a different sort, but it was not shame. Elena believed that if she never failed, it was because she had never tried, whether it was something truly difficult or not. Lucas had taught her that long ago. So, no, it was not failure that was causing her this pain, it was grief.

She turned to Jacob, who was sitting quietly, as if waiting to learn the next move.

"Where are we going from here?" he asked.

"I don't expect you to do this." Even as she said the words, she knew that she did not mean them.

"Elena, we've already had this conversation," he said wearily. "You can't do this alone. Stop letting your pride instead of your brain dictate your actions."

She felt Dieter's eyes on her and thought him wise to say nothing.

"It's not pride," she said, stung by the accuracy of his words. She resented being so easily read. "It's because I don't want to get you even further involved in something dangerous."

She looked sideways at him. He was looking away, but she could have sworn that there was humor in his face. She felt foolish, but she knew he understood perfectly well what she was doing, and why. She even knew what he was going to say next!

"This is germ warfare, Elena, which is appalling beyond any imagination. Even yours, as good as it is. But this isn't about you or me, or even about Fassler. It's about doing the right thing, the only possible thing."

"I . . ." she started, and then stopped.

"He's right," said Dieter, moving toward the door. "Stay in the room and I'll be back, as soon as I get the contact information for you. They were drawing it up when I hung up the phone earlier."

Before Elena could respond, he slipped into the hallway and closed the door.

Elena sat on the bed, lured by the thought of crawling under the covers and sleeping . . . for days.

Jacob leaned back in the chair and closed his eyes.

They remained like this, quiet, pensive, until there was a light tap on the door. Elena crossed the room and opened it.

Dieter was there, balancing a tray of tea and biscuits. "Your tea, madam," he said, entering the room.

The moment the door was closed, he pulled a scrap of paper from his pocket. "I have the address, and you're to go now. It's too dangerous for Fassler to remain there for the night."

She took the paper and handed it to Jacob.

"Yes, I know this area," he said.

As Dieter was about to leave, he turned back. "Oh, and I thought you'd want to know that your grandfather has safely landed and should be home soon."

"What does any of this have to do with my grandfather? And landed . . . from where?" She was confused. She was also angry.

A look of chagrin crossed his face. "Damn, I think I just spoke out of turn. He was here, in Berlin. And don't ask me what he came for. And if you could do me a favor . . . please don't tell anyone that I said anything."

She was puzzled, yet nodded her agreement. At the same time, she felt her chest tighten.

"There's a doctor treating Cooper now. She's very skilled, and can see the darkness on the horizon. She's risking her life to treat the wounded, and does so quietly enough to give us time to help our people escape."

Two hours later, Elena had checked out of the hotel, having explained that there was a family emergency, and was driving with Jacob to the safe house. Silence filled the car. Elena was exhausted, yet knew that she had no time to sleep, not even rest. A man's life was at stake. She couldn't fail again.

"It's not your fault that Hartwig died," Jacob said, as if reading her thoughts.

Elena looked at him. He knew her so well, perhaps too well. True, Jacob had been by her side when she was in danger, feeling grief and distress, but it bothered her that she should be so easy to read. "I know . . . maybe."

He took one hand off the wheel and touched her arm. It was brief, but more powerful than words. Then he gripped the wheel again and merged into the flow of traffic.

"I wish we had something to eat," she said. "I should have thought to get us both something, and I didn't. I'm sorry."

Again, his smile was a bit twisted, but it was definitely still a smile. "Yes. Very thoughtless of you. Perhaps we can blame Fassler for that."

She smiled. The reproof was fair. Her emotions were in the way. It was past the time to put them away and devote her attention to Fassler.

As they drove, she watched the narrowing streets, noted the poorer neighborhood, until they came to the address where Alex Cooper was in hiding. Jacob found a place to park on the same street, which was little more than an alley. He parked the car and they went past a pile of rubbish and up to a scarred door, its number nearly worn off. She knocked, and then stepped back.

Nothing happened.

She repeated the knock.

An upstairs window opened and a young man looked out. He was pale, and leaned on the sill awkwardly.

"Cooper?" She was almost sure. He looked like the man in the photograph she had memorized, but much thinner, his face tense with pain.

"Are you Peter Howard's girl?" he asked.

"I hadn't thought of myself like that," she said, realizing it was probably his way of identifying her. "But yes, I suppose I am. Can someone let us in?"

Cooper disappeared and the window was closed. A few moments later, the door opened and an older, dark-haired man with a serious and highly intelligent-looking face stood just inside. He did not speak to them at all, but stepped back to allow them in.

Jacob thanked him.

The man nodded, but did not introduce himself.

Surely he could only be Fassler.

The man ascended the flight of stairs, Jacob and Elena following behind. He took each step carefully, as if he expected a loose board or even a missing stair. They entered a room and the man locked the door behind them.

Alex Cooper was half lying, half sitting on a mattress near the window. His right leg was heavily bandaged, with strips of gauze around the wound. It was soaked with fresh blood. Clearly, the bandage had been applied by someone with expertise.

Elena recognized him more easily from his photograph now, despite his face marked by pain, and possibly the shock to his system from loss of blood. But the golden-brown tousled hair had the same hairline, the same wave; his eyebrows the same individual shape. The difference was that his shoulders were hunched and his whole body sagged.

"Ellen," she said simply. "This is Jacob. I gather a doctor has been

here. I'm told she's very good indeed, and is used to working discreetly."

"I can't go with—" he began.

She winced, hating what she was going to say. "You're no use to
any of us dead." It sounded brutal, but she could not afford to be
misunderstood. "I was asked to share a message: rest assured that the
doctor will stay near you, and you can trust her. She knows very well
the price you will pay if you're caught. Don't endanger her by not
doing as you're told. I'll take Dr. Fassler and get him out of Germany.
At least, I'll do my best."

That was difficult to say. Did Cooper know Hartwig was dead?

Cooper relaxed a fraction. "I'm afraid I can't do much now. I—"

"I can see that," she replied. "But you've done well to get Fassler
safely out of sight. We'll take it from here."

Cooper hesitated.

"The doctor will continue to take care of your injury," she repeated, hoping to assuage some of his fear. "And then she'll see you
to safety," she went on. "That's what she does. As soon as she comes
to assess you, we'll leave. I don't know exactly where we'll go yet, but
I wouldn't tell you if I did." She smiled at Cooper, who was clearly
in pain. "Get better. There's going to be a lot more to do. Especially
for someone like you, who can pass as German."

"Can you?" he said curiously.

"Yes. I lived here for years, some while ago. Now please, try to
relax and heal, and let us take care of Fassler."

Cooper gave a brief, wincing smile, and stopped struggling to
sit up.

The doctor arrived five minutes later. She was a small woman,
her gray hair curling softly around her face. She looked like a
middle-aged housewife, except for the sharp intelligence in her face.
She carried a heavy leather doctor's bag, presumably with all she
was likely to need in an emergency call.

Elena did not ask her name, nor did she give the woman hers. She
simply accompanied her upstairs and then told her to call down if

she needed an extra hand, more linen, hot water. Then she went downstairs to get acquainted with Fassler.

She passed through what seemed to have once been the sitting room and into the kitchen. It had a chaotic look, and she wondered if only the kitchen, bedrooms, and bathroom were now in use.

Fassler was standing by the sink, staring at a single hotplate on a metal stand. He was making coffee. He turned round as Elena came in. "If you're looking for your friend, he's outside with the car." He turned his attention back to whatever he was doing with old coffee grounds and a filter. "This is barbaric."

"There's a lot of that around," she said tartly.

He looked surprised. "Coffee?"

"No, barbarism," she corrected, and forced a little smile. "Unless Jacob discovers something wrong with the car, we should leave as soon as possible. We might have to help the doctor get Alex into her car, but after that there's nothing here. We must get as far as we can toward the border before morning. I'm not sure if we can cross in the middle of the night or not."

"For God's sake! Don't any of you know what you are doing?" Fassler demanded from just behind her. "You don't know this, and you don't know that! The Gestapo could be on your heels!"

"Of course they could," she replied. It took some effort to hold her voice steady. "They always could be, and you know that even better than I do. But let's get this clear, Professor. I don't know how to do your job, and you don't know how to do mine. We don't tie ourselves to ironclad plans, because the situation can change, and we might have to change the plans as well. Do you play tennis, Professor Fassler?"

His expression darkened. "What! What the hell has that to do with this? Yes, I do. Quite well."

"Do you plan the game before you start? Where you will stand? Which way you will hit the ball—backhand, forehand?"

"Of course not! That's a—"

"Stupid question?" she asked, her eyebrows raised.

"I take your point," he replied, with a sharp gleam of understanding in his eyes. "Do you do this all the time? Get people out of countries that want very much to keep them from leaving?"

"Among other things," she replied. "The last time was treacherous."

"But you got him out anyway?" There was a light of amusement in his eyes.

"No," she said. "Actually, I killed him."

"I . . . I don't believe you." It was a challenge.

She shrugged. "You asked." She smiled and saw the uncertainty in his face. And then she saw Fassler become serious, all humor gone.

"Hartwig," he said. "Is he safe?"

Elena lowered her head for just a moment. "I'm sorry," she said, her voice barely above a whisper.

"He's . . . my God, is he . . . dead?"

The grief crossing Elena's face answered his question.

Before Fassler could speak, Jacob entered the house and rushed upstairs.

In less than a minute, Elena heard more footsteps on the stairs. Ignoring Fassler, she walked over to the landing and saw Jacob come down the stairs backward, guiding Cooper and taking most of the man's weight on himself. The doctor followed behind, supporting the MI6 agent, her hands gripping him by the shoulder.

Cooper could hardly put any weight on his left side. He winced as he descended, and smiled bleakly as he passed Elena. His face was very white, ashen, and she could only guess at his pain.

"Thank you for looking after Fassler," she said quietly to him. "Now, get better. We'll need you soon enough."

She looked at the doctor, but no words were necessary.

Fassler rushed into another room and returned with a small suitcase.

Elena gave a questioning look.

"This holds thirty years of research," he told her. "Papers, microfilm, everything I've worked on. It comes with me."

Only five minutes later, Jacob, Elena, and Fassler were driving out of the alley where the car was stowed. As they hurried, Elena spotted motion out of the corner of her eye. She saw a familiar man gazing at them across the way. At first she couldn't place him, and then she realized: he had been following her on the university campus when she first arrived.

"Jacob," she whispered, "someone is watching us." She nodded slightly in the strange man's direction.

Jacob peeled out of the alleyway, heading north and away from the center of a city roiling in chaos.

It was nearly three o'clock in the morning before they were out of the metropolitan area and on the open road. They went several miles in silence. There was nothing to say.

"Where are you going?" Fassler said suddenly. "This is north! We've got to go south, man. Have you no sense of direction? I assume you can read."

"You want me to turn around and go back into Berlin?" Jacob asked.

His voice was level, but Elena heard the anger in it, now that she knew him so well.

"I want to get to England," Fassler replied. "And get there alive."

Jacob did not answer. Elena saw the temptation, and his struggle to remain silent. She put her hand on his arm. Several replies came to her lips, but she bit them back.

"First you want to get out of Germany," Jacob corrected him. "We need to go the way they least expect."

She glanced back at Fassler's face. He looked angry, but she wondered if it was actually fear she was seeing. She could not blame him for that. It must have been difficult to elude his watchers. That in itself was a feat. The man he had trusted with his life had been seriously wounded, and had passed him over to two strangers who were expected to protect him, and who now appeared to be driving him in the exact opposite direction he wanted to go. And presumably, like Hartwig, he was leaving behind any friends he had, or even family. Almost certainly, he had not been able to tell anyone that he was going away, never mind why. His anger might well be grief disguised, and pain, loneliness, and vulnerability he chose to hide. It was a very private wound.

Behind him, out the rear windshield, she could see a gray car just off in the distance. She focused her attention back on the road in front of her.

"The police have probably been looking for you to go south or west," she said. "Actually, Poland is the nearest border. Do you want to go to Poland?"

"No," Fassler said decisively. "Do either of you speak Polish? Do you even have people there?"

"No idea," she replied. "If I do, I don't know them. Our first thought is to get you out of Germany."

"Into the Baltic Sea, judging by your sense of direction," Fassler snapped.

"Presumably, you do not want to go there?" Elena asked, biting back yet again the words she would have preferred to use. Fear took people differently, but this man was getting on her nerves.

"Of course not. That's an idiotic question," he replied.

"Shut up!" Jacob said sharply. "We have to keep you alive! And out of the hands of the Germans, who are looking for you. The only thing worse for us than your death would be to have you taken alive."

Fassler said nothing.

"If we're stopped, you could say we took you against your will," Jacob went on, his voice bitter. "I don't suppose they'll believe you, but it's a good story for the public. You are loyal to the Führer, and you were kidnapped. Now you are rescued and safely returned to your work, where you can finish your plans to wipe out half of humanity with some filthy disease. *Heil Hitler.*"

"We were also working to find the protection against it. Or better still, a prevention," Fassler said, his voice quieter, the harsh edge blunted. "I don't blame you for being frightened about this research," he added. "I am myself. I didn't go looking for it. I stumbled on it..." He did not finish. Perhaps it was completely true, but it would sound like an excuse, and he was clearly a man who did not make excuses.

Elena felt a wave of pity for him. He wasn't a pleasant man, but carrying a burden like that, how could he look at it as anything but a nightmare that had chosen him, rather than one of his own creation? And even if it was his own, perhaps he realized the horror of it only when it was too late.

"Let us get you out," she said more gently. "It doesn't matter in which direction. The Gestapo will be spreading the net as wide as they can. They need to get you back."

"I'm sorry about that." For an instant, Fassler's voice carried real regret. Then the coldness returned. "But this is your job, just as germ warfare, and its prevention, is mine."

"Be quiet," Elena told him. "And please, go to sleep and let Jacob keep his eyes on the road."

She felt no satisfaction when Fassler did not answer.

CHAPTER
24

They drove another hour in silence. Elena was beginning to feel herself drifting into sleep. The road was excellent, but tedious. It was purely by chance that she glanced into the rearview mirror and saw a police car a hundred yards behind them, alongside that same gray vehicle she'd noticed before.

"Jacob!"

"I see it," he replied. "I wouldn't mind, except that there's another one a few hundred yards behind that one. I know this area a bit. In half a mile, there's a turnoff."

He sounded perfectly calm, but she could see the tension in his face. "To where?" Suddenly, she found it hard to swallow. Fassler was right: the Germans wouldn't kill him, and they might prefer to take Jacob and Elena alive, in case they could torture them into giving useful information. And then they would shoot them without regret, if that seemed the wiser choice. She wondered with a stab of pain if anyone had found Hartwig's body.

"In a few miles, there's a farm," Jacob replied, jerking her back to the present. "The farmer will help us, if he can."

"To do what! Jacob, the police have guns! Is he going to take a rabbit gun to them? And what will happen to the farmer?"

"He has a small plane," Jacob said steadily. "It will get us as far as Denmark, if we're lucky. That is, if there's fuel in it."

"Do you know how to fly a plane?" she asked.

"Fortunately, I do. That at least is not a problem."

Elena knew that he would not add that there would be no time to fuel up now, and they would be lucky to get it out of whatever shed it was kept in, and even luckier to get it off the ground. She did not reply. There was nothing meaningful to say. She glanced again in the mirror. The police were out of view.

Suddenly, Jacob saw a break in the traffic and moved to the right, and then a hundred yards later took a side road. Within seconds, he slowed to take another hard turn, this time onto a rough country road, little more than a track.

Fassler sat upright with a start and nearly spoke, but then it sounded as if he were choking off the words.

Elena glanced back. His posture was rigid, and he seemed disorientated, as if having been awakened from a sleep.

"What's happening?" he asked, alarm in his voice.

"It won't take them long to find us, but it might be long enough," Jacob said quietly.

"Long enough for what, for God's sake?" Fassler demanded.

"Long enough to get a small biplane out of a shed, onto the runway, and off the ground," Jacob said. "Pray that the farmer is around the house, not working out in some field."

Elena did not bother to add anything. The risks, the chances, were all there, but there were no alternatives. Besides, how many farmers tended their crops before the sun rose?

They were roaring along through ripening fields, tall stalks of grain slapping against the side of the car. Another few weeks and it would be time to reap the rich crops.

The road was dusty. If the police could see any distance, they would see plumes of dust in the air, and the dry dirt marking where the car had been.

Jacob took a corner a little too fast and had to struggle to right the car. No one said anything, as if knowing they could do no better.

It seemed like an age before they were racing again through silent fields. In a dark green meadow, several cows standing near the road looked up at the disturbance. A working tractor sat nearby.

The land was motionless, idyllic.

Jacob swung around the last corner and pulled into the yard of an old farmhouse, next to two barns. Without speaking, he climbed out and strode right up to the back door of the house.

Elena was silent. So was Fassler, for once.

Jacob knocked on the door. Waited, and then pounded on it urgently.

Somewhere, hens were disturbed and started cackling, a dog began to bark.

Seconds ticked by like a minute, stretching out in the near silence.

The farmer came to the door, pulling a robe around him. He spoke with Jacob for a few moments. Jacob nodded, and walked round the corner of the house and disappeared.

The farmer came across the dry earth of the yard. He stopped at Elena's side of the car. When she lowered the window, he spoke to her in German. "Please come with me. Jacob is getting the airplane out of the barn. I think there is no time to lose. Please."

She scrambled out of the car and turned to order Fassler out, but he was already opening the door.

They ran after the farmer, across the yard, round the corner, and over a stretch of patchy grass to the barn. Inside, there was a small biplane with its cockpit door open. Jacob was in the pilot's seat.

There was no time to argue or question. The sound of car engines was already audible in the distance. It would be the police, led by the gray vehicle.

"Get in the back!" Elena ordered.

"You—" Fassler began.

"We have to get you out. If you leave me behind, it doesn't matter."

There was a flash of appreciation in his face, then he did as he was told, pulling his suitcase after him.

"Come on!" Jacob shouted at her.

"Will it take me as well?" she asked, eyeing the small passenger space.

The farmer looked to Jacob, then put his hands on Elena's back and gave her a firm lift and push. She nearly fell into the seat beside Jacob just as he hit the throttle. The plane jerked forward, rolling out of the barn doors and onto the dry earth. It swerved a little, then made the grass landing strip.

The engines were so loud that Elena covered her ears. Then she realized that some of the noise was the roar of the police cars as they rounded the bend and headed toward the plane.

Jacob pushed the plane harder. They were racing along the runway, having covered at least half the length of it.

Elena gripped the side of her seat. If they did not lift off soon, they would crash into the hedges at the far end. She gulped, tension tightening her muscles. At least death will be quick, she told herself. But there was something more: Peter had been very clear about it. If she didn't get Fassler out, she was expected to kill him. She'd been told that quite unhesitatingly. But not to kill Jacob! Or get herself killed! She hoped to God that Alex Cooper wasn't the only one to get out of this alive.

She heard the first shot rip through the fabric of the plane's wing. Before she could react, they were airborne.

More shots rang out, but this time they missed.

The plane was climbing steeply. Could the engines tackle such an ascent? She wondered how soon they would be out of range. She looked at Jacob. His face was tense, the muscles in his neck and jaw like knotted ropes.

There was another volley of shots, but none of them struck the plane.

They were still climbing. There was no visible sun, but Elena saw the first blue sheen of the sea, far to the north. And then she was gripped with fear. She remembered Hartwig, seated in the back of the car, saying nothing, dead. She turned quickly to look at Fassler. His face was white with fear, but he was unhurt.

"Thank you, God!" she said quietly. Then aloud, "Well done, Jacob."

"We have a way to go yet," he said, his voice barely audible above the roar of the engines. "North until we hit the coast, then northwest. I will feel much better once we're over the water."

"Who is the farmer?" Fassler asked from the rear seat, his voice a little rusty, as if the tension in his throat had all but choked him. "Why did he give you his plane? And what will he tell the police?"

"That I stole it at gunpoint, I imagine," Jacob replied. "That's what I told him to say."

"Why?" asked Fassler. After a moment he added, "I'm grateful that you've done this for me."

It was the first kind or gentle thing he had said since they had met him.

Elena looked down, but she could not see land. There was a deepening blue sky, and she imagined the darker blue sea below them. Soon, the air would glow with the rising sun.

Just as Elena felt herself begin to relax, she heard a sound that drove fear through her like a knife. The engine gave a cough, seemed to die, and then caught again.

For an instant, she tried to deny this to herself. She had imagined it. They were high in the sky, part of the whole, silent, exquisite world. They were nearly there.

And then the engine coughed again.

She looked at Jacob, then at the fuel gauge. "Can we . . . ?"

"I don't know," he replied. "I'll try to make the nearest land, but it's not where we're meant to be."

"Didn't you damn well check the fuel?" Fassler demanded.

"Yes," Jacob replied levelly. "However, I did not take into account the fact that a bullet would strike the petrol tank."

"Wonderful! Are we going to go up in flames?"

"More likely drown," Elena said, before she thought about it. She saw Jacob roll his eyes, but he smiled.

Fassler swore with fatalism rather than anger.

They were losing height. Not quickly, but Elena could see it on the altimeter.

If they had to land in the sea, how long could they float? And would it matter anyway? The end would be the same, just slower.

"Ahead," Jacob said quietly. "Those lights. I think that's Denmark."

There was no point in asking him whether they could make it. Elena sat in silence.

The engine coughed again, twice.

How long before the horizon showed signs of daylight?

Through the diminishing darkness, with new light reflecting off the water, it was clear that land was ahead.

"How far?" asked Elena.

"One mile, perhaps two," said Jacob. He adjusted their course. The lowest part of a cliff was becoming visible.

The engine coughed, then once again, and then it fell silent. They could hear the wind whining as they slipped through it, dropping lower, gliding now, closer to the island and the wrinkled surface of the sea.

Elena could see individual waves.

No one spoke. The wind slapped against the aircraft's body and set it shaking.

Elena sat rigid, trying to breathe, not gulp. The island seemed miles away, then suddenly it was there, rushing toward them, huge cliffs towering up, waves crashing on the thin thread of beach.

It all happened at once. They were low, racing over the waves, and then they hit the surface of the water violently. Elena was thrown forward and, almost immediately, felt the ice-cold water on her feet, her legs.

She was disorientated, unable to determine where she was in relationship to the water. And then she felt Jacob's hands pulling on her. The water was freezing. She took a deep breath.

"Up!" Jacob shouted at her. The water was there again, everywhere. She struggled for breath. Then her head was above it; she gasped and drew in a deep breath. The plane was just beyond the line of breaking surf. Jacob held her above the rising water. Was the plane sinking? It was! They had to get free of it or it would suck them down with it. She was trapped, one leg under something heavy.

Where was Fassler? She twisted in Jacob's arms so she could look behind her, where Fassler had been. He was still there, strapped in, but not moving. Was he unconscious? She had to bring him back!

The plane tipped a little and sank a fraction deeper. It was going quickly. Elena tried to reach for Fassler, and was able to grab a piece of his jacket, but it slipped out of her grasp. In desperation, she tried to free her leg, fighting panic.

Jacob pulled her sharply. "Come on! If you don't get out, you go down with it! It's breaking up!"

The look on his face told Elena that he finally realized she couldn't move.

He pulled himself back into the cockpit and managed to free her leg. This time, when he grabbed her arms, she was jerked free.

The next few moments seemed endless . . . and terrifying. One second she was free and above water, in the sharp dawn light, and the next she felt the powerful current take hold of her and drag her deeper, until the surface was over her head and her mouth was filled with the taste of salt. In those terrifying moments, she saw her parents, her sister, her brother who had died in the war. She saw Lucas and Josephine, and was gripped with a profound grief not for her own death, but for the pain these people would feel. As the water filled her mouth and nose, she thought of the husband she would never have, the children she would never hold. With such loss engulfing her, she lashed out, arms moving wildly. Suddenly, something caught her hand. She was totally confused, and so cold she felt as if she had already drowned. Everything was chaos. Chaos and terror.

The world around her was dark, but she could breathe.

"Elena! Elena!" It was Jacob's voice. He was touching her face.

She took a shuddering breath. Air filled her lungs. She was shaking with cold, but there was a blanket around her. A dry, warm blanket.

"Fassler?" she asked, her voice a harsh whisper.

"I couldn't get him out," Jacob replied.

She was too cold and confused to absorb this news. "Where are we? We're not in Germany, are we?" She looked around her at the beach, clear in the rising sun.

He pulled the blanket closer around her. "I think this is Denmark."

A man came to them with more dry blankets and offered them a nip of whiskey. When he spoke, whatever he said was not in German.

Perhaps Jacob was right after all: this had to be Denmark.

"Fassler?" she asked again, as if Jacob hadn't already told her.

"I'm afraid he's dead," he said gently. "And all his secrets with him. The sea took his papers as well. At least for now, no one knows what he discovered. In a way, I guess it's for the best. A sort of success."

The light was broadening across the sky, clear and beautiful.

"Yes," she whispered. "A success . . . for now."

For more international intrigue in pre-war Europe,
turn the page to sample

The Traitor Among Us

An Elena Standish novel

BY ANNE PERRY

CHAPTER

1

Lucas Standish was not asleep in his chair—not quite. The September sunlight lay in a soft, bright pool on the floor, picking out the colors of the carpet and the patches worn by the passage of feet over the years. He could still hear the soft chattering of the birds from the garden. When the telephone rang, its shrill noise startled him fully awake. It must be important for anyone to call at this time on a Sunday afternoon.

He reached for the phone and said quietly, "Standish."

"Sorry," the voice at the other end replied.

Lucas recognized it, even from that one word. It was James Allenby, back in England after two years in the United States. He did not bother to say that it was urgent. Of course it was. He would not call Lucas for anything less.

"What is it?" Lucas did not waste time with trivia.

"I'm afraid it's bad."

Lucas knew Allenby well enough to recognize how the man's carefully controlled voice betrayed the depth of his emotion.

"John Repton is dead," Allenby told him. "Shot and left in a ditch in the countryside. In the Cotswolds, near a private estate called Wyndham Hall. Single rifle bullet to the heart. I think he was killed somewhere else, and then moved. Not enough blood on the ground where he was discovered. Not visible from the road. In fact, it was only by chance that he was found at all."

Lucas felt a sudden intense pain of loss. He had known John Repton for years. They had worked together in MI6 during the Great War, which had spread ruin across half the world, from the late summer of 1914 to November of 1918. That had been sixteen years ago. Now, in the waning summer of 1934, the prospect of conflict was returning. Less than three months ago, Adolf Hitler had silenced, banished, or executed thousands of his most dangerous enemies within his own country. Those who had survived were forced to live in mute obedience. The events, which had come to be known as the Night of the Long Knives, were still fresh in Lucas's memory.

"What was he working on?" Lucas asked. "I thought John was retired."

"There's always the one last time. And he was passionate about this particular project," Allenby replied. "You understand."

Allenby was referring to the fact that Lucas had more or less retired. He was well over the age when most men sat back and relaxed, taking up gardening or beginning that book they had always intended to write. But Lucas could not leave the job alone: He cared too much; it involved every part of his life. He had been willing to be called on by those who had previously worked for him, and eventually he returned as an adviser and, sometimes, more than that. He had a good idea that John Repton had been doing something similar.

"John was looking into personal influence," Allenby continued. "That is, people who were using their influence to back some candidates for Parliament and ruin the reputations of others. There's a lot of sympathy for Germany, and admiration for the way it is rising to power again. So many think the Treaty of Versailles was a recipe for future disaster, punitive beyond sense, and—"

Lucas interrupted him. "We know all that, James. But it's too late

to undo, even if we could. What can we do now? Germany is rebuilding at a hell of a pace and beginning to prosper. Specifically,
what was Repton looking into that got him killed? Are you absolutely sure it wasn't personal, or even accidental?" He knew that
Allenby had more sense than to have jumped to a conclusion without proof. Still, he had to ask.

There was a moment's hesitation before Allenby spoke again, his
voice completely unchanged. "He was sixty-two and lived alone, so
the chances of it being personal exist, but they are unlikely. Repton
had no close personal relationships. Most of his family are dead;
there are a few living abroad. He has a house, inherited from his
parents, in Lincolnshire, miles from the Cotswolds or Wyndham
Hall."

"Have you been there?" Lucas pressed. "That is, to his home."

"Only once, briefly," Allenby answered. "I've had no time to research what I might be looking for; it's too soon. But I wanted to see
if Repton left any kind of note, or evidence."

"And did you find anything useful?"

"Lots of newspapers."

"Specifically, which ones? Did he cut anything out, or mark anything? Dates?"

"It was just one whole cupboard of newspapers. A lot of them
Bagby's titles."

Bagby was a newspaper magnate at both ends of the popularity
scale. He published the exploits, relationships, and personal griefs of
the social elite. The readership was small when compared to the
millions who bought his other newspaper, in which the gossip and
scandal often descended to the level of the gutter. At a glance, that
paper featured the complaints and aspirations of the working man,
and gave a loud and eloquent voice to the injustices of society and
the anger that they rightly caused. It took a fairly critical eye to see
how much it followed and how much it led mass opinion.

"Curiosity?" Lucas wondered aloud. "Or was John following
something in particular?"

"If there was something in particular, I didn't see it." There was a catch in Allenby's voice, as if he knew he had missed something. "He marked some of the letters to The Times, even though they seem on the surface to be little more than a diary of gentlemen's parties, sports, messages, and advice on the stock exchange. And, of course, the bit of scurrilous gossip that everybody despises, but still reads avidly."

"He wouldn't select any piece without reason," Lucas knew for certain. "Or keep them at all, for that matter. And don't tell me it was to light a hundred winter fires."

He was snapping at Allenby only because the man was being careful, perhaps too careful, just as Lucas would have been. John Repton's death hurt. He had been a good man, careful and quiet; he loved cider and creamy Lancashire cheeses and, above all, a good joke. He was gifted at telling shaggy dog stories, long and meandering, but always with a great laugh booming at the very end. He probably had no idea what a hole he would leave behind, what a sense of loss.

Allenby hesitated for a few moments before answering. Was he hiding his own grief as well? "There were several articles about Robert Hastings, the member of Parliament for the area around Wyndham Hall. Highly respected. There is even talk of him as a possible prime minister in the near future. He has the courage to face a battle, if there is one, without backing down. Next best thing to Churchill coming back from the wilderness," he told him. "And articles about the sermons of Bishop Lamb, who's also from around that area. Looks harmless enough, all about forgiveness and peace in our time. But then his comments would be, wouldn't they? Coming from a bishop." That was not really a question.

Possibilities ran through Lucas's mind, raised by what Allenby had shared. The war was the most horrific in the history of the world. Hardly anyone was left untouched by it. No sane person wanted that again—ever.

Lucas pushed these thoughts away. This was about John Repton, a man who had been easy to see but not really noticed. He'd dressed casually. He could have passed for a law clerk or the owner of a small business, except for his shoes. His shoes had always looked well made and expensive. It turned out they had been personally made for him because his feet were slightly different sizes. He had mentioned to Lucas once that his only regret was that his job made it impossible to have a dog since he was away too often. Lucas remembered how he had stopped and spoken to other people's dogs in the street with such joy.

And now he had discovered something that got him not only shot dead, but left in a ditch for no one to find.

"Lucas," Allenby interrupted his thoughts. "Are you still—"

"I'm here, and I understand," Lucas cut him off. "That's part of what MI6 is for—to stop a plot before it is fully grown and it is too late." Lucas paused for a moment, and then asked, "Why are you telling me this? You don't report to me. In fact, we haven't even spoken since the Washington incident."

"Because John Repton was your friend. And because you have the courage to think the inconceivable," Allenby answered. "And, if necessary, to deal with it. I know you don't want war any more than the rest of us, but I also know that you will do what you can to prevent it by facing the possibility. And you may have friends in the aristocracy, but you have no illusions about them."

Allenby left the rest of it unsaid. They both knew about the ties the royal family had to Germany, never mind the rest of English aristocracy, and how war weariness and grief still crippled the defeated country.

"Do you know why Repton went to the Cotswolds? Or is that the next thing to find out?" Lucas asked.

"All the land around there is owned by the Wyndham family, and has been for centuries. Repton's body was found on Wyndham land. David Wyndham is a quiet sort of man, but he doesn't miss much. His wife is well known in high society and has connections to everyone of influence. If we could send someone with access to Wyndham

Hall, it would be the swiftest way to learn something of value," Allenby told him. "I don't quite know how, but we need someone within the house. The local police don't seem to be connecting Repton's death to anyone yet. John was left . . ." Allenby's voice dropped, as if he was finding it difficult to finish his sentence. "Lucas, he was left like rubbish—dumped into a ditch. As if he were a drunken tramp, and—"

"All right!" Lucas cut him off more sharply than he had meant to. It was hard to hear. Allenby's emotion surprised him. He had always struck Lucas as quick, loyal, clever, but emotionally uninvolved. Lucas liked him better now that he cared more than he could hide. "I'll get someone there," Lucas promised. "Do you know who's in charge of the investigation locally? The chief constable?"

"You mean who's investigating a tramp's death?" Allenby spat bitterly. "The chief constable is a fellow called Algernon Miller. Got his eyes on a knighthood one day, if he plays his cards right. But he's good at it, I'll grant you that. He's got the grip of an octopus to hang on to what he wants."

"Don't make a move until I tell you," Lucas instructed. "Allenby, you're back in England now, and you'll do as you're damn well told!" Again, he spoke more sharply than intended. It was fear that he heard in his own voice, and grief over the loss of yet another of the old guard, the MI6 of the past.

"Yes, sir."

Lucas wasn't sure if that was amusement he heard in his voice, or relief that someone else had also seen the shadows.

"Let's continue this face-to-face." It was agreed.

After Allenby said goodbye, Lucas stayed still for a few more moments, the sun warming the chair where he sat. He remained there, quietly turning over what Allenby had told him. It brought a sudden surge of grief that he had not expected. Despite it having been several years since he had seen John Repton, he could remember him as clearly as if it had been just last week. He had trusted Repton's judgment many times, mainly because he had always been reliable and never jumped to conclusions.

"What is it, Lucas?" Josephine's voice interrupted his thoughts. He had not heard her come in, and yet she stood beside him. He looked at her now. Her long hair was pinned up in a loose knot at the back of her head. She had never submitted to the modern fashion of cutting it short. That pleased him. Actually, it pleased him rather a lot.

"What is it?" she repeated, breaking him out of his trance.

"Did you ever meet John Repton?" he asked her.

Josephine had been a decoder during the war, and she knew far more than Lucas had ever realized. He had never told her that he worked in MI6, as one did not tell anybody, even one's most intimate family, for their own protection. It took only one careless word, one person who was trusted and should not have been, and the results could be the unintentional betrayal of unknown numbers of people. He had discovered only recently that she had always known about his position, which was not as one of the many MI6 agents, but head of the entire organization. Perhaps it had been in something she had decoded or pieced together. It had been a relief when they had finally revealed all they knew about each other's roles. He had never felt comfortable hiding anything from his wife, the woman he considered his best friend.

Yet today, he could not remember if she had ever met John Repton.

"Once," she answered quietly. "He was a kind man. Lonely, I thought. But there were times when we all were. Has something happened to him?" She looked at Lucas with a certain softness, as if in anticipation of what he was going to say.

Was he really so transparent to her? Yes. That was the only possible answer. "Allenby called to tell me that John Repton has been killed." He had long ago abandoned wrapping things up in soft-edged words for her.

"I'm sorry," she sighed quietly, her eyes looking down. "In the line of duty, I presume. Did you know what he was up to?"

"No. Allenby just said he had been watching Wyndham Hall, in the Cotswolds."

"Belongs to David Wyndham? Nice man," she commented. "We've met him a few times, do you remember? Some charity events? Very gentle, and I always thought pretty straightforward. Has he changed so completely?" she asked thoughtfully. "Or was I wrong? Has he got caught up in this 'Never Again' movement?"

There was disappointment in her face, very slight.

As always, he told her the truth. She was the one person he could not dissemble with. "Repton was shot. His body was moved and left in a ditch near Wyndham Hall. We need to find out why he was killed, who is responsible, and what it means."

"Knowing that is certainly important," Josephine agreed wholeheartedly. "I suppose Allenby couldn't be mistaken? About the murder, that is."

Lucas did not bother to answer that.

She nodded, smiling slightly, and touched his shoulder as she passed him. She did not offer tea. That would come at four o'clock, as always. It was good to have fixed things, something certain in a time of uncertainty.

As Josephine closed the door behind her, Lucas pulled over the telephone and dialed a number.

"Peter?"

"Lucas." Peter Howard's voice was guarded at the other end, as if he was certain that a call from Lucas at this time on a Sunday afternoon could not be good news.

Lucas could tell by the question in Peter's voice that Allenby had not yet spoken to him, which meant he knew nothing of John Repton's death. He told Peter briefly what Allenby had said—that Repton's body had been discovered close to Wyndham Hall.

There was silence at the other end of the line while Peter absorbed the shock. For a moment, Lucas wondered if they had been cut off.

Finally, Peter spoke. "I see." He swallowed nervously. "I'm sorry. Repton was a good man."

Lucas knew that Peter was trying to keep the emotion out of his voice, but he was failing.

"David Wyndham has already come to my notice, I'm afraid," Peter went on. "He mixes with some pretty strong Hitler admirers, although anyone in society will meet a few. Mosley and his crew from the British Union of Fascists, Unity Mitford and some of her sisters, just to name the most obvious. Even the Holy Fox is a good deal more benevolent toward them than I'd wish." There was bitterness in his tone. They both understood whom he was referring to: Lord Halifax, a prominent member of the government and a vocal sympathizer with Hitler's political victory and the rebuilding of Germany. "I don't mean that they're traitors—"

"I know that!" Lucas exclaimed sharply, cutting him off. "But the damage is the same, whether you mean it or not. Daft optimism is just as dangerous as intentional sabotage. Is it Wyndham himself? I mean, is he active or merely an enabler, deliberately turning a blind eye? Whatever he is, I don't think he's a fool."

"Most people can be fools where their own families are concerned," Peter said grimly. "We see what we need to see, what we can live with. That's the only way it's bearable for us. We've all got to be allowed to make as big a fool of ourselves as we wish, or we'll never truly be alive. And we'll never love anyone. It's too much of a risk."

That caught Lucas by surprise. It was the most tolerant thing he had ever heard Peter say. He did not comment on it, in case Peter spoiled it by backing away.

"Better look into it," Peter continued. "Inconspicuously, of course. And you say it was Allenby who told you?"

"Yes."

"Good."

"What's good about it?"

"He worked well with Elena over that miserable business in Washington," Peter told him. "Handled it pretty deftly. Could have become a lot worse. I'm . . ." He paused, as if looking for the right word. "I'm sorry," he finally said.

Peter took a breath, a moment's silence, then continued. "I'll send Elena to join up with Allenby. She's the best person I've got for that sort of thing and . . ." He trailed off. He seldom wasted words. "Thank you."

"Good," Lucas replied, and replaced the phone on its cradle. It was only then that he noticed Josephine had come back into the room.

"Peter?" She was not really asking a question. She knew it was, just as she had always known for years when it was a business call, an MI6 call.

"Yes," he answered. "He's going to send Elena to find out what Repton was onto. At least it will be mostly watching and listening. That might take a little while to organize."

"No, it won't."

He shifted in his chair a little to look more directly at her. Her comment puzzled him.

"Margot is staying at Wyndham Hall next weekend," she told him quietly.

"Did you tell me?" He struggled to keep the concern out of his voice. Was he losing his memory? The thought was terrifying. He tried to cover this up by saying, "She goes to so many places, weekend parties and so forth. Dinners, receptions, theaters."

"No, my dear," she assured him gently. "I didn't tell you. I am . . . a little nervous about it."

"About David Wyndham in particular?" he asked. "Or that she is getting about so much? She's looking for something, for someone, we know that. She has never really got over losing Paul." Her grandparents never stopped worrying about Elena's older sister, Margot.

Her husband had been killed in the last days of the Great War, leaving behind a nineteen-year-old widow. "From what I've seen, Wyndham is a decent man," Lucas added. "More than that, he is quiet and brave, and really very good company. The sort of man I think Margot might like to marry."

"He is already married," Josephine pointed out. "It's his wife's brother, Geoffrey Baden, that Margot's involved with. And before you ask, he's definitely single, and extremely eligible. He's in his late thirties, independently wealthy, good looking and with considerable charm. Not to mention—"

"Really?" He leaned forward in surprise. Was it possible that happiness would come to Margot again at last? She had borne grief with considerable grace, but he knew that sometimes she found it almost overwhelming.

"Lucas?"

He brought his attention back to Repton's murder. "Yes, of course. Best answer would be that Repton was mistaken in his interest in the Wyndham family, but we need to know as much as we can about why he was killed. We can't leave it just because we might not like the answer."

"Are you hesitating because you think investigating at Wyndham Hall will be too much for Elena because it's politically complicated? Or because Margot is emotionally involved and could not bear the ugly truth, if that is how it turns out?"

He did not answer immediately. Was Josephine right that he was only trying to protect his granddaughters?

She put a comforting hand on his shoulder. "If the problem is in that place, then Margot will need Elena's help. You cannot alter the truth, and you must not. But Margot will have to make her own decisions. Possibly David Wyndham is involved in whatever Repton was looking into, but I doubt it. Elena may be able to prove that Wyndham and those around him are misguided, but nothing worse."

"I know." He put his hand over hers. "I know."

An hour later, Lucas was walking across the early autumn fields with Toby, his golden retriever. The dog was practically treading on his heels in excitement. To Toby, any walk was good. But now the dog was clearly hoping they were about to meet with Peter Howard, who always made a terrific fuss over him. There was no such thing as too much attention.

Lucas looked at the long sweep of the land, the gold stubble rising toward the deep blue of the sky. Old-fashioned stooks stood in rows like small pointed tents. A light breeze carried the smell of grain drying in the sun.

There was a figure in the distance, walking steadily toward them. Toby stiffened. He was used to it being Peter Howard, but this time he was not certain.

Lucas put his hand on Toby's head and patted him in reassurance. "It's not Peter, boy. Just hang on a moment."

Toby moved forward, then stopped, uncertain. Allenby reached the dog and offered his hand to calm him.

Lucas had recognized Allenby from a considerable distance away. He was tall, even taller than Lucas, and between one and two generations younger, which made him perhaps a few years short of forty, with no gray in his dark-brown hair. He came across as mild, with a keen sense of humor, but Lucas knew that he also had a temper, although it was seldom out of control. In all, he suspected that James Allenby was a man of deeper emotion than he had so far displayed.

"Thank you for coming," Lucas said when they were standing face-to-face. "There are a few things about this that I would rather tell you personally."

Lucas started to walk up the incline from which Allenby had just come. Allenby turned and followed him, and Toby, satisfied that all was well, galloped out into the field, leaping over the stubble and, to his delight, sending a variety of birds swirling into the air.

"I haven't told her yet, but I'm sending Elena to Wyndham Hall," Lucas told him.

"How are you going to explain her presence?" Allenby's voice was slightly on edge.

This told Lucas that Allenby had emotions regarding that decision, and that was worrying. How much was there about the Washington business, and her relationship with Allenby, that Elena had not told him? She had been distressed profoundly. But that would have been unavoidable, whether the person helping her were Allenby or anyone else.

No one knew what this was going to involve. Lucas knew that it would not end as the Washington incident had, but it might still be awkward, even painful, especially if Margot was seeing Geoffrey Baden. She appeared assured, but Lucas knew that she was far more vulnerable than she pretended.

Allenby did not repeat his question. There was no sound as they walked across the straw, and it was silent but for the faint sigh of the wind through the bare branches of the hedges.

"Lady Wyndham's brother, Geoffrey Baden, has far more influence than he appears to," Allenby said. "One way or another, there's a huge amount of power just beneath the surface. I'm referring to weapons."

"Weapons?" Lucas echoed. "Do you mean the production of them?"

"Eventually." Allenby glanced at him, then at the path they were following. "Beginning with steel and other heavy industry and skilled staff, he manufactures first-quality armaments, particularly guns and tanks. It's not Geoffrey Baden's firm, but that of a man named Landon Rees." He paused for a moment. "Landon Rees is married to Wyndham's sister."

Lucas had known about Landon Rees's steel interests, but it was still chilling to hear somebody else stating these facts, especially those about his family ties to David Wyndham and Geoffrey Baden, the man who was linked to his own granddaughter. He was debating with himself as to how far he should trust James Allenby. He did not know him well, not personally, and Elena had said very little. Did that mean she disliked him? Or that her feelings were deeper than she wished to discuss? And could Lucas allow her emotions to matter?

"My other granddaughter, Elena's sister, is going to be at Wyndham Hall next weekend," he informed him, although he suspected Allenby might already know this. "Margot Driscoll."

"I know," Allenby replied quietly, eyes down, still watching where he was putting his feet on the rough, stubbled ground. "That's what I want to speak to you about."

Lucas felt the knot in his stomach tighten. "Margot? She has nothing to do with MI6. She doesn't even know I was with MI6, nor that Elena . . ." His voice trailed off.

Allenby's smile was very slight, a momentary acknowledgment of irony. "I know that, too," he said softly. "But I believe Margot is the one they are interested in. John Repton called me. It was pretty brief, from a call box. He didn't say much, but he was sure that Margot, although a striking woman, graceful, and comfortable in all sorts of company, might be appreciated more by the Wyndhams as a way to access her father." After a pause, he added, "I didn't want to tell you this over the phone."

Lucas drew a sharp breath. His son, Charles, was a former ambassador to Berlin, Paris, and Madrid. He was well connected.

Lucas froze. "Are you certain?"

"No. But I fear it. And so did Repton. It is certain that Margot doesn't know Elena's part in MI6, so she is the perfect person to send."

"Is it?" Lucas demanded. "Are we sure Margot doesn't know?"

"Yes," Allenby confirmed. "And as for Elena—well, you haven't seen her in the field. She's very good."

"Is she?" It was a serious, demanding question.

"Yes." No embroidery, just the one word.

Toby came back with a stick in his mouth and offered it to Allenby.

"He's testing you," Lucas said, pushing aside the conversation for a moment.

Allenby smiled, scratching the dog's head. "Thank you, Toby."

He picked up the stick and flung it a considerable way across the field.

Toby galloped after it, swerving around stooks, leaping over clumps of uncut stalks.

Lucas smiled, still avoiding the subject at hand. "That was some throw!"

"Cricket," Allenby explained, but then his smile vanished. "But Margot spent quite a lot of her youth in Berlin," he went on. "She still has friends there, some of them rising now in the Nazi Party. I'm sorry." His voice turned quieter, but harder. "I wish I could deny this, but it seems extremely probable that someone in Wyndham Hall wants to use her connections to strengthen their own. At the very least, she will be another easy and natural avenue of contact to some very influential people. I know her father, your son, was ambassador to Germany for a lot of her growing-up years. It's—"

"I understand," Lucas interrupted. "Margot is . . ." He felt that he was betraying her vulnerability to a man whom he knew only by reputation, not personally. He wanted to protect her from intrusion, let alone tragedy.

Allenby stopped walking. "I do understand," he said quietly. "If Margot is being used in this way, Elena will do anything she can, even warn Margot, if she'll listen."

"And what are you going to do?"

"Go to Wyndham Hall as an old friend of Elena, in whatever relationship she is comfortable with. Except professional, of course." His expression hardened. "And find out who killed John Repton. And, if possible, see that they pay for it."

"Be—" Lucas began.

"Careful," Allenby finished for him. "I won't let anger drive me. It's a lot more than that. I know revenge isn't a luxury any of us can afford. It's not about me. It's not even about John Repton, although loyalty counts. It's about finishing Repton's job, whatever it was."

Lucas did not answer. It was not necessary.

ANNE PERRY was the bestselling author of two acclaimed series set in Victorian England: the William Monk novels and the Charlotte and Thomas Pitt novels. She was also the author of a series featuring Charlotte and Thomas Pitt's son, Daniel, as well as the Elena Standish series; a series of five World War I novels; twenty-one holiday novels; and a historical novel, *The Sheen on the Silk,* set in the Byzantine Empire. Anne Perry died in 2023.

anneperry.us

ABOUT THE TYPE

The text of this book was set in Janson, a typeface designed about 1690 by Nicholas Kis (1650–1702), a Hungarian living in Amsterdam, and for many years mistakenly attributed to the Dutch printer Anton Janson. In 1919, the matrices became the property of the Stempel Foundry in Frankfurt. It is an old-style book face of excellent clarity and sharpness. Janson serifs are concave and splayed; the contrast between thick and thin strokes is marked.